THE
SORCERER

THE
SORCERER
BOOK ONE OF DARKNESS RISING

Paul B. Spence

Asura Press

THE SORCERER

An Asura Press Book

PRINTING HISTORY
First Paperback Edition 2023

Cover Art by: Paul B. Spence

ISBN: 978-1-929928-47-7

www.paulbspence.com
author@paulbspence.com

For my gamer friends that helped this happen.

CHAPTER ONE

Geoffrey Meeks cursed as he died *again*.

"I don't understand why you keep playing those games, if they only bring you frustration," his housemate said from the easy chair by the bookcase.

Jason Grey had been reading one of Geoffrey's history books and snickering occasionally. The book was about the Second World War; it wasn't humorous, but Jason often read Geoffrey's history books and laughed at what he found. Evidently, he'd been taught something else growing up. Which was funny, because Jason couldn't be more than a few years older than Geoffrey.

Geoffrey didn't know much about Jason.

The house was Jason's. He was a private and somewhat paranoid guy who didn't like uninvited people in his house. At least, that was how he'd explained it, the time Geoffrey had come home late and hadn't announced himself, and found a knife at his throat.

Jason was a good guy; he'd apologized about the knife. He was just… weird.

Geoffrey had never been able to determine Jason's ethnicity.

He looked somewhat Hispanic, with dark brown hair and eyes and olive skin. Spanish, maybe? He wore a bandana and engineer boots all the time, which Geoffrey thought made Jason look like he was in a gang. He didn't have any kind of accent, but that didn't mean anything.

Geoffrey paused the game and slipped the headphones down. Jason had that look that said he wanted to talk.

"I don't know," said Geoffrey. "I think I just like exploring the worlds in games. They're cool."

"Uh-huh."

"They help me relax."

Jason shook his head. "So I see."

"Well, yeah, it's frustrating when you die, but it's just a game. There are elves and dragons, and you've got all these cool spells and armor and stuff..." He trailed off at the look on Jason's face. "Most of the time, the game isn't so hard. Then it's a relaxing way to escape reality for a while. Think of it as like your woodworking."

"Except I have something to show for my time after I make something."

"My point is, you do that when you're stressed out. Although I don't know what you have to be stressed about. All you do is hang around the house and read all the time."

Jason gave him a cool, appraising look. "And what are you doing?"

"Don't begrudge me my time to relax when I'm not working."

"Is an unpaid internship at a museum really work?"

Geoffrey had been working at the Cincinnati Museum Center for most of the summer. The Museum Center was built into the old Union Terminal, a train terminal dating to the nineteen thirties, big, sprawling, and covered with beautiful industrial-era mosaics. The museum itself had taken over the adjacent wings of the building, off the huge half-dome.

Geoffrey loved working there on the weekends. Well, *volunteering* there, anyway. He was an unpaid intern, but that was sort of like work. At least, that was what his history advisor at the University of Cincinnati had said.

Volunteer work looked good on a résumé.

Geoffrey had just finished his sophomore year toward a history degree. The old stone Museum Center was certainly full of history. He could feel it in the air, in the way the floor shook as hundreds of people walked between the museum wings. The displays in the museum itself almost felt like an afterthought. A glorious afterthought filled with wondrous things from faraway places.

The degree had seemed like a good idea when he'd started, but Geoffrey didn't have a clear idea of what kind of job might be available after he graduated. Maybe he'd teach or go to graduate school. The internship was hard work but great experience, if he ever made it out of school. It was unpaid, but that wasn't the point.

"You sound like my family," Geoffrey finally replied.

"Ouch."

"Thanks a lot." Geoffrey was from a rural county in Kentucky. Most of his family didn't understand why he'd even wanted to go to school, much less why he'd work for free. But then, Geoffrey had never had much in common with the rest of his family.

Museums had always been special refuges for him. He'd grown up in the backwoods of central Kentucky. Some of the towns there had small museums, but not many people went to them. That just made the museums more special for Geoffrey. He could go and study for school without his cousins or the town bullies hunting him down.

History was safe.

Other than the local museum and the library, there had never been anything to do in Mount Sterling. Geoffrey craved adventure; he didn't want to just read about it. He loved adventure movies, books, and video games. At the very least, he wanted to travel and see exotic places.

Maybe meet exotic women.

Geoffrey sighed. He was currently between girlfriends and had that odd feeling of both freedom and loneliness. He was young, and his mind often turned to thinking about girls. He sometimes thought about asking out the girls in class with him, but they seemed focused, and besides, he didn't have a car. No reliable transportation made it difficult to date.

Geoffrey paused his game again. "Any ideas about dinner?"

"Pizza?" Jason suggested. Jason preferred foods he could eat with his hands. Or maybe he was just lazy and didn't like to cook. Not that Geoffrey was eager to cook, either. In any case, they ate a lot of pizza.

"Sure."

Geoffrey ordered the pizza and then flopped back down bonelessly on the sofa to resume his game. He had to wear a headset when he played, because Jason didn't like the noise from the games, but at least Jason didn't mind Geoffrey hogging the television. Jason never watched anything by himself, as far as Geoffrey could tell. Jason hadn't even owned a television when Geoffrey had moved in.

Someone pounded on the door.

"Thank god. The pizza," said Geoffrey, scooping the cash off the coffee table.

Geoffrey wasn't paid for his summer work, but he didn't have to worry that much about money. His mysterious uncle, brother to the deadbeat father he'd never met, had set up a college fund for Geoffrey when he was born, back in ninety-one. It wasn't a lot of money, but it was enough. Sometimes he thought about picking up another job, maybe at Walmart or something, so he could afford his own place. He didn't mind having a housemate, but Jason was a pain in the ass sometimes.

It wasn't the pizza guy at the door.

The man standing in the doorway was half a head taller than Geoffrey and covered in blood. At least, that was Geoffrey's first impression. The man's face was bloody, and he was swaying and clutching his side.

"Help me," the man begged as he slowly collapsed.

Geoffrey caught him. "Jason!"

Together, they managed to get the man inside and lay him on the floor. He was tall but thin and gaunt. His head and side were bleeding, and Geoffrey grabbed the first aid kit from the hall bathroom.

"Were you in a car accident?" Geoffrey asked him.

The man was unconscious.

Jason shook his head and pointed. "Those aren't wounds from a car accident."

Someone else pounded on the door.

"This is going to look great," said Geoffrey. "Shit."

"Wait," said Jason. "That might not be the pizza. Someone might be after this guy."

Geoffrey glanced out the hall window. The house was surrounded by the strangest people he'd ever seen. They wore black outfits that looked a bit like some kind of martial arts gi, but not really. Their heads were covered in hoods and masks, and they carried medieval swords. They were also wearing shiny aviator sunglasses. It was too weird to even process.

"Not the pizza," Geoffrey said. He surprised at how calm his voice sounded. "The house is surrounded by ninja."

"Call the police," said Jason. He was wrapping a bandage around the head of the guy on the floor.

Geoffrey grabbed the handset on the wall, but the line was dead. He tried the hook a couple of times, but it was still dead. "They cut the line."

"Bet you wish you'd bought that cell phone last week."

Geoffrey *had* almost bought a cell phone when they'd gone

out shopping, but he couldn't justify the expense. Now he wished he'd gotten it anyway. He laughed to dispel his fear and grabbed his baseball bat out of the hall closet.

The wounded man moaned and sat up. "Thanks," he said, touching the bandage on his head, and then the one on his side. "I didn't know where else to go. I'm too tired to jump again."

Geoffrey exchanged a glance with Jason, who shrugged.

"Yeah, man, you shouldn't try to walk, much less jump," said Jason. "There are... ninja outside. They after you?"

"Ninja?" The man laughed softly. "I guess that figures. They must have followed me. If one of you could get me back to the Eternal City, I'm sure I could find help there."

Geoffrey exchanged another glance with Jason. "The what?" Geoffrey asked.

"Is neither of you non-local?" the man asked. He was searching Jason's face. "Shit, I must have gotten here too early. That's the trouble with precognition: sometimes it isn't very precise. You're both connected to what I need, though."

"What are you talking about?" said Jason. "Who the hell are you?"

"Call me Jon," the man said. "If that bat is the best weapon you've got, we should get the hell out of here. Either of you have a vehicle?"

"I have an old truck in the garage," Jason replied, "but I don't think we'll get past the guys outside. What's going on?"

"I'm sorry to drag you both into this, but I didn't have much choice." He was quiet for a moment, scowling. "No, you're both definitely connected to me getting back. I just can't see how. We'll have to play it by ear."

"What are —?" The sound of breaking glass in the kitchen cut off a complaint from Jason.

Geoffrey was breathing hard, scared but not as freaked out as he'd thought he would be. This whole situation was too weird for his brain to process. A ninja came down the hall from the kitchen, and Geoffrey moved to intercept him. A part of him noticed that Jason had a strange, white-bladed knife in his right hand. It looked sort of like a kitchen knife, and Geoffrey didn't have time to wonder where it had come from.

The ninja swung his sword at Geoffrey. He knocked it out of the way and jabbed the man in the face with the end of the bat, and then followed up by smashing him in the side of the head. The man dropped, and another sprang past him, stabbing at Geoffrey.

The sword left a fiery line of pain across Geoffrey's left arm, but he caught the man in the chest with his next swing and knocked him back. The man's sunglasses fell off, and Geoffrey felt a little bit dizzy as he looked into the man's solid grey eyes: no white or even a pupil visible.

He wasn't human – not with those eyes.

"Look out!" Jason shouted.

Geoffrey spun around just in time avoid being run through by one of the men who'd come in from the living room. They must have broken the window there, he thought. He blocked a wild swing of the sword and smashed the bottom of the bat into the man's temple. The man crumpled to the ground.

In the hallway, Jason had helped Jon to his feet. Another man came running out of the living room, and Geoffrey was surprised to see Jason grab the man from behind and slash his throat open with his white knife.

Bright red blood sprayed across Geoffrey, and he felt sick. He could hear sirens and hoped that one of their neighbors had called the police. Normally Geoffrey didn't have a lot of confidence in the police; now, he just wanted them here to stop the insanity.

"Geoffrey!" Jason was shaking him, and Geoffrey wondered how he'd ended up on the floor. His head hurt, and he thought maybe he'd fainted; his face, hands, and feet had that odd tingly sensation. "Geoffrey, we need to get out of here."

"What?" Geoffrey carefully shook his head. Then, "Look out!" he shouted. One of the ninja had come into the room behind Jason and was raising his sword.

Suddenly Jon grabbed the man from behind and slammed him headfirst into the door jamb. Geoffrey couldn't figure out how Jon had gotten behind the man; he'd been in the hall just a moment before. Geoffrey pushed himself up off the hall floor and picked up his bat, just in case.

Before he could say anything, the front door burst open, and soldiers in riot gear crowded into the hall. The soldier in front pointed a weird, boxy gun at Geoffrey, and he felt a sharp impact on his chest. All of his muscles spasmed, and then he fell into blessed oblivion.

☉

The man arrived too late to stop what happened.

He was angry. It was not a feeling he normally cultivated, but someone had entered his Realm and attempted to interfere with his work. Now, the one he'd kept an eye on was gone, and he didn't know where. Someone had taken him. For what purpose, he did not know.

The local police had cordoned off the area around the house.

Men who were not police brought bodies in black bags out of the house. They placed the bodies in an unmarked van with government license plates. The men were armed, possibly soldiers, but he was unconcerned about that. Their weapons couldn't harm him, even if he allowed them to try.

Walking past the police and soldiers, the man approached the van. Only one of the soldiers noticed him, but the soldier's mind was easily clouded, and he looked away, never to be certain if he'd seen a man or not. The body bags didn't hold the one he sought. He'd known they wouldn't, but he had to check.

The dead men, however, were familiar to him. The eyes

could mean anything, but the tattoos on their shoulders… No, they couldn't be here in this place, and yet they were. Someone must have guided them here.

The man had been angry before; now he was furious. The presence of the dead men with the solid grey eyes was someone sending him a clear message. Someone had interfered with something that belonged to him, and he would not respond kindly. However, he still had to find the one he sought.

The man glanced again at the troubled soldier. Yes, the soldier would know where the others had been taken. He would have that information before he left.

CHAPTER TWO

Jason was afraid.

He'd spent most of his life running from soldiers and governments. His current identity was good, but not good enough to hold up to a close look from government officials. He hoped his arrest was just a misunderstanding, but he didn't have much faith in that.

The men who burst through the front door had seemed to know what they were doing. They'd been ruthless and efficient, although they hadn't been needlessly cruel. Jason was grabbed, a bag was thrown over his head, and he was marched out of the house into a waiting van. He pulled the hood off as soon the doors were shut.

At least Geoffrey and Jon were with him.

Jason sometimes thought it had been a mistake to rent out his spare bedroom to Geoffrey, but he had been alone for a long time, and he craved companionship. He needed a friend more than he needed the money. Now he'd come to care for the kid, to feel almost as if Geoffrey was a younger brother. He would never have chosen to get Geoffrey mixed up in his troubles, but now it looked as if there wasn't much choice. Once the government figured out who Jason was, Geoffrey would be in trouble just for knowing him.

Unless all of this was because of Jon. Strangely, Jason also felt a kinship with him, even though they'd just met. Jon had come to Jason's house – being pursued – and asked for help. Jason would give that help if he could, although under the circumstances, he had no idea how that would work. Jon was a mystery. Geoffrey assumed Jon had been in a car accident, but there had been no vehicle. The men who'd attacked them weren't human, which shook Jason more than the attack itself.

They weren't human.

What they were, he couldn't say, but with those eyes, there was no way they were human. It was important to Jason to discover where they'd come from. If they could attack him here in Cincinnati, they could attack other places. Were they after Jon, or someone else?

Jason glanced over at Jon. He'd been quiet so far. Jason thought that was probably for the best. The soldiers might be listening in case Jason or Jon revealed anything, although what, he couldn't guess.

Geoffrey was still unconscious. Jason hoped he wasn't hurt too badly. He didn't know much about Tasers, but they seemed nastier in real life than they were in movies. Geoffrey looked pale and sweaty, and his pulse had been a little erratic when Jason checked it.

Jason leaned back against the cool side of the van and gathered his strength. If there was a chance for them to escape, they had to be ready to take it. They would all take it together.

He wouldn't leave the others, Jason decided suddenly. No matter what, he wasn't going to run away and leave friends again. He'd spent too much of his life running. He'd stay with these men until the end.

Whatever that might be.

☉

Geoffrey woke up suddenly, rolled over, and threw up on the floor of the van.

Jason caught him and kept him from falling face-first into the mess. Geoffrey sat back against the side of the van and looked around. It was just Jason and Jon in here with him. He'd expected to see at least one soldier.

"What happened?" He felt a swaying that suggested they were in a moving vehicle, but his brain wouldn't process what it meant.

"Those weren't police," said Jason. "At least not normal police. I think they were military. They shot you with a Taser as soon as they breached the door. I assume it was because you were the only one with a visible weapon."

"That damn baseball bat." Geoffrey cautiously sat upright. His stomach hurt. "Never should have played baseball. I hate the game. I thought they looked more like soldiers than police. Why would they be at our house?" Distant thunder rumbled outside the van.

Jason shrugged and glanced at Jon. "Maybe because of who or what had just attacked us? They asked us some weird questions, threw hoods over our heads, and rushed us out into this van."

"They didn't read your rights or anything?"

Jon laughed humorlessly. "You don't have much experience with this sort of thing, do you?"

"Weird guy showing up on my doorstep bloody? Sorry, Jon, but seriously, alien ninja and stuff? Paramilitary forces kidnapping me? Nope. Can't say I have any experience with that."

"They're probably listening, Geoffrey," Jason said quietly. "And technically, it was *my* doorstep."

"So what?" Geoffrey said. "Damn."

"What?"

"I left the TV and the game console on." Geoffrey frowned. "And what happened to the pizza?"

"I think we have other things to worry about."

"Maybe, but I really wanted that pizza."

Now that the nausea was fading, he was hungry. He'd ordered a large pepperoni-and-sausage with extra cheese. He could imagine the smell and the taste of it. Hopefully, the pizza place wouldn't blacklist him for not paying for it. Surely being attacked by ninja and then kidnapped by the military was a good excuse.

He sighed.

The van squeaked to a stop, and the engine cut off. A few minutes passed before the back opened, and one the guys in riot gear ordered them out of the van. Geoffrey wasn't even tempted to run. They were in some underground facility: a parking garage, maybe. The other police – or soldiers or whatever they were – had submachine guns.

Geoffrey hopped out of the van and immediately had his hands pulled behind him and zip-tied at the wrist. He glanced around. The van was wet; it *had* been raining. A black hood was thrown over his head then. The soldiers weren't unnecessarily rough, but they didn't seem to be too worried about hurting Geoffrey, Jason, and Jon, either. He heard Jon grunt in pain as his arms were pulled back, and Geoffrey worried about the man's chest wound.

It was strange and disconcerting to be led along by a firm hand on his arm when he couldn't see, and Geoffrey didn't like it at all. He could think of a dozen bad ways this whole thing could end, and not a single way for them to get out of it alive. His whole life had suddenly been turned upside down. *How could helping someone lead to this?* he wondered.

An elevator ride up, a long corridor, and then another elevator ride up, and Geoffrey was led into a room and shoved down into a hard chair. It hurt, with his hands behind his back. How long he sat here, he couldn't say. He needed to pee. Or maybe he was thirsty. Or both. He wasn't sure, but he hated sitting here. He didn't even know if the others were with him. All he could hear were his own breathing and the muted sounds of the storm outside.

He must have dozed off, because he woke to feel a cold blade slipping between his wrists to cut the zip tie. Then the bag was pulled from his head. The room was dark except for lights directly in front of Geoffrey and each of the others; Jason was to his right, and beyond him, Jon. Lightning flashed outside the tinted windows, and Geoffrey thought he could see other buildings he recognized.

Still in Cincinnati, then, he thought.

A man was moving behind them, but Geoffrey didn't dare to turn and look. He was really scared, if he was being honest with himself. He hadn't had time to think about it when the house was being attacked, but now he did. Those men who attacked hadn't been human. Their eyes...

"I'm sorry about the circumstances of you all being here, but I hope you're more comfortable now," said a man from behind them. "I don't have much time before you're transported to the Pemberton Institute, and I want to speak to you first. One of you has some impressive tech, and I've been asked to evaluate it. You cooperation would be greatly appreciated."

"I'd feel much more like cooperating if I hadn't just been kidnapped from my house," Jason said as he straightened his bandanna. Geoffrey envied him a bit; he always looked cool and collected.

"At least one of you isn't what he appears to be," the man said. "And I have to caution you not to try to run. The exits are all guarded."

"Hey, look," said Geoffrey, "my friend here and I were just waiting on pizza, when this other guy shows up wounded. Then we get attacked by freaking alien ninja."

The man came around from behind them: a sophisticated-looking older man, maybe in his sixties. "Why do you use that word?"

"*Ninja*? Because they were dressed in black and had swords."

"Don't play stupid, Mr. Meeks. Why did you say they were alien?"

"The solid grey eyes seemed like a clue. And then your Men in Black showed up and zapped me."

"Maybe you are what you say," the man said, walking past Geoffrey to Jason. "Maybe you are, as well, Mr. Grey." He walked over to Jon. "You, I can't find any record of."

"No, you wouldn't," said Jon. "These kind gentlemen helped me when I was in need, so I feel more than a little indebted to them. You, however, I feel nothing but contempt for."

"Strong words," the man said. "What is your name?"

"What's yours?"

"I am Klaus Gerhardt. What is your name?" he repeated.

Geoffrey had heard of Gerhardt; he was an industrialist. Which didn't really explain anything.

"You can call me Jon Livingston. You'll not find any records of me. I'm not local, and this is my first time here."

"I thought as much, from your implants. The military is very interested to know what they do."

"I'm sure they are."

Geoffrey had no idea what they were talking about. He was about to ask, when his thoughts were interrupted by a loud flapping noise that could be heard over the storm. It sounded like something from the game he'd been playing. An impossible shadow was cast across the room as a lightning bolt flashed nearby.

"What is that?" Gerhardt demanded.

"I don't know," said Jon. "However, such noises are rarely

good to hear. You might want to call for the soldiers."

Gerhardt didn't hesitate. "Guards!"

There was a stunning crash as one of the long windows exploded inward. A man stood silhouetted against the storm; he appeared to be holding a sword in his right hand. Geoffrey couldn't see any other details because of the lightning.

The guards opened fire on the intruder as he walked forward. The bullets seemed to flatten and fall a meter from their target. The figure gestured, and the guards screamed and collapsed, writhing on the floor, their bones *glowing* through their skin as if they were burning from the inside out.

Gerhardt clicked a button on a remote, and the lights came up in the room. The man with the sword flinched slightly. At first, Geoffrey had thought the stranger was one of the ninja, because he was dressed in black and carrying a sword. With the better light, he could see that he wore a black leather trench coat and what looked like close-fitting armor underneath it. He was tall and had long, red hair in a ponytail or queue. His eyes were a brilliant green and slightly slanted. There was something vaguely Asian-looking about his face. His ears were very pointy, as were his teeth.

Jon stood suddenly.

"Don't," the man said. He sounded somewhat British.

Jon staggered, although Geoffrey couldn't see why.

"What are you?" Gerhardt demanded.

"Angry," the man replied. He walked around them, and Geoffrey couldn't help but shake slightly. This man, whatever he was, radiated danger. "You," he said, stopping in front of Jon. "Explain yourself."

Jon stood his ground. He was taller than the man but seemed much smaller. "I have done nothing to you," Jon said. "What business do you have with us?"

"You reek of Cynosure."

Jon flinched. "So you're one of them."

"One of whom?" the man asked, eyes flashing.

"Joseph told me about the Ruined Courts. The enemies of the Eternal City, who are able to walk the worlds. Sorcerers and madmen."

"He would know," the man said. He turned to Jason and Geoffrey. "I don't know you."

"We just happened to be in the wrong place at the wrong time," said Jason.

"Why is it that I doubt your sincerity?" the man asked.

"You can stick your doubt up your ass," Jason replied.

"I like you."

He gave Geoffrey a cool, appraising glance as he walked past, and Geoffrey felt as if he was sitting naked before everyone in the room. He felt vulnerable and afraid. This world of death and swords was far from the games he'd played. This felt real, in a way he'd never imagined. He could still see, in his mind, those guards writhing as they burned, and the smell...

"This Realm is under my protection," the man said. "I have a vested interest here, and I don't like it being invaded."

"I'm not invading," said Jon. "I came here because I was being pursued by assassins. These two were simply where I happened to enter this place. They gave me aid and protected me from those who would do me more harm. You should let them go."

"I will not let them go, for no reason other than that you wish it. I will have answers from all of you before I leave this place. If you wish to live, it would be wise to be honest with me."

"I have been," Jon said quietly.

"We shall see."

CHAPTER THREE

The storm continued to rage outside. Rain puddled around the shattered window, but the positive force of the building's air-conditioning kept most of it out. Strangely, the man stalking around the room didn't appear to be wet, nor did he leave wet footprints. That was almost stranger than how he'd entered the building.

"Who are you?" Gerhardt demanded.

Geoffrey thought Gerhardt sounded like a man trying hard to maintain control of a situation he knew was out of his control. Geoffrey was familiar with the feeling; he'd never had much control over his life. Just now, he was trying to be small and unnoticed.

The man bowed mockingly in front of them. "You may call me Daeren Drake. I'm a prince of the Ruined Courts and the General of the Army of the Rim – much good may the information do you."

Drake had an odd way of speaking. The rhythm of his words wasn't normal. He'd pronounced his first name *Day-ren*. His titles sounded impressive, even if Geoffrey had no idea what any of them meant.

"What did you do to my guards?"

Drake looked surprised. "I killed them. Or where you asking for the specifics? Very well. I caused them to be boiled alive from the inside out. A fate you could share with them if I am not satisfied with your answers to my questions."

Caused to be boiled? It had to be magic, Geoffrey thought. *He used magic.* Of all of the ways he'd thought he might die today, being killed with magic hadn't even made it onto his list for consideration. He wasn't sure what it meant, that he'd been making such a list. Maybe he was being a realist, or maybe it was just his way of trying to maintain a little control.

"Those men weren't a threat to you," Jon said angrily. "Their weapons couldn't even touch you."

Geoffrey thought Jon was being brave, if a bit stupid. Whoever this big, red-haired man was, he didn't seem the type to take any shit off people. The dead guards smelled of roast pork; it was nauseating.

"Those men attacked me. I don't allow that to pass unanswered."

"What did you mean," asked Gerhardt, "when you said this realm is yours?"

"I didn't," Drake corrected. "I said it is under my protection."

"What did you mean by *realm?*"

"Curious, aren't you?"

"I've always been curious about the unknown. That's why these men are here. Also, I'm old, and you can only kill me once."

"So you might think," said Drake. "You would be wrong. As for your answer, a Realm is an Earth, one of many. For your information, your security systems have been disabled. You are stalling for time by asking me questions, but it is to no avail. No one is coming, and even if they did, their fortune would not end any better than it was for the last guards. They would die for no reason."

"What do you intend to do with us?" Jon asked.

"I *had* intended to kill you," said Drake. "However, now that I know you entered this Realm only because you were pursued, I wish to know more about that. The ones who drove you here are the ones responsible for the intrusion. They shall receive my full wrath. I would have that information from you."

Geoffrey felt a faint hope at that.

Jon glanced over at Gerhardt. "You really want to have that conversation here, in front of him?"

"Are you not all together?"

"No, we were *his* prisoners before you arrived. Now, I suppose we're yours."

Drake glanced at Gerhardt and frowned. "Why were you keeping these men prisoner? What have they done to you?"

"Aliens had just attacked a house, and these men were there. The military picked them up and brought them here. I am a contractor for the legal authorities and protectors of this country. It is standard procedure to quarantine and question anyone who has had possible contact with... something so unusual. These men have information the government needs to know."

"They have information I need to know, and I care little at all for your government," said Drake. "By *aliens*, I presume that you mean the men with the grey eyes."

"Yes. And possibly you."

"They weren't aliens in the sense that you are thinking." Drake shook his head. "They were not from some other planet in space. It would seem that much of this unpleasantness could have been avoided if you had but spoken to these men before taking them. I find I now regret the death of your guards. I thought you aligned with... my enemies. I shall allow you to live if you give up your interest in *these* men."

"There are worse things than death," said Gerhardt.

"Yes, there are. Would care to sample a few of them?"

"I would not."

☉

Jon thought he was keeping himself together fairly well.

He'd been having a difficult day, and the scary sorcerer from the darkly enigmatic Ruined Courts was a final capper. This Drake, whoever he was, was coldly dispassionate about dealing death. And yet, he didn't seem to be an unthinking killer.

His new friends confused him. Jason was hiding something, for all he'd been kind to Jon. Geoffrey seemed like an ordinary university student, but there was something about him that made Jon doubt it. Neither of them had hesitated to risk their lives for a stranger, something that Jon had found was quite rare on any world.

Not that he was complaining. Quite the opposite. He just didn't understand their motivations. Gerhardt, he understood. The man was a corporate bloodhound who saw an opportunity to get ahead by understanding the technology Jon bore implanted in his body. It was a fool's errand. This world's technology couldn't understand or interface with his, but he had no doubt Gerhardt would try anyway. Jason and Geoffrey were clearly just in the wrong place at the wrong time, and Jon wasn't sure why his precognitive sense had guided him to them.

Drake was something else.

Jon had no idea what to make of Drake. He hadn't seen him in any vision. Drake was an unknown variable in the ongoing equation of Jon's reality. To make matters worse, Drake didn't show in Jon's visions when Jon did try to see him. Instead, all he could sense was fire, pain, and madness.

It wasn't reassuring.

☉

Geoffrey couldn't imagine staying so calm in the face of this deadly man. He was ready to piss himself, and Drake had hardly paid any attention to him. Of course, he'd had to pee anyway.

"You are not, at the moment, a threat to me," Drake said to Gerhardt. "Who knows? I may have a use for you in the future. Remember that I let you live when I easily could have chosen otherwise. These men, I will be taking."

Gerhardt glanced at the dead guards. "I don't see that I have any way to stop you."

"You do not. Now, I will be taking my leave." Drake turned his back to Gerhardt. "We need to talk," Drake said to Jon, and to Jason and Geoffrey, "You two may have valuable information, as well."

"We're not going—" There a sense of disorientation, and a rainbow flash fading to a bright afternoon sun. "—with you," Jason finished. "Where the hell?"

"Albuquerque," said Drake. "There is a place here with excellent enchiladas." He turned to Jon. "I'll ask you not to run. It would be inconvenient and uncomfortable for you if I have to bring you back. I just want to talk to all of you. If, after we talk, you have no desire to know who attacked you or why, then I shall return each of you to the place of your choosing." His eyes lingered on Jason for a moment.

"Well, since you could have simply killed us back there, why not?" Jon looked down at the blood on his shirt. "We might stand out a bit."

Geoffrey felt an electric tingle crawl across his body. When he looked down, the bloodstains had all disappeared, and his clothes were mended. More magic, it seemed.

"You cleaned our clothes?" asked Jason.

"Yes. I even provided you with that ceramic toy knife you've been thinking of. Now, let us sit, eat, and tell sad tales of the death of kings."

Geoffrey wasn't sure if Drake was paraphrasing Shakespeare or if he just talked that way all the time. The man was terrifying, and yet there was something about him, an almost magnetic charisma, that inspired trust.

Jason looked conflicted. He was very protective of Jon, for some reason, and also seemed to want to trust Drake but wouldn't allow himself to. Geoffrey wasn't sure about Jon, but he was certain Drake could have killed them and had chosen instead to be nice. That had to count for something.

Drake led them through a throng of tourists to an old restaurant where a tree grew in the center of an enclosed courtyard. Geoffrey thought it was odd that no one around them seemed to think Drake was strange, since he was in armor and had pointed ears. Geoffrey thought that was almost stranger than Drake himself.

The hostess flirted with Drake as they made their way to a table. Geoffrey wondered if she saw the same thing they did, or if Drake was hiding himself somehow. The table was separated from the others by a low wall that did a good job of blocking the noise of the restaurant.

"I assume you're buying," said Jon. "I doubt they take the money I'm used to here."

Geoffrey paused from reading the menu at that. He knew Jon had said he was a traveler, but he hadn't really thought that Jon was... well, alien. He thought about the earlier conversation between Jon and Drake, and wondered.

"Despite the unpleasantness of our meeting, I'd like you to consider yourselves my guests," Drake said. "I just want to get to the bottom of what is going on."

Geoffrey excused himself and went in search of a restroom. He was slightly tempted to run and not look back, but Jason was his friend. He couldn't and wouldn't do that to him. Geoffrey took care of his business, washed his hands, and returned to the table in time to hear Drake order drinks and appetizers in fluent Spanish. It made sense, he supposed, looking at Drake; he doubted English was his native language. Not that he thought Spanish was, either.

Geoffrey ordered a soda.

The chips and salsa were good. The salsa was a little hotter than he was used to, but he figured that in New Mexico, the Mexican food was a little closer to its roots than in Kentucky. Everything from earlier today was starting to fade from Geoffrey's mind. It had all been too strange. He kept expecting to wake up on the couch, and hoped he'd get to eat first.

Geoffrey's arm started hurting again, and it started to sink in that all of this was really happening.

"I feel that we should wait until after we eat to discuss important matters," said Drake. "Tempers will be more muted with full bellies."

"I'm not sure what you might think important," Jon said. "Honestly, it's nice to not be hunted for a little while. It's been a rough week."

Geoffrey noticed Jason looking uncomfortable. "You okay, buddy?"

"I'm fine," Jason replied. He was glaring at Drake.

"Something troubling you?" Drake asked Jason.

He was spared a reply by the waitress returning with drinks and little bowls of queso blanco for each of them. Drake was drinking Dos XX with lime, which seemed odd. Geoffrey had never thought of fruit juice and beer going together. The pale cheese dip was amazing.

"So…," Jon drawled after a few minutes. "You're not like the people I met in the Eternal City."

"Neither are you," Drake replied. "I take it you are fairly new to the family there."

"You know them?"

"Most of them, only by reputation. I was away during most of the last war with them."

"War?"

"Did they not mention that their people had waged war against mine recently?"

"Unprovoked, I supposed you'd say."

"Not at all. I believe the enmity is generally universal."

Geoffrey was fascinated by what wasn't being said as much as by what was.

"The flapping before you arrived – what was that?" Jon asked.

Drake smiled, and Geoffrey noticed his fangs again. "That was me. I'm a shapeshifter, of course. Did they fail to mention that about my people?"

"So why do you look the way you do now," Jason asked. He sounded angry.

"For much the same reason as you," said Drake. "I was born this way."

Geoffrey wondered why Jason was angry, and why Drake's response seemed to scare him.

The waitress returned with a lot of food and more drinks, and everyone seemed content to eat in silence. Geoffrey watched his companions as he ate. There was more going on than he thought, but he didn't know what it could be. The food was really good, though, so he didn't mind too much.

CHAPTER FOUR

Geoffrey had ordered the enchiladas, since Drake said those were good. They weren't just good; they were amazing. Geoffrey had never had Mexican food that tasted so good. Jason ordered tacos, but then, he usually preferred food he could eat with his hands. Drake and Jon had also ordered the enchiladas, although Drake had ordered a double plate-full. It seemed like an obscene amount of food to Geoffrey, but Drake ate steadily and finished before Geoffrey did. Jon only picked at his food, which was probably why he was so skinny.

It was difficult for Geoffrey to remember the fear he'd been feeling only a few hours ago. He'd never had anything truly bad happen to him before. Not like that. He'd been beaten up a few times in school, and he'd had the normal minor injuries kids got when growing up in the country, scrapes and such, but he'd never actually faced death. His mind was still shying away from it.

After collecting the plates, the waitress brought a plate full of steaming, triangular buns that looked a little like doughnuts. Geoffrey asked her about them, and she said they were *sopapilla*, good with honey, which was on the table in a squeeze bottle.

Geoffrey had never had a sopapilla before, but it was quite good with the honey, just as she'd suggested it would be. The honey had a faintly spicy taste, and Geoffrey wondered if it was just a local variety, or if the locals actually put peppers in it. In any case, it was good.

"Well, I imagine you are all somewhat more at ease now," said Drake when they'd finished eating. "If I understand the situation correctly, Jon, you were pursued by strange forces who were trying to kill you, and for some reason you ended up at Jason's house. Jason and Geoffrey then protected you and themselves against the attackers."

"That sums it up rather well," Jon said. "I imagine the devil is in the details, though. I went to their house for help because that was where I needed to be. I don't really feel like explaining it further, and I suspect you know anyway."

Drake smiled. "Then, if they wish, I will return Jason and Geoffrey to their home, and we can continue our business."

Geoffrey had mixed feelings about that. While the day had been terrifying, it had also been exhilarating. He'd never had an adventure, much less imagined being on one with magic and stuff. He didn't want that to end. He'd always wanted more out of life. Now that he'd had a glimpse of that, he didn't want things to return to normal.

"You're not getting rid of me that easily, sorcerer," said Jason. "Jon came into *my* house, wounded, and we protected him. He is *my* guest."

Geoffrey thought that was taking the Southern hospitality thing a bit far. Jason had lived in Georgia at one time, but Geoffrey had always suspected he was from farther away, South America or someplace. Geoffrey also suspected Jason was using hospitality as an excuse. He hoped it worked. He wanted to see how Jon's problems, whatever they were, all turned out.

Drake frowned. "I see. That is a powerful thing to invoke. I think, maybe, that you don't hold the guest obligation in the same regard that I do."

"Try to do something to him and find out," Jason snapped.

"You forget yourself," Drake responded coldly. "I invited you to eat with me as my guests. Had you forgotten?"

Jason blushed. "I had not, but I didn't know in what regard *you* held it."

"Now you do. Do not insult me again."

Geoffrey was suddenly feeling scared again.

"Perhaps we can clear this up easily," said Jon. "Jason, I appreciate the help you both gave me, but I'm all right now. I trust Drake, although I'm not completely sure why. I would happily relieve you of any guest burden you feel."

"Sadly, you cannot do that," Drake said. "Only he can, and I don't think he trusts me as much as you may."

Jason nodded sharply to Drake. "I am obligated to see you safe, Jon. I don't think you will be until this whole business is resolved. I'm a part of it now. Like it or not."

"Well, shit," said Geoffrey. "Count me in, too, I guess. I'm not going to leave my friend at the mercy of strangers. Those guys attacked us in our house. Hell, I was cut defending Jon. I'd like to know why."

"You were wounded?" Drake asked; his voice sounded odd.

"Just a cut on the arm, not deep. Gerhardt's men bandaged it." To tell the truth, Geoffrey had hardly thought about it. The cut didn't hurt much.

Drake glanced away and then waved the waitress over to settle the bill. Geoffrey noticed that Drake gave her a rather generous tip, as well. Geoffrey wondered where he got the money. Hell, maybe he just conjured it. Geoffrey wouldn't have put it past him.

"That's not going to turn into leaves at midnight, is it?" Jason asked.

"I'm an elf, not a fairy," said Drake. "Besides, it would be rude, and difficult for the lovely young lady. What part of me saying that I like this place and come here often did you miss? There is a park near here that I also enjoy. We can talk further there without being overheard."

They stood and straightened their chairs. Drake excused himself to use the restroom, and Geoffrey suddenly thought again about running. Strangely, the others simply waited for Drake to return. Jon was an unknown, but he'd have expected Jason to get out of this situation as fast as he could, hospitality or not.

Maybe he didn't Jason as well as he thought.

"Ready?" Drake asked when he returned. When they nodded, he gestured, and the feeling of disorientation swept over them again. Then they were standing on a ridge overlooking a vast city – Geoffrey assumed it was Albuquerque. A river glinted in the distance. The air was cool and a little thin. Geoffrey was surprised that none of them seemed to have trouble with the transition: Cincinnati was near sea level. Geoffrey wasn't sure what Albuquerque's elevation was, much less the high ridge they stood on. Aspens grew along the trail where they found themselves, and both snow and bright flowers spread across the ground.

This place was beautiful and isolated.

Drake sat on a nearby fallen tree trunk and gestured for the others to settle in. "I think I like this place because it reminds me of home," he said.

"Where is that?" Jason asked. For once, he didn't sound hostile or sarcastic when speaking to Drake.

"Someplace lost in the mists of time. I haven't been able to return home since I left long ago. However, we are not here to have *me* tell tales."

"I suppose you'd like to hear my story," Jon said.

"It would seem to be the most relevant."

"The circumstances of my birth aren't important to the

story," Jon said, "except, of course, that I wasn't born on Earth. I'm a starship pilot. A job I took led me to Earth – not this one – where I met a group of strangely dressed people in a bar. They seemed to think I was related to them, although I knew I couldn't be. They told me a strange tale about an Eternal City in a Golden Kingdom, and a power to walk between different worlds. Ordinarily, I would have laughed and walked away, thinking they were drunk or con-artists, but there was something about them that made me believe what they said. Being between contracts at the time, I thought, *Why not?* I told them to show me, and they did. They took me to see the Eternal City, and it was just as glorious as they had promised. As for the Cynosure, well, they weren't going to take me home if I didn't at least try to gain its power. I wasn't entirely unwilling, as I wanted that power for myself, if I could have it."

"So you *are* of the Royal Family," said Drake.

"That isn't possible."

Drake seemed amused. "They didn't tell you that the Cynosure is gene-locked to their Royal Family? Anyone not of that bloodline dies – horribly, as I understand it."

Jon looked shaken. "I didn't know."

"I'm not surprised. Many of them are ambitious and cruel. You have some of the look of that family. You could be a son of Joseph or Dominic. Well, any of them, really, since they all have the look of their sire. You could even be a by-blow from the old king. He was quite the goat, as I understand it."

"Joseph was kind to me when I was there, although he denied ever having been near my home universe. As I said, I didn't know about the thing with bloodlines, so I didn't ask around too much. In any case, it was some of the younger members of the family who took me there. I hadn't thought about it until now, but I think they'd been looking for me, specifically, there on Earth."

"They may have simply thought it would be funny to lure

someone to the Cynosure and watch them die," Drake suggested. "However, the odds are against such an accident. I would put little past many of that family, although Joseph always seemed honorable. If he said you aren't his, I'd believe him. Speaking of honorable men, did you ask Dominic? You are of a similar build."

"I did, and I was given a curt negative answer. He didn't seem amused. Nor did he elaborate."

"He is rather dour," Drake agreed. "I am also uncertain of his sexual predilections."

"You seem to have a lot of personal information about a people you say you've been at war with," said Jason.

"I also said we are no longer at war. I met some of them before the war, some after," said Drake. "I am a general, and a soldier must have good information about the opposition. I am also not as young as I look."

"I would never have assumed you were," Jason said. "What is this damn *Cynosure* you both keep talking about?"

"Thank you," Geoffrey said quietly. "I was wondering about that."

"You want to field this one?" Jon said to Drake. "You probably know more about it than I do."

"Almost certainly, and I have no desire to divulge most of it. Let us say that the Cynosure is one of the primal Powers of the Realms, ancient and terrible. With its power, an attuned person can walk the worlds. They can move from Realm to Realm, universe to universe. At least, they can walk the Earths."

"Well, after I was joined with the Cynosure – a weird experience, let me tell you – I found it had meshed with my own mental mathematical construct of reality," said Jon. "I felt I had the knowledge of how to move through that reality. I was enjoying just seeing how it all worked, at least until those bastards tried to kill me."

"The younger people who had taken you there?"

"Yes. I don't know why. Most of them left when I didn't die. I had one of my premonitions, turned my head, and a crossbow bolt just missed my eye. That's how I got the cut on my cheek. I'm normally faster, but the world seemed sluggish there. It was difficult to move. I took another glancing blow to the head and was hit in the side. The guy with the crossbow didn't stop to monologue, and I didn't wait around to find out why he was attacking me. I jumped into the void."

"What do you mean when you say *jump*?"

"I can apport – move from place to place."

"I know what apportation is," Drake said. "You may have noticed that I do it myself."

"I assumed you were using some magical power. I could apport by will alone, before I gained access to the power of the Cynosure," Jon said. "I just couldn't apport to different universes. Never thought to try, anyway."

"So you made one of your apports, augmented with Cynosure. Where did you aim for?"

"That's the thing. I panicked and didn't pick a destination. I just jumped *away*, and then I found myself falling through... something. I don't know how to describe it. I fell, and then finally I focused my will enough to try to go somewhere I would find help. I landed outside their door, and these gentlemen were kind enough to help me."

"I thought at first you'd been in a car accident," Geoffrey added.

"Interesting," said Drake. "And the assassins?"

"I had never seen them before they attacked us at the house. I don't know where they came from or how they got there. From what I saw, they weren't human."

"Hmm. *Human* is a fluid term," said Drake. "I do know where the assassins came from: a Realm very far from where they died. The people there cannot move through the Realms without assistance, so someone must have taken them to that

Realm to kill you."

"Why would they do that?"

"To send me a message. To implicate me in your death, perhaps. The Realm they are from is mine, as is the Realm where they ended up. I claimed both long ago. I need to go now to the place they're from and discover who sent them."

"You think someone might still know?" asked Jon. "Wouldn't whoever sent them have covered their tracks, gone back and killed anyone who knew them, and so on? Gods, I sound Machiavellian."

"I'm counting on that person trying to cover their tracks. Time doesn't run the same in all Realms, and it takes time to travel across them, if you're walking or riding a horse. Whoever it is, it will take them some time to return to Nandegurth. In fact, we have a little over an hour, at the soonest, before anyone could have gotten back there using Cynosure. I plan to be there to meet them."

CHAPTER FIVE

The sun was setting on the far horizon, and the air was turning cold. Jason felt exposed on the top of that mountain. The jagged rocks below them reminded him of other mountains, far from here. He didn't want to think about those mountains and the sense of longing he felt for a home he could never return to.

Jason didn't like this arrogant man, Drake.

It wasn't just the way in which Drake had taken control of their fates, taking them from Gerhardt. He had a way of talking that just got under Jason's skin, and Drake's casual display of power when he killed the security guards had shaken him. Drake had killed them horribly just because they had dared to resist his will. They weren't a threat, only in his way. It was monstrous, and yet the others didn't see it.

Geoffrey appeared almost smitten, as if Drake were a hero riding out of some comic book to save them. Jason needed to shake Geoffrey out of that mindset. He didn't know what Drake was, but he certainly wasn't a hero. There was no proof that Drake wasn't responsible for the attack on Jon and the invasion of Jason's home.

Jason wasn't sure about Jon, although they had the bond of hospitality between them. Jason was obligated to help the man, but it was starting to sound as if his story was every bit as complicated as Drake's. Jon said he could move around the way Drake did, and that he had access to a power of a kind that was similar to Drake's.

The bond of obligation wasn't as extreme as Jason had made out. If Jon proved untrustworthy, Jason would walk away from him.

On the other hand, Drake had said that he could get them all home. He'd been looking at Jason when he said it, too. If Drake really could get him home, and maybe help smooth things over... Jason didn't want to allow himself to hope again. It had been too long since he'd been home, although he'd tried in the past... No, best not to think about it.

"If it takes so long for the enemy to get to this Nandegurth place, how are you going to beat them there?" Jason asked.

"Because, young man, I'm not using Cynosure."

Jason ground his teeth at being called a young man. Drake seemed to be toying with him, not to mention that Drake barely looked to be over twenty-five. *Don't let it show,* he thought to himself. *Don't let him know that you know he knows.*

"The people of the Ruined Courts don't use the Cynosure?" said Jon.

"Certainly not," Drake replied with mock offense. "My people have access to an older and far more powerful... magic."

"Of course they do."

"We should head for Nandegurth as soon as we're finished here." Drake paused and looked pointedly Jason. "You're sure that you still wish to come along?"

"You're not going to get rid of me so easily, sorcerer," Jason snapped. "I told you that before."

"Just offering," Drake replied amicably. "And you, Geoffrey?"

Jason wondered why Drake was interested in Geoffrey. He hoped it wasn't something weird and sexual. Geoffrey was young and vulnerable. Jason would personally slit Drake's throat if he tried anything, sorcerer or not.

"I'm sticking with my friend Jason," said Geoffrey.

"So be it."

Ο

Drake wondered what he was doing.

It made sense to use Jon to lure out whomever was behind the attack. Drake told himself that he cared not at all what might happen to Jon after he was done using him. He knew he was lying to himself, though. He liked these people. He wanted to protect them. Whoever was behind the attack on Jon was also targeting Drake, to some degree. They would soon learn why that was a bad idea.

Drake knew he should drop Jason and Geoffrey back in Cincinnati and forget about them, but he'd bartered for their lives, and that made him somewhat responsible for them. The people after him and Jon wouldn't stop until they were forced to. That meant they would go after anyone who might be leverage of any kind. There was also the possibility that Gerhardt wouldn't stop going after them himself. Drake had inadvertently made their lives more complicated.

No, it was better for his own…conscience, to take them both with him and keep them safe. Jason was an interesting problem, since he was obviously running and hiding from something. What, Drake didn't know and didn't really care about, as long as it didn't become a problem. He also liked Jason for some reason he couldn't quite pin down. Maybe Jason reminded Drake of himself in his youth, so long ago. He couldn't say. Maybe he just liked the man's spirit. People who would stare into the face of death and spit were few and far between.

Drake liked his attitude.

"Traveling to Nandegurth will not be as easy as apporting across the continent," Drake said. "Also, we are going to be gone for some time. If you travel with me, you may never make it back here. I just want you all to understand that. I am agreeing to bring you with me; I cannot guarantee your safety."

"I wouldn't expect any less from someone like you," said Jason.

Drake frowned. There was a fine line between an attitude and insolence. Jason was crossing that line. He held a smoldering anger for Drake that seemed to go beyond their current circumstances. What Jason blamed Drake for, he couldn't guess. At some point, they were going to have to clear the air between them.

"I will promise you all that I will not kill, harm, or betray you while you are in my care. I will protect each of you to the best of my abilities, which are not inconsiderable. You will also have my hospitality and the hospitality of the House of Drake, a noble house of the Ruined Courts. While you are with me, I will ask that you do not kill except in self-defense, or otherwise engage in any activity that may reflect badly upon my honor or that of my House."

Jason broke his eye contact, perhaps sensing he'd gone too far. Maybe he was embarrassed by Drake's generosity. Drake had just pledged far more than he'd intended.

"Why are you helping me?" Jon asked. "Us?"

Drake smiled reassuringly. "It isn't entirely out of a sense of altruism. I mentioned before that someone was sending me a message. You'll understand that better when we get to Nandegurth."

"Where is this place?" asked Geoffrey.

"The Realm is very far from here."

"This universe, or another?" Jon asked.

"Another."

"Then why not just say that?" said Jason. "Why say *Realm*? Why not *universe*, or *Earth*, or *planet*, or whatever?"

"Because I like to be precise. A Realm is an Earth in another universe, no matter how different and strange. Another universe might not have an Earth and therefore could not be a Realm."

"That seems to be a very Earth-centric view of the cosmos," Jon said. "What makes Earth so important?"

"Absolutely nothing," Drake lied. "I don't have time to explain the metaphysics to you at the moment. We should get going."

"Waiting on you," Jason said, folding his arms over his chest.

☉

Geoffrey was worried about Jason.

He'd never known his friend to be one to bait the bull, but Jason was antagonizing Drake, and Geoffrey couldn't figure out why. Given everything that happened to them in this very long day, Drake didn't even seem that strange. Geoffrey was inclined to trust him, although he had to admit a part of it was that he wanted to see the wondrous places Drake and Jon talked about. What was the Eternal City, and why was it called that? What were the Ruined Courts? What was Nandegurth, or the Realms? Why did Drake look like a wicked elf?

A part of Geoffrey that he hadn't even known was there was crying out for adventure.

"I brought you all up to Sandia Crest because the air on Nandegurth is thinner than this Earth's atmosphere is at sea level," Drake said. "I thought coming here first would make the transition easier. That world is very different from this one."

"We're ready," Jon said with a nod to each of them.

Geoffrey hoped he was ready.

Drake gestured, and the world disappeared in a blaze of rainbows. This apport was different from the previous times. They stood in a grey, swirling tunnel that swept past them, or maybe they swept past the walls; either way, it was disorientating. Then came another burst of color, and they were standing on a rock ridge overlooking an appallingly dreary landscape.

Geoffrey turned around and saw a stunning, tall spire of rock rising into the…sky. That sky was bright white, with black clouds. In the distance, Geoffrey could see snow-covered mountains of rock floating, with rivers falling out of them; all of the rocks were shades of grey. The air was clear but cold and thin.

"Where…?" Jon seemed at a loss for words.

"Nandegurth," said Drake. "It's a demi-Realm in the Black Realms, the subjugated Realms of the Ruined Courts."

"A demi-Realm?"

"What you see is what you get. There's not much universe beyond this planet. We're in a crater about fifteen kilometers deep and a hundred fifty kilometers across – roughly the size of Ireland, if you know that place. Call it about two-thirds the size of the State of Ohio."

Jon shook his head. "I know of Ireland; I don't know Ohio. Why can't we see the walls of the crater?"

"On Earth, you can see only about five kilometers at ground level. It is no different here. The atmosphere here is similar in composition, with slightly less nitrogen, a little more neon and argon."

"Is that healthy to breathe?" Geoffrey asked.

"It's essentially the same atmosphere as on the Earth you just left."

"Oh." He wished he'd kept his mouth shut,

"The gravity is slightly less," said Jon.

"Yes, hence the thinner atmosphere."

"Where does the light come from?" asked Jason.

"There's a glowing shell of plasma around the planet, out to about three light-minutes, where the universe ends. The plasma is energized by the slow collapse of the outer wall of the universe."

"The universe is collapsing?" said Jon.

"Yes. At the present rate, the outer veil will reach the planet in about a billion years, so I think we have time to conduct our business, assuming there are no other questions."

"Just about," Jon said. "How does something like this even happen? I assume the atmosphere of the planet is restricted to the crater."

"I've always assumed a large cometary impactor struck the planet, when the universe was larger. I wasn't here to see it, so I can't be certain."

"So, what now?" said Jason.

"We aren't far from my citadel." Drake turned and gestured toward the rock spire in the distance. "Only a few kilometers to get there. Walking will help acclimate you."

They began walking down a wide, graded stone path. The edges of the path were high and jagged, as if the rock had been blasted aside. Which, for all Geoffrey knew, it had been. The air was cold and bit damp; it reminded Geoffrey of winter in Cincinnati. There was snow in the shadows along the road.

"Can I ask a question?" said Geoffrey.

"As long as you keep walking, yes."

"Why is there a rainbow when we apport?" he said cautiously.

"Light is refracted along the field-effect displacement boundary of the dimensional transit."

"It happened during the apport from Cincinnati to Albuquerque," said Jon.

"Your point?"

"It doesn't happen when I apport. And we weren't

apporting to another universe."

"Psionic apportation is a quantum displacement effect, so no rainbow," Drake said. "Apportation using one of the Powers is always cross-dimensional."

"Even within one universe?"

"What do you think you jump through?"

"I hadn't thought about it. I haven't had much time to study it. I only just gained Cynosure this morning."

"What was it like?" asked Drake. "Attuning yourself to the Cynosure?"

Jon shrugged. "Weird. There wasn't much to see. They led me onto a mountaintop, to a ring of stones with a sense of power about it. They stood and chanted as the moons rose over the horizon. One of the moons was framed by a rock with a hole bored through it, and my mind was filled with a vision of *something*; I couldn't hold onto whatever shape it was."

"I have always imagined attunement with the Cynosure to much like the power of the Courts, I see that it is different, and yet similar," Drake said. "At least in the effect on the mind."

"It extended into strange dimensions like nothing else I've ever seen," Jon said. "There was a... presence about it. An intelligence I felt against my mind. I reached out and made contact somehow. I felt myself drawn into it, and it into me. I felt as if I was on fire. I felt changed by it, and not just mentally, from the experience. I felt as if it had rewritten me at a fundamental level."

Drake was nodding. "You are encoded with it now. I sensed that when I first encountered you. I think a part of the device's quantum signature overwrites your own. You carry a piece of it with you, which is how you can navigate the Realms. You're entangled with it now."

"You're a strange one, Drake," Jon said. "The people I was with before referred to the Cynosure as if it was a god; they talked of magic and rituals. You speak of such things as science."

"If you get a repeatable, testable effect, it's science. No matter how strange."

Geoffrey was having trouble following what they were talking about, but he found it fascinating. He wished he were related to Jon, so he could attune himself with a Power and walk the worlds. It was really cool.

CHAPTER SIX

Jon thought about magic and science.

Until a few weeks before, he never would have considered magic as anything except a lot of mystical bullshit. Then he'd traveled to the Eternal City. The trip there had been much like the one he'd just experienced, coming to Nandegurth. His companions then had spoken of magic as if it were a real thing. He'd had no reason to doubt them, not once they'd shown it to him. Now, here was Drake, doing things even more astounding and calling it science.

He'd traveled to some strange worlds as a starship pilot, but none as strange as Nandegurth.

The road they walked opened up onto a vast plain with the spire of black rock in the center.

A huge army was encamped on that plain, with tens of thousands of tents aligned in neat, orderly rows, divided by wide, unpaved lanes. It was obviously a well-organized army. Metal signposts stood at the intersections of the lanes, topped with unlit, caged torches. Jon supposed that the presence of torches implied that there must be a nighttime here. He wondered how that would work. How could there be night on a world with no sun?

With his enhanced abilities, Jon sensed the mass of the planet under him and the fragile envelope of life-giving atmosphere within the crater. The planet *felt* odd. The entire planet hummed slightly, on an odd frequency outside his previous experience, as if the planet were a vast machine. The outer envelope of plasma held currents and eddies; the planet must be producing an enormously powerful magnetic field.

His perceptions shied away from the edge of reality, the boundary of the universe itself in this Realm. He couldn't sense any other planets or even asteroids, but there was a metallic mass in orbit, just under the plasma. It was too big to be a starship. He wondered if it had something to do with the creation of the magnetic field.

Could these people have space travel? Nothing Jon had seen indicated that.

All of the visible technology seemed very primitive to him. Jon thought about what Drake had said earlier. He hadn't really bought into the magic-and-gods bullshit that the people in the Eternal City had talked about, and he'd never been religious.

The power to walk the worlds *had* to be science, just radically more advanced than he'd ever seen before. The people in the Golden Kingdom believed the mysticism, though – he was sure of that. And then there was what Drake had done. Apporting the whole group of them without effort, much less how he'd killed the guards. How could that be science? How could it *not* be?

Drake called the Cynosure a device, Jon suddenly recalled. *A powerful artificial intelligence with godlike powers? That would track. The people in the Golden Kingdom used swords and crossbows. Was this advanced technology something they'd lost, so long ago that they don't even remember what it was?*

What the hell have I gotten myself into?

Soldiers marched, doing drills and singing in loud voices.

The cadence of the songs was familiar, even if the words were foreign. The soldiers were a mixed lot. Some of them looked human, some mostly human, and some not human at all. Many of the soldiers had all-grey eyes like the men who had attacked them on Earth.

Some of the soldiers were bestial in form. They had bent legs, and goat heads, complete with horns. Were they actually human?

I guess I need a new definition of human, Jon thought.

The universe he came from only had humans, at least in the explored space within twenty light years of Sol. Humans had explored most of the local cluster and found nothing more advanced than trees and insects on any of the planets, although they had certainly found traces of an alien race: the Precursors his people always worried would come back. He wondered whether the people in Nandegurth really were human, or whether they were some other humanoid species. *Does any of that even apply, in a place like this?*

Jason and Geoffrey were from an Earth. Were they human? Was Jon himself? He wasn't from any Earth, but his ancestors had been. *How does anyone ever keep any of this straight?*

The black-uniformed soldiers they passed on the road saluted. Some of them spoke briefly with Drake. All seemed to hold him in great respect, although there was none of the obsequiousness Jon had expected to see. Drake was an arrogant bastard, but he had earned the respect of these people, not just their loyalty. He'd called himself a prince and a general. Jon was inclined to believe it, after seeing this place.

"So this is how you knew where the assassins came from," Jason said. "They were yours."

"The world is mine," said Drake. "The people, I had thought universally loyal to me. I didn't send the assassins, if that's what you're insinuating. Besides, none of these people are originally from this Realm. Personally, I have trouble believing any of my soldiers would ever betray me."

Jason shook his head.

"That's why you said someone was sending you a message," said Jon. "The assassins can't be native to this world, can they? In an infinite number of universes, aren't there other worlds where the people have those same grey eyes?"

"I'm sure there are many places like that," Drake said. "However, the assassins all had tattoos of the white dragon." He gestured toward the pennants that could be seen flying from the citadel and a few tents: black, with a white dragon displayed on it, wings wide. "That symbol is mine. My troops commonly wear that tattoo."

"They were definitely from here, then."

"So it would seem. I didn't have the time to interrogate the dead, so I can't be completely sure."

Jon didn't want to think about the implications of that casual statement.

Drake led them to the gates of the citadel. The guard there spoke to Drake and then waved them through.

Jon wished he knew the language spoken here; it seemed somehow familiar, a bit like his native Cymric and also a bit like Hindi. He'd heard something like it before, he was sure. He shook his head. No doubt the language wasn't at all related to any he'd ever heard.

How could it be?

A ragged bit of memory of a woman's voice, speaking that language, came to him. He'd not thought about her in a long time. If she had been speaking the same language, then what did it mean?

O

Jason was more shaken than he cared to admit.

Despite what Drake looked like, Jason hadn't truly believed

the man could travel to different worlds. He'd thought Drake was pulling some kind of con. Drake was just another human, right? Drake couldn't *actually* be some kind of alien. It just wasn't possible. However, this place...This place was certainly not the world he was used to.

This wasn't Earth.

Nandegurth looked sterile. Nothing grew here, at least nothing within range of the central spire. Jason could see motion of some kind on the closest floating...mountain. It looked as if there might be trees growing up there, and something huge and sinuous gliding among the rocks. Whatever it was, he didn't think it was a snake.

The guards at the gate of the citadel were human enough, except for their all-grey eyes. The courtyard Jason entered was flanked by pillars of stone with carved dragons on them. He shuddered a bit when he looked at those. They were stone, but he felt dread at the thought of getting close to them, as if they might come alive and eat him.

"You doing okay, buddy?" Geoffrey asked quietly.

"Just a bit overwhelmed." Jason didn't know how Geoffrey was holding together; he hadn't struck Jason as being mentally strong. Geoffrey often freaked out when the bus was late. Jason had to admit, though, that Geoffrey was doing well with the current situation. Maybe he was just in shock; Jason thought he might be, himself.

"Yeah, me, too," Geoffrey replied. "This place is just... Wow."

The spire was of natural, dark grey stone – if anything about this place could be called natural. The citadel had been carved from the basaltic stone of the spire itself. It reminded Jason of the Temple at Petra, or the ones in India where the whole temple was carved from the stone. It was an impressive edifice. Maybe Drake had something to be arrogant about besides his looks.

"What do they keep saying to you, Drake?" asked Jason.

Drake glanced back and smiled. "They greet me as their general. As I have said before, I am a Prince of the Ruined Courts and the General of the Army of the Rim. The army you saw as we came in is that army."

"It didn't seem very big for an army, or am I just biased? The United States military fields millions of soldiers."

"The twenty thousand troops of the Army of the Rim, which you see here, are what you would call Elite Special Forces," said Drake.

"What the hell are you fighting," Jon asked, "that you need so many Special Forces? That's a larger army than the Eternal City fields, and I was told that they'd fought the Courts to a stalemate during the last war."

"My army was engaged elsewhere. The forces from the Golden Kingdom only fought the Royal Guard at the Imperial Plaza. It was the only world of the Courts they could reach, as it is the only remains of the Earth there. The House of Drake alone fields several billion troops."

"Billions?"

"There are millions of worlds in the Ruined Courts. Well, parts of worlds. We weren't the aggressors in the war. If we had been, we'd have won."

"We should just take your word for that?" said Jason. He didn't know what war they were talking about, but anyone who kept that many troops around was spoiling for a fight.

Drake shook his head. "One day, we may get to the Courts, and you'll see it for yourself. My people's armies mostly fight the armies of the warlords who rise up and fight their way in from other Realms. Most of that fighting takes place in the universes closest to the Courts, the Black Realms. To be honest, my people have little interest in what happens beyond the Black Realms."

"You being the exception?"

"I am an exception to many things."

Black-liveried servants bowed to Drake as he entered the main vestibule. The hall was huge, spanning the entire interior of the spire. Jason believed they could fit twenty thousand people in here. The ranks of tables alone were incomprehensible.

A servant spoke and gestured. Jason thought the person might be a woman, but it was difficult to tell with the people that were part animal. Part of his mind was gibbering at the concept. The solid grey eyes were weird enough, but goat people?

"Speak English," Drake commanded, "for our guests."

"Of course, My Prince," the woman said. She had an odd accent and a bit of a lisp. "We had word you were coming in, and rooms have been prepared. Will you be dining in the hall?"

As she talked, Jason realized he didn't think her form was so odd, after all. She looked different from anyone he'd ever seen before, but she was obviously a person. She was even pretty, with her grey-striped black fur.

"I think perhaps we will dine in the conference room adjacent to my quarters," Drake replied. "I think we will need the privacy."

"Very good, My Prince."

"I need to speak to the steward. Please have our guests escorted to their rooms, and comply with their requests." Drake turned to address Jason and the others. "You're in good hands here with Housekeeper Tasia. I need to start the investigation. Please join me in an hour for lunch."

Drake leaned close to speak to Jason, so the others couldn't hear, before he left. "The metal you see here is galvorn. There is no iron or steel on this world. You have nothing to fear here."

Jason was still shaking as he was led to his quarters.

CHAPTER SEVEN

Drake strode out of the citadel.

He put the people he'd traveled to Nandegurth with out of his mind. They weren't important to his current plans. Either the operational security of the training Realm had been compromised, or someone had gone to extraordinary lengths to make him think it had been. It mattered little which, since it would take an intimate knowledge of his army to fake it. Either of those scenarios was bad.

His captains were waiting for him in the command tent. He nodded to them and accepted a glass of wine from Maelindefel, captain of the first division. Her thoughts were composed, as were the others'. If there was a traitor on Nandegurth, it wasn't one of his trusted officers. He relaxed a little and sipped the wine.

It was the Courts variety that he preferred, purple and tasting of cloves.

"We have a problem," Drake began. "I left so abruptly because I was informed of activity in a distant Realm I guard, where family resides. Assassins were sent there to kill a member of the royal house of the Golden City. The assassins appeared to have been from here."

Maelindefel nodded. "A squad was missing this morning at roll call, General. We sent out search parties, but no trace of them could be found. We have not investigated other possibilities."

Drake sighed. It was as he'd feared. Someone was trying to make it look as if he wanted a war with the North. He did not.

"Did they succeed?" asked Torvus, his third division commander, a huge beastman with black fur. Drake had known him for almost a hundred years. He was loyal.

"They did not succeed, and some of the soldiers may have been missing, if it was a full squad. I'm not convinced they were our soldiers. As I said, they appeared to be, but the target was not particularly well-equipped for battle, and they failed."

"Were any captured?"

"Unknown," said Drake. "I counted six bodies. If they were our missing squad, then four are unaccounted for. Either they were killed because they wouldn't go along with the assassination plot, or they were captured by the inhabitants of that Realm."

"Does the Golden Kingdom know?" Aubriella Scylla asked. She was his second division commander, fairly new to his circle of officers but very talented. She'd risen quickly through the ranks. She was a sorcerer from one of the sept houses of Drake.

"Not that I know of. The locals had captured the royal from the North. He is here now as my guest. He's on the run from the Golden Kingdom; I am unsure as to why. Some of the younger royals tried to kill him when he was there. The timing is too much of a coincidence for me. Either someone from the North interfered here, or they are working with someone from the Courts who did."

There were grumbles at that. None of his officers had been involved in the recent war, but they all knew someone who had been. Many soldiers of House Drake ended up in the Royal

Guard. It was unthinkable to them that someone from the Courts would collude with someone from the Golden Kingdom.

"I don't like the idea, either," said Drake. "Is there any information about the missing squad?"

"We hadn't thought they might have left Nandegurth," Maelindefel said. "We can ask the guards at the Waypoint, but no one reported any unusual activity. I think they would have reported it if a team had left that way."

"If someone from the Golden Kingdom was involved, they could have used Cynosure to walk the Realms."

Several of his commanders made the sign of the Eye with their fingers, to ward off evil.

"The other option being someone from the Courts using the Omphalos. Neither option is satisfactory, as I would have felt the use of a Power within this Realm." Drake shook his head. "The wards are also intact. No, the Waypoint remains the most likely point of vulnerability. Who was in charge of security overnight?"

"Sergeant Oisin was on duty, General," said Maelindefel. "Should I fetch him?"

"I think we should question him before we go further with our investigation."

Maelindefel nodded and left.

"General, is it wise to have one from the Golden Kingdom here?" asked Torvus.

"Wise? That's hard to say. He is a member of the royal family there by blood only, and too young to have been involved in the war. I want to know more of his story, as there is something strange about him. If I can get him on our side…"

"Understood, General. I didn't mean to sound as if I was questioning your judgement."

"I didn't take it that way."

Maelindefel came back in with a beastman sporting a red-dyed mohawk. The man bowed deeply before coming to stand before Drake. "General."

"Sergeant Oisin, did Commander Maelindefel explain why I've asked you here?"

"No, My General."

"You were on duty last night? At the Waypoint?"

"Yes, General. Is this about the team that left?"

Drake glanced at Maelindefel, who looked surprised. "Yes. Tell me about that, sergeant."

"It was a standard squad, sir. Their papers said they were doing reconnaissance in the forest outside Darkton. The papers were all in order, sir. I had no reason to question those papers. Did I do wrong, sir?"

Darkton was a town in one of the Black Realms. There had been reports of monsters in the forests, and Drake had sent teams there before for hunting practice. "No, you did well. Thank you, sergeant. That will be all."

Drake waited for him to leave and then sighed again.

"I didn't issue those papers, General," said Maelindefel. "However, the squad is from my division, and I take full responsibility for them and their actions. Should I relieve myself of duty, sir?"

"Don't be rash," Drake said. "I need you where you are, and I trust you with my life."

"Thank you, sir."

"Don't thank me yet. I want you to take a team and go to Darkton. Find out if anyone saw our soldiers there, or anyone else. Strangers will be talked about in that town. Find out what you can and report back in the morning."

"General!" She saluted and left, calling out orders as she went. Maelindefel was a confident and competent officer. She'd get the job done.

"General, with your leave, I'll take a team and guard the Waypoint personally," said Torvus. "As you said, we could have a vulnerability."

"Thank you, I'd appreciate that."

The other commanders left with Torvus, and Drake finished his wine, alone with his thoughts.

☉

Geoffrey had never stayed in a room as opulent as the one given to him.

The room was carved from basalt, like the rest of the building, but the walls were covered with rich, monochrome tapestries and silvery velvet draperies. The furniture, including the chandelier, were intricately shaped from some dark metal. A filigreed window looked out over the landscape, where he could see one of the strange floating mountains drifting past.

He was surprised to find hot and cold running water in the bath, along with bars of scented herbal soap and a glass bottle of shampoo. There was no toilet paper, but there was a bidet. He'd actually expected that.

A glint of red drew his eye to the tapestry next to the window. Braided hair had been picked in intricate detail with coppery wire. The figure could only be Drake or one of his ancestors. The detail on the figure's armor and sword was superb, as was the detail on the monster he was fighting. It looked like something from a Cthulhu story: lots of eyes and flailing tentacles.

He wondered if the scene had actually happened.

The other tapestries were also scenes of battle. In every one of them was a red-haired man fighting. Geoffrey wished he knew what the story was. It looked interesting.

There was a knock on the door.

"Enter," he called.

"Young sir," said the servant, "Prince Drake has called you to lunch." The servant's tone implied that it was a great honor.

Geoffrey wondered again just how powerful Drake was. When he'd called himself a prince, Geoffrey hadn't thought much of it, but this whole world seemed to belong to him.

"Please lead the way," Geoffrey said.

The others were waiting when he arrived, and he moved to stand with Jason. His friend was looking pale. He wondered what had happened, or if Jason was just worn down. Geoffrey was feeling seriously jet-lagged himself.

Drake arrived and waved them inside. He took his place at the head of the table and gestured for them to sit down. The room and table were smaller than Geoffrey expected, something more like someone might find in a boardroom.

"We aren't terribly formal here," said Drake, "at least not for a casual lunch."

Servants brought out glasses and a thick, blue-purple wine. Other servants placed plates in front of each of them piled high with roast meat and mushrooms that smelled amazing. Small bowls of something that might have been white carrots were placed next to the plates.

"Any luck with your investigation?" Jon asked.

"I have some leads; they are being followed even now," said Drake. "Please eat. We'll have time to discuss important matters after."

Geoffrey sighed and carefully cut a little of the meat. It was tender and cut easily. He tried it. It was just beef, roasted with herbs. He could taste rosemary and onions, among other herbs. He'd almost been afraid to try it. The root vegetable *was* carrot, glazed in something sweet, maybe honey. Servants placed plates of steaming rolls with butter next to each of them and left.

The food was excellent, if strangely mundane. Geoffrey had been expecting something weird and horrible, like monkey brains or haggis or something. He was glad it wasn't that.

Even Jason seemed to enjoy the meal, once he brought himself to try it. Geoffrey knew Jason preferred finger foods, but sometimes Geoffrey liked to have a real meal. It was the first formal meal he'd had since leaving home for college.

The wine was odd. It was like nothing Geoffrey had ever tasted. It smelled and tasted of sweet cloves, with an underlying smoky flavor. It was thick but seemed to turn to mist on the tongue. It was good, but he suspected it was also very strong. He felt lightheaded after just the one glass. He asked for water after he finished it.

Drake waved the servants out after they had collected the plates. Geoffrey couldn't remember ever feeling so full, or so satisfied. A small hearth held a fire crackling, and he realized he was happy. Just… happy. He felt as if he'd been missing this all his life.

"Now that we've eaten, maybe we can sort out a little of this long and confusing day," Jon said. "How was it that you arrived in time to rescue us, if that is what you actually did? If you don't mind me asking."

"I sensed it when you entered that Realm," said Drake. "As I said before, I have a personal interest there. I traveled as quickly as I could, but you had already been taken by Gerhardt's soldiers. I scouted out the building and then entered in the manner I felt would cause the least disruption to the locals."

"You burst in through a window on the twentieth floor. How did you even get up there?"

"I have my ways."

"Hmm. Would any of those ways be why I saw the shadow of wings before you burst in? I heard a bit about your people when I was in the Eternal City, and you did mention being a shapeshifter."

"I'm sure you heard many things. My people are mostly myths and legends to the people of the Golden Kingdom. The members of their royal family know better, of course, having just fought a war with us," Drake said. "I understand that most of the Golden Kingdom infantry involved in that war died."

"They said you could change your shape. I was just wondering if this what you really look like. If you're even human."

"I am not human. However, this is my true form. I see no reason to disguise myself in my own home."

"But you *can* change your shape," Jon insisted.

Drake smiled, and it took Geoffrey a moment to realize what he was seeing. Drake's pointed teeth shortened into normal incisors; his ears became rounded and his skin slightly darker. Drake stood up, and his skin blanched suddenly to white and turned rougher. His hands became clawed, and his face extended to become something alien and reptilian. Wings burst from his back and extended across the room.

It was so startling that no one moved or spoke.

As quickly as it had happened, Drake shifted again into his normal form and sat back down. "Are there any other tricks that I could perform for you? Shall I dance a jig?"

"Thank you, no," said Jon. He sounded shaken, and Geoffrey didn't blame him. He couldn't have spoken just then if his life depended on it. Jason was pale, and his fists were clenched so tightly that Geoffrey could see the bones of his knuckles. His friend was seriously freaked out.

"Now you know how I got up to the window," Drake said.

Geoffrey found his voice. "Could I have another glass of wine?"

CHAPTER EIGHT

Jon knew how Geoffrey felt.

"What's in that wine, anyway?" Jason asked.

"Nothing hallucinogenic," said Drake. "Herbs, and a molecule similar to alcohol."

Jon had been a little surprised that he felt relaxed from the wine. Usually, alcohol didn't affect him in any way; his implants filtered toxins, and his nervous system had been rewired to improve his reflexes while piloting. He had to admit, he liked feeling a little buzzed. It had been a long time.

"Can everyone from the Ruined Courts do that?" Jon asked. "Shapeshift, I mean."

"Not everyone can change their form, and of those who can, most not as easily as I do. The ability to shapeshift is mostly confined to the Royal and Noble Houses of the Courts. I've always had a talent for shifting, even when I was very young." Drake seemed sad for a moment.

Jon couldn't imagine Drake ever having been young. When Drake had said he was older than he looked, Jon had thought the man might be in his thirties or something. He realized now that he might have been off by an order of magnitude, or three or four. That shape-changing was more impressive, and more frightening, than anything else he'd seen so far. Everything else that had happened could be explained by the use of advanced technology, but this... No.

Servants came in, poured them all more wine, and left.

"Well, I guess some of the things they told me were true," said Jon.

"That all of my people are sorcerers and madmen?" Drake said. "Not quite."

"You're not all madmen?" said Jason.

"No, we're not all sorcerers," Drake replied with a toothy smile.

Jon wasn't sure whether Drake was serious or not.

"There are tapestries in my room," Geoffrey said into the uncomfortable silence. "They're mostly about fighting and have a figure that looks like you."

"I'm something of a living legend to my people," said Drake.

No one could ever accuse Drake of modesty, Jon thought.

"Did you fight all those things in the tapestries?" Geoffrey asked.

"Well, I haven't seen the tapestries you speak of, but probably. I've lived a long life and fought in countless wars. I am a general, you know."

"I'm curious as to what you've been fighting," Jon said. His precognitive abilities were giving him visions of endless, bloody war. Drake couldn't possibly have fought in everything he was seeing: he'd have to be ancient. "You said you didn't fight in the war against the Golden Kingdom. What could have been more important?"

Drake looked away. "I didn't know about that war until it was on our doorstep. I believe it was started over the succession to the throne of the Eternal City. It spilled down to the Ruined Courts because our bloodlines are mixed. Our emperor has a claim to both thrones – not that he wanted either. To be honest,

I wouldn't have wanted to get mixed up in that sort of thing anyway."

"Wait – your bloodlines are mixed?" said Jon. "What does that mean?"

"That you and I are related, of course." Drake grinned wickedly. "Don't worry, we're only very distant cousins."

Jon shook his head. People kept insisting he was related to the royals in the North, when he knew that he couldn't be. He knew his origins. "So the people in the Golden Kingdom are related to yours."

"That would seem to be what I was saying, yes."

"And I thought this day couldn't get any stranger."

"Things can always get stranger," Drake said. "You should remember that."

☉

After lunch, Jason felt like being alone. He went for a walk around the sprawling citadel.

The fortress was huge.

Despite the opulence of many of the rooms, it was obviously a building meant for war. It could have easily held the tens of thousands troops camped on the plain, and Jason wondered why they weren't housed inside. The lower levels held armories where hundreds of artisans were toiling away, creating weapons and armor.

Jason didn't know what galvorn was, but it was certainly the metal of choice in this place. True to what Drake had said, there didn't seem to be any iron or steel in use. It wasn't until he reached the lowest levels and saw the mines that he started to understand. The meteorite that had formed the huge crater must have been made of a particularly useful metal.

It would explain why Drake's people were on this world in the first place. There didn't seem to be any other reason; the place was desolate.

Jason stopped and watched a woman dishing out a helmet with swift, precise blows of a hammer. He couldn't see what powered the forge, but it didn't produce smoke or fumes. Jason was a woodworker by choice, but it gave him pleasure to see another artisan with obvious skill creating something beautiful. It occurred to him that there probably weren't many woodworkers in a place like this, since only trees he'd seen had been on the floating mountain.

The woman stopped to wipe sweat from her brow and saw Jason. She smiled and said something in the local language. Jason smiled back, nodded, and walked on. It was inconvenient that the locals didn't all speak English – not that it was his first language, but he'd spoken it for so long that he almost didn't remember his native tongue.

That made him sad, and he walked outside.

He'd have given almost anything to feel some sun on his skin. The strange sky glow on this world just didn't feel the same. It gave light but not much in the way of warmth.

Two of the floating mountains were in view now, and Jason wondered whether they kept to some set path or just wandered about, dumping water on everything. Higher above, the black clouds were thickening, completely opaque, and Jason could see how they would make for a long, dark night if they were regular.

Nothing about this world seemed natural.

Shouts drew Jason around the side of the citadel, toward the encampment. He'd noticed the stone arch along the road before but hadn't paid any attention to it. It was no stranger than anything else here. Now, however, he stopped, stunned. The center of the arch was filled with a film of quicksilver. He was surprised because he'd seen something similar once before, long ago, and had never expected to see its like again.

From the angle at which he viewed the arch, he could see the film was only visible from the front. Men in green and black armor stepped from the hole in the air and joined others fighting Drake's men. He'd thought it some kind of training exercise at first, until he saw a bright splash of arterial blood. It took his brain a moment to realize that this world was being invaded. The enemy soldiers were headed for the courtyard, but he might be able to get there first if he ran.

He spun on his heel and ran for the gates. He didn't think he could get there fast enough to close the gates, but he could give warning. That might be enough.

Enough for what, he wasn't sure.

Servants were in the courtyard, placing baskets of raw meat at the base of each of the pillars.

"Run!" he shouted. He hoped they knew English.

Several of them screamed as they saw past him. The guards near the entrance to the citadel ran past him toward the enemy, whoever they were. There was a *whoosh* in the air, and Jason felt a sharp, nauseating burst of fire in his right arm. A crossbow bolt shattered against the pillar in front of him. He was pretty sure it had just gone through his bicep.

"Drake!" he screamed.

He turned to face the enemy. He didn't know what he'd be able to do, but he'd fight if he had to. One of the guards was down, and the other was holding back a dozen of the enemy troops; he wouldn't last long alone. Jason threw his knife into the throat of one invader, stepped in, and grabbed the haft of a spear that was about to be driven through the guard. He was lifted from his feet by the man on the other end of it. Whoever they were, they were unnaturally, inhumanly strong.

Jason was thrown almost six meters to hit one of the pillars. His legs gave out, and he fell to his knees. The man with the spear turned on him, and all Jason could see was the half-meter-long steel blade coming at his chest, when suddenly his view was blocked. Drake had appeared out of nowhere. The spear struck Drake squarely in the chest and shattered.

Drake held a long sword with edges of pure blackness. Jason couldn't see what happened next, but he heard the scream. The man who'd been holding the spear fell to the ground in pieces as Drake ran forward into the group of enemy soldiers. Nothing stopped that blade as Drake moved like a whirlwind through them. Pieces of men and weapons flew away in sprays of blood. The bodies seemed to dissolve slowly away into nothing.

One man surprisingly held his own to exchange a few blows before being taken down. It took Drake almost a minute to kill him. Jason wondered who the attackers were, and what they had been trying to do.

It was all over before Jason could catch his breath.

Drake helped him to his feet. "Are you all right?" he asked. His face was covered with spatters of blood.

"My arm," Jason said. His right arm was numb, except for the part that burned. Blood flowed down to drip off his fingers. It hadn't hurt much at first. That was changing quickly.

"Sword, or something else?"

"Crossbow bolt," Jason gasped. The pain was now unbearable. His vision was wavering.

"Oh, my god! Jason, are you okay?" Geoffrey had run out to see what was happening.

Drake met his eyes, and Jason shook his head slightly. *Please*, he thought.

"He'll be okay," said Drake. "Crossbow bolt. Poisoned, from the look of it."

Thank you.

"Anything I can do?" Geoffrey asked. He looked pale. Jason thought Geoffrey was too young to see things like this.

"Have him sit down. Wrap it with this." Drake handed Geoffrey a cloth bandage. "Apply pressure. It will hurt him, but you need to control the bleeding until I can work on it. I need to make sure this was the last of the enemy soldiers and regain control of the Waypoint. Stay here!"

Jason sat down and let Geoffrey wrap his arm with the bandage. He hadn't expected Drake to be so understanding. Geoffrey gripped his bicep, and it hurt like hell, but Jason knew it was needed.

It seemed like forever before Drake returned. He looked angry, and Jason wondered if he should be concerned. Drake shook his head as if aware of Jason's thoughts, and knelt down next to him.

"Not angry at you," Drake said. His voice was rough with emotion. "I lost a friend at the Waypoint, one of my captains. Six of my men were killed. Two others might not make it. I'm angry at whomever attacked here. I'm angry that they even knew to attack here. Not at you."

"Is he going to be okay?" asked Geoffrey.

"I'll look. Go help Jon," Drake said.

"I want to stay with Jason."

"I don't want you to pass out on me," Drake said in a hard voice. "Go help Jon. He needs you."

Geoffrey stood up and reluctantly walked away.

Drake held out Jason's bandana, which Jason slipped back over his head with his left hand. He was a little surprised that Drake had bothered. Geoffrey would have seen him without it. He'd been sitting right there, holding his arm. A part of him didn't even care anymore.

"I clouded his mind," said Drake. "He's in shock from seeing all that blood. What I did will help him forget all of this, not just you. Now, let me take a look at your arm."

Jason watched with a numb detachment as Drake unwound the bandage on his right arm. The crossbow bolt had torn through the muscle, and Jason could see blood well up out of a hole the size of his thumb. The skin around the wound had turned white, as happened when he was poisoned by iron. Bits of shattered bone were visible. Jason knew that, with a wound like this one, he'd probably lose his arm.

"I'm going to fix this," Drake said. "It will hurt."

"Am I going to lose it?"

"Not if I can help it."

Drake gripped his arm above and below the wound, and Jason felt something like fire flow into his arm. Sharp bursts of pain pulled a scream from him, and his vision greyed out. Drake didn't stop, though, and the pain went on and on.

Eventually, he slipped away into darkness.

CHAPTER NINE

Geoffrey sat with Jason as the sky slowly darkened outside the window. He was worried about his friend. He couldn't believe Jason had been stupid enough to stand there and fight soldiers, much less soldiers who would dare to attack Drake in his citadel. What had Jason been thinking?

Jon came in with a plate of food at the same time as a servant, who lit the candles in the chandelier and left. The room didn't feel brighter with the candles, as their light only deepened the shadows. Geoffrey had felt safe in the citadel, but obviously they weren't as safe as they'd thought.

"That for me?" Geoffrey asked.

"Yeah. Thought you might be hungry," said Jon aid. "How's he doing?"

"Pretty good, I think. He's sleeping." Geoffrey took the plate: roast beef and potatoes with bread. It smelled good. Tasted even better.

"Do you know what happened?" Jon asked, glancing at Jason.

"Only that some people came through some kind of portal and attacked."

"I'm surprised Drake would leave it unguarded."

"He didn't. He said six of his people guarding it were killed, included a friend. He seemed really angry."

"I can imagine. I saw what he did to the soldiers."

"Yeah, he carved them into pieces."

"Pieces that dissolved," said Jon. "We need to get some answers. There's something going on that we don't know about. I don't believe in magic, but this place could convince me. Drake could, anyway."

Jon pulled the cover down to look at Jason's arm.

Geoffrey had to swallow hard against the memory of what the wound had looked like. Now, there was just a really pale area about the size of a quarter on his arm. Jason was breathing evenly, and stirred a little in his sleep, mumbling something that Geoffrey couldn't quite make out.

"What did Drake do to heal it?" Jon asked.

Geoffrey shook his head. "I don't know. It was a pretty bad wound."

"Went through the bone?"

"Yes. I saw bits of bone and stuff." Geoffrey didn't want to think about that.

"Sorry, I've been trying to figure Drake out. He heals as well as he kills, apparently. He didn't have any tools or machines with him, and back where I'm from, it would have taken a full medical lab to fix an injury like that one. Maybe even nanotechnology. Even still, Jason might have lost his arm."

"You think Jason will be okay?"

"I don't think Drake does anything half-assed. Yeah, he'll be fine. I don't know what he did, but the wound looks like it's healing well."

Drake came into the room then, holding a bottle of wine and four glasses.

"I doubt you need four," said Geoffrey. "He's still asleep."

"No, he isn't," Drake replied. "He's awake. His heartrate

increased by twenty beats a minute around the time Jon joined you."

Jason sat up in bed and grinned sheepishly. "I didn't want to interrupt what was becoming an interesting conversation."

Geoffrey gripped his shoulder. "Glad you're doing better, buddy."

Jon shook his head. "How did you know his heartrate had increased? Do you have a monitor on him? In the bed?"

"I heard it," Drake said, pouring the wine.

"You *heard* it."

"Yes. Yours is slow, even for one of our people, barely fifty beats a minute. Geoffrey's is fast, at almost ninety. Jason's was slowing down, but it is now racing again at around one hundred. I suspect he's feeling a little anxiety as he remembers the battle."

"Just what the hell are you, Drake?"

Drake ignored him and handed out the glasses. "A toast to our friend's health," he said, raising his glass to Jason.

"Mocking me, sorcerer?" Jason asked.

"Not at all," Drake said after taking a drink. "You perplex me, but I am in your debt."

Jason flexed his arm carefully. "Seems like I'm more in yours."

"You were wounded while protecting my people. Your warning undoubtedly saved the servants in the courtyard. You stopped the one with the spear from killing my guard, who is alive only because of you. Your shout also caught my attention so I could end the attack. The least I could do was repair your wound."

"Do you mind if I ask how you did that?" said Jon.

"I take it you wouldn't accept the answer of magic."

"No, I don't think I would."

Geoffrey would have accepted that answer; it had *looked* like magic.

Drake sighed and contemplated his glass. "It's hardly a state secret," he said. "And by now, I suspect, you've figured out a fair amount of it all. The people in the North have a Power they refer to as the Cynosure. A Power you now have access to. You've deduced it's a machine, I'm sure."

Jon nodded. "Yes, an artificial intelligence. I'll come back to the North thing; please go on."

"Here in the *South,* we have a Power known as the Omphalos. It has an older name that few know: the Instrumentality. It is an ancient and intelligent machine that most people don't even realize *is* a machine. My people are bound by tradition and religion."

"Religion?"

"Many worship the Omphalos, which is how it likes things. I'm sure you noticed the same in the Eternal City."

Jon nodded. "Some of them seemed like fanatics. So this machine, this Instrumentality – it does what?"

"Anything you want."

"Care to elaborate?"

Drake smiled. He looked tired, Geoffrey realized. "Back home, there are universities devoted to the learning of sorcery. Students are taught to focus their will and desire using spells."

"Sorcery?" Jon sounded skeptical.

"It's all bullshit, of course. It does, however, work." Drake finished his wine. "The important part is the focus. The Instrumentality was built in ancient times to free people from the toils of labor. It was to be the final instrumentality of technology. No other tools would ever be needed. In the beginning, if you were attuned, all it took was the will and the focus, and the machine would make your desires real."

"But people forgot."

"It has been a very long time, and there were a few major wars that accelerated the loss of knowledge. A few people still remembered it was a machine when I was a child, but the cult of the Omphalos was starting to catch on, even then. Now, almost no one else remembers that the Instrumentality is a machine made to serve us, and not the other way around."

"People actually worship it?" asked Jason.

"Hard to argue with a god you can see, that grants your wishes. Not to mention that it might destroy you if you try to argue or question."

"Damn," Jon said. "And the healing?"

"Nanotechnology, as you guessed. I had to knit each piece of bone into place, and sew up the arteries and tissue at the molecular level. There may have been a better way, but this was what I had available."

"The shapeshifting?" said Jason.

"Natural," Drake said. "Purely a biological quirk of my species. It can be done with the Instrumentality, but that's something a bit different. If you all stay with me, you'll see examples of that eventually. It's popular in the Ruined Courts to wear exotic bodies."

"Exotic bodies?" Geoffrey asked.

"Daemonic forms that humans normally just see in nightmares: bodies of flame, or swarms of insects, that sort of thing. Anything you can imagine, you can create, if you have access to the Power."

"How is that even possible?" Jon asked. "The energy needed..."

"Would be astronomical?" Drake said with smile. "Yes. You'll understand soon enough. I've done the math on the energy available; it is essentially infinite."

"You're a bundle of contradictions, Drake," said Jon. "You wear armor and fight with a sword but have access to the most advanced technology imaginable. You talk science like a physicist and religion like a priest."

"A sword works in any place your biology will function. I should add a word of caution there: it is possible to walk the

Realms and end up in a place where there is no air, or where the laws of physics are different. Just be sure of *where* you want to go. That blind jump of yours could have ended very badly for you."

"You seem different, Drake," Jason said. "You weren't this chatty before."

"Suspicious of my motivations?" said Drake. "I'm somewhat drunk, and I trust you all a little more now, after earlier. Jason, you risked your life to save my people. I'm not going to forget that."

"You only trust us a *little* more?" said Geoffrey. He was surprised to find that he felt hurt. He'd come to trust Drake; he'd thought it was mutual.

"Don't take offense. I've lived a long time because I'm always very cautious," Drake pulled out Jason's ceramic knife and placed it on the table. The point was broken off. "You left this in an enemy soldier. I thought you might want it back."

"Thank you." Jason slipped it under his pillow.

"Do you know who attacked?" asked Jon.

Drake frowned. "The soldiers wore the gear of House Cyryth; it's one of the Royal Houses in the Ruined Courts, and one that my House has vendetta with. I'm more worried about how they knew to get here than about the fact that it was them, if it was."

"If it was?"

"The vendetta is well known, and I was too angry to leave much of the enemy behind to examine."

"Can I ask why the vendetta?" said Jon.

"I executed the duke of their House for cowardice two thousand years ago at the Battle of Longfalls. They have never forgiven me or my House."

"Two thousand years ago?"

"I told you I'm older than I look."

"Just how long *do* you people live?"

"Most live five thousand years or so. I'm older than that."

"Shit."

Drake laughed; it was strangely musical. "You didn't know? Joseph is almost two thousand years old, and Dominic closer to three, I think. Time moves differently in different Realms, so it is difficult to keep track."

"Will I live that long?"

"That depends on who tries to kill you, and if we can stop them."

Geoffrey couldn't even imagine living that long. Drake could have seen the fall of the Roman Empire. He could have watched as Stonehenge and the Pyramids were built. The entire written history of Geoffrey's species had unfolded while Drake was alive.

"*We?*" said Jon.

Drake nodded. "You were attacked while under my protection as guests. Jason was injured. I will not let that pass unanswered. Someone is behind all of this, and they are powerful, to have gotten in here."

"I saw a shimmering portal," Jason said hesitantly. "Under a stone arch. The soldiers came out of that."

Drake nodded. "A Waypoint," he said. "Part of the ancient network that joins together worlds across universes."

"Not just Realms?" Jon asked with a grin.

"No, actually. If you know the proper code and how to access it, the Waypoint can take you to almost any world. Any world my people visited before... a long time ago."

Geoffrey was certain Drake had been going to say something else, instead of *a long time ago*.

"Do these Waypoints ever just work?" Jason asked sleepily.

"Yes. Some of them are programmed to open at certain times or under certain conditions. Some of them have strange locks on them that allow them to open only if you turn around three times first, for example."

"You're joking," Jon said.

"I'm afraid not. A lot of people have messed with the Waypoints since the ancients built them."

"The ancients?"

Drake sighed. "I feel as if I'm the only one talking. I think perhaps that is a tale for another day. Jason has fallen asleep, and Geoffrey is almost unconscious."

"Fine, but I'm going to want to know more someday," Jon said.

"If we live long enough, I'll happily tell you."

CHAPTER TEN

Drake didn't get much sleep that night – not that he normally slept much. There were times when all his years of toil came back and sat on him, gibbering. Tonight was one of those times. He wished, not for the first time, that he could slay those demons as easily as he'd slain the ones he'd spent most of his life fighting.

The attack against his citadel didn't make sense. House Drake had been at vendetta with House Cyryth for thousands of years. That didn't mean much, most of the time. Occasionally one of their young idiots would challenge him to a duel. It served little purpose except to entertain the crowds at the dueling arena. House Cyryth just wasn't stupid enough to attack him so openly. Houses had declared war over far less.

The problem Drake had with believing the attack had come from Cyryth was that the vendetta between their Houses was too well known. None of the enemy soldiers had survived to be interrogated, and his sword Maegril didn't normally leave bodies to be interrogated after the fact. That ancient blade would carve through anything and destroy whatever was left.

It was a great weapon for war, but not so good for casual

defense.

Someone could easily have guessed he'd use his favorite weapon to stop the attack, someone who might want him to dismantle a Great House of the Ruined Courts, which would weaken the Courts. It felt like something the people up North would engineer. He couldn't be certain, however. Then, there was also the problem of how someone got the assault force through the Waypoint in the first place.

It was secret known to very few in the Courts and none outside it, save one.

Together with what Jon had told him, Drake had to believe that parties from both sides were involved. Probably even working together. He made a list in his head of the people who could pull it off. It was a short list, and one he didn't like to review. Too many people on that list were ones he trusted.

Drake got up early and had clothes made and delivered to his guests' rooms; his companions looked a bit outlandish in their clothes from Earth. Drake wondered again about Jon. The man hadn't seemed that out of place in the Realm Drake had found him in, but Jon had indicated he was from somewhere more advanced. Drake needed to follow up on that at some point, too.

Too many damn things to look into.

Drake waited at the Waypoint until Maelindefel returned.

She noticed the different guards immediately. The dried blood on the ground was less obvious, but she noticed that, as well. "Torvus?" she asked, guessing the truth.

"'There was an attack yesterday afternoon," said Drake.

She closed her eyes in pain, and then her face got hard. "Are we going to retaliate?"

"Those who did the deed are dead. As for who sent them, I'm working to discover that, and then, yes. You know me well enough to know that I'll make them pay in blood for what was done."

"Torvus was a good soldier," she said. "And a good friend."

"To me, as well," Drake replied. "We'll have a ceremony tomorrow tonight, but first I need to know what you found. I'm sorry. It is pressing, and it may be related to what happened."

"No, you're right, My General. Duty first. Torvus knew this. He died fighting?"

"Yes. He died with honor."

She nodded. "Darkton is a still a shithole. The locals didn't want to talk to us, but with a few well-placed bribes, we eventually found out what we needed. The missing team had been there before," Maelindefel said. "Two other times in recent weeks. They met with a stranger who wore black. Unhelpful, I know. I spoke to the guards on duty, and they all said the same thing: our team had headed west with the mysterious man."

The rest of her team came through the portal carrying cloak-covered bodies.

"Captain, what is this?" Drake asked.

"Our missing team," she replied. "Killed with sorcerous fire, by the look of things. We mostly identified them by their gear."

Drake released an explosive exhalation. "So the men I found on that distant Earth Realm *weren't* ours. I should feel relieved, and yet there is the matter of the tattoos. Someone wanted those men found on that distant world."

"There is more, General. The missing team had orders signed and sealed with the Imperial seal."

"Our Imperial seal?"

Maelindefel nodded.

"Well, that complicates things. At least I know where to go next."

"You'd go before the emperor?"

"I'd go into the Eye itself to discover who was responsible for our men dying."

The soldiers around him stirred as he said that. They knew he'd done exactly that at least once before. His exploits were the stuff of legend to them, yet they knew it was no idle boast. He would go to any extreme to find those responsible.

"Sir, given the circumstances, it would be understandable if you suspected me," said Maelindefel.

"Captain, I'd rather cut off my arm than doubt you. I know all my captains are loyal. Rest easy there. Tomorrow night, we will celebrate the lives of Captain Torvus and the men who died with him. The day after, I will stand before the emperor and demand answers."

Maelindefel saluted. "General!"

Drake turned and walked back into the citadel. Nothing was going as it should. Torvus shouldn't have died at the hands of common soldiers. Drake had actually had to expend effort to kill one of them; the man had been very skilled.

Almost too skilled for even House Cyryth.

☉

Geoffrey found the new clothes the next morning.

He'd taken a quick bath, and the clothes had been on the made bed when he finished. Drake's servants were stealthy and efficient. The clothes looked odd to him, but he could see how he'd fit in better wearing them. There were all of black velvet and silk. Geoffrey felt as if he should be going to a Renaissance festival. He wondered if the others were getting new clothes, too, or if it was just him who was going to look silly.

Looking at himself in the mirror, though, he didn't feel as silly as he'd thought he would. The clothes looked good on him. He was in good shape, kept himself fit. He'd played sports in high school, although he'd had never enjoyed playing. It was just something one did. Looking at his reflection, he did wish he'd been given a sword – not that he really knew what to do with it. Maybe a dagger.

A servant came and led him to the place where he'd had lunch the day before.

Was it only yesterday? Geoffrey thought. It seemed like a lifetime ago.

"You look good, Geoffrey, almost a local," Drake said as he entered.

Geoffrey wasn't sure how he felt about that. Some of the locals didn't seem very human. Of course, Drake wasn't, either. So maybe he'd meant it as a compliment. Or maybe Geoffrey was just being self-conscious and overthinking things.

Or all of the above.

Jon was wearing a blue jacket and pants, with a white tunic underneath, which seemed like a good idea. The blue suited him; it went with his grey eyes. Besides, the man was too thin to wear black.

Jason was wearing dark grey clothes, a coif and wide-brimmed hat. Drake had obviously noticed Jason's fondness for keeping his head covered. Jason had once told Geoffrey that his scalp burned easily, although Geoffrey doubted he'd have to worry about that in a place with no sun. In either case, Jason was scowling and looking dangerous.

Drake was dressed in armor and leather, the same as Geoffrey had seen him wearing before. A part of him wondered if Drake ever wore anything else. Not that it mattered; the man would look good in anything. Maybe it was the pointed ears. Or the cheekbones.

Breakfast was steak and eggs, with fried potatoes. Geoffrey was noticing a bit of a pattern to the cuisine: beef with every meal. Not that he was complaining. The food was good, and there was coffee. Drake, he noticed, was drinking tea.

"I hope everyone got some rest last night," said Drake.

"Well enough," Jon said.

Geoffrey had passed out the night before, which he

suspected had something to do the wine. He wasn't really a drinker. He was just glad the stuff didn't seem to cause a hangover. That would have been bad.

Jason nodded. "Before the unpleasantness yesterday, I explored a bit. I had a long list of questions that were put aside. Can I ask what the metal is you're mining here?"

"It's not a secret. If you spoke the language, I'm sure anyone would have been happy to tell you. It's an alloy called galvorn, which I think I've mentioned. It has some very useful properties, as well as being fairly lightweight."

"An alloy of what?" Jason asked.

"Zirconium, platinum, and niobium," said Drake. "Strong as titanium, although heavier. It's still lighter than steel, for the thickness. It is virtually impervious to neutrons and acids."

"Fight against a lot of neutron weapons?" Jon asked. "Or acid monsters?"

Drake smiled enigmatically. "It is strong and lightweight and not damaged by extreme conditions. That's enough to be useful."

"So... what? It was in the meteor that hit?" said Jason. "Seems convenient."

"I'm pretty sure it was a rocky comet that struck this world," Drake said. "The metal is what the planet was constructed out of."

"Wait – *constructed?*" Jon said. "You mean that literally, don't you?"

Drake nodded. "The entire world is a machine, a world engine, made by my ancient ancestors to harness the power of the collapsing bubble universe. The outer fifty kilometers of the crust are made of galvorn, with a thin layer of dirt and rock over it here in the crater. It's easier to mine the metal than to try to create it using the Instrumentality or to import it."

"Just how old *are* your people? When was this built, and what did they need that kind of power for?"

"That is difficult to answer," said Drake, "and we have other things to discuss."

Jon sighed. "Drip-feeding me knowledge."

"Keeps you coming back for more." Drake finished eating. "I've gotten some more information about the attack on you back in the Earth Realm where we first met. The soldiers did *not* come from here. A patrol of my troops was ambushed. The assassins who went after you used some of their equipment and attempted to pretend to be my troops. We'll need to go to my home to discover who sent them, and why."

"I thought this was your home," said Jason.

"It's more where I work. This Realm is just for training and outfitting my elite troops. We'll have to head to the Ruined Courts, if we want more answers."

"That should be interesting," Jon said.

"Indeed, it shall. I foresee that we'll have to go to the Golden Kingdom, too, to find all the answers we seek. It may take some time to unravel the plots that seem to be springing up."

"When do we leave?" Geoffrey asked. He was excited to see those places.

"In two days," said Drake. "First, today we need to prepare the service for the fallen. Then, tomorrow afternoon, we'll have the actual service. I must be there for my soldiers. You need not attend if you don't wish to. It will be in Thari, but you'd be welcome."

CHAPTER ELEVEN

Geoffrey wasn't sure why he'd agreed to go on the hunt with Drake and his men. Having grown up in the backwoods of Kentucky, he'd gone deer hunting with his cousins, and he hadn't enjoyed it. He didn't like to kill, but he did like meat. He just preferred to buy it at the store.

His cousins always wanted to use musk, salt licks, and deer blinds. To Geoffrey, that had seemed like cheating. If you were going to hunt, you should stalk your prey. It should be something romantic, like the frontiersmen used to do, or something.

He realized then that he really didn't have a clear idea of how frontiersmen had hunted. He thought that maybe it was something like in that *The Last of the Mohicans* movie. You run through the woods and then shoot the deer, say a few words over the body, then cook it and eat it. He wondered if Drake had hunted with frontiersmen.

However he felt about it, hunting with Drake was something he shouldn't pass up.

Drake hadn't paid much attention to Geoffrey since they'd been traveling together. Geoffrey had been content with that, for the most part. Drake was scary. However, he was also becoming something like a father figure to Geoffrey. That was something he'd missed, growing up. He knew how absurd that was, and yet it was true. Geoffrey looked up to Drake.

That morning after he'd asked Geoffrey to go one the hunt, Drake had given him a change of clothes more suited to traipsing through the woods. The grey twill was thick and warm, and the fabric looked sturdy, although Geoffrey couldn't have said what fiber the fabric was made of. It didn't feel like cotton. The long knife that came with the outfit was welcome, as well. It was single-edged and as long as his forearm, almost like a narrow machete.

Two dozen soldiers were waiting with Drake when Geoffrey got to the courtyard. A dozen of the people carried axes, saws, and ropes. The rest carried long spears with little cross-hilts. Geoffrey suppressed his feeling of disappointment. He'd thought they were hunting alone. Drake was in his usual attire, but he carried a wicked-looking glaive.

"What are we hunting?" asked Geoffrey. He'd only ever hunted deer and rabbit, and those with a rifle. He was a pretty good shot, but he'd never hunted with a spear.

"Wild boar," Drake replied. "They roam the high forests."

"I haven't seen any forests here."

Drake pointed into the distance where one of the floating mountains was visible. Geoffrey could just make out trees and snow on the flanks of the mountain. He realized that Drake intended for them hunt high up there.

"I've never hunted boar before."

"They usually squeal before they charge. When you hear that, turn toward it and set your spear like this." Drake braced his weapon against his foot and crouched, bring the point low. "The boar will charge right onto the spear. The cross lugs are to keep the animal from charging up the shaft and goring you. They have long tusks and are vicious. They can be deadly, so be careful."

"Why do those soldiers have axes and saws and stuff?"

"We'll need the wood for the funeral pyres."

Geoffrey nodded, sorry he'd asked. It was sobering to remember that people had just been killed the day before. His friend Jason had almost been killed. His mind shied away from the details, but Jason's injury had been bad.

Drake led them around to the side of the keep Geoffrey hadn't seen yet. A stone pier had several wooden ships tied to it, although there were no bodies of water visible in any direction. It was so strange that Geoffrey stopped and stared: the ships were floating on air.

"Come along, Geoffrey."

Geoffrey followed Drake. The ship bobbed slightly as they embarked. The soldiers with Drake sprang to work, untying the ship and working in the rigging. A woman in an officer's uniform took the wheel and gave it a spin. The ship moved out across the ground. Geoffrey couldn't tell what made the ships float.

Magic, for all he knew.

The ship slowly moved higher into the air, sailing the air currents. They circled around the keep once, gaining altitude, and then moved toward the distant floating mountain. The air was damper, higher up, but not much thinner. Geoffrey found it somewhat frightening but also exhilarating.

The floating mountain was larger than he'd realized. As they got closer, he could see that it was actually many mountains, with valleys and dales. Water poured from several caves around the edges, and snow glinted from the central peak. Thick forests of pine and aspen rose up along the flanks. It was beautiful.

The soldiers expertly guided the airship to dock at a small stone pier.

"Are there other animals up here?" Geoffrey asked. "Besides boar?"

Drake nodded. "Elk, deer, bear, and salmon in the rivers.

There are probably a few dragons, but they won't bother you if you leave them alone."

"Dragons?"

"They live in the caves, mostly. Don't you have dragons on your world?"

"Only in the folklore, as far as I know."

"Interesting. I could have sworn I saw one there once. In any case, don't worry about the dragons. For that matter, most of the animals will run away as we get close to them. Only the boars are so territorial as to attack armed men."

"No snakes?"

"No, just the dragons."

"The dragons are snaky?" Geoffrey wriggled his hand. "I was thinking huge and winged."

"The ones here are more like what you might think of as Chinese dragons."

Geoffrey wondered how he knew about China. Drake looked somewhat Asian, mostly in the eyes and cheekbones, so Geoffrey wondered if he was from a place like China. He still didn't know much at all about Drake, and he was too afraid of the man to ask a lot of questions.

Drake gave orders to the others in their language and then gestured for Geoffrey to follow him. The forest smelled amazing; Geoffrey loved pines. Thick ferns, and bushes with dark purple berries, were the only groundcover. He wondered if the berries were edible – they looked good. He might have tried them if he'd been alone. Maybe not, though. He wasn't really daring when it came to things like that.

"Tell me about yourself, Geoffrey," Drake said as they walked.

Geoffrey suddenly felt self-conscious. "Not sure what to say. I don't even know if you'll understand my cultural references."

"I've spent time on your Earth before," said Drake, "in the United States. Favorite restaurant in Albuquerque, remember?

I'm just curious as to how you and Jason came to be living together. I like to know about the people I'm traveling with."

"We're just friends," Geoffrey said. His cousins had given him shit about living with a guy, but they didn't understand about renting rooms from people in the city. Most of them still lived with their parents, in trailers. Of all his relations, only his cousin Alan was a decent person. Drake wouldn't care about any of that, though.

Drake nodded and kept his eyes on the trail.

"I needed a place near the university while I was going to school. Jason had a room for rent. At first, I didn't think it would work out. You might have noticed that he's weird." Geoffrey shrugged. "We've known each other almost two years now. He's a good guy. Keeps to himself, mostly. We hang out some. I think maybe was he in a gang or something, when he was younger."

Drake nodded. "And you? You're not from Cincinnati, I think."

"No, I'm from Kentucky. Montgomery County. I grew up near Mount Sterling."

"Family?"

"Mom, some cousins – one I like – and an uncle I've never met."

"I was wondering why you wanted to come along on this adventure." Drake paused and seemed to be looking at a small waterfall. It was pretty. "Not the hunting trip."

Geoffrey shrugged. "Loyalty to a friend?"

"It wasn't that," said Drake.

"I wanted the adventure," Geoffrey admitted. "Once I knew about you and other worlds. I had to see it for myself."

"Even if it's dangerous?"

"Wouldn't be much of an adventure without danger."

"Fair enough." Drake turned and gestured up the slope. "I can hear boar in the highlands. The other hunters have already killed six to the east of us."

"How can you know that?"

"I heard them squeal when they died."

"You have freakishly good hearing."

"Not human, remember?"

"Not most of the time, no," Geoffrey said. "Never met a person that wasn't human before, so I think of everyone as human. No offense."

"No taken. To be fair," Drake said, "I'm not much like most of my own people, either. My mother was Eldalië, an ancient people. My father was from the Ruined Courts. They died when I was young. I think I take after my mother more than my father."

"Kind of hope I take after my mother, too," said Geoffrey. "Never knew my dad. Mom never had anything good to say about him, though."

Drake raised his hand for silence and gestured ahead of them.

Geoffrey took the hint and shut up. Thinking about his father had depressed him a bit, and he didn't want to think about that anymore. He wanted to think about how strange it was that he was hunting a wild boar on a floating mountain on an alien world.

That was worth thinking about.

There was a rustling sound, and suddenly a huge boar rushed out of the bushes. It was much bigger than Geoffrey had expected, almost shoulder-high to him. He dropped the point of the spear and braced it as Drake had shown. The shock of impact felt as if it dislocated his shoulders. The animal squealed loudly and slashed the air with half-meter tusks. Geoffrey didn't know how much longer he could hold it back.

Drake stepped in and thrust once with his glaive. The boar squealed again and died.

Geoffrey stumbled forward as the pressure came off.

"Next time, aim a little lower on the chest. You'll hit the heart and take it out cleaner."

Geoffrey nodded. He felt sick.

Drake gripped his shoulder. "It was well done, especially for your first hunt."

"I've hunted before."

"Boar? With a spear?"

"No."

"Then relax. You did well." Drake whistled shrilly, and two soldiers came up with wooden poles and started to truss the boar. Geoffrey hadn't even known they were back there. "The animal didn't suffer."

"Thank you."

"Come, we'll need one more for the feast tomorrow." Drake handed him his spear, which Drake had pulled from the animal.

Geoffrey took a deep breath and nodded. He didn't think he'd be able to eat any of the meat, but he was happy to help feed others. He wasn't squeamish; he just didn't like to kill.

He wondered if Drake liked to kill. Geoffrey thought he seemed indifferent to it. He wasn't sure, though. Drake was almost impossible to read. Something about his eyes suggested he was troubled more by killing that he let on.

Maybe even to himself.

CHAPTER TWELVE

Jason felt uncomfortable in the clothes Drake had given him.

Everything fit him well, even the boots. The style and cut were just a little too familiar. It was as if Drake had pulled the outfit from Jason's mind. It bothered Jason to think that Drake could look into his mind. If Drake could read minds, it would also explain a lot about how Drake knew about Jason's actual identity.

On the other hand, if Drake could read his mind and didn't care about what he saw there, then why should Jason worry himself about it? Because he'd spent so much of his life running? Drake wasn't like the people Jason had run from. Drake wasn't like anyone he'd ever known.

A servant came by and announced that the funeral service would be starting soon.

Jason didn't want to attend the service, but some of those people had died trying to protect him, so he felt as if he should. He found Jon and Geoffrey easily enough when he walked out to the encampment. Jon was a head taller than almost everyone else, although a few of the beast...*people* were even taller than

Jon.

Seventeen tall, wooden funeral pyres bore draped forms. Jason hadn't realized so many people had died in the attack. A raised platform stood on the other side of the square. The sky was darkening, and the wind had picked up. Pennants and standards snapped in the wind, sending a shiver up his spine.

The soldiers kept bowing to him with their arms crossed over their chests. He didn't know what it meant, but it made him uncomfortable. He wished again that he spoke the local language so he could ask them. He didn't see Drake around. Jon looked calm, but Geoffrey was blushing for some reason.

"Any idea how long this will be?" asked Jason.

Jon shook his head. "From what Drake said, it will go on all night. I think this part of the ceremony will be preceded by a eulogy, then the cremation. Drake said there would be a... wake, of sorts, afterwards."

"They don't seem to be a cheerful lot. I can't imagine them having a wake. How long are you going to stay?"

Jon shrugged. "I'm curious about the culture. I'll stay through the first part, out of respect. I'm not sure about what comes after. I've never been one to party."

Jason gestured at Geoffrey. "What's up with him?"

"Drake told us about the typical after-funeral party."

"Fertility rites?"

"Something like that."

Jason chuckled. Geoffrey was still very young, only twenty or so. Jason didn't even know if Geoffrey had ever had a serious girlfriend, but he hadn't dated anyone while he'd been living with Jason. At least, he'd never brought a girl home. Geoffrey had a lot of growing up to do, if he was going to travel with someone like Drake. Not that there *was* anyone else like Drake.

A...*being* in red robes mounted the platform. The person looked like an anthropomorphic salamander. He – Jason assumed for no reason that it was male – had black, shiny skin with neon blue stripes. Actually quite handsome, for a lizardman.

The man spoke for a while in that lyrical alien language that Drake spoke sometimes. The voice was exactly in the range between male and female. Jason shrugged. It didn't matter whether the priest was a man or a woman, other than what it might say about this culture. The priest finished his speech, and then he bowed with a wide gesture.

Drake stepped up to the platform. He was in the form of a white dragon with large wings, and yet he was still somehow in the armor and coat he'd been wearing before. Even his wings were encased in armor. He opened the wings wide as he spoke, embracing the crowd.

Drake spoke briefly. All of the assembled soldiers, tens of thousands extending out into the darkness, shouted, and he joined them, fist raised to the sky. Five people of various shapes in officer's uniforms stepped forward with torches and lit the pyres. The wood caught instantly and burned bright and hot. The wind carried the smoke and sparks high into the sky.

Jason felt unexpected tears in his eyes.

The words had been foreign, but the meaning had been clear. These were honored fallen soldiers given a deeply respectful sending-off. Jason wished he'd understood the language. He thought if he did, he might understand Drake more.

Drake came back to Jason and Jon in his normal form. His eyes were unabashedly wet. "Well, companions, we should retire to the citadel for the evening. Let the soldiers have their wake in peace."

"You don't join them?" said Jon.

"It wouldn't be proper. They wouldn't truly be able to relax in the presence of their general and prince. Come, there will be a supper laid out in the upper hall for us, and we can talk some more about the other matters that press us."

They turned and followed Drake – Geoffrey somewhat reluctantly, Jason thought.

⊙

Drake led them up to the room where they always ate. Food was laid out in metal dishes, as he'd said, but there were no servants present. Jon assumed they'd been released for the night. The meal was, unsurprisingly, beef and mushrooms with a side of potatoes. Plates of rolls were in a covered dish to keep them warm. Drake gestured for Jon and the others to serve themselves as he poured the wine.

"Drake, can I ask you something?" said Jason.

"You want to know why the soldiers kept bowing to you."

"Reading my mind?"

"No, it seemed the most likely thing to have bothered you," Drake said. "They honor you. You fought with them. They respect you."

Jason nodded and took a quick drink of wine.

"You are not a soldier, and so you may not understand what that bond means to them, and to me. I will not forget what you sacrificed."

Jon toyed with his food. It was good, but he never had much of an appetite. "Drake, I don't want to be disrespectful…"

"But you'd like to know more about what's going on," Drake finished.

"Yes, please. I have so many questions. I spent a few days in the Eternal City before everything happened, but I haven't even had a chance to really understand what I can do. I know you're probably not the best person to ask about using the Cynosure, but you're the only one around who might have answers."

Drake smiled. "No, I'm hardly a good fit for such questions, but I will help you as I may. The two great Powers are related."

"You're not worried about helping an enemy?" Jon said with

a smile.

"I don't automatically think of everyone from the North as my enemy."

"Perhaps we could start with that," said Jon. "What is this *North* and *South* thing all about?"

"Completely arbitrary, as you probably guessed. Leftover notions of terrestrial navigation applied to cosmological principles. Those from the Ruined Courts think of the Instrumentality as being in the South, because the first universe was the wellspring of all others. Any direction away from the Instrumentality is North. Those who are accustomed to such things can sense the distant presence of the primal Powers, like the needle of a compass. When walking the worlds, it helps if you think of it as moving between two poles: the Cynosure at one end, and the Instrumentality at the other. If you can hold that in your mind, you'll be able to know where you are and navigate."

"Aren't there an infinite number of possible universes?"

"No, it's a finite number, although higher than I could ever count. Well, sort of finite. The Realms as you think of them are the peaks of harmonics in the probability waves. It gets infinitely recursive and fractal between those peaks. If you travel down into the variations, you'll find yourself chasing the rabbit down the hole, so to speak. Don't do that. Stick to the finite peaks."

"I'm already lost," Jon said, laughing.

Drake seemed to have an understanding of physics that was a little different from what Jon had learned at university. He often sounded religiously reverent when he spoke of science, and somewhat skeptical when he spoke of religion.

"I'll see if I can get the emperor to talk with you about it. He is a bearer of both Powers."

"How does that happen?" Jon couldn't imagine why anyone would want both, although it suggested interesting things about the emperor's parentage. He must have had a parent from the Eternal City and well as from the Ruined Courts.

"You'd have to ask him that."

"Okay, so back to navigation. Can you actually walk from one end of reality to the other?"

"Of course. At the most basic level, you set a destination in your mind and walk to it, holding the Power – Cynosure or Instrumentality – in your mind as you move through the Realms. Keep in mind that you can only walk from Earth to Earth. I suppose, though, you could walk from another planet to the variation of that planet in the next universe. I've never tried it, but you could probably walk from Mars to Mars, for example."

"So, if I held the thought of the Earth where I was before, where Geoffrey and Jason are from, I could walk there from here?"

"Theoretically, although I wouldn't recommend trying it. The Realms on either side of this one didn't get the comet. There is no air on those worlds. That's part of what makes this Realm so secluded and secure. Normally, you can enter only via the Waypoint."

"We didn't come in that way," said Jason.

"No, but the Cynosure and Instrumentality aren't the same, and I'm not an average sorcerer."

"Could I apport there from here?" Jon asked.

"Possibly, but you'd probably not make it past the wards."

"Wards?"

"Realms can be sealed, at least with the Instrumentality. I'm not sure about the Cynosure, but I don't see why it couldn't be used that way. Wards are encoded energy fields embedded in the walls of the universe. Think of it like a lock. I have a key. You don't."

"So we're stuck here until you decide to let us leave?" Jason asked. "Otherwise, we could just leave with Jon?"

"You're stuck here until you ask to leave," said Drake. "You'd be stuck here anyway without me. Jon doesn't have the experience yet to move a group with him through the Realms."

"That could be done?" Jon asked. "By me, I mean. I know *you* can, obviously."

"Certainly. Only the royals in the Eternal City have the Cynosure. They took an army South, remember."

"I had wondered about that."

"If they'd had access to the Waypoints, they could have marched straight there in one step. Instead, they fought through all the Realms between the Eternal City and the Imperial Plaza. As I understand it, they didn't have an easy time." Drake chuckled.

"Why?" Jon asked.

"They wanted a war. The Realms tend to reflect one's desires to some degree. They moved through most of the wars in existence on the way South. Blamed us, of course. The truth was, they made their own bed and wallowed in it."

"Can you explain that *reflect desires* thing?"

"You said it yourself," Drake replied. "When you jumped away from your attacker in the Eternal City, you desired a world where you'd find help, and you landed on Jason and Geoffrey's doorstep. They helped you, and then I arrived to help more. Was that not a reflection of your desire?"

"You went there to kill me," said Jon.

Drake shrugged. "I changed my mind, didn't I?"

"And that was because I found a place where that would happen?"

"Makes you think, doesn't it?"

"Wouldn't that mean that free will is null and void?"

"Not at all. I chose to do what I did based on my own information. I was using a Power, too, remember."

"What about us?" Geoffrey said. "We *had* to help?"

"You chose to do what you would have done. He just picked

the world that had you both, and where you would be willing to help. The next universe over might have a Jason who would've knifed you, Jon, as soon as you fell in the door."

Jon shook his head. "Are the worlds branched from a common source, or what?"

"Not that I've seen. I think any of the Realms in a single harmonic form a cluster that are going to be similar. There is almost certainly a quantum exchange of information. As for if they all have a common source, you know the answer to that."

"News to me." Jon couldn't remember Drake mentioning it.

"Everything started with the first universe."

"Okay, where is that?"

"The Ruined Courts."

CHAPTER THIRTEEN

Drake could tell that they didn't believe him.

Well, Geoffrey might have, although belief and understanding were opposite edges of a sword. Geoffrey looked a bit stunned. Jason and Jon didn't seem to understand, and Jon *needed* to understand. His life depended on it. Drake was probably telling them all too much, but he found that he trusted them, as strange as that seemed. It had been a long time since he'd had friends who weren't under his command.

"Let me tell you how it all began," said Drake, "at least as I understand it. In the beginning, there was just one universe, with one large galaxy. The people thrived as they conquered the worlds there. They had a galactic empire, but eventually the universe began to collapse. They tried to flee to other universes, but there wasn't any other place to go. Legend has it that those ancients built the Instrumentality to hold back the forces of their collapsing universe. Then they built an even more powerful machine, the Plaza of the Worlds. This machine was said to have started the reaction that formed all the other universes."

"Said to have?"

"Well, I wasn't there, so all I have is the history of my people to go on. Not a lot of written history survived the later wars. You'll understand when you get to the Courts."

"And the Plaza of the Worlds?"

"Lost in time, if it ever existed. There was a great war a hundred thousand years ago, in the first universe. Based on the time differential, that would be hundreds of thousands, if not millions, of years ago in most universes."

"Time differential? You mean something different from relativity, I think."

"Yes and no. You'll understand better when we go to the Ruined Courts, but time moves slower there than in other places."

"Okay, what was the war about?"

Drake smiled. They weren't ready to know that, and he wasn't ready to talk about it. There was a difference between trust and foolhardiness. "That was a long time ago. Ask me when we get to the Courts, and I'll take you to the Monument of the Forgotten War in the Imperial Plaza. Tell me why a war on your world was waged a thousand years ago, much less a hundred thousand."

"Fair point," Jon said. "My home planet was settled only a few centuries ago, and I wasn't taught much Earth history."

"My point exactly. Knowledge gets lost. I know about it at all only because I'm older and have searched for answers. I have spent normal human lifetimes scouring the Realms for the smallest bits of knowledge about our past."

"So time moves at different rates?" Geoffrey asked. "How much time is passing back home?"

"In relation to here?" said Drake. He thought about it for a moment. "Every hour here is three hours in your Realm, roughly."

"So half a week has gone by?" Geoffrey seemed worried.

"Roughly, as I said."

"And time in the Courts?" said Jon.

"Roughly? An hour there is a day here."

"Shit."

Jon shook his head. "Doesn't work, Drake."

"What doesn't work?"

"Your story. My home… *universe* is billions of years old. It wasn't made a hundred thousand years ago."

"Time moves faster in younger universes. Time starts slowing down at around twelve billion years or so, once a universe hits the inflationary plateau. I think it was designed to give time for universes to develop to the point of having life-bearing planets, for colonization."

Jon shook his head again.

"You'll see," Drake said. "Once you get out there, into the Realms, you'll see it for yourself."

"Drake, other than getting Jon to see your emperor about his Power, why are we going to the Ruined Courts?" Jason asked. "If time there moves so differently, why waste the time?"

"When we first came here," Drake said, "it was because I thought the men who had attacked you all were from this place."

"You as much as said so when we arrived."

"I was mistaken. My missing soldiers were found dead in one of the Dark Realms. They were sent there by Imperial Order. None of my other soldiers are missing, and frankly, it makes far more sense this way."

"How does that make more sense?" Jon said.

"Because if my soldiers had tried to kill you, you'd all be dead."

"The attack did seem a bit… amateurish," said Jason. "Seeing your men fight here the other day, I wondered how we could have possibly gotten the upper hand."

"I'm not trying to take anything from you or Geoffrey," Drake said. "You fought well, but my soldiers are highly trained. There is also a little matter of timing."

"How did they find me so quickly?" Jon said. "I wondered about that. They arrived there hours before you did."

"I don't think they were meant to succeed; I think they were meant to be seen making the attempt."

"Seen by whom? And to what purpose?"

"As for who, I don't know. The purpose? Possibly to start a war. If you were killed by my soldiers, or even attacked and wounded, it could be considered provocation for a war. If someone is looking for a reason."

"I'm not sure," said Jon. "This doesn't feel like the whole story."

"I agree, because I'm not sure why they tried to kill you in the Eternal City. To get you to run? Why, then, the elaborate setup with soldiers who looked like mine? I would have killed you and dumped your body near the bodies of people I wanted to frame. We'll need to speak to the people from the North who may be involved."

"They're going to love that, back in the Eternal City."

"I think they'll see reason."

Jon laughed. "Maybe you know something I don't, but they didn't seem like reasonable people when I was there."

"I can be very persuasive."

Jon laughed again. "I can see that."

"Well, we should call it a night," said Drake. "We have much to do in the morning."

☉

Jon awoke suddenly in the deep of the night.

He'd been dreaming, but the memory of the dream was elusive and faded as he woke. All that lingered was a sense of impending danger. Something was wrong, and it was immediate and close. He stood and dressed quickly.

The citadel was quiet, except for a faint susurrus of the ventilation system, whatever powered that. Jon extended his senses. Jason and Geoffrey were asleep. Drake was awake and pacing in his suite. Nothing seemed out of the ordinary.

Jon trusted his intuition.

There was a threat nearby; he just didn't know what it was.

Lanterns in the hallways cast small pools of radiance. Jon probed ahead as he walked. He didn't like those shadows. He normally wasn't particularly superstitious, but that night the dark held a dread for him he couldn't quantify. Nevertheless, he needed to discover what was wrong. The danger he felt was specific to him, not like what he'd felt the other day when those soldiers attacked.

The citadel was vast, much larger than the palace where he'd grown up. Jon carefully kept his thoughts from straying too far into the past. He didn't want to think about the family he'd lost; that world and that life were gone now. He'd lost them long before he'd run into some strange people in a bar on an island off the coast of California.

Very few of the servants were in their quarters, and none were about in the lower halls as Jon made his way there. He figured most of them were out with the soldiers celebrating the wake. It was a fascinating culture, and he wished he had the time to learn more. Not that he was an anthropologist, but he liked learning about the people he met when he traveled.

He always had.

Jon stepped out into the night. The air was clear and cold, without a trace of pollution. In the distance, the funeral pyres were still smoldering. He could see people out there dancing and hear the faint sounds of a fiddle. A low breeze stirred the pennants. There were no sounds of insects, he realized. There never had been. This world truly was desolate.

Nothing seemed out of the ordinary. The night was lovely. He was about to walk down to the fires when he heard a soft scrape of metal nearby. The sound of a blade being drawn was distinctive, even when done stealthily. It sent a chill of premonition up his spine.

Jon felt around with his mind but sensed nothing unusual. His psionic abilities were telling him no one was nearby, but he knew they had to be here. He'd heard the blade, and his sense of danger was telling him to run. He crouched in the shadow by the stairs, suddenly glad he was wearing dark colors.

He could hear someone moving now. Or not so much hear them moving as sense the displacement of the fine sand over the rocks as they moved. Whoever was out there was *good*. No one moved that quietly unless they had ill intent.

What to do about it, though? he thought. Calling out seemed like a bad idea. Whoever it was, they were too close for him to make it back inside before they reached him, unless he apported, and he wasn't sure he was ready to try a blind jump in this place. Short-range jumps where he knew his surroundings were all right, but this whole world was strange to him.

For that matter, since the person with the blade was so close, they might have seen him come out of the citadel, which meant —

He moved to the right just as a thrown knife flashed by. It would have struck him in the eye if he hadn't moved when he did.

The assassin stepped out of the shadow of the column to Jon's right. Jon recognized him: one of the young men who'd taken Jon to the Eternal City. He was the one who'd shot at Jon with a crossbow and managed to hit him. His face was twisted with contempt and something Jon wasn't sure he had a name for.

"You should have let us kill you back home," the man said quietly. "Would have been easier for everyone."

"Sergei, right? Strangely enough, I'd prefer not to die," said

Jon. Sergei was wearing a small oxygen tank. That answered how he'd crossed the airless void between worlds, but it must have been very uncomfortable. Jon hoped so, anyway.

"That was never an option. You were born to die. The only question was the fashion in which you'd go, and how much harm you'd do first. Can't let you do that." Sergei saluted mockingly with his sword.

"Do what?" Jon asked. "I would never have known about you people if you hadn't taken me from that bar."

Sergei laughed softly. "As I said, you were made to die. Funny that you don't know it."

Drake! Jon sent a mental plea. Drake was sensitive; maybe he'd hear the thought. Jon didn't want to fight Sergei. Jon didn't have any weapons, and he tried not to kill if he could avoid it. Sergei didn't look as if he'd just give up, though.

Jon was usually good at avoiding a fight.

He hadn't had much luck with that recently.

CHAPTER FOURTEEN

Jon backed away as Sergei advanced.

The courtyard suddenly felt much smaller than it actually was. The pillars with carved dragons had seemed huge before; now they appeared to be slender – not capable of hiding a man. Normally Jon would apport away, if facing a deadly opponent, but he didn't know his way around the citadel well enough for that. His room wasn't even distinctive enough for him to get a lock on it with his mind.

He didn't want to just randomly apport away, either. He didn't know what kind of defenses Drake might have set up against intruders, but he figured those defenses would be powerful. Apporting into an area where he shouldn't go would almost certainly be bad for his health. Of course, staying where was looked to be bad for his health, too.

"Just stand still," Sergei suggested. "I'll be merciful."

Somehow, Jon doubted that.

"Listen, do you even know where you are?" Jon asked. "The guy who runs this place isn't going to like you trying to kill me. You might even start a war. I don't think anyone wants that."

Sergei paused then, shaking his head. "Stop trying to

confuse me. You're here in the far South, which only reinforces
the need for you to die. You're working with *them*, just as I was
told. As for a war, one is coming, no matter what, and I know
that I'm on the right side of it."

"I'm not working with anyone. I'm just trying to stay alive.
So far, you and your people are the only ones who've attacked
me. I don't want a war, and I don't think you do, either. From
what I've heard, the last war with the Ruined Courts ended in
a stalemate, and they weren't even active participants."

"You're stalling for time," Sergei said. "Enough!" With that,
he lunged, a thrust that would have impaled Jon if he'd still
been there.

Just as Sergei moved, Jon apported away.

He couldn't safely apport any real distance, but he could
reach someplace in line of sight. Jon apported to the other side
of the courtyard. It didn't help that much. Sergei was fast, far
faster than Jon had thought humanly possible. *Maybe he is
related to Drake,* Jon thought as he apported away again.
Maybe he isn't human at all. I just thought *he was, because he
looks like me, but if Drake is right, maybe I'm not as human as
I thought I was, either. At least, not any more.*

"Stand still!" Sergei said with a growl.

Jon needed to defuse the situation. "Sergei, just stop, and
let's talk about this."

Sergei didn't stop, though. He chased Jon all around the
courtyard, Jon trying to reason with him the entire time. If
Drake showed up and killed the man, or was killed by him, it
would start a war. Jon didn't want that kind of blood on his
hands. He could easily sense what that future would hold:
endless, bloody battles across an unimaginable number of
universes. Those precognitive visions were nearly
overwhelming.

Eventually, Jon miscalculated, or maybe Sergei anticipated
Jon's apport. In either case, Sergei moved almost in a blur,

seized Jon, and lifted him from the ground with one hand. Jon kicked at the sword to keep from being impaled. Sergei was having a hard getting into a good position to thrust with the blade, and Jon didn't intend to make it easy on him.

There was *whoosh* of air, and then Sergei dropped him, pulled backwards by someone much stronger than either of them. Drake had aported behind Sergei and thrown him to the ground. Jon hadn't realized just how strong the Sergei was, until Sergei had picked him up with one hand. Sergei wasn't a big man, under one hundred eighty centimeters tall and slightly built. He was a full head shorter than Jon, and lean. Drake was even stronger than Sergei, but then, he *was* a big man.

Sergei had rolled to his feet and brought his sword between himself and Drake.

Jon's mind was again filled with visions of bloody war.

"Don't kill him!" he shouted.

Drake growled but sheathed his sword. "What is the meaning of this?" Drake asked. "Who are you?"

Sergei didn't answer, instead thrusting with lightning speed at Drake's chest.

Drake made it look slow as he slapped the blade out of the way and punched Sergei in the chest hard enough to send him flying several meters. Sergei hit the ground and again rolled to his feet, and Drake was on him before he had time to raise his weapon. There was a loud crack, and Sergei dropped his sword. Drake had broken Sergei's wrist with a chop of his hand.

Sergei raised his other hand and shouted a word. There was a flash of lightning and the smell of ozone. Drake gave no sign of having been affected by the flash, but smoke rose from his coat. Drake gestured, and a bubble, looking for all the world like a soap bubble, appeared around Sergei. Jon could see the man gasping and trying to get his respirator mask in place. Sergei looked afraid for the first time since he'd arrived.

Drake gestured again, and the man staggered under the

thunderclap of returning air.

"Surrender!" Drake demanded.

Suddenly Sergei was gone with a rainbow shimmer in the air.

Drake frowned for a moment at the space where Sergei had been. Then he turned and helped Jon to his feet. "He's actually gone. Are you all right?"

Jon laughed humorlessly. "You mean other than almost being impaled by that guy? Yeah. Thanks, by the way. I thought I was dead there for a moment."

"Why did you shout for me not to kill him?"

"I know him," said Jon, "and I don't want to be responsible for a war."

"Tell me about him."

"His name is Sergei. He's the son of Prince Joachim, from the Golden Kingdom."

Drake sighed. "Yes, that could have been awkward. Joachim was one of the architects of the last war. Killing his son could have been bad."

"Sergei said something about killing me before I could do join with someone or something," Jon said. "He didn't specify, but he seemed genuinely angry at me. I don't understand what's going on with him. Are you okay, by the way?"

"He caught me off guard with the lightning spell. The North doesn't have many sorcerers."

"Yeah, but are you *okay*? Your coat is still smoking."

"What?" Drake took off the coat and cursed in what sounded like several languages. His armor was unmarked, and Drake seemed unharmed. "I liked that coat."

Jon laughed again, as much to relieve stress as anything else. "They aren't going to stop, are they?"

"Not until we make them stop, no."

"Any idea how to do that?"

Drake's soldiers ran into the courtyard then, shouting and

looking around in confusion. *Better late than never*, Jon thought. His sense of time told him only a few minutes had passed since Sergei arrived, but the chase around the courtyard had felt like hours.

Drake shouted some orders to the soldiers and then turned back to Jon.

"Well, first we need to find out why they want to kill you," he said. "Then we'll deal with it. Hopefully without a war."

"Yeah, I don't want to be responsible for a war," Jon said. His precognitive sense wouldn't let him ignore the possibilities of what a war between the Golden kingdom and Drake would be like. Entire worlds would burn. Untold trillions of people would die.

"You won't be responsible for whatever happens. I don't know why someone wants you dead, but that's on them, not you."

Jon nodded. "Promise me you'll try to avoid a war with the Golden Kingdom."

"I'm truly not looking for one," Drake said quietly. "I have enough to keep me busy. Whatever is going on, it can probably be solved diplomatically. At the very least, a duel or two should solve things. No one even has to die, unless they insist on doing so."

Jon closed his eyes against the visions – not that it helped. Drake was difficult to focus his precognitive sense on, and when he did, he wished he hadn't. So many possible futures involved death on a scale he'd never imagined, war across the universes. He felt as if there was a thin thread he could follow through the probabilities. If dying would stop those universal wars from happening, he'd willingly lay down his life. However, so many of those conflicts seemed to start with Jon's own death.

He'd take it.

He didn't want to die.

If living prevented the wars, so much the better.

O

Geoffrey rubbed the sleep from his eyes and carefully nursed his coffee.

When Drake told them to get a good night's sleep, Geoffrey hadn't expected Drake to wake them up in the middle of it. Only as he listened to Jon explain what had happened did he really wake up.

They had been attacked. Again.

What the hell was going on?

"I thought you said no one could just walk in here," said Jason.

Jason had gotten over his shock from the day before and was back to being suspicious of Drake. It was almost refreshing; Geoffrey had been worried about him.

"I did, for good reason," Drake said.

"Sergei was wearing an oxygen tank," said Jon.

"He also must have gotten the key to my wards. That's the part that really worries me."

"Where could he have gotten that?" Jason asked.

"Very few people know it. Believe me, we'll be asking *each* of them."

"So we're still going to the Courts?" Geoffrey said. He was barely able to keep his voice steady. He really wanted to see where Drake was from.

Drake nodded. "It's just Black Sky Rising at Drake Manor, which is where we should head first."

"*Black sky rising?*" asked Jon.

"The homeworld of the Drake estates is near the center of the cluster of worlds this millennium. It will slowly orbit out to the edge and be closer to the edge of the universe. When the Eye, the black hole in the center of the galaxy, rises above the horizon, it dominates the sky for half the day. That is Black

Sky, when the world faces the black hole. The other half of the day, it faces outward toward the light of the Red Sky. Black Sky Rising means the day is ending and we have a few hours before the dark of Black Sky."

"Sounds like a very... unusual place," said Jon. "What about the other side of the planet?"

"There are no complete worlds in the Ruined Courts," Drake replied. "They are aptly named."

"That sounds *interesting*, if improbable."

"The machinery of the worlds keeps the atmosphere in place and the gravity normal. You'll be fine." Drake stood. "Is everyone ready to go?"

"Should we take our other clothes with us?" asked Geoffrey. He'd dressed in the fine black velvet clothes Drake had given him.

"No reason to."

"Then I'm ready," Geoffrey said. The others nodded, as well.

Drake led them out to the Waypoint, where Maelindefel was waiting for them with a double squad of soldiers. Drake had sent word to her as soon as he'd awakened the others. Geoffrey thought she looked tired. He could still hear music in the distance.

Maelindefel saluted. "We'll be vigilant, My General."

"Trust no one else until I return," said Drake. "I don't care what orders they have. I've changed the watchword on the wards, as well, so no one should be able to just walk in. Defy the emperor, if you have to. I'll back you up and make it right."

"Yes, General."

Drake gestured, and the stone arch suddenly filled with a vertical, silvery pool. It reflected light but also seemed to shed just a little of its own. Geoffrey thought it looked wondrous, like something from a movie. He found it a little difficult to believe he was actually travelling through different universes; he kept expecting to wake up.

"The Ruined Courts await," said Drake.

CHAPTER FIFTEEN

Jon expected the transition through the Waypoint to House Drake to be similar to when Drake took them to Nandegurth. It wasn't anything like that. Instead, it was like stepping through a door. One moment they were in Nandegurth, and the next they were standing on a stone platform beneath an arch. The house before them was enclosed in high walls and was more military compound than palace, although still elegant.

Jon could believe people related to Drake had built it.

Two guards with drawn blades stepped forward as they appeared. His senses shied away from those swords; the blades were somehow cutting spacetime along their edges. An officer carried a silvery sphere. She held it out to Drake, who touched it and spoke briefly. She bowed again and held it out to Jon. He wasn't sure what he was supposed to do.

"It is the Orb of Truth," said Drake, "a genetic scanner used for identification, the Ritual of Recognition. I've identified myself. Now Captain Byrwynn wants you to touch it, so they will know you when you come back."

"I'm not sure I like the idea of it reading and storing my DNA."

"The Orb can't be read. All it can do is verify an identity based on a previous scan. No one can pull your data. If it helps, mine is also in there, and I wouldn't allow that if someone could use it against me."

"Either I trust you, or I don't," Jon said. He sighed and touched the orb. He didn't feel anything, but the captain nodded and then held the orb to the others. Only Jason hesitated; Jon wondered why.

"I'm going to have to teach you all Thari," said Drake.

"Are we going to be here long enough for it to matter?" Jason asked.

"They speak Thari in the Eternal City, too, not to mention many other Realms. Come on inside. We'll get you settled."

Jon stood rooted on the spot, though. He'd looked up past the wall. Half of the sky was a deep, textured red; the other half was dominated by a semicircle of pure blackness. It could be nothing other than a black hole, and Jon had never seen one so big, or from so close. Or was it even larger than he thought, and they were farther away than he thought? He couldn't tell. An impossible arch of metal spanned the sky over the black hole, faintly visible.

"How big?" was all Jon could ask.

"The black hole itself is three hundred thousand lightyears across," said Drake.

"As large as the Milky Way," Jon said. "What's the arch? That can't be solid."

"It *is* solid. I've stood on it. The arch is known as the Walls of Matter, the Instrumentality itself. The machine that keeps this universe from collapsing, or the black hole from finishing the job of swallowing the galaxy."

"There aren't any stars."

"My ancestors dismantled them for material, or fed them to the black hole to increase its mass," Drake said. "The same for all of the non-inhabitable planets. I'm not sure if the rest of the worlds were broken in the war or partially dismantled for raw materials, but there aren't any intact planets left here. They are all ruined."

"I never imagined…," Jon breathed. He shook himself. "I guess I know why you call it the Eye."

Drake nodded. "Most people here think the Eye is where the Power comes from. Be careful not to speak of these things to others. They may take it badly."

Jon shook his head. Now that he could tear his eyes away from the black hole, he could see hundreds of other partial worlds in the sky, and that was just the immediate vicinity. His mind kept trying to calculate the orbital positioning data for the planets and moons he could see. It was too complex for the data he had available. He wondered whether Drake's ancestors had invented a new math or left it to AI. Probably the latter, he guessed.

"The gravity feels perfect," Jon said. "This isn't Earth, is it?"

"No," Drake replied. "The Imperial Palace is on the remains of Earth, or so I suspect. We don't have records going that far back. It's along the line of Realms, though, so I have to assume it is."

"I have so many questions, I don't even know where to start."

"How about we start by going inside?" Drake suggested. "Come along, Geoffrey and Jason. Let's get inside and find rooms for you."

Jon nodded.

Drake led them inside. The same polite informality existed in the manor as had been the norm on Nandegurth. People greeted Drake, but there was no bowing or scraping. Jon had to admit he was impressed.

Jon's brief stay in the palace in the Eternal City had been very different. The ordinary people in the city and palace weren't mistreated, but there weren't treated as equals, either.

The servants there were *servants*, and knew it. Jon liked this better.

"How many of these people are you related to, Drake?" asked Jason.

"Just about all of them, to some degree. Everyone in the Courts is distantly related."

"I meant how many are closely related?"

"Few, if any."

"No kids?" asked Geoffrey.

"No," Drake answered curtly.

Jon didn't think he was telling the truth, but he understood why Drake might want to keep any children of his secret. They would be leverage to be used against him, and Drake didn't seem like the kind of person who'd allow anything to compromise him. He was driven, although Jon couldn't have said by what.

It had something to do with the visions of war Jon kept seeing. Drake was a general, and Jon suspected the army they'd seen was only the tip of the iceberg. If the Special Forces were twenty thousand strong, how large was the rest of the army?

⊙

Jason was no less moved than the others by what he was seeing.

He just wasn't as obvious about it as Geoffrey or Jon.

He'd learned the hard way to keep his thoughts to himself most of the time. The world he was on was almost incomprehensible. Jason knew one thing, though: Drake had lied to them. There wasn't a single person here who looked the way he did, so either Drake had lied about his true appearance, or he'd lied when Drake said the Ruined Courts were his home.

Of course, Jason knew as well as anyone that *home* could have many meanings.

Drake may have been from somewhere else and still called the Courts his home. It wasn't as if Jason was from Cincinnati. Thinking of his home brought tears to his eyes. He'd have given almost anything to be able to pick up his fine vanadium-bronze chisels and just... make something. Geoffrey had been right; Jason liked to relax by woodworking, and he hadn't been able to do that for a while now.

As Drake led them though the estate, he stopped occasionally to say something about a piece of armor or artwork or whatever – Jason wasn't paying much attention. He wasn't like the others; he didn't crave adventure. Not anymore. It was enough just to have a home he could call his and be safe there.

Sometimes they passed someone who said something to Drake in Thari. It always echoed around inside Jason's skull. The language was so familiar. It reminded him of a language he hadn't heard in a long time and had never hoped to hear again.

Eventually they ended up in a smaller room with paintings of strange creatures on the walls, and odd toys on the floor. At least, Jason thought they were toys. Strange machines stood along the wall; they reminded Jason of old hairdryers.

"Here we are," said Drake. "This is where children learn Thari."

"Cute, Drake," Jason said. "You want us to take classes with the kids now?"

Drake shook his head. "These machines are used to put the information directly into your mind."

"How safe are they?" Jon asked, examining one of the machines.

"They are made for children."

"Yes, but not for *human* children," Jon said. "Will it work on our physiology?"

"First of all, you aren't human," said Drake. "And yes, it will work on any mind in a humanoid template. None of you has any physiology that is too different for a machine that works on shapeshifters."

"Forgot about that part," Jon said. He sighed. "Okay, what do I do?"

"Each of you, come over and sit facing a machine."

"I'm not sure I want to do this," said Jason.

"It's safe," Drake said. "I swear on my honor to that."

"You can't know that."

"Yes, I can. Please, just trust me."

"Damn it, Drake, I *will* haunt you if this kills me."

Jason sat in front of one of the machines. Up close, the hood on the machine looked like plastic, although Jason was sure it was some kind of ceramic. There was no obvious mechanism.

Drake raised his arms, and glowing holographic displays appeared around each of the headsets. He moved close, did something to the headsets, and gently pushed the hoods down over Jason's and each of the other's heads. Jason felt nervous, but nothing else.

"Okay, it's done," said Drake.

"I didn't feel anything," Jason said, pulling back from the hood. The displays were gone. "Say something in Thari, so we know if it worked."

"I just did," said Drake. "So did you."

"What?" Jason examined his thoughts, but he didn't feel any different.

"After a few days, your brain will settle back to the language it normally uses, and you'll have to concentrate to use Thari, the same as you would any other language."

"That's some pretty impressive tech, Drake," Jon said. "I didn't feel anything, either."

"It's very old technology. Pre-war, I think. These devices are probably a hundred thousand years old or more. The House of Drake is one of the few that still has functioning technology like this."

"And those swords?" Jon asked. "The ones the guards

outside had?"

"Annihilation blades. Ancient relics. They cut though spacetime itself, as I am sure you noticed. Very little can stop one of those blades from cutting."

"I believe it."

"Now what?" asked Jason.

"Now we get you settled, and then Jon and I will visit with the emperor," Drake said.

"I'd like to go, too," said Geoffrey.

"Sorry, not this time. This is a business trip, and it could get ugly if the emperor is behind Jon's attempted murder. We need to go carefully. Jon can get out on his own if I have to fight."

"Are things really that dire?" asked Jon.

"I hope not. Emperor Emrys is an old friend. I don't want to think he's behind this, but he is a suspect."

"And if the emperor orders you to hand Jon over for execution?" said Jason.

"Then I'll tell the emperor to jump into the Eye," Drake said. "You'll be safe here, Jason, and Jon will be safe with me."

"You said we'd be safe on Nandegurth, too."

Drake sighed. "What more assurances can I give you? I cannot foresee every possibility. I do the best I can."

"I'm sorry, Drake," Jason said, and he was. "I'm just overloaded. We'll be fine here."

Drake gripped his shoulder. Jason normally found physical contact uncomfortable, but he didn't mind Drake's touch, for some reason. A part of him trusted the madman.

What does that say about me? he thought.

"Come," Drake said. "I'll introduce you to the steward."

CHAPTER SIXTEEN

Drake took Jon though the Waypoint to the Imperial Plaza.

It had been some time since Drake had been here, but nothing ever truly changed in this place – not in normal lifetimes, anyway. The intricate patterns of the paving stones still invoked feelings that he didn't quite understand. Near to the Waypoint stood a worn statue with raised arms, facing the Eye. Drake walked with Jon to stand before it.

Drake brushed sand away from the carved tablets at its base, but the words had faded since his youth, illegible now. It was sad, that so much history was gone. Who now, besides him, remembered what had been written there?

"What does it represent?" asked Jon.

"'Look on my works, ye mighty, and despair.'"

"Shelley? You surprise me, Drake."

"I have always been a fan of good poetry. This, however is the Statue of the Forgotten War," Drake said. "It was a monument to the Great War, and to the Armistice that followed. I suppose now there are very few who remember it."

"How long ago was the war?"

"Here? A hundred thousand years, give or take a few

decades. The tablet was legible when I was younger. It's been a long time since I've come here to look at it."

"You weren't here when it was constructed, were you?"

Drake laughed. "I'm not *that* old, no."

"Whew. Had me worried, Drake."

"What difference would it have made?"

"You'd be scarier than you already are?" Jon shrugged. "I don't know. No difference, I suppose. What was the war about?"

"It's complicated." Drake hadn't intended to get into a discussion about those matters, as the war was still ongoing. He was usually more secretive about his vocation. Perhaps Jon had a part to play in the upcoming war that Drake didn't understand yet. He hoped not, for Jon's sake. "It was something like a civil war, across all of existence. Countless worlds and even universes were said to have been destroyed. You're looking at what little of the first civilization survived the war."

"Your people don't do anything on a small scale, do they?"

"Our ancestors certainly didn't," said Drake. "Come, we should head to court."

"Did you send word ahead?"

"Certainly not. Why allow my enemies time to set up an ambush?"

"You really expect to be attacked?"

"Always."

Jon just shook his head as they walked.

"It's customary for one to change into daemonform when entering the Imperial Court," Drake said.

"I'm not a shapeshifter, Drake."

"I know that. I just don't want you to be surprised when I change."

"Oh."

Drake shifted into his draconic form and called upon the Instrumentality to shift his clothes and armor to suit his form as he did. It was all a very fluid change for one as experienced as he was. He shrugged to settle his wings and approached the gates of the palace.

The guards at the gates bowed to Drake and allowed him and Jon to pass. They recognized his chosen form, and since he'd have slain anyone else who dared to wear a body too similar, they never doubted he was the Prince of Drake. He didn't feel as comfortable with that as he might have in the past. They should have used an Orb of Recognition to verify his identity, but they were not as safety-conscious as the House of Drake.

Or not as paranoid, maybe, he thought.

The courtyard was a study in frozen fountains and time-locked flame. It was pretty, if a bit ostentatious for Drake's tastes. The guards at the entrance to the palace opened the doors for him with a bow.

Drake and Jon were immediately intercepted by a glowing apparition of swirling smoke and flame. "Your Highness, if we had known of your pending arrival, we would have prepared refreshments," the majordomo squeaked. "We could have even sent word that His Majesty is not seeing supplicants at this time."

"Well, then, it's a good thing I am neither hungry nor seeking anything from him. Out of my way."

"Please, Your Highness, His Majesty has a guest and gave explicit orders that he was not to be disturbed."

That gave Drake pause for a moment. "Who is with him?"

"I couldn't possibly divulge that information!" the majordomo gasped.

"Is it a woman?" Drake demanded. Emperor Emrys liked women and often entertained them in his quarters. It was the one thing Drake wouldn't consider interrupting.

"Certainly not, Your Highness!" The gasbag seemed scandalized.

"Then get out of my way before he has to find himself a new majordomo."

The man squeaked again as he lost control of his abilities and shifted into a trembling human form and bowed. His head almost touched the floor.

Drake walked past him, shaking his head. He knew that the majordomo position in the palace was a coveted one that usually went to young members of the Noble Houses, but they always seemed to be grotesque little suck-ups. He hated people like that. He'd rather be insulted than be adulated to no purpose.

"That was... *interesting*," said Jon.

"Sniveling little brown-nosers like that are not uncommon."

"I meant the form. When you said *exotic*, I didn't imagine you meant *non-biological*."

Drake laughed. "I hardly noticed. Sorry. Yes, young shapeshifters sometimes get a bit too theatrical."

"But how?" Jon asked. "You said the shapeshifting ability is biological, but that couldn't have been."

"I said it was biological or done with the Instrumentality. He used the latter."

"I still don't understand how."

"Patterned energy and magnetic fields. He would say it was magic. I'd say the form was held together with nanomolecular machines. Think of it as a robot piloted remotely. His trueform was folded away into a pocket space."

Jon shook his head. "I think I'll give up for now on making sense of it."

"Probably for the best."

The massive bronze doors of the Imperial Audience Chamber stood open, and the chamber itself was empty. The Fire Throne glowed with the baleful intensity of time-locked flame, but Emrys wasn't on it. A faint light was visible from under the door behind the throne. Drake could hear the murmur of voices from the room.

Drake shrugged back into his normal form. There was no reason to keep up appearances if there was no one around to impress. Emrys rarely wore a daemonform anyway.

"No one around?" asked Jon.

"He's in his private study." Drake gestured to the back of the room.

"Should we come back?"

"No. Now come along." Drake paused by the throne and gestured. "The Fire Throne."

"It's warm," Jon said. "What's it made of?"

"Time-locked fire."

Jon frowned. "If it's time-locked, which I assume is like stasis, how can it be warm?"

"*Time-slowed* might be a more accurate term. It loses energy at one-billionth the normal rate. Eventually it will fade, but until then, it makes a nice theatrical prop."

"That isn't enough energy loss for it to feel warm."

"The stasis field effect slows the heat exchange in the air near the throne."

Jon just shook his head.

Drake rapped sharply on the door.

"Enter!" a voice commanded.

Drake opened the door and paused. Two men were seated before the small fire, glasses of red wine in their hands. Emperor Emrys was young, only in his sixties, although he looked barely twenty-five. The other man, Drake was less happy to see, having before met him only on the battlefield. He was the supreme military commander for the Golden Kingdom, and the emperor's uncle.

"Pardon me, Your Majesty. I didn't realize you were with family."

"Drake, don't get formal on me now. You've met my uncle?"

"Dominic," Drake said holding out his hand.

"Fate is a funny thing," Dominic said, standing up. He was maybe ten centimeters taller than Drake, about the same height as Jon. His sandy hair was greying, and his eyes were a cold steel grey. "I came here looking for *you*, to ask if you knew what had happened to *him*."

Drake lowered his un-shook hand. "Well, now you've found us both."

"Something I should know about?" Emrys asked. He seemed unconcerned, and sipped his wine, but Drake knew he was an accomplished sorcerer. Drake didn't want to find out just how good he might have gotten since he was young.

"Almost certainly," said Drake. "May I ask *you* a question first?"

Emrys stood. "I've not known you to hesitate to speak your mind. What's up?"

"It's complicated, and I'm not sure if you'd want me to speak of these matters in front of your uncle."

"I'm sure it would be fine. Please have out with it."

"Very well. Did you issue orders for some of my men to be dispatched to the forest outside Darkton, and did you have them killed there?"

"I didn't do either one," Emrys said, glancing at Jon with curiosity. "Perhaps we could all have a glass of wine and discuss the matter. I'm not sure I like having you and my uncle looking as if you want to draw swords. I like the furniture in here too much for that."

Drake nodded. Emrys wasn't a liar. He'd often gotten into quite a bit of trouble as a child for telling the truth, when a lie would have been more polite. If he said he didn't do it, Drake believed him.

"Perhaps a glass would soothe things," Drake said with a slight bow. "May I introduce by friend, Jon."

"Your Majesty," Jon said.

"You speak Thari now," said Dominic.

"Drake taught me."

"That was fast."

"Magic, of course," Drake replied. "Emrys is not the only sorcerer in the Courts."

"Nice to meet you, Jon. You're obviously family. Call me Emrys. Please, have a seat." Emrys gestured, and two more overstuffed chairs appeared.

"Thank you," Jon said. He accepted a glass of wine, and Drake sat opposite him.

"So...," Drake said before taking a sip of his wine, a fine merlot, "why were you looking for me, Dominic?"

"Obviously, I was misled," said Dominic, settling back into his chair. "Jon disappeared rather suddenly from the palace. When I tracked him back to an Earth, he was gone from there, as well, but there were bodies present. Bodies that looked like your men."

"I wasn't aware that you were so well-versed in the forms my troops take."

"Well, they weren't human, and they bore your device. Seemed like they would be yours."

"I can see how you might think that."

"If they were yours, then you have some explaining to do."

"I see no reason why I should explain anything to you."

"Enough!" said Emrys. "You two can cool it down! Just tell me what the hell is going on. Jon, you don't seem as inclined to measure your dick as these two. Maybe you can tell me."

Jon laughed. "I'm not sure where to begin."

"Well, I've never met you, so you must be new to the family. Since my uncle here is looking for you, I assume you're from the North? Who are you related to?"

"I've known about all of this for less than a week. I honestly don't think I'm related to any of you."

"He is attuned to the Cynosure," said Drake.

"Then you *must* be family," Emrys said. "You look a bit like Dominic, here. Your build and eyes are the same, at least."

Jon shook his head. "He's denied any connection."

Dominic smiled. "No offense intended, Jon. I just know that I'm not your father. I don't know who that might be, but it wasn't me."

Emrys shrugged. "I suppose it doesn't really matter. So you attuned to the Cynosure only days after learning about it? That was ambitious."

"Less ambition than ignorance. I was given little instruction and no warnings."

Emrys glanced at Dominic. "What's this?"

"Jon was with some of the younger crowd," Dominic said. "You ran with them yourself for a while. You remember how wild they could get."

"I didn't think they'd pull something like that. He could have died."

"I don't think they cared overly much," said Jon, "as they tried to kill me just after I succeeded. Crossbow. It's how I was injured." He gestured to the steri-strips on his head.

Emrys glanced at Dominic. "Got to watch the young ones with crossbows."

Dominic just snorted at what seemed to be a private joke.

"Then what?" Emrys asked.

Jon shrugged. "I got out of there as quickly as I could. I ended up on an Earth I didn't know. A couple of people there helped me, and then I was attacked by some strange people dressed in black. I was arrested by the local government, and then Drake showed up and rescued me."

"Out of the goodness of your heart, no doubt," said Dominic.

"Of course not," Drake said. "I showed up to kill the interloper who had dared to invade a Realm I protect. However, Jon wasn't to blame, so I started investigating instead. That led me here, where I have found you."

"And your men who tried to kill him?"

"They weren't my soldiers. My only missing troops were killed with sorcery outside Darkton. The men used to attack Jon were imposters. They certainly weren't well trained."

"How do you know that?"

"My troops wouldn't have been killed by two locals wielding a baseball bat and a kitchen knife."

CHAPTER SEVENTEEN

Geoffrey wasn't sure what to do with his time.

Normally he'd watch television or play a video game when bored, but that wasn't an option in this strange place. He'd discovered that the language he learned was only for the spoken version. The books he found were still indecipherable to him, although some of the pictures were interesting.

Jason didn't want to talk, either, so Geoffrey went exploring.

Drake Manor was a huge, sprawling complex filled with tens of thousands of people working and living here. Almost everyone was wearing a black, military-style uniform. A glimpse of the daily life of these people was interesting, but it wasn't particularly informative. Geoffrey was an outsider, and while he'd in come here with Drake, that didn't mean people were going to be open and trusting with him.

He went out into the courtyard for a while, but the baleful stare of the unblinking Eye made him anxious. Drake had said it was just a galaxy-sized black hole, as if that made things better. An accretion disk was just barely visible inside the unconceivably big wall that surrounded it.

The engineering needed to construct that wall was

incomprehensible to him. People back on his Earth had trouble making bridges that didn't fall down. Here was a wall untold millions of *lightyears* across, that had been here for at least a hundred thousand years.

He imagined he could feel a malign intelligence staring down at him from the deep black Eye. It made him shiver. Drake had spoken of the Instrumentality, an ancient machine. Geoffrey wondered if the Eye had anything to do with it.

He went back inside and wandered the halls. He tried to imagine what the Imperial Palace looked like. He couldn't. He'd wanted to go with Jon and Drake. He'd thought he and Drake had bonded a bit on the hunting trip. Drake had certainly seemed more talkative with him then. Drake had told Geoffrey that he couldn't go to the palace, though. That had hurt.

A room full of paintings drew his attention, and Geoffrey stopped to look at them. The paintings reminded Geoffrey of the tapestries in his room on Nandegurth. The paintings were all of brutal battles, and filled with fantastical creatures and people, achieved with exquisite and horrifying detail in vibrant colors.

Whoever had painted them, those artists had been masters.

A few of the paintings held a familiar draconic figure.

The next room contained portraits.

Drake's was easy to find. He looked much as he did now, and Geoffrey wondered how long ago the painting had been done. The other people in the paintings all had a similar family resemblance. Some had red hair, like Drake's; others were blond or even brown-haired. One or two had black hair. The shapes of the faces, particularly their cheekbones and noses, were similar to Drake's. They all had a vaguely Asian look that Geoffrey couldn't quite define.

Geoffrey was pleased to see that the Drake family were just normal, healthy, good-looking people, although none of them were as handsome as Drake. Geoffrey wasn't sure why that pleased him, too.

Maybe it just made him feel better about himself.

All of the rooms in this wing of the manor seemed to hold artworks. Some of the sculptures were achingly beautiful and would have made Michelangelo cry with their perfection. Some were of things that Geoffrey thought might end up giving him nightmares.

The final room in the gallery held armor and weapons.

Geoffrey had seen a display of armor and weapons at the Cincinnati Art Museum once on a school trip. Those had been on loan from the Tower of London. This display put those arms to shame. It wasn't just the workmanship of the pieces, which was exquisite; it was the variety of the arms and armor.

The armor and weapons here hadn't been made by humans, or at last not by people Geoffrey normally would have thought of as humans. The people of the Courts were shapeshifters, and the armor and weapons reflected that. Some of the armor was grotesque, hinting at strange forms for the wearers.

Some of the blades looked normal enough, although all were beautifully made. Others were blackened, barbed horrors meant to rend and tear. Geoffrey was afraid of those blades. Several of them were actually glowing in the dim light of the gallery.

One blade, near the center, looked very much like Drake's sword. Geoffrey hadn't gotten to look closely at Drake's, and the one here was beautiful, with an intricate pattern etched into it. Something about it called to him.

He hesitantly reached out to touch it.

"I wouldn't do that, if I were you," a voice said from behind him.

Geoffrey started and then turned guiltily.

The speaker was a beautiful woman of about his height. She was dressed in the black uniform he'd seen on the other soldiers of House Drake. Her hair was black and cut short, and her eyes were a deep green, like Drake's. She was smirking.

"Some of the things down here will kill people who shouldn't be here," she said. "Who are you?"

"Geoffrey Meeks," he replied. Her hand was resting on her sword hilt. "I came here with Drake."

"That's informative," she replied. "They are a lot of Drakes here. Which one?"

"Daeren Drake."

"Oh, *the* Drake, I didn't know he was back." Her hand dropped from the sword. "What are you doing down here?"

"I'm sorry, I didn't catch your name."

"I didn't give it. Now answer the question."

Geoffrey sighed. That never worked for him. "I was just exploring, looking around. Drake went to see the emperor; he said to stay here in the house. No one said I couldn't explore."

She sighed. "Well, someone should have warned you about the dangers, at least. Did you speak to the steward?"

Geoffrey nodded.

The woman shook her head. "I'm Sergeant Revna Södersjö sept Drake. I'll speak to the steward about it later. You're not related to the Drake?"

"No, I'm human."

"What am I, chopped liver?" she asked, eyes flashing. "No, wait, it's probably a translation error. You just learned Thari using the hoods, right?"

Geoffrey nodded, confused.

"The teaching hoods tie your thoughts together. It links the name of our people to the name you use for your own. Somewhat inconvenient, if you ask me." She frowned. "You're from an Earth Realm?"

"Yes," Geoffrey replied. That seemed safe to say.

"Interesting. I wonder why he'd bring you here." She waved her hand. "None of my business. If I needed to know, I'd have been told."

Geoffrey felt a little awkward, as she didn't say anything else or leave.

"Could you tell me about this sword?" he asked. "It looks like the one Drake carries."

Revna smiled, obviously happy for the change in topic. "It's an ancient weapon, dating back to the founding of the House in the Before Times. Some say it was held by the first Drake." She shrugged. "I don't know anyone who would know. I suppose maybe Prince Daeren Drake might, if anyone did. You can ask him, if you're brave enough."

"You seem to have something more than just respect for him."

"Don't you?" she asked, obviously surprised. "He's ancient, himself. He's the oldest living Drake. That means he's the best of us. Have you seen him fight?"

Geoffrey nodded.

"Then you know what I mean."

"I don't know enough about the rest of you to have anything to compare him to," said Geoffrey. "He's amazing and scary but seems pretty cool, too."

"I envy you, Geoffrey Meeks. I've never even spoken to him."

"You could show me around, and I could introduce you," Geoffrey suggested.

Revna laughed. "You may walk with me as I do my rounds down here. As for the other, I have no need to call attention to myself."

"How long are you on duty?"

"Shift change is with dinner, about a quarter tuning from now. Surely you will not find my company too onerous until then."

Geoffrey smiled. She was gorgeous. He knew he didn't have a chance in hell of anything happening with a woman like her, and that actually made it easier. He could relax and not worry about trying to impress her. He was only twenty, and he had no idea how old she was. She could be thousands of years old, although she looked to be only in her early twenties.

"I'd like that," he replied.

☉

Jason lay in the firm bed in the room he'd been given, and brooded.

He'd checked on Geoffrey, but the young man wandered off somewhere. Jason didn't have any desire to do that himself. This world was too strange. At least he could speak the language now; that machine Drake used had put the knowledge right where he could use it.

That would have made things so much easier over the years.

English hadn't been his first or even second language, and it hadn't been easy for him to learn. Spanish hadn't been too hard; the structure was similar enough to his own tongue. German had been difficult, but that had been at a bad time in his life anyway, one he didn't like to think about.

Jason has roamed about the planet when he was younger, never settling in any place for long. It hadn't been easy for him, since he didn't age as humans did. Because of his wandering, he hadn't owned a home in a long time, and somewhat resented being separated from his home now. He wasn't entirely sure why he'd extended the bond of guest obligation to Jon. Maybe it was just because Jon was being hunted. Jason knew what that felt like. He'd been hunted, himself, over the years. Once, many years ago, someone had extended the guest bond to Jason. He hadn't known why, but it had been very welcome.

Jason sat up and moved to the end of the bed. There was a mirror on the dresser. Even in this private room, he didn't let his guard down. His long hair and bandana had sometimes caused problems of their own over the years, but they generally kept him safer.

Drake was a problem, though.

Jason realized he'd drawn his knife and was carefully testing the edge. The point had broken off, and he hadn't dared to ask for a new knife. No doubt Drake would have given him one, and then Jason would have felt as if he owed the man something.

What, exactly? he thought. *Loyalty? Friendship?*

Maybe that was what scared him: the thought of having someone as a friend who didn't care about his past. Drake seemed to actually be an okay... *person*, if a little scary.

Drake was almost like a force of nature. You didn't hate the tornado when it knocked down your house; you just nodded and rebuilt. Drake was like that. He was capable of terrible things, but Jason didn't feel as if Drake meant anything evil with his deeds.

Drake's eyes said he'd seen a lot, and much of it dark and ugly. Yet Jason thought Drake hadn't been as touched by that darkness as others would have been. Drake was friendly, accepting, and easy-going. Jason could be himself around him.

Now he just needed to figure who that was.

He'd been hiding and pretending for so long that he didn't really know anymore.

CHAPTER EIGHTEEN

Jon sipped his wine and watched the interplay of emotion and personalities. He hadn't spent much time in the Golden Kingdom, but he liked Dominic. Watching him and Drake verbally spar was somewhat fun. He was just glad it was only words. Dominic was said to be a formidable swordsman, and Drake...Well, Drake was Drake.

"How certain are you that those locals actually killed the soldiers?" asked Dominic.

"As certain as one can be without being there," Drake replied. "If you saw the solders being taken away, why not intervene and interrogate them? If you were so certain they were mine?"

"Those high middle Realms can be tricky," Dominic said, "as you are no doubt aware. I admit that the wounds on those I examined are consistent with your narrative. The bodies showed small knife wounds and blunt force trauma."

"How kind of you to admit the truth."

"It does seem improbable that any soldiers of yours could have been bested in such a way, Drake," Emrys agreed, obviously trying to smooth the tension between Drake and

Dominic. "You taught me to use a blade, and I've watched you duel. Any soldiers you trained would be more than a match for most locals on a random Earth Realm. I cannot see how *any* troops of yours could be so easily overcome, killed, or captured."

"I will apologize, if you wish," said Drake, "for my tone when I first entered. Our dead soldiers were found bearing Imperial Orders. It has made me somewhat distraught."

"What?" Emrys shouted. "The orders weren't faked?"

Drake pulled a set of papers from inside his coat and handed them to Emrys.

Emrys spread the papers out on the side table and examined them. For just a moment, Jon thought he could see a sign or symbol floating in the air before Emrys. Then Jon blinked, and it was gone. It had looked much like the disk shape he'd seen when joining with the Cynosure.

"The seal is authentic," said Emrys. "No wonder you were pissed off when you got here. I can assure you that I had nothing to do with this."

"I believe you," Drake said. "I hadn't wanted to suspect you, but you can understand why, I hope."

"Of course, old friend."

"I'm not sure that I do," said Dominic. "What do these papers prove?"

"That someone in the Imperial Court issued authentic orders to my troops, and then had those troops killed, I assume so that imposters could be used in the attempt on Jon's life."

"That seems a bit contrived."

"Not if whoever it was wanted to start a war."

"If I may interject something, Your Majesty...?" said Jon.

"You're a royal cousin, at the least," Emrys said, "as well as a friend of Drake. I would wish you to speak at will, here in private."

"Thank you, Your Majesty. Drake hasn't mentioned the

timing yet. I was attacked in the Eternal City by people I had thought trustworthy, and then again by people pretending to be Drake's troops within *minutes* of arriving in that Realm. They couldn't have gotten there from his citadel that quickly. I was later attacked by someone from the Eternal City while with Drake."

"While under my protection as a guest," Drake said. "I'll settle up with that one later."

"Well, shit," said Dominic. "You're certain the troops weren't yours, Drake?"

"Absolutely. My captains perform a roll call every morning. Only the one squad was missing. That squad was later found dead, to the last soldier. The body of the sergeant on the patrol was the source of the Imperial Orders."

"To be honest, I had thought the tattoos seemed oddly fresh. They were still pink on one of the corpses," Dominic said.

"You saw them firsthand? We must have just missed each other."

"You didn't detect me enter your Realm?" Dominic said with a smile. "Good to know I still I have my ways."

"Hmm."

"The locals also captured four men alive. I heard them talking about moving them to a secure location."

Drake nodded. "Well, I know where to go and whom to question, when I have the time."

"Jon, who tried to kill you, later?" asked Dominic.

"Sergei."

"Joachim's son," Dominic spat. "That bastard wanted to keep fighting after the last war. He's always said the treaty was a mistake. He stops just short of actual treason, but he isn't in high regard with the king."

"Joachim, or Sergei?" Emrys asked.

"Well, both, actually."

"Joachim is Dominic's brother," Drake said to Jon.

Jon nodded. "I think I knew that."

"Half-brother," said Dominic. "I don't care for them. I have little use for men with no honor."

"Any idea why any of them would want to kill me?" asked Jon.

"None. It doesn't make tactical sense to have you attune to the Cynosure and then try to kill you. What purpose would it serve? Why not kill you without granting you a Power, if they wanted you dead?"

"Drake, you don't think the Ancient Enemy could have a hand in this, do you?" said Emrys.

Drake frowned and glanced at Dominic.

"My uncle knows," Emrys said. "Some of the people up North fight against them, as well."

"I know that," said Drake. "I just didn't know Dominic is one of them."

"To defend out kingdom, I needed to know about the Ancient Enemy," Dominic said. "I was trained to fight them by my uncle, the previous Lord Protector."

"Am I allowed to ask who this enemy is?" said Jon.

"Remember when I told you there had been an ancient war a hundred thousand years ago, and that who was involved was complicated?"

"I think so, yes."

"Some of those enemies are still around and fighting," said Drake. "That is the purpose of my army."

"I take it they're formidable?" Jon said. They would have to be, for Drake to have an army such as he did.

All three of the other men nodded solemnly.

☉

A quarter turning was about an hour, Geoffrey learned. Revna showed him the rest of the art gallery, which wasn't as interesting as the weapons and armor, or the company. Geoffrey thought Revna was the kind of woman his cousin Alan would have called a heartbreaker. She flirted with him, but in a friendly, completely non-sexual way.

She told Geoffrey about the House of Drake and about the command structure of the House armies. Everyone in the House, it seemed, spent a few decades in the House military. *Decades,* he thought. It must seem like such a short time for people who lived practically forever.

Sometimes things didn't translate as well, if Geoffrey didn't have an English term in his mind that matched the concept she was expressing. Mostly, it had to do with the Courts and the relationships of the other Houses. Geoffrey didn't understand most of it, but it was interesting to spend time with her.

After her shift was over, Revna led him to the dinner hall, pausing only for a brief conversation with her guard replacement. The man who replaced her looked at Geoffrey with curiosity but asked no questions. Everyone seemed so… *professional.*

Geoffrey wondered if he should go find Jason but then decided his friend could take care of himself. Jason was good at that, if nothing else. Jason would find the mess and eat, or he'd do without, as the mood struck him.

The mess was different from what he'd expected. Geoffrey wasn't sure exactly what he'd been expecting, maybe something like the food Drake had served, but the food here wasn't anything like that. It was served buffet style, which he *had* expected. It was a military chow line, after all. He'd seen them in movies, if nowhere else.

He didn't recognize any of the food, except maybe what looked like whole fish and what was probably brown rice. Everything smelled like food to him. It was exotic, to say the least.

"What's wrong?" Revna asked.

"Not sure what any of this is."

"Just grab a tray. I'll toss some good stuff on there for you."

Geoffrey went through the line with her, and she piled his tray with a plate of small, oily, and salty-looking fish; well-cooked sausages; rice; mixed vegetables he didn't recognize, and a knot of twisted, dark bread with coarse salt on it. Some of the vegetables had strange shapes, like stars and pyramids. Revna placed an empty ceramic cup on his tray, as well.

Pitchers of something reddish-purple that smelled and tasted of root beer stood on the tables. It wasn't very sweet but had a strong aroma. It wasn't carbonated, and Geoffrey could see pieces of what looked like roots in the bottom of the pitcher. The beverage was smooth-flavored and pleasant.

Revna introduced him to the other non-commissioned officers at the table where they sat. Geoffrey couldn't keep track of all the names. They all seemed to be sergeants or corporals, and they all had strange names.

The fish tasted better than it looked, although he had to remove the head. The bread turned out to be rye or something like it. Everything tasted strange but good. The spices were *odd*. He hoped he wouldn't have stomach problems from the exotic food. He hadn't yet, but this food was a lot different from what he'd been eating.

Everyone seemed friendly, if a little reserved. Geoffrey wasn't military, so he sort of understood why they wouldn't be as open with him as they might have been otherwise. A few people had questions about Drake that he didn't know how to answer. Everyone seemed to think Geoffrey had been accorded a great honor.

Geoffrey thought much the same, if for different reasons.

He had wanted adventure, and so far, he'd had a good one. He didn't think Jason was having as good a time. However, if Geoffrey had been shot in the arm with a poisoned crossbow bolt, he probably wouldn't have been having as much fun, either.

After the meal, Revna led him back to the VIP quarters. He wasn't sure which room he was in, but she asked a passing steward and got directions. Geoffrey was suddenly fairly nervous when they got to his room. He was uncertain if he should ask her in. He decided against it, because he wasn't sure if he was ready for her to say yes. He definitely wasn't ready for her to say no.

He wasn't inexperienced with women, but neither was he super comfortable with them.

Revna seemed to understand, or maybe she didn't want anything, either. She thanked him for the company and left. Geoffrey felt bad about not being able to introduce her to Drake. He'd make a point of doing so later, if he was able to.

Geoffrey couldn't help but think that he'd missed an opportunity with Revna. He just wasn't sure how he felt about it. He knew he should feel disappointed, but he mostly felt relieved. He was tired, and the world was strange, and she may have been achingly attractive, but she wasn't human.

It shouldn't matter, but it did.

Or maybe he was just making excuses.

He had difficulty falling asleep that night.

CHAPTER NINETEEN

Drake wasn't happy about the emperor telling Jon even a small part of the truth about the secret war. On the other hand, Jon had seen Drake's Special Forces and had guessed that the army wasn't used for conventional purposes. Jon wasn't stupid, and he seemed to have an uncanny knack for prediction. Drake wasn't sure whether he was good at calculating probabilities, precognitive, or both.

"I take it that your army has been busy fighting this enemy, Drake," said Jon.

"Indeed, we have been, for a very long time," Drake replied. "I've lost millions of troops over the millennia. Of course, we've killed millions of the enemy."

"Excuse me – did you say *millions?*"

"I did, and the enemy has lost millions more than that."

"Where do they come from?" Jon asked. "The enemy, I mean. I assume the troops are raised from the Drake estates."

"The troops are from Drake and allied Houses in the Courts. As to the enemy, that is a complicated question to answer. Suffice to say that many of them are scattered throughout the universes, waging wars and feeding on the pain and despair. They are concentrated in some places, dark worlds filled with terror and suffering."

"They can be found in many Realms," said Dominic. "I've often encountered them at the head of armies. They are the stuff of nightmares. You're not experienced enough to fight them, Jon. If you find yourself facing one, run. As fast as you can. Many of them can follow a man through the worlds, so don't be content to just walk a few Realms away. It may not be enough."

"Sounds like good advice," Jon said. "Not that I'm sure I'd know if I did face one. Any idea if they *are* involved in this?"

Drake shrugged. "We don't have enough information at this time."

"So you can't rule it out." Jon shook his head. "This week has been the strangest in my life, and that's saying something."

"If you live long enough, all your weeks will seem strange," said Dominic.

"In regards to the Ancient Enemy, I'd appreciate it if you said nothing of this to any others," Emrys said. "Knowing about the Ancient Enemy can make a person their target."

"Of course. I wouldn't wish that on anyone. I assume you had good reason to let me know," Jon said. He straightened his shoulders to relieve some of the building tension. "I feel as though I'm already a target. Knowing the Ancient Enemy are out there doesn't make me feel much better."

"Drake, if I may ask," said Dominic, "who else in the Golden Kingdom knows about all of this?"

"I assume you've told the king," said Drake. "Joseph may know; he seems to be the type to get into this kind of trouble. Otherwise, Monika knows. I don't know who else might. "

"Monika?" Dominic raised an eyebrow. "I'd heard a rumor that the two of you..."

"That was before our last war," Drake replied. "She and I had met while tracking a particularly nasty old monster through a Realm just North of the Dancing Mountains. I believe the thing had attacked a Realm she kept for her own. I was traveling through when I detected it and started a hunt of my own. She is quite knowledgeable about the Ancient Enemy. She indicated that she'd learned about them from her grandfather while learning sorcery."

"Really?" said Dominic. "Now I wish I'd spent more time with him."

"I see I still have much to learn," Jon said. He laughed. "To think I once thought I understood how the world and universe worked. My reality was much smaller a week ago."

"It can be a shock," said Emrys. "Hell, I never thought I'd end up an emperor."

"So what do we do now?"

"As I see it, we have a few paths forward," Drake said. "We need to understand what's going on in the Golden Kingdom, and why some of the people there want to kill you. We also need to discover who your father is, as that may have a bearing on the first question. Beyond that, I'd like to know who sent the Imperial Orders to my men. I want their head to send back to my troops. We lost some good people. Morale has suffered since that loss and the attack on my world."

"There was an attack on Nandegurth?" said Emrys.

"A highly trained force came through the Waypoint. I stopped them, but not without losses."

"I understand even more why you came here. Very few even know of that world. We'll get to the bottom of that before you go. As for the other, do you plan to go to the Golden Kingdom?"

"I do," Drake replied. "I think I'll find some answers there."

Dominic nodded. "I believe you'll need to tread carefully, if going to the Golden Kingdom is your plan. Please don't let the actions of a young fool cause you to do something rash. Some of us in the North understand just how close the Golden

Kingdom came to being wiped out in the last war, even if some fools deny the possibility. I'm aware of your troop capabilities down here, Drake. I'm glad you chose to stay out of that squabble. If you'll allow me, I'll return home and try to find what I can. I'll let you know what I discover."

"I'll abide by that," Drake said. "I trust your honor. However, at some point we will need to travel to the Golden Kingdom ourselves. I trust that won't be a problem."

"We're not at war," said Dominic. "Don't kill anyone there unless they attack you, and it shouldn't be an issue. I'll speak to the king on your behalf."

"As for the Imperial Orders," Emrys said, "there are very few people who could have issued them. We should be able to clear that up quickly. If you want their head, you can take it."

"I don't suppose it will be easy, and one of the people is from House Cyryth," Drake said.

"No. Although…"

"What?"

"I'm not sure which House the sept Nichols is beholden to."

"Cyryth," said Drake. "I take it there's a Nichols here."

"The Imperial Dispatcher."

"Perfectly placed to do the deed," Drake agreed. "What would you like me to do about it?"

"Perhaps now would be the best time for me to excuse myself," Dominic said, standing.

Drake stood and shook his offered hand. It was rough with sword callouses, much like Drake's own. "May all our misunderstandings be as easily resolved," said Drake.

"Indeed. I suppose I'll see you in the North soon." He turned slightly. "Jon, I'm glad to have found you intact. Drake is an honorable man. You'll be safe with him."

"Thank you," Jon said. "I'd figured that out."

Emrys walked out with Dominic for a few private words, and Drake forced himself not to listen. He doubted it had anything to do with him anyway. He'd made a career out of avoiding politics. What would he do with a throne if he had one?

"I sent the guard to fetch Noel Nichols," Emrys said as he reentered the room. "Even if the man didn't have anything to do with it, the order would have gone through his office."

"Then he had his hand on it," said Drake.

"Drake, you mentioned trying to find my father," said Jon. "Why is that so important?"

"Actually, I said we needed to discover who you're related to. However, I assume you know your mother wasn't one of the Royal Family from the North, in which case it must be your father who is. There is a slight chance you received some mix of genes from older ancestors that recombined to make you able to receive the Cynosure."

"I've never heard of anything like that," said Emrys. "The genes usually dilute over time. I've never heard of anyone being able to attune who wasn't a direct descendant, and even then, only until the second or third generation. I remember just a couple of years ago, Giovanni lost a daughter in the attempt to attune."

"Well, until we discover Jon's genealogy, we won't know that for certain."

"I'm not sure how comfortable I am with this," Jon said. "What does it matter?"

"Because people hold blood debts for a long time," said Drake. "Cyryth's vendetta with Drake has lasted two thousand years. I understand they have something similar to our vendettas in the North, except between the brothers and sisters of the old king."

"Great. So I'm the victim of a blood feud that has nothing to do with me?"

"You're related to them somehow."

"Can we talk about that later?"

"Certainly."

Emrys offered them more wine, then sat back by the fire. "So, Drake, how were things going before all of this happened?"

"Well enough," Drake replied. "There hasn't been any activity along the border forts in the past few weeks. We had a single incursion in the Court of the Broken Prince, but our man Count Sima resolved it quickly enough."

Emrys nodded. "I've heard you brought a couple of humans with you to the Courts."

Drake grinned. "Your spies work quickly. The two men in question protected Jon when he arrived in their Realm. I felt they now have an interest in his wellbeing."

"That Earth Realm is one of *your* Realms, isn't it?"

"Well, I watch over it. I have a personal interest there, in the American Southwest. I believe you know why."

"I do, indeed." Emrys glanced at Jon. "I find it interesting that you ended up in that Realm, of all places, Jon. What made you stop there?"

Drake was glad Emrys hadn't mentioned what that personal interest was. Drake knew that he knew, and he didn't want anyone else to.

Jon shrugged. "When I escaped the Golden Kingdom, I left without a destination in mind. I was falling through the worlds, and I tried to reach a place where I'd find help."

"Hmm. I can't help but suspect that there's more to it," said Emrys.

"I checked him for a geas," Drake replied.

"I was thinking more of a Realm Ward. Perhaps to guide him to a place where they knew you'd respond?"

"What are you talking about?" Jon asked.

"Sorcery," Drake said with a grin. "A geas is a magical compulsion; a Realm Ward guides a Realm-walker to make a certain choice. There was certainly something more than just blind luck involved. The imposter troops arrived within minutes of his arrival," he added to Emrys.

"There is no Waypoint near there?" Emrys asked.

"No, there's a node in the vicinity, but the only Waypoint is in New England. If the North was involved, they couldn't have used it, anyway."

"So it was just a normal Earth Realm. Why did you bring the two humans with you?"

Drake shrugged. "They had been arrested and would have been ill-used by the local authorities for having met one of our kind. It seemed kinder to bring them along, and they wished to come."

"That was well done."

There was a knock on the door.

"Enter!"

"Your Imperial Majesty, we've brought the clerk you asked for," a guard said. She gestured back over her shoulder into the audience chamber.

"We'll sit in official judgement," said Emrys.

The guard nodded and left.

"Shall we, Drake?"

"Certainly, Your Majesty."

CHAPTER TWENTY

Jon was curious about what justice was like in the Ruined Courts. He suspected that if Drake was involved, justice would be swift and decisive. Drake didn't seem to waste time being subtle, and with power and skill like his, why should he?

Emrys was an unknown factor, though. The emperor didn't appear to be much older than Jon. Jon knew looks could be deceiving with these people, but Emrys didn't *feel* old. The man must have been accomplished, to have ascended the throne at so young an age. Also, Drake genuinely seemed to respect Emrys. Jon didn't think it was just a matter of Drake respecting the office, either.

Jon followed as the emperor and Drake moved back out into the Imperial Audience Chamber and Emrys mounted the Fire Throne. Emrys had used a Power to change his clothes into rich black robes with silver chains of state. A crown of flame appeared on his head. He held a wicked looking scepter in his hand.

It was all very impressive.

Guards flanked the throne and held long pikes that sparked with energy.

The prisoner was held on his knees before the throne by two other guards. He was a nondescript, grey-robed little rodent. Literally: his form was that of a large, humanoid rat with beady red eyes.

Jon thought that under the circumstances, the man could have chosen a better body for himself. Maybe it didn't have the same connotations in this culture, though. Still, the man didn't seem like an assassin. He didn't seem like much of anything.

Other people in various bizarre and improbable bodily shapes filled the seats along the sides of the hall. Some were quite lovely, while others were terrifying to behold. Jon wondered why someone would *choose* to look like a monster.

"Noel Nichols, Imperial Dispatcher, do you know why we have called you here before us?" Emrys asked.

"Objection, Your Majesty!" a daemonic figure in full robes shouted. "This man is of a sept of our House." Jon thought the man looked like an alien from an old horror movie he'd seen once. He liked Drake's daemonform much better; it was actually beautiful, not meant to inspire fear.

"No charges have been laid, to object to, Duke of Cyryth," said Emrys. "We are curious: to what do you object, specifically?"

"I object to this man being brought here without charges, Your Majesty. I object to that man–" he pointed at Drake "– being here at all."

"We may choose what advisors we will," Emrys said. "Prince Drake is here as our guest. We suggest that you respect that."

"Of course, Your Majesty. We meant no disrespect to *your* august personage."

"Now, Noel Nichols, you will answer our question."

Jon didn't miss the glance Noel gave the Duke of Cyryth before bowing from his knees and answering. "I do not know why I am here, Your Majesty."

"We have had you brought here to answer for irregularities

from your office of the dispatch," Emrys said. "We–"

"Objection, Your Majesty!" the Duke of Cyryth shouted. "This man has the right face his accuser!"

"Interrupt us again, and you'll be beside him," Emrys said coldly. "We have made no accusations, but merely stated that there were irregularities. What say you, Nichols?"

"I don't know of any irregularities, Majesty."

"We know that orders were dispatched from your office. Orders that resulted in the death of our soldiers. We would have answers to that."

"I know of no such orders, Majesty."

"We do not believe you."

"I am just a humble servant, Majesty."

"Either you dispatched the orders, or you knew about them," said Emrys. "All dispatches are approved by you, are they not?"

"Yes, Majesty, but I issued no such orders."

"Then tell me who did, or you will be put to the question."

Jon didn't know if Emrys meant to imply torture, but it certainly sounded bad.

The little man glanced at the Duke of Cyryth and then squared his shoulders but didn't say anything.

"Drake?" Emrys said. "Make him speak."

Noel exploded up from the floor, hamstringing the guard on his right and driving a long knife into the belly of the guard on his left. The two guards beside the throne leapt forward. The little man didn't even try to back away. Jon hadn't thought Noel could be so quick and violent.

"Don't kill him!" Drake shouted.

Noel flipped his knife in the air and drove it into his own eye to the hilt.

No one spoke as he fell to his knees and then face-down on the marble floor.

"Drake." Emrys gestured.

Drake stepped past the guards and picked Noel up by his head, like palming a basketball. He raised him until his feet were dangling from the floor. An inarticulate moan came from the man's open mouth. Then he screamed. It was the most horrible sound Jon had ever heard, born of soul-wrenching horror and pain.

"Who issued the orders?" Drake demanded from the corpse.

"Duuuke Cy–Cy–Cyr–" was all that came out of Noel's mouth. Then he screamed again.

"Enough, Drake," said Emrys. "Let him go. He damaged his brain too well."

Drake dropped the body and stood with his shoulders heaving.

"What know you of this, Duke of Cyryth?" Emrys asked.

"The man was obviously deranged, Your Majesty," said the duke. "His sept has always caused problems for our House."

"Isn't it bad enough that you had the man commit treason?" Drake said in a cold voice. "You have to malign his sept, as well?"

"Just what are you implying, Drake?"

"Nothing that you'd have the balls to act on."

The duke stood and left the audience chamber without even bowing to the throne. Jon couldn't help but think that wouldn't be forgotten by Emrys. Such an insult would have resulted in arrest and death in some places.

Drake turned back around, and Jon knew he was right about the man. Drake appeared to be in pain from what he'd had to do, yet Jon could understand why he'd done it. He had to know who was responsible for his men's deaths. That he knew it was the Duke of Cyryth didn't seem much comfort to him.

"We are sorry, old friend," Emrys said quietly.

Drake nodded. "I... May we have your leave, Majesty?"

"Of course."

"Would you have the head of this man sent to Captain

Maelindefel on Nandegurth? She can display it to the troops, so that she'll know our troops have been avenged."

"It will be done."

"Thank you, Your Majesty. Jon?" Drake pointedly bowed, then turned and strode from the chamber.

Θ

Drake hated having to make dead men talk.

Dead meat should be allowed to rot in peace and not have to understand that it was dead. He'd gotten more from Noel's mind than he'd shared. The Duke of Cyryth had given Noel his orders, but there had been another man with him. That man, Drake didn't recognize; he had been wearing a mask, which was not a fashion in the Courts. Drake suspected, since the man had been in human form, that he was from the North.

It made a certain kind of sense.

Drake knew that someone from the North had orchestrated this whole farce with someone from the South. Jon had been driven to run from the Golden Kingdom with an attack. Jon's arrival and subsequent assault by imposter forces there on that Earth Realm had been too perfectly arranged. Drake himself would've had difficulty pulling off the timing.

"Drake?"

He'd almost forgotten about his companion. "Yes, Jon?"

"Are you all right?"

"No. I'm sorry that you had to witness that."

Jon glanced away. "Me, too, but it wasn't your fault."

"I'm glad that you think so, but we now have no leads here in the Courts."

"I figured as much. Tell me, were you *hoping* the Duke of Cyryth would challenge you?"

Drake smiled. "The thought had crossed my mind. No, he is too much of a coward. He wears the body of a monster, and he is one, but he would never get his own hands dirty. Not if there was a chance he might lose them, anyway."

"I've known men like him," Jon said. "Bullies."

"Unfortunately, this bully has the power of life or death over billions of souls. He'll probably go home and whip a servant to death to make himself feel better."

"Is Cyryth really that bad?"

Drake shrugged. "I admit I'm biased, but you saw what just happened. That poor dispatcher was so afraid of what Cyryth would do to him that he killed himself."

"You got more from him than he said, didn't you?"

Drake nodded. "It doesn't help. I think all we can do now is focus on the other side of things. Starting with which of the princes your father is."

"Drake, about that...," Jon began.

"Bide a moment." Drake activated the Waypoint. "Let's return to safer grounds before we talk further."

Drake followed Jon though the Waypoint to the grounds at Drake Manor. The ritual of identification was a relief after the past few hours. Drake saluted the guards and then led Jon around the side of the manor to an area dominated by tombs and mausoleums.

"How far did we travel?" Jon asked. "Can we see the world we were on?"

Drake shook his head. "Trillions of kilometers, and no, we can't see the homeworld from here."

"Homeworld?"

"The first Earth," Drake replied, "the wellspring of creation."

"I don't doubt you, but it's hard to believe."

"I understand that." Drake sat on a stone bench beneath a red leafed tree. "So what were you going to say back there?"

Jon sighed. "Everyone keeps saying I'm related to the House in the North, and yet I know I can't be."

"Are you that certain of your parentage?"

"That's just it: I had only one parent, and she was definitely local."

"Explain."

"My mother wanted to have a child but couldn't. She had me engineered from her own genetic material so there would be no outside claimants to the throne on my world. My brother was king, but she didn't want an outsider to have even a secondary claim to the throne."

"You realize it would take some serious genetic engineering to create a Y-chromosome from an X."

"I do, but my family had plenty of money, and she was adamant about her choice."

"I believe you, but the Cynosure doesn't make mistakes, Jon. You'd be dead if you weren't directly related to that family somehow."

Jon shrugged.

"Can we ask your mother?"

"Dead."

Drake sighed. "Well, there must be records someplace. The lab that produced you. Something."

"You think they slipped something into my genes?"

"I think that's the only explanation."

"I don't know."

"Look, how did those kids from up North know to look for you where they did?"

"That was random chance."

Drake laughed. "Oh, Jon... It was anything but. A single coincidence, I can swallow, but this? No. They were there for you."

"I think I see what you mean, but why?"

"Maybe we'll get lucky and find someone we can ask."

CHAPTER TWENTY-ONE

Geoffrey borrowed Jason's ceramic knife the next morning to shave.

He hadn't realized that he'd gotten so scraggly. His hair was going to need a trim soon, too, but he wasn't going to try that with a kitchen knife. At least his hair didn't look too bad. A part of him realized he was being a bit vain. It didn't really matter what he looked like, but his evening with Revna had made him somewhat self-conscious.

Geoffrey returned Jason's knife as they all sat down for breakfast in a small conference room not too different from the one in Drake's citadel. The food was blessedly mundane: scrambled eggs, bacon, grilled ham, sausage, fried diced potatoes, and biscuits.

It was strange how quickly eating meals with these people had become normal. Jason was a familiar companion, of course, but the other two were something else. Jon and Drake seemed a bit subdued this morning, and Geoffrey decided it was the better part of valor *not* to ask what had happened when they'd gone to the palace.

He had wanted to get Drake alone to ask about Revna, but

when Drake started talking about travel plans, he realized he needed to speak up. Revna been friendly to Geoffrey, and she hadn't needed to be. Geoffrey wanted to uphold his promise about her meeting Drake.

"...so we'll be heading out shortly after breakfast," Drake finished.

"Drake, before we go, could I ask you a favor?" said Geoffrey.

"You want a weapon?"

"I still have that hunting knife. No, it's something else."

Drake just looked at him expectantly.

Geoffrey sighed. "I sort of made a promise to someone yesterday..."

"What was her name?"

Geoffrey felt himself blush. "She was nice to me."

"I'm sure she was. Did you sleep with her?"

Geoffrey wasn't sure why that was Drake's business. "No, it wasn't like that."

"Then what did you promise?"

"She showed me around. You came up in the conversation, and she said she hadn't ever met you..."

"You promised an introduction, and she didn't even sleep with you? You need to try harder, Geoffrey."

"I wasn't trying for that," said Geoffrey. "We just hung out and had dinner together in the mess. It wasn't even a date."

Drake sighed. "Her name?"

"Revna."

"Any other identifiers?"

"Sergeant Revna Södersjö. About my height, black hair, green eyes."

"Made an impression, did she?"

Geoffrey realized then that Drake was gently teasing him, and grinned. "Well, she gave me a tour of the art gallery and then got me dinner in the mess."

Drake nodded. "I'll see what I can do."

"Thanks, Drake."

"Actually, Drake, I have a request, too," Jason said suddenly.

"I thought you might," Drake replied. He reached behind his back and pulled out a sheathed dagger about the length of his forearm. He slid it across the table in front of Jason.

"You anticipated I'd ask," Jason said quietly.

Drake nodded. "Yours was broken in the defense of my people. I had this one made for you before we left."

"You didn't just conjure it?"

"Sadly, real craftsmanship has to be paid for in time and labor. The dagger's name is Calacarca. She is made of mithril and galvorn."

"Mithril?" Geoffrey asked, surprised.

"My ancestors called it that. The material is a platinum-iridium alloy," Drake replied. "Very strong. Why?"

"I've heard the word before, that's all."

"Interesting."

Before he could continue, a man in red livery came in and bowed. He was escorted by two guards in House Drake uniform. He handed Drake a folded message sealed with black wax and black silk ribbon.

"What is this?" asked Drake.

"There is a guild meeting this afternoon for masters of the Omphalos," the man replied.

Drake sighed. "I am quite busy. Can this be postponed? Or done without me?"

"You are a Grandmaster, prince. Several members of House Drake are being elevated."

Drake broke the seal and read the message, frowning slightly. "Do you wish a written response?"

"If you please, prince."

Drake gestured; black parchment, a quill and ink, and bar of white wax appeared in front of him. He wrote quickly, with a sweeping, looping handwriting. Geoffrey didn't recognize the language. Drake blew across the parchment to dry the golden ink and then rolled it up. He melted the bar of wax and dripped some on the parchment to seal the opening, and then he stamped it with a signet ring Geoffrey hadn't realized Drake was wearing.

"When?" Drake asked as he handed over the message.

"Half-sky Eye, prince."

"Very well. Inform them I'll be there. I will be bringing guests."

"Such is not normally allowed, prince."

"Those are the conditions of my attendance," said Drake. "Make it allowed."

The man bowed and left with the guards.

"What was that about?" asked Jon.

"An inconvenience. We will have to wait until after the meeting to leave for your Earth Realm."

"It's not my Earth," Jon said, "but yeah, I understand. What is the meeting?"

"Periodically, there are meetings of the masters of the Omphalos to induct new members. Since there are members of the House of Drake being inducted, I need to be there, to honor them."

"How long is that going to be?"

"We will be finished before Black Sky. Then we can leave. I hate to delay our departure, but it cannot be avoided in this instance."

"You said you'd have guests," Geoffrey said. "Does that mean us?"

"I am loath to leave any of you unattended at this time, even here in Drake Manor. There are forces moving against us. In particular, to leave Jon here would be to invite an attack against this House. While it would fail, some of our people would be injured or lost. I will not abide that."

Geoffrey didn't mind at all.

He was excited to see more of the Ruined Courts than just this one manor. He'd talk to Drake and make sure they could still stop by and say hi to Revna; she deserved that. Then he'd be off on a new adventure.

He couldn't wait.

"Drake?" Geoffrey said as everyone stood up. "About that other matter…"

"Let's go say hello and impress the young lady, Geoffrey."

"You know her?"

"I know of her," Drake replied. "I've seen the duty rosters."

"Do you mind if I ask how old she is?"

"It isn't polite to ask a lady that."

"That's why I'm asking you."

Drake laughed. "I am uncertain of her exact age. Södersjö is a lesser House allied with Drake. Most of the members of the lesser Houses don't live much more than a thousand years – too much blending with the people from the outer Realms. To be a sergeant in this House, she must have served for a decade or more. Does her age really matter so much to you?"

Geoffrey shrugged. "I don't know. Maybe?"

"Do not be offended, but you are *very* young. You should understand that the women of the Courts are no more beautiful than the ones from your own Realm. They are just more exotic and new to your eyes. That they may be older than you is both alluring and abhorrent to you. I think you'll find as you get older that age doesn't matter as much as you might think it does."

"Humans where I'm from don't live nearly as long," said Geoffrey.

"Of course not," Drake replied. "But if you reject every person who is older than you, you are limiting your options. I'm not saying you should have done anything with Revna. I'm just saying you should keep your options open. Relax. Enjoy your adventure."

"What's it like?" Geoffrey asked.

"What? Being with a woman? I would have thought that by your age—"

"No!" Geoffrey said, blushing. "What is it like being so much older? Do you still remember when you were young? Did you always know you'd live as long as you have?"

Drake sighed. "I remember being your age. It was very long ago, and I was in love. And no, I had no idea I'd live as long as I have."

"You still remember her?"

"You presume it was a woman," said Drake. "But yes, that time it was, and do I still remember her. She was very lovely. A powerful warrior and hunter. She was of my mother's people, and a bit older than I."

"Do you ever go see her?"

"That was a *very* long time ago, Geoffrey. I am much older than you think. She is dust now, no doubt. I'm not even sure that world still exists. I have not been there in since my youth, and that was before your species had civilization."

Geoffrey swallowed hard and looked away from the pain on Drake's face. He hadn't actually expected Drake to open up to him, and now he wasn't sure if he wanted him to. *Drake's not human*, he reminded himself. *He isn't remotely human, no matter what he looks like.*

О

Jason finished breakfast and went back to his room to pack the few things he had with him.

He wondered what had become of his house in Cincinnati. By the time he returned home, weeks would have gone by. Jason hadn't truly felt safe since the attack. It wasn't just that the sanctity of his home had been violated. His entire worldview had been overturned.

Jason unsheathed the dagger he'd been given.

Calacarca, he thought. He wondered what the name meant, and why Drake would name a dagger. He and Drake were going to have a talk soon. They needed to clear the air between them.

The dagger was lighter than expected, the hilt black and the blade silvery, with fine, script-like runes etched into it. He assumed that was the name, although he couldn't read it. The dagger felt as if it would be well-balanced for throwing, despite the length.

Drake confused him.

By giving Jason the blade before he'd actually asked for it, Drake was relieving him of the obligation of a request. There was the matter of gift obligation, but Drake had said the dagger was a gift to repay Jason for his service.

It was almost as if Drake understood Jason better than Jason did himself.

Jason had to admit that he was starting to like the man.

He was startled by a knock on his door.

"Enter."

It was one of the soldiers, with a bundle of items in his arms. "Prince Drake had these made for you." He laid a leather backpack, boots, sturdy brown clothes, a leather hat, and a black robe on the bed.

"What's the robe for?" Jason asked.

"The Drake requests that you don the robe over your clothing and meet him and the others at the Waypoint in the yard as soon as you may."

"Is there more than one Waypoint?" Jason asked suddenly.

"There are several here at Drake Manor," the soldier replied. He bowed and left the room.

"Well, Jason," he said to himself, "I guess we get dressed and find out what this guild thing is."

When he opened the backpack, he found a liter bottle of

water and a small stack of wafers in green wax paper. He assumed they were travel rations. There was plenty of room for his old clothes and shoes in the pack. He placed his old knife in there, as well.

CHAPTER TWENTY-TWO

Drake nodded in satisfaction as the others arrived, dressed in the black robes of the guild and carrying their backpacks. Dressed as they were, they would not call attention to themselves and would blend in well enough.

"Place your packs here on the ground," said Drake. Once they did, he called on the Instrumentality to lift the packs up and tuck them away for easier transport.

"What did you do?" Jon asked.

"I placed the backpacks into a folded space."

"Handy, if a little unnecessary. I would have been happy to carry mine."

"Space is easy to fold here, where spacetime is twisted into knots anyway. The backpacks would be identifiers, and I want you all to be as anonymous as possible during the guild meeting."

"The fact that we aren't shapeshifters won't be a problem?" said Jason.

"None at all. Everyone there wears a humanoid form – their own, preferably. Everyone tries to be as anonymous as possible, so you should withhold your names."

"Your robes are rather more ornate," Jon said. "Doesn't that make you stand out?"

"I wear the robes of a Grandmaster. There will be others present in the same robes. Also, I am not worried about myself."

"What do we do there?" asked Geoffrey.

"Be silent, for the most part. The ceremony will take a few of your hours. If anyone asks your affiliation, you may answer *House of Drake.* Enough of us will be there that you won't stand out. Don't answer any other questions. No one should ask any, but you never know."

"Drake, I can feel a build-up of energies here," Jon said.

"We are close to the place where one attains the Instrumentality," Drake replied. "Also, many of the people attending will have magical wards in place. Call forth your mental image of the Cynosure, if you feel you need to see more."

"Won't that attract unwanted attention?"

"It could. The choice is yours."

Drake pulled up his hood and gestured for the others to do the same. When he was satisfied with their appearance, he laid his will upon the House Gate and led them through to another. They exited a little-used gate on the far edge of the Drake Estates.

This planetoid was closer to the Eye. The huge black hole dominated the sky, and the Walls of Matter could be seen clearly. It was a magnificent view that never failed to move Drake, although he'd mostly come this way for his guests.

He walked around the gate three times, and the runes etched upon its metal face changed. He selected seven of them, and the Gate opened for them again. This time they came out into a dark chamber lit mostly by torches. A few summoned spheres of ball lightning swirled across the vast ceiling, providing little more illumination.

The chamber itself, carved from black basalt, was a vast

circular, covered amphitheater. Thousands of people were already present, all of them robed and hooded. Many were moving away from the Waypoints in the outer ring and finding seats. A few even conjured cushions to sit on.

That's a waste of time and energy, Drake thought. Not to mention how soft it made the sorcerers look.

Drake led his companions close to the inner ring, where the grey-robed initiates stood in a circle. "Have a seat here," he said. "I'll be nearby. Try not to get into any fights."

"What if something happens?" Geoffrey asked quietly.

"Stand your ground. Call my name. I'll hear you and come very quickly. Now, is everyone good?"

They all nodded.

Drake turned and made his way to his reserved seat in the inner, raised circle. As a Grandmaster of the Omphalos, he sat in judgement of the new initiates. As a prince, and Duke of his House, he sat here to defend the honor of members of his House, if anyone was foolish enough to judge them unworthy.

Given the trouble he'd recently had with Cyryth, he had no hopes for a smooth and easy ceremony. During the ceremony, each initiate would stand forth, throw back their hood, and declare their name and allegiance. Other Grandmasters could challenge their right to be here.

It was an ancient tradition. Normally, nothing ever happened at these things.

Normally.

A smaller robed figure moved close to him and whispered his name.

"Eliza," he replied quietly. "I'm sorry I haven't been to see you recently. How have you been?"

"I've been well," she replied. "You're quite the talk around the Courts."

"Hmm. Anything interesting?"

"You expect me to give you that for free?"

"You brought it up. Besides, this is hardly the place for the usual game."

"Fair. There has been the usual boring stuff from Cyryth: death to House Drake, and all that," she replied. "And, of course, the rumor that you're harboring someone from the North."

"He's here tonight."

Eliza hissed softly. "He isn't a guild member!"

"What are they going to do, kick me out?"

"It would almost be worth the disclosure to see them try."

"Eliza, don't you dare!"

"I did say *almost.*"

Drake laughed quietly. "What brings you here tonight?"

"My granddaughter just completed her training and is being inducted tonight."

"Congratulations," Drake said sincerely. "You've strengthened House Torenvey with another sorceress."

"The House was always strong; that's why I married into it." She leaned close. "In my heart, I'm still a Drake, of course."

"That is not something that anyone can take away," Drake said with a smile.

He was proud of Eliza. Her mother was dead, but Drake knew his daughter would have been proud of her, as well.

☉

Geoffrey was bit bored, truth be told.

The bench was hard and cold, and he envied the sorcerers who'd conjured pillows. It might have seemed frivolous, but it was cool. Geoffrey imagined all the things he would create if he ever had a Power like that.

He laughed to himself. That wasn't ever going to happen.

It was maybe half an hour before everyone finished trickling in. A large, robed figure stood up in the center and began speaking. The voice was in that tenor-to-alto range that made it difficult to determine whether the speaker was male or female. Geoffrey couldn't see their face inside the deep hood they were wearing. They were also speaking with such a strong accent that he had trouble understanding them. He'd thought they weren't speaking Thari until he picked up a few words he recognized.

The androgynous speaker sat back down, and another stood up. This one was as tall as Jon and looked thinner. Geoffrey was surprised to hear a strong feminine voice come from the figure. *I need to stop expecting anything to be normal,* he thought.

The group in grey all chanted something together that he couldn't quite make out, and then one of them threw back their hood and said their name and house affiliation. Geoffrey wondered what was going on. No one else seemed surprised, so he figured it was normal. As each figure said their name, there was a pause, and then a person in the center stood and accepted them.

He wondered what would happen if they weren't accepted, and he didn't have long to wait to find out. A tall, good-looking woman with shoulder-length blonde hair stood and declared her name.

"Gillian of House Torenvey," she said.

A woman in the center stood, but before she could speak, a man jumped up.

"Objection!" he shouted.

"On what grounds?" the woman demanded.

"Her blood is impure!" he growled.

A man stood up next to the woman and put his hand on her shoulder. "Membership in our guild is not about bloodlines." Geoffrey recognized Drake's voice.

"Of course you would say that, Drake," the man sneered. "But you're not being called out. Torenvey is. What say you, Torenvey?"

"On the contrary," Drake replied, "Torenvey is allied to

Drake, and this young woman is of my bloodline. To call her impure, suggesting it's because of me, and not allow me to respond is not our way. Tell us all your name and House, or are you too cowardly?"

"Drake wants whoever that is to fight him instead of the woman," Jon said quietly from next to Geoffrey.

"Yeah, I got that."

"*You* call *me* a coward? You're the coward, Drake. Always cowering behind your armies. You have not the nerve to call me out on it, either."

"And allow you to set the terms of our duel?" Drake laughed. "You called out my bloodline. I responded. Now accept or recant. Your choice."

"I call out a different House, and yet you respond. Somehow I am a coward because you hope to use your magical sword against me."

Geoffrey realized from the mutterings that there were quite a few others who agreed with the man. Drake seemed exceptionally skilled with a blade, but Geoffrey hadn't really seen him use much else. He wondered how the man wanted to duel, if not with blades.

"I have called you a coward, Cyryth, and you have insulted my bloodline and called me a coward in turn. Very well. I call you out. Set your terms. As long as the duel is not postponed, I will agree to any you set."

"We will have it here and now," the man said. He threw back his hood. "I am Loranth, son of the Duke of Cyryth, and heir. I accept your challenge on these terms: You will relinquish your sword to a second. Then we will fight here and now, not with blades but with sorcery, as our ancestors meant us to fight."

"Your ancestors were cowardly pigs who wallowed in filth."

"For that you will die, Drake."

Suddenly a man stood up in the center of the circle. "We

object! Duels here are to second blood only."

"No, Your Imperial Majesty. This man has insulted us and our ancestors, and do not forget that our Houses have a declared vendetta. It will be to the death."

Geoffrey could see Drake talking to the emperor, but he couldn't hear what was said. The emperor nodded sharply. Drake pulled off his robe and handed it to the short Torenvey woman who'd spoken before.

The emperor turned to the Cyryth man. "Very well. To the death it shall be. Know this, however: if you prevail, it will not be for long, for you'll face our wrath next, and you will die screaming." He then gestured, and people cleared out from the center.

The Torenvey woman went to speak with the younger woman, Gillian, who'd been called out originally. Geoffrey could see them talking. He wished he could better hear what was going on. He pushed through the crowd to the two women.

The shorter woman spun around; a knife in her hand was at his throat before he even realized she'd moved. Geoffrey could see dark red hair and green eyes under her hood. The younger woman with the blonde hair bore a close resemblance to her, although she was taller.

"Who are you?" the woman asked quietly.

"A friend of Drake," he said. The edge of the blade was cold and sharp. He felt a slight burning pain and a single bead of blood rolling down his throat.

"Are you the Northerner?" she asked.

"No. My name is Geoffrey. I just came here with Drake and a couple of others."

"What do you want?"

"I just want to know what's going on. I saw him talking to you. I'm worried for him."

She nodded abruptly, and the knife vanished.

"My name is Eliza," she said. "There is little need to worry.

The Cyryth child is a fool to think the Drake can be bested."

Geoffrey wished he felt as confident.

CHAPTER TWENTY-THREE

Jon had moved closer with Jason and Geoffrey.

He'd almost stepped in when the woman had drawn on Geoffrey. He was surprised at just how fast she was. It was something he was going to have to get used to. These people weren't normal humans; they were something older and more powerful.

Emrys was talking to Drake and shaking his head. Finally, he turned and stepped down from the platform to stand with the Torenvey woman. Jon didn't know exactly what was going on, but after the display the day before in court, he suspected there was a power struggle in the Ruined Courts.

Drake had indicated that Emrys was young. Jon wondered if House Cyryth felt they had a better candidate for the throne, although it certainly wasn't the man facing Drake. He looked nervous, as Jon would have expected anyone to be, facing Drake.

"Jon," Emrys said quietly, "come meet Eliza, Duchess of Torenvey."

"Your Grace," Jon said with a slight bow. She was a lovely woman. There was something about her facial features that suggested a closer relationship to Drake than others he'd seen. He wondered if she might be Drake's daughter. It would explain a few things.

"You're the one from the North," said Eliza. "You have some of the look of Dominic."

"So I've been told."

"Don't let her fool you," Emrys said. "She loves to ply her trade as an information broker."

"I have little information of interest," said Jon.

Just then, Jon felt an odd pressure, almost painful. Emrys noticed the look on his face and gestured toward the center platform. "What you feel are the wards going up. They keep stray magics from leaking out."

Jon nodded. He'd wondered how they would prevent that.

From his point of view, a wall of almost solidified spacetime had manifested around the platform. Drake had suggested that Jon would be able to see and understand more if he called forth a mental image of the Cynosure, but he was loath to do so in this place; there were too many people in the room who might take offense.

Jon saw manifestations of the Instrumentality hovering before the two on the platform, and before a few others around the chamber. He found it interesting that while he could sense they were manifestations of the same Power, they looked different. The Cyryth man had a ring of fire with a burning eye that was also somehow a black hole. Drake's was almost more interesting: a ring of glowing white light, with no center at all.

Jon wondered if the difference had to do with the individual's understanding. Drake obviously knew the Instrumentality was a machine, whereas the other man seemed to view it as a dark god. Jon wondered how that would affect the use of the Power.

An immense bell sounded somewhere above, and the Cyryth man shouted a word and gestured. A tornado of fire swirled around Drake. For a moment he was obscured, and then Jon could see Drake inside, unharmed. He appeared to have curved spacetime away from himself so that none of the heat could affect him. Jon could almost feel the immense fields Drake had manifested to defend himself.

This pattern continued with waves of fire, ice, and even a rain of knives. Drake seemed unconcerned and merely watched as the Cyryth sorcerer, Loranth, became more and more frustrated and desperate. Some of the spells Loranth called out were long and complex. Nothing fazed Drake.

"Stop toying with the poor man," Emrys muttered.

"Why should he?" asked Eliza. "The boy was a fool to try this. No one has challenged Drake to a sorcerous duel in millennia for a reason."

"I think he's made his point."

The Cyryth sorcerer seemed to feel the same way. His spellcasting faltered, and he looked around, bewildered. "Are you going to duel me or not?" Loranth shouted.

"Is that what this was?" asked Drake. "I thought you were practicing. Very well, if you insist."

Drake gestured, and Loranth began to scream. He was convulsing, but Jon couldn't see what was wrong until the man's clothes fell off as ashes, his skin striped with angry red lines. The lines continued to form over his entire body and even up his neck and head. He was screaming and shaking but didn't seem able to otherwise move as he slowly rose into the air.

"Let us all see what you are made of," said Drake.

Starting at his feet, Loranth's skin began to detach itself in one long ribbon of flesh. Jon had to look away and wished he could block his ears, as well. The screaming went on for an improbably long time before devolving into whimpers and gurgling noises.

Jon forced himself to look.

Loranth was still somehow alive; Jon could see his chest

heaving as he breathed. Drake had done something to keep Loranth from bleeding to death. He looked like an anatomy model. It was ghastly, and Jon felt nauseated.

Geoffrey and Jason were pointedly not looking. Jon wished he had done the same. However, he felt it important to know what Drake was going to do. He understood the importance of making an example of the Cyryth man, even if what was done was horrible.

Drake gestured again, and something Jon couldn't quite focus on began at Loranth's feet and again worked its way up his body. The formless nothingness consumed the man's body, bones and all. Loranth was so far gone that he didn't even scream as it devoured him. Nothing was left of him but the long ribbon of skin, which fluttered around the platform. Eventually even that was destroyed.

Drake clearly hated what he'd done. There was pain on his face, and a hardness Jon hadn't seen before. At a wave of Drake's hand, the barriers fell.

"Let no one *ever* dare to insult my family again," Drake said loudly. He voice echoed around the huge chamber. No one said anything as he stepped down from the platform and joined Emrys.

"Out of professional curiosity, Drake," said Emrys, "what would you have done to him if the duel had been to the standard second blood?"

"Much the same at first, then slashed his cheeks and sent him on his way," Drake replied.

Emrys nodded.

"My dear Eliza, you are satisfied?"

"Our House honor is secure."

Drake smiled. "Once again, I'm sorry you had to witness that, Jon." He turned to Geoffrey and Jason and seemed unsure of what to say.

"Perhaps we should take our leave," Jon said.

"Take the others to the Waypoint." Drake gestured to the one he meant. "I'll follow along in a moment."

Jon saw him turn to speak to Eliza and the blonde woman. He touched Jason on the shoulder.

"Don't," Jason said quietly.

"We need to go."

Jason started walking toward the Waypoint, guiding Geoffrey, who was stumbling slightly. Jon understood exactly how they both felt. He felt much the same, sickened and horrified at what Drake had done.

"Can you operate this thing?" asked Jason.

"No," Jon replied. "Are you okay?"

"You're joking, right?"

Jon sighed. "Drake did what he had to. He didn't kill the man that way for pleasure. He did it to keep anyone else from attacking people more vulnerable."

"It was fucking nauseating."

"That, it was," Jon agreed. "Did you see the things the other man tried to do to Drake? Those would have been pretty horrible, too."

"I just want to go home," said Jason. "We both do."

"I understand that," Jon said, "but do you think it would be safe?"

Jason shook his head. "So we're just supposed to accept what happened?"

"Yes. You already accepted him killing people. He didn't kill Gerhardt's guards easily, or the man who almost killed you. Don't forget the man you killed, for that matter."

"That was self-defense," Jason snapped.

Jon laughed sourly. "So was this. I know you don't want to hear it, but Drake did what was necessary – this is from a guy who tries for a non-lethal option whenever possible. Drake had to make it a horrible, memorable death, to discourage others. He had to send a message."

"What kind of message could be taken from that?"

"'Fuck with me, and you die,'" Drake said. He'd walked up to them silently. "'Fuck with my friends and family, and you die horribly, screaming and whimpering for death.' That was my message. I believe it was well delivered. We're done here in the Courts. Are you ready?"

"We're done, Drake," said Jason. "Geoffrey is practically catatonic. We want to go home."

Drake nodded. "You wouldn't be safe back at your house."

"You call being with you safe?"

"Safer, yes."

"Fine, Drake. It's not as if we can force you to take us home."

"You weren't forced to come along," Drake said. "You chose to come with us. That's on you. What did you think they were going to do to you at the Pemberton Institute?"

"It doesn't matter."

"They would have taken steel scalpels and dissected you. They wouldn't even have bothered to kill you first, and you know it."

Jason spun around and struck Drake in the face.

Jon thought Drake had let Jason hit him. Drake certainly didn't react to it.

"Feel better?"

"Fuck you."

"Yeah, fuck me," said Drake. "You ready to go? We're leaving. Come along or not, as you wish." Drake gestured, and the backpacks fell to the stone floor. He then turned and stepped through the Waypoint.

Jon hesitated a moment, but he really didn't have a choice. Drake was his best chance of finding out who was trying to kill him, and why. He shrugged, picked up his pack, and stepped through the gate.

⊙

Jason clenched his fists in anger.

Drake had left them here, after what he'd said before. He'd promised to get them home and then just left them.

"Jason?"

"Geoffrey? Are you okay?"

"Yeah. Kinda shaky."

"Geoffrey, I'm sorry. Drake and Jon just left."

"I'm in shock, Jason, not dead or deaf."

Jason sighed. "Yeah, sorry."

"The gate is still open."

"What?"

"Drake left the gate open behind him," Geoffrey said. "Don't you think we should follow him?"

"After what just happened?"

"Him killing the guy, or you hitting him?"

"The *first*," said Jason.

"Well, we're going to have to talk about both eventually. Personally, I'd rather do that someplace safer."

"You think you're safer with him than with me?"

"Jason, don't. Okay? Just don't. This isn't a you-versus-Drake thing. Drake, or maybe Jon, is our only way home. You think someone here is going to be kind to us after what just happened?"

"Shit."

"We don't have any choice about this, and Drake has been a decent guy so far."

"You call what he did *decent?*" Jason could still hear the sounds that man had made while dying.

"I think he didn't kill that man that way out of joy in doing stuff like that. If he was the monster you keep trying to make him out to be, he'd have killed us both a long time ago, just for being a bother. I say we follow him and see what happens."

"Still craving adventure?"

"Today was just as hard on me as it was you. Don't be more of an asshole than you have to be."

Jason bit down on a sharp reply. Geoffrey was the only friend he had in this place. Hell, he was the only friend Jason had at all, really. Maybe he was right.

He certainly wasn't wrong about them not having much choice.

CHAPTER TWENTY-FOUR

Jon stepped hesitantly through the Waypoint.

He wasn't worried about what he'd find. Despite everything, he still trusted Drake. He just didn't like the idea of leaving Jason and Geoffrey in the Ruined Courts. Drake was right, though; the choice to follow or not was up to them.

The Waypoint came out by a natural-looking rock shelter in a cliff. A gravel path ran past the shelter. Jon could feel as much as hear a deep bass rumbling from the ground and indeed, from all around them. He felt mildly nauseated when he looked up and saw the tops of the surrounding mountains shifting and swaying like the boughs of a tree in the wind. The sky pulsed to the same rhythm.

Jon was relieved to see Jason and Geoffrey come through the Waypoint before it closed.

"Pilgrims' Rest," Drake said, sitting down on a worn stone. "We're at the midpoint through the Dancing Mountains. Don't wander – there be demons and monsters here. Travelers are often lured away to their doom."

"You've mentioned the Dancing Mountains before," said Jon. "I didn't realize the name is literal."

Drake nodded, and Jon thought he looked worn out. He had seen Drake tired before, but this appeared to be complete exhaustion. Using the Instrumentality to deflect spells powered by the same Power must have taken a great personal toll.

"Standing wave in the quantum flux," Drake muttered. He lay back and closed his eyes.

Jon decided he'd ask about that later.

Jason and Geoffrey settled down near the rock face. Jon didn't blame them. The constant shaking and rumbling caused rocks all around them to clatter and roll. It was nerve-racking, not to mention frightening.

Jon moved over and sat next to Jason. "I'm glad you decided to come," he said quietly.

"Geoffrey talked some sense into me."

Geoffrey laughed feebly and lay down on the ground, using his backpack as a pillow.

"Seriously, I'm glad you came," Jon said. "I need someone normal to talk to."

"Damn, if you're talking about me, you're in deep shit."

"Well, *normal* is relative."

"Fair enough."

"You know, Drake didn't enjoy what he did. I saw his face as he ended it."

"Can we not talk about this right now?"

"Yeah. I just thought you should know."

They sat together in silence for a while.

"What the hell is this place, anyway?" asked Jason. "This isn't a normal world."

"Drake called it the Dancing Mountains. This alcove, he called Pilgrims' Rest."

"That's informative."

Jon smiled. If Jason was being sarcastic again, then he was all right. "I think we're somehow supposed to walk from here to Catalina Island."

"That's off the coast of California," Jason said. "Near Los Angeles, right?"

"It was on the Earth I'm from."

"Is it a lot different?"

"What?"

"Your Earth. I've been thinking about picking up a summer home."

Jon laughed quietly. "I don't think my Earth would be good for that. The planet is a mess. We didn't take good care of it before leaving for the stars."

"Yeah, that seems pretty common."

"How's Geoffrey doing?" Jon asked him.

"Geoffrey is doing fine," came Geoffrey's muffled voice from under his arm. "He's just not available to take your calls right now."

"Tired," Jason translated. "He's tired."

"Yeah, I think we all are." Jon hesitated. "Listen, I just wanted to thank you. I haven't really had a chance to do that since all this started. Thank you for helping, back there on your Earth. It seems as if it's just been one thing after another since then."

Jason shrugged. "People should help other people in need."

"They should," Jon agreed. "I've found that not many do."

"Why *did* you knock on my door, of all the houses along that street?"

"That's hard to explain." Jon took a moment to collect his thoughts before continuing. "I didn't pick your door, per se. I arrived just outside it. When I was falling through the worlds, I was confused, hurt, and I just reached out for a place where I would find help."

"We sort of talked about that before. I still don't understand it."

"I don't, either, to be honest."

"That's fair."

"Look," Jon said, "I don't know how all of this will end, but I'll do my best to make sure that you both make it home, okay?"

Jason sighed. "I hate to admit it, because he was being an asshole, but Drake was right. Without some way to smooth over with the government what happened during the attack on my house, we can't go home. They've connected us to beings from outside our world. That will have to be dealt with."

"Well, I don't know if I could fix that, but I'd try."

"Thanks, Jon."

"If I can offer a piece of friendly advice, you might want to tell Geoffrey the truth. He'll find out eventually. It will be easier if it's from you."

Jason's posture turned rigid. "Care to elaborate?"

"Do you really want me to?"

"No, actually. Not at the moment." Jason shook his head. "Thanks for the advice. I'll think about it."

Jon nodded. "I'm going to try to catch a nap while Drake's out."

"That sounds like a plan," Jason said, yawning. "I think I'll sit up a bit, keep guard and all that. Someone has to be responsible."

Θ

When Geoffrey woke, he was cold and stiff. His head hurt, and his nose was stuffy. It took him a few minutes to remember where he was. When he did, he wished he'd stayed asleep.

"I feel like crap," he groaned as he sat up.

"You should see what you look like," Jason said quietly.

"Ha-ha," Geoffrey replied, rubbing his eyes. "Everyone else still asleep?"

Jason yawned. "Yeah. We've been here a couple hours, I think. For a place where everything changes, nothing really changes, you know?"

Geoffrey looked around at the pulsing mountains and sky. They looked the same as when he'd arrived.

"Yeah, I get you."

"Bushes over that way," Jason said, gesturing to his left.

"Thanks." Geoffrey went and took care of his suddenly urgent bodily business.

Drake was still sprawled on his back on the rock where he'd collapsed. Jon was near Jason, resting his head on his arm and facing the rock. Jason looked like he was ready to pass out, leaning back against the rock face.

"Why don't you get some rest?" Geoffrey suggested. "I'm awake now. I wish I had some coffee, though."

"I wish you hadn't mentioned coffee," Jason grumbled. "Yeah, I think I might rest for just a moment." He slumped over until he was laying on Geoffrey's backpack and began to snore softly.

Geoffrey shook his head at his friend and walked round the rock shelter. Here and there, people had carved their initials and even a lewd cartoon on the ancient rock face. Bits of old bottles, faded tin cans, and cigarette butts showed that the place was used by others, at least sometimes. It was all felt so oddly *normal*. Ignore the surroundings, and the rock shelter looked like any similar place he'd find in a state park back in Kentucky.

He walked over to the path, worn with the passage of many feet over the years. Geoffrey wondered how many people had walked it, and why. It seemed odd to him to think there might be so many people walking the worlds that they'd wear a path.

Were they all Drake's people? Jon's? Someone else? He didn't have enough information to speculate. The name *Dancing Mountains* seemed evident enough, but why *Pilgrims' Rest*? Pilgrims suggested a place to journey to. A holy place? Holy to whom?

Geoffrey sighed and kicked a rock.

The rock bounced down the path, hitting other rocks and

making quite a lot of noise. As the sound of clattering echoed back to him, he thought he heard something else: a voice calling for help.

Geoffrey struggled with his indecision.

Drake had mentioned demons and monsters luring travelers away from the path, but there were obvious signs that people traveled through here. There really could be someone in trouble. The voice called out again; Geoffrey took a step toward it. A stone clattered away down the path.

"Is someone there?" the voice called.

It didn't seem very far away, but he couldn't go off looking without some backup.

He ran back to camp and shook Jason. "Wake up!"

Jason sat up suddenly. "What's wrong?"

"Shh! Come with me."

"Geoffrey, can this wait? I need to piss."

"Be quick. Then come with me."

Jason groaned and stood up. He stumbled over to the bushes and then was back after a minute. "Okay, let's go."

Geoffrey led him out to the trail. All was quiet.

"How long was I asleep?" Jason grumbled. "Couldn't have been very long."

"Quiet – listen."

They heard nothing but the wind and the faint grinding of stones.

"What are we doing here?" asked Jason.

"I heard someone calling for help."

"Classic bandit ploy. Or worse. Drake did mention demons."

"And monsters. I know. I don't think that's what this was."

"Geoffrey, I swear…"

Geoffrey picked up a rock and threw it. The rock clattered down the path, echoing back to them.

"Hello? Is someone there?" a woman's voice called. "Can

you help me?"

"There!" Geoffrey exclaimed. "You heard that, right?"

"Yes, and I think it's probably a demon."

"Come on, Jason, we need to check it out."

"Would you be so eager to help if it was a man's voice?"

"I helped Jon, didn't I? I'm not as shallow as you seem to think."

Jason sighed. "Fine, lead on. If I die..."

"You're haunting me, I know."

Not far down the path, a narrow track led off to the left of the road. Geoffrey couldn't see very far down it because of the fallen boulders. He thought he could see stone ruins in the distance. Small boot prints led away from the main path.

"This feels like a trap," said Jason.

"Maybe it was, for whoever is calling for help."

Jason shook his head and drew his dagger.

Geoffrey drew his own knife and moved as quietly as he could.

A small woman was sitting next to a stone pillar. She was dressed in blue jeans and a black tee shirt printed with the words *Harrison Denmark Fan Club* and a picture of a band he didn't recognize. A rough, black stone pendent glittered on a cord around her neck. She hadn't seen them yet. Her leg appeared to be caught under a large fallen stone. There was a dark cloak or something behind her.

She suddenly looked up at his face and then frowned as she saw the knife in his hand. She flicked a quick glance past the rock at Jason. "I guess passing pilgrims were too much to hope for," she said.

Geoffrey was surprised; she spoke English with a faint Hispanic accent. She looked Hispanic, as well, with long, dark hair in a braid and dark eyes. She wouldn't been out of place in Albuquerque. She was more cute than pretty – not that she was bad looking.

"If you're planning to rob me, I don't have anything of value. If you're thinking of anything else, know that I'll fight you. I'm tougher than I look."

"Sorry," said Geoffrey. He sheathed the knife. This woman couldn't possibly be a demon – or any other kind of threat, for that matter. "We were kind of expecting a trap when we heard you calling."

"Yeah, I got lured into one myself, as you can see."

"Are they still around?" Jason asked.

"Who?"

"Whoever lured you into the trap."

"Oh, it was just the one demon," she said matter-of-factly. "It's probably still lurking around here somewhere."

Geoffrey dropped his hand to his knife again, although he didn't know what good it would be against a demon.

"Not to seem ungrateful or anything," the woman said, "but do you think you could help me get free before it gets back?"

"Jason, will you stand guard?"

"What do you think I'm doing?"

"Right." Geoffrey crouched down and got his hands under the rock. It was heavy. Damn heavy. "Hold on." He shifted around to the other side of the woman and tried again. The rock moved a little.

"Hurry up," Jason said. "I hear something."

"Working on it, buddy." Her leg was bloody under the rock. It didn't look broken, though. "Try to pull your leg out as I lift."

"Just say when."

Geoffrey heaved, and she pulled her leg out from under the rock with a grunt of pain. He heard a rustling noise and looked around at her. She wasn't wearing a cloak. Black-feathered wings arched out from her back. One was slightly droopy.

"Thanks," she said. "I've been sitting on my wing for hours. It hurt like hell."

CHAPTER TWENTY-FIVE

Geoffrey just gaped at the woman and her feathered wings. She was impossible. He'd seen many strange things while traveling with Drake, but not this. It couldn't be real.

She laughed, holding out her hand. "I'm Erin. Thanks for the rescue."

"Geoffrey," he replied automatically, shaking her hand. "You're–"

"No."

With those wings, she had to be, even if the feathers *were* black. "But you–"

"Nope." She shook her head.

"Geoffrey, did you move that rock yet?" Jason came around the pillar and stopped suddenly.

"Hi, I'm Erin. Nice to meet you."

"Uh, hi. I'm Jason. You're a... Your leg is bleeding."

"I noticed, thanks." She gave them a lopsided grin. "Not my biggest concern right now. I hate to impose upon you both further, but do you think you could help me out of here? That demon is definitely still around. I'd rather not have to try to fight it, in my condition."

"Sure," Geoffrey said. How could they say no? She didn't look big enough or tough enough to fight off an angry cat. *Why did I think* cat*? Because of the bird wings?* "We're camped just up the path."

"At Pilgrims' Rest?" she asked.

He nodded.

"Perfect." She pulled a leather biker jacket from under the rubble and tied it around her hips.

Geoffrey carefully slipped an arm around Erin's slender waist. He didn't want to crush her wings; they looked delicate. Jason shook his head and took up position on her other side, and together they got her back to the road. She couldn't put any weight on her leg. She wasn't heavy, but her feathers kept tickling Geoffrey as they walked. Occasionally one wing would – embarrassingly – bump him on the ass.

They didn't take long to return to camp.

Drake had his back to them as they walked up. He was talking animatedly to Jon. He suddenly paused and turned around as if he sensed them. Maybe he'd just heard them. His hearing had to be extremely good, though, to have heard them over the rumbling of the mountains.

"I was just about to come looking for you two," said Drake. "I see you've already gotten into trouble. You seem to have knack for finding strays."

Jon did an almost comic double take and then came over to help them. Together, they got Erin to the raised rock Drake had slept on. Jon looked as if he had a lot of questions but didn't know where to start.

"Hi! I'm Erin," she said cheerfully.

"Hi," he said as he focused on her injured leg.

"I know what you are," said Drake.

"And I know what you are," Erin replied, grinning. "I'll not hold it against you."

"You're an angel?" Jon said quietly.

She laughed, shaking her head.

"She's no angel," Drake said.

"Neither are you, pointy."

"You two know each other?" asked Jason.

"No!" they denied in unison.

"Yeah, that was convincing," Jason muttered. He sat back down by the rock wall and shook his head.

"What happened to you?" Jon asked Erin.

"Demon lured me off the road and ambushed me. Pushed a rock over on me. Pinned my leg. I mean, I'm buff," she said, flexing a thin arm. "Check out those guns! Just not strong enough to move the rock when pinned under it. Luckily, these two strapping young men saved me."

"What demon?" Drake asked.

"Relax. It was just a normal roadside demon," Erin replied. "As embarrassing as it is to admit that to you, of all people. What you're thinking of wouldn't have sat back and waited for me to die before eating me."

Drake nodded sharply. "I guess I should look at that wing."

"Yeah, I think I dislocated it," she said. "As you know, I can't put 'em away like that."

Geoffrey went over and sat down next to Jason. "Well, it wasn't a trap."

"Says you." Jason laughed and rubbed his face with both hands. "You know, this whole thing is so crazy. I mean, *angels?*"

"Not an angel!" Erin called.

Jason groaned and hid his face.

Geoffrey knew how he felt.

☉

Drake had been worried when he awakened to find Jason and Geoffrey missing and Jon asleep. He'd been worried that they had tried to find their way home. It was just barely possible that they'd have been able to do it without one of the Powers, since they were on the path between worlds. It was more likely that a demon would find and eat them first.

He frowned as he worked carefully on Erin's wing. He hadn't met *her* before, but he'd met her kind over the years. Her people were at least as ancient as he was. They weren't angels, but they were probably what people had seen when they started those myths in the various Realms. Probably where the myths of demons as fallen angels had come from, as well.

After all, not all of them were benevolent.

In fact, many of them had worked with the Ancient Enemy.

Her people, whatever name one gave them, were cunning adversaries with powers that rivaled his own, although he didn't know where that power came from. He hadn't met one of Erin's people for many years. He'd almost begun to think they were all dead, hunted to extinction by the Ancient Enemy.

Drake didn't sense any ill intentions from the woman in front of him. His enemies were good at hiding themselves, but not that good. Drake was in physical contact with Erin as he fixed her wing; it would have been very unpleasant for him if she were one of the enemy. He would have known, and then it would have been very unpleasant for *her*.

"You're worried about me," she said, looking up at him. Her eyes were dark pools reflecting the millennia she'd lived. Drake knew they had many things in common, and at least one thing that set them apart from each other on a level few others shared. *He'd* never been tempted by the darkness. He could feel her guilt: she had once Fallen.

"Not all of your kind are trustworthy."

She nodded. "Sadly true. Of both our peoples." She shook her head and grinned wryly. "I didn't catch your name. You look a bit like a guy I know. He was one of your people, long ago."

"My name is Drake."

"Lots of Drakes down South," Erin said. "Can you be more specific?"

"Daeren Drake."

"I *have* heard of you. No one told me you were handsome." She winked. "What about him?"

"Jon."

"Just Jon?"

"Livingston," Jon replied. He patted the bandage into place on her leg. "That should do it."

"Jon Livingston?" she asked with raised eyebrows.

Jon shrugged. "That's what I go by."

"Okay, why not?" She seemed amused.

"This may hurt," said Drake. He'd found the wing joint that was out of place. At Erin's nod, he popped it back into position. She grunted but didn't cry out. Those of her people he'd met before had been tough, too. Almost impossible to kill.

She rolled her shoulders and flexed her wings. "Many thanks," she said.

"You're welcome."

Her wings folded back, and then they disappeared. She pulled her leather jacket on carefully. "Still a little tender, but much better. Holding those things up was wearing me out. I'm not normally one to casually show off my wings. Always seemed a little intimate to me."

Jon held out some food and water. "It isn't much, but you're welcome to it."

"Thank you, Jon." She unwrapped the wafer he'd handed her and took a delicate bite. "Mmm, haven't had lembas in a long time."

Drake shot her a glare.

Erin laughed. "Oh, come now. You're sporting those ears, and cheekbones that could cut a girl, and you didn't expect me to tease you?"

"I don't think Drake expects anyone to tease him," said Jon.

"Well, you should more often, then. He needs to lighten up."

"It isn't lembas bread," said Drake.

"Close enough. I mean, that isn't your true form, either, is it?"

"It is, actually."

"Oh, sorry. Wow, I've never met a half-elf. Cool."

Drake shook his head. This woman wasn't like the others of her kind that he'd met. The good ones had been sad, and focused on ridding the worlds of the scourge of the rest of their kind. The bad ones... Well, he'd dealt with them as he did other threats.

Erin was... *frivolous.*

"Gods, I hope so," Erin said with a grin. "If I ever get too serious, run me through with that annihilation sword of yours, O Lord of the Abyss."

"None of my people have gone by that title in a score of millennia."

"No offense was intended, Prince Drake. Despite my seeming irreverence, I have a great respect for what you and your family have done over the years to protect the Realms from the evils of our peoples' shared past."

Drake nodded sharply. Her praise was somewhat embarrassing. He had devoted his life to ridding the Realms of the Ancient Enemy, but it hadn't been out of altruism. She would know that better than most people would.

"So... Which way are you gentlemen headed?" asked Erin.

"I don't think you need to know that," Drake replied.

"Still don't trust me, huh?" Erin sighed. "I just wanted to warn you that there have been more Reality Storms of late at the North edge of the High Plains. Hellhounds have been seen prowling along the path through the Desolate Plains in the South."

"How bad are the storms?" Drake asked. He hated giving

out even that much information, but this woman didn't feel like a threat to him, and he trusted his instincts. She might even be a useful ally. She looked small and frail, but he knew she could have torn a normal man in half with her bare hands.

Erin grinned. "You shouldn't have too much trouble, if you're walking the main road through the Realms. If you stray too far from the path, you might get into rough weather."

"Thanks," said Drake.

"I'm headed that way myself, at least for a while."

"I'm not sure that would be a good idea."

"Oh, come on, Drake. We can pull out our wings and take turns scaring the locals. You can be the dragon, and I can play the angel. Might be able to make a little coin along the way. Earn it, I mean – you're the only one of us who can actually *make* coin. It'll be fun!"

Drake finally laughed. The strange winged woman's humor was a salve for the pain he'd felt after the Guild meeting. Maybe it wouldn't be a terrible idea to have her along. She might help soothe Jason and Geoffrey, and her good cheer would be a welcome change.

He looked around at the others. Jon had a faint smile on his face, and even Jason didn't seem too unhappy. Geoffrey looked as if he'd been hit over the head with a club, but then, angels were revered in the mythologies where he was from. Not to mention that Erin was lovely.

"Fine," said Drake. "How far are you headed? We're not going all the way."

"Neither will I, naughty boy. Don't think I haven't heard about you."

Drake sighed. *Maybe this is a mistake,* he thought.

CHAPTER TWENTY-SIX

Jon stood and stretched his long frame.

He wished he could take a shower or even bathe. There didn't seem to be any source of water around, though, and he didn't want to waste the little they had with them on washing. It wasn't just because of Erin that he wished he was clean. His skin itched where he'd been sweating.

Their new traveling companion was talking with Drake. Jon hoped Drake knew what he was doing. Erin seemed very likable – almost too likeable. On the other hand, Drake didn't trust easily, and he wouldn't have put them all in danger if there were any doubts about the woman.

She looked up and grinned at Jon as if aware of his thoughts.

Drake had that uncanny ability, too.

Jon shook his head. Erin wasn't what he'd first thought, but Drake seemed to know what she was. She wasn't just a shapeshifter; she didn't seem to be able to do anything other than hide her wings. Even that was different from what Drake's people could do. Jon was just going to have to accept that there was a lot he needed to learn about.

"Everyone ready?" Drake asked. After everyone nodded, he

walked over to Jon. "This next part is on you."

"What do you mean?"

"I've never been to your Realm, so you're going to have to get us there."

"Drake, I've only done it the one time, and that without instruction."

"Well, it's a good thing I'm here to give you instruction."

Jon nodded. "Isn't the Instrumentally a lot different from Cynosure?"

"Yes and no. I asked Emrys about it, privately. The two Powers function much the same. You'll need to hold your private version of the Cynosure in your mind, and then hold a distinct thought of the place you want to go. Hold them both together, and just walk there. It may take some time, but eventually the worlds will change around us, and we'll be in your world."

"Nifty!" Erin interjected. "I always wondered how you guys did it."

Drake glared at her.

"Right, sorry. Silent as a blackbird in flight."

"I think I get it, Drake." Jon walked out onto the path and stared down it. He understood what Drake meant; he just had to figure out how to do it. He pictured the Cynosure, and then he mentally sketched an outline of it. That was easier to keep in his mind. The destination was harder, until he realized he could simply focus on his ship.

He'd never forget the *Chwyldro*. His beautiful starship. She was made for him, literally. The ship had been custom-built as part of the same program that had made him a pilot. Well, extensively refurbished, anyway. She was one of a kind.

"Jon, just two other things," said Drake.

"Yes?" Jon said, annoyed. He felt as if he'd had it for a moment.

"The first is not to forget to include us as you walk."

"Right, yeah, okay. What's the other?"

"You're facing South. Your world is in the North. It actually is important."

Jon sighed and turned around. Time to try again. He brought up his mental image of the Cynosure, and then thought about the *Chwyldro,* and about his companions. Time seemed to slow down as his engineered nervous system slipped automatically into flight mode. His other abilities merged with his ideogram of the Cynosure, and suddenly he could *see* the pulse waves moving through spacetime, the waves that made the mountains dance. Drake was right; they were a standing wave of probabilities.

He took a step forward, and light waves interacting with his body blurred across the dimensional interface, refracting back as rainbows. Jon kept thinking about the *Chwyldro*, holding the ship in his mind as he walked. Suddenly the blurring became intense and merged with the pulsing to form a swirling kaleidoscope of light. The world spun away into a tunnel of confusing colors.

Jon felt a hand on his shoulder and lost his concentration. The world spun back to normal, and he realized he felt a little bit nauseated. He closed his eyes until everything settled down.

"Sorry, Jon," Drake said. "I should have warned you about that. I didn't think you'd pick up on it as quickly as you did."

"What happened?" Jon asked. "What did I do wrong?"

"You didn't do anything wrong."

Jon could hear someone getting sick.

"Doesn't feel that way," Jon said. His head hurt behind his eyes.

"You just pushed too hard. You moved through too many Realms with each transition. Think of the Realms as stepping stones in a pond. The pond is deep, but that doesn't matter. You don't have to run across the stones."

"I only took a few steps."

The mountains were nowhere in sight. The path ran across a plain of tall grasses. The sky was a pale blue, and the air was crisp, with a steady breeze from the right. There was a faint scent of lavender in the air.

"You moved us halfway across the High Plains with those few steps," said Drake. "It's an important skill to have, but not one that you want to use all the time."

"That's what you did when you took us to Nandegurth," Jon exclaimed with sudden insight. "That grey tunnel..."

"It was similar, yes. I didn't completely take us through the Realms, but the method was the same."

"What do you mean, not through the Realms?"

"I did and didn't. We walked above the normal reality."

"He walked you through hyperspace," Erin interjected. "Didn't you? Not many can walk those paths. I'm impressed, Drake."

Drake nodded. "Not many know the paths are there *to* walk them."

"Okay, so how do I move more slowly?" asked Jon.

"I suspect you drove us with your will to get back to your ship," Drake said. "Try to feel for the veils between the universes, and step through one veil with each step."

Jon closed his eyes. "I feel many veils."

"You're sensing the Realms within each Clade. You only need to focus on the dense veils. Those are the important ones."

Jon sighed. "All right, let's try again."

Θ

Geoffrey still felt ill.

Whatever Jon had done to move them, it had been frightening and sickening. His inner ear still wasn't happy about it. They'd gone from mountains to plains in just a few steps. He wondered how many universes they'd traveled through.

Jason had gotten sick after the first part of the journey. He looked pale now but walked steadily just behind Geoffrey. Jason hadn't wanted to talk when Geoffrey tried. Now they were sort of avoiding each other.

Only Drake and Erin seemed unaffected by the rapid travel.

Geoffrey thought Erin was… *interesting*.

He found her attractive, but then, he thought most healthy women were attractive. He'd never been particularly picky about looks, but she was truly pretty. She was obviously really smart, and her personality was fun. She reminded him a bit of a girl he'd dated in high school; she'd been cheerful all the time, too. Even when she'd broken up with him because he didn't have a car.

In any case, Geoffrey was happy Drake had agreed to allow Erin to travel with them.

What was most intriguing to him was her wings. He wondered if she could actually fly. He suspected not, but then, why have them? She'd shapeshifted, but not like Drake did. She only seemed to be able to either have wings or not. Drake had seemed to indicate that her wings were a part of her true form. It would have been cool to have wings.

Erin said she wasn't an angel, but she sure looked like one.

"Tell me about yourself, Geoffrey," she said, slowing to walk next to him.

He blushed. She'd probably heard his thoughts.

"Your thoughts are pretty quiet, actually," she said. "I heard that last bit, but otherwise I just felt your regard."

Geoffrey shrugged. "Not much to say about myself. I'm not that interesting."

"I wouldn't say that," Erin said. "How'd you come to be traveling with these guys?"

"Jason and I are housemates. Well, I rent a room from Jason for college. Jon and Drake, we haven't known that long."

"Long enough," Jason muttered from behind them.

Erin laughed. "I guess all this must be a lot to take in."

Geoffrey nodded.

"Are you a shapeshifter, like Drake?" Jason blurted.

"Nope," Erin said. "I'm not anywhere close to his league."

"But you *are* a shapeshifter," he insisted.

"Well, you don't see my wings, do you?"

"That's not an answer."

"It's a kind of answer," Erin replied. She took off her jacket and handed it to Geoffrey. "Hold this for me."

The jacket was warm and smelled of cinnamon and leather.

"Check it out." Erin turned so they could see her back as she walked. Her tee shirt had two long slashes down the back.

Geoffrey could see a lot of smooth olive skin there.

Suddenly, wings sprouted from the slashes. Erin extended them wide. Each wing was longer than she was tall, and covered with large, glossy black feathers.

"Okay, yeah, seen 'em," said Jason.

"This is how I really look," Erin said. "Like Drake's ears, these are a part of who I am. My people all have them."

"So are you a shapeshifter or not?"

"Only with my wings," Erin replied. She folded the wings away and then took back her jacket.

"Are you one of Drake's people?" Jason demanded.

"Only distantly related. You need to lighten up, man. You kind of come across as a dick."

Geoffrey had to suppress a laugh. She wasn't wrong.

Jason evidently didn't think it was funny. He started walking faster and moved up nearer Jon. His shoulders were hunched a bit as he walked.

Geoffrey wished his friend would relax. He thought that maybe the problem was that Jason had just started to trust Drake, and then that duel at the guild meeting had made him draw up into himself again.

Erin seemed to have lost the interest in talking, which annoyed Geoffrey – he blamed Jason. He liked Erin, even if he had just met her. It wasn't that he expected or even wanted anything to happen between them; it was just that she a new person who seemed nice and could be a friend.

Erin pulled a small, flat, black box and headphones out of her jacket.

"Is that an iPod?" asked Geoffrey. "I haven't seen one of those in years."

"Thanks for making me feel old, Geoffrey."

"I'm sorry," he stammered.

Erin laughed then. "I'm kidding. I'm ancient, like Drake, but I *love* listening to rock while I walk the Realms. Gets my groove on."

She raised her arms, dancing and strutting down the trail, and Geoffrey couldn't help but laugh. Her positive attitude was infectious. He hoped maybe Jason would catch some of it.

Before Geoffrey was forced to strangle him.

CHAPTER TWENTY-SEVEN

Jason wanted to talk about what had happened during the duel, but Jon was concentrating on moving them through the Realms.

However that worked.

Drake was walking to the side, looking stern. Jason wasn't ready to talk to him yet. Geoffrey and Erin were a short distance behind him. Geoffrey was obviously infatuated with Erin. He couldn't really blame him; she was a very attractive woman.

Whatever species she was.

Jason felt lonely and was acutely aware that it was his own fault. His questions to Erin had come off as more aggressive than he'd intended. Even Geoffrey had seemed irritated with him.

Around noon, Jon slowed down and then stopped moving them though the Realms. The path had become old, cracked blacktop at some point. Ahead was what looked like a covered picnic shelter. Jon made for that and sat down.

He looked exhausted.

Drake collected the others' water bottles and took them over to a drink fountain to refill. He didn't even look at Jason. Jason took his bottle out of his pack and joined him. Drake just held out his hand for the bottle without saying anything.

"Drake?" Jason said quietly.

He turned, took the bottle from Jason's hand, and filled it. Then he handed it back before speaking. "Yes, Jason?"

"Can we talk?"

"That depends," Drake replied. "I'm not in the mood to be insulted. You want to have a conversation? We can do that. You wish to yell at me, or strike me again? Keep it to yourself. You only get the one free hit without response."

"Look, I know you can flatten me anytime you want, okay? I just want to talk, to have a conversation."

"All right, go ahead."

Drake wasn't going to make it easy for him.

"Did you tell Jon about... me?"

"*That's* what you lead with?" Drake sighed. "It isn't my secret to tell." His expression softened. "I think you should tell them both, but I'll not force the issue. Not at this time, anyway."

"Jon sort of indicated that he knew."

"He's a very intelligent and perceptive man. He probably figured it out from observation, as I did."

"Drake, about what happened..."

"You hitting me, or before that?"

"I'm sorry that I hit you, and thankful I'm still alive to say it. Okay? I mean about the duel, or whatever it was."

"It was a duel. I did what I felt I had to do. You may accept that or not, as you see fit."

"You didn't enjoy it, right?" asked Jason. That was really the important part, to him.

"I am not a monster. The woman he challenged..."

"The blonde?"

"Yes. She is the granddaughter of my granddaughter. She would not have survived a duel with that man. He would have torn her apart. The small, red-haired woman is my granddaughter. She is powerful but also would have failed to overcome the skill of her opponent. Which would have meant death."

"You were protecting your family," Jason said quietly. "I didn't realize."

"I don't let many people know that I have relatives who can be harmed to hurt me. That he evidently knew bothers me a great deal. If he knew about Eliza and Gillian, he may have known of others. I can't be everywhere and protect everyone."

"I can understand that," Jason said. "Why tell me?"

"Because I trust you, Jason," Drake said. Only he hadn't said *Jason*. Drake had said his name in a language Jason had never expected to hear again.

Jason choked as his throat constricted. He felt dizzy, and his vision greyed out slightly. He felt Drake catch him and help him sit. He hadn't heard that name spoken aloud in a long time. He heard Drake saying something to the others about Jason being tired. Then his vision turned black, and he faded away.

He dreamt of the friends he had lost, so long ago, and awoke with tears on his face. The sky had darkened, and most of the others were sitting by a small campfire at the edge of the shelter. Drake was sitting nearby in a lotus position.

"Feel a little better?" Drake asked. "I suppose I did hit you over the head with that rather suddenly."

Jason hadn't moved or made any sound, yet Drake knew the instant he woke. Now he sat up. Drake handed him a wafer of food and a bottle of water. Jason hadn't tried the food yet; it was light, crisp, and a little salty. It didn't taste like anything he'd ever eaten before, but it was good. Just a little of it filled him up.

"What did you tell them?" Jason asked quietly.

"Only that you were sleeping. Jon needed a nap, as well. He isn't used to moving through the Realms, and it can be exhausting. Even just following along can be exhausting."

"Thank you."

"I don't have so many friends that I can afford to alienate one," Drake said with a smile. "Now get your ass up and join us by the fire. We'll camp here tonight. I might hunt some food."

Jason nodded. He had a lot to think about.

Ο

Geoffrey had been worried when Jason passed out.

He'd seen Jason and Drake talking, which also worried him. Drake didn't seem like the forgiving sort, and Jason had hit him, back in the Courts. However, it had turned out that Jason was just really tired. Geoffrey was, too. He took off his pack and stretched.

Jon sprawled on top of one of the picnic tables and fell asleep.

Geoffrey leaned back against the table and dozed off. When he awoke, the sky was getting dark. Erin and Jon sat by a small fire, talking quietly. Drake was watching over Jason, who was still asleep. Geoffrey stood up, stretched, and walked over to sit by Jon and Erin.

The warmth from the fire felt good.

"Feeling better, Geoffrey?" asked Jon.

"Much. How about you?"

"Better," Jon said. "Drake makes it look easy, but moving through the Realms is exhausting."

"I think Drake makes a lot of things look easy," Erin said. "He likes to act tough."

"Seems pretty tough to me," said Geoffrey.

"Oh, he is."

"You said you didn't know each other," Jon said, "but you act as if you do."

Erin laughed. "I knew *of* him, but I hadn't met him. He'd met others of my kind."

"Winged not-angels?" said Geoffrey.

"Exactly."

"What is it between you two? How do you know of him?"

"I'm not sure that's my story to tell."

"Does that reluctance have something to do with the Ancient Enemy?" Jon asked.

"He told you about them? Okay, well, did he tell you there was a war? A very long time ago?"

"Drake said the war was something like a hundred thousand years."

"Longer than that in most places, but yeah, that would be right for the Ruined Courts."

"He called it a civil war, at one point."

Erin chuckled. "I suppose you could call it that. The Ancient Enemy were his own people, but something twisted them into monsters."

"You guys seem to be having a fun conversation," Jason said as he sat down. "Mind if I join you?"

Geoffrey looked around but didn't see Drake.

"Hi, Jason!" said Erin. "Feeling better?"

"Yeah. Listen, I'm sorry I was a dick, okay?"

"We're good."

"You were talking about monsters," Jon said to Erin.

"Right." She sighed. "My own people are related to Drake's. After the war, many of them were imprisoned, many killed. Many of my people had served the monsters, and a few of them were monsters themselves. It gets complicated after that, but some of us fought back against the monsters. We still do."

"Are they still out there?" Jason asked. "The monsters, I mean."

"Many of them, yeah. Drake fights against them, too; that's how I heard of him. I suppose you could say that we're on the same side." Erin poked at the fire. "He's a good guy. You don't have to agree with everything he does, but he usually has a good reason for it. I think he's just gotten hard, fighting the Ancient Enemy. He's been doing that for tens of thousands of years."

"I didn't realize he was that old," said Jon.

"I think he tries to hide that," Erin said. "But my people have long memories, and I heard about *him* when I was *young.*"

"You know you're telling us how old *you* are with that, right?" said Jason.

"I think I still look good for my age," Erin said with a grin. "Most girls start getting wrinkles long before fifty thousand."

Geoffrey choked on the water he'd been drinking.

"Don't aspirate the water, Geoffrey," said Erin. "Breathe or swallow. Don't try both at the same time."

"I don't think any of us realized…," said Jon. "Is Drake of a comparable age?"

"At least," Erin replied. "As I said, I heard stories about him back then. Of course, I was on the other side then, and they were mostly cautionary tales."

"Two things there," Jon said. "First, are you sure it's the same Drake?"

"Absolutely."

"Okay. Now, what do you mean, you were on the other side?"

"Most people mean it metaphorically when they say they were monsters as teenagers. I really was. It isn't a time in my life I'm proud of." Erin rubbed the stone pendent around her neck.

"Does Drake know?" asked Jason.

"Of course. He knows about many things. He certainly knows as much about the Enemy as anyone alive. He knows about my people; that's why he didn't trust me at first."

"Was *he* like that? A monster?"

Geoffrey was glad Jason had asked. He hadn't had the nerve, but he wanted to know.

"No." Erin poked at the fire again. "He never fell. I don't he could."

She seemed sad, thinking about the past. It didn't suit her.

Drake returned then. He was carrying a stick with five fish tied to it; they looked a little bit like trout. Their heads had been removed, and they had been expertly gutted. Geoffrey suspected Drake had been giving Erin and Jon time to talk.

"I hope everyone likes fish," Drake said as he set them over the fire to cook. "I didn't see any signs of civilization near here, other than the road and shelter. No game worth going after, either."

"Looks good, Drake," said Erin. "Thanks."

Geoffrey thought she sounded a little guilty. Probably embarrassed to have been caught talking about Drake. Geoffrey doubted Drake cared, though. Drake didn't seem to care what other people thought about him.

"I would have gotten you guys a pizza," Drake said with a wink a Geoffrey, "but I didn't want to order from here. Thought it might call too much attention to us."

CHAPTER TWENTY-EIGHT

The next morning, Jon bathed as best he could in the cold fountain and then ate a little of the wafer from his pack. It was lighter and more filling than he'd expected. He couldn't quite identify the taste, but it didn't have much of one anyway.

Erin bathed after everyone else did. She stripped to the waist, with her back to them. Jon watched the muscles play across her back as she washed, and wondered where her wings went when she put them away. He could see the graceful curve of her small breasts as she pulled her tee shirt back on. He looked away in embarrassment.

He'd always wanted wings. It was big part of why he'd become a pilot. That, and necessity.

"Can I ask you something?" he asked as Erin walked past.

"Go ahead," she replied. If she'd been aware of him watching her, she didn't seem to care.

"Why wings? You can't expect to fly with them, can you?"

She shook her head. "Not in this gravity, no."

"So you didn't evolve in Earth-normal gravity? You move well here, if not."

"I'm not sure that applies to my people," Erin said.

"Evolution, I mean, at least past a certain point. My people didn't have a homeworld. We were from a smoke ring."

"A smoke ring?"

"A protoplanetary ring of rocks and atmosphere around a star. I don't know whether or not it was natural. Almost certainly not. I grew up playing amongst the rocks and flying around the ring. We had a lot of space there."

"Was it at normal planetary distances?"

"Sol-type star, with a ring at one hundred fifty million kilometers out. The ring of gasses was about twenty thousand kilometers thick, with an unbroken ring of metal in the middle of it all. I think that ring gave the gravity to hold the atmosphere in place, and a strong magnetic field to block stellar flares. There wasn't much else in the system, so we never worried about asteroids or anything. It was a very long time ago for me, dim in my memories, like another life."

"I didn't mean to sound as if I was grilling you," said Jon. "I'm just curious. So you could fly, growing up? That must have been amazing."

"Yeah," Erin said. "Still do, sometimes."

"How?"

"It isn't hard to find Realms off the beaten path with lower than Earth-normal gravity. I've also been in space, in a few places. Zero-gee isn't quite the same thing, but if you're on a spin station, it feels close enough. Sometimes I can find a big O'Neill habitat that gives me room to fly."

"I can almost imagine you scaring people by showing your wings and flying around."

Erin laughed. "Keeps them on their toes."

"You like shocking people, don't you?"

"I may have given up on being evil a long time ago, but I didn't give up on having fun."

"Would it be rude of me to ask what kind of Power you have?"

"My power over men is entirely natural," Erin purred. "Women, too, for that matter."

Jon cleared his throat; he wasn't unaffected by her charms. "I mean, how do you normally move through the Realms? You don't have Cynosure or Omphalos, I'm guessing."

"No, I don't," Erin replied with a wink. Then she vanished. She appeared next to the fountain, took a drink, and then apported back to Jon. "As you saw for yourself, all natural."

Jon ignored her innuendo. "Can your people can just apport through the Realms without one of the Powers?"

"Not exactly."

"She isn't going to tell you," Drake said from over by the tables. He walked toward them. "Her people use a Power, but they don't talk about it."

"A long time ago, we used a Power," said Erin. "We haven't had direct access to it for a long time. You use it yourself when you draw your sword."

Drake nodded. "One of the old Powers, Jon. Older than the Cynosure."

"I didn't realize there *were* other Powers."

"There are many Powers across the Realms, and even out in the universes. Some of them are ancient."

"Some are even older than the Instrumentality," said Erin.

"How can that be?" asked Jon.

"Time differential," said Drake. "The Ruined Courts are the first universe, but it's barely six billion years old."

"Just long enough for a couple of star cycles," Erin said. "Then *blam*!" She slapped her hands together. "Collapse! Poor little things." It seemed to amuse her, for some reason.

"My own universe is almost fourteen billion years old," said Jon.

"Pretty common age," Erin said with a sniff.

"Your universe was probably formed less than half a million years ago, as time in the first universe goes."

"I just can't wrap my head around that yet."

"You understand Einstein-Lorentz contractions, right?" said Drake.

"Sure. Basic time-dilation equations for space travel."

"All right, so apply that in reverse to the rapid inflation of a universe after a precipitation event."

"You mean like the Big Bang?"

Drake pointed a finger at Erin. "Don't," he said. "And yes, Jon, exactly like that."

"You're no fun," Erin complained.

"You're saying that if time compresses as spacetime does, then the inverse is true, and time accelerates when spacetime expands."

"Basically," Drake said. "Up to a certain point. As the expansion slows down, the universe slowly syncs up with the first universe. There's still some variation, and it doesn't always work right. I don't know why. Remember that those other universes were created by us. My ancestors wanted to colonize them all."

"So you look human because all of us are descended from colonists?"

"It isn't that simple."

"None of this feels *simple*."

"Some of the people in the Realms are descended from first-universe colonists," said Drake. "Her people, for example, or even your people up North."

"I'm not related to them," said Jon.

"That doesn't matter right now. Some people are descended from colonists; some people evolved in those places. Think of it as a parallel evolution. The universes started at the same point, so most of them end up being very similar."

"Geoffrey and Jason's Earth seemed similar to mine, then, not because they branched off each other but because they started at the same point?"

"It's–"

"More complicated than that," Jon interrupted. "Yeah, I figured."

"There is exchange of information between universes at a quantum level," said Erin. "There are also people moving around, spreading ideas and materials between the universes. You'll find clusters out here that are very similar. You'll find worlds where everything is strange."

"What do you mean by *strange*?" Jon asked.

"Exotic chemistries and laws of physics. Places where something went wrong with the creation of the universe, and nothing is quite is as it should be. Down in the South, you'll find artificial worlds, and micro-universes that have only an Earth.'

"Like Nandegurth," said Jon.

"I don't know that one."

"Drake's fortress is there."

Drake looked as if he was displeased with Jon for mentioning Nandegurth, but Jon didn't care. Drake hadn't forbidden him from talking about the place, and if Drake had been telling the truth about that strange world, it was inaccessible anyway.

ʘ

They left the picnic shelter around midmorning.

Drake would have preferred to leave earlier, but then, he wouldn't have stopped for the night if he'd been traveling alone. The shelter hadn't exactly been defensible. Most of his companions weren't accustomed to walking as much as he did, though. They were worn down, even after the long break.

As Jon walked them through the Realms, trees began to appear along the road, and now it widened into a six-lane highway. Sometimes they moved through places where the cars lay rusting in the road. Drake encouraged Jon to move them along from there as quickly as possible. Realms that had suffered apocalypses were rarely safe for travelers.

Erin stayed with them until they stopped at noon.

"This is me, guys," she said.

Jon paused, and a truck roared past them, horn blaring. They moved to the side of the road. Drake could hear a jet passing in the distance. This was one of the central Earth Realms, where technology hadn't advanced very far. It could have been close to Geoffrey's Earth.

"Come on," said Erin. "Bring it in!"

She hugged the others and then stopped before him. "Well, big guy?"

Drake sighed. She was too cute to deny. "Fine."

She gave him a quick squeeze. "Thanks for letting me tag along. It's been interesting. I hope I'll you see again, Drake, but if not, you take care of yourself."

Drake nodded. "Before you go, may I ask you something?"

"Sure."

"Why walk the Realms along this road?"

"I'm not a big, tough fighter like you," said Erin. "I have to be a little more discreet most of the time. Walking in along the road doesn't make detectable waves."

"You can sense when someone uses a Power?" he asked. It was a disturbing thought.

"We can sense when someone apports in from far away," she replied. "So can the enemy."

Drake nodded. "I can, too, if I'm in the Realm or have set up watch over it."

"There you go, then. I walk in, to stay quiet. You barge in and swing your sword around, and then leave." She waved her hand to demonstrate. "I can't afford to do that. If nothing else, what I'm hunting might run."

"I'll keep that in mind. Safe travels to you."

"Thanks, Drake. 'Bye, guys!" She waved, stepped off the road, and started walking down a path that looked as if it led to a river.

"Is she going to be all right?" Jon asked. "She seems so… delicate."

"She'll be fine," said Drake. "She's much tougher than she looks. She wouldn't have lived as long as she has, if she wasn't. We should keep moving."

Jon nodded and went back to moving them through the Realms.

Drake knew Geoffrey missed Erin already. Hell, so did he, a little bit. She'd been fun to have around. Not to mention being interesting to talk to. He'd never had a chance to have a conversation with one of her kind before. He'll killed many of them, but never talked to them.

The sun moved lower in the sky with each step they took. It would be night soon, and Drake wasn't too sure about traveling after dark. Jon wasn't experienced enough to keep them on track with fewer visual clues.

Even once they reached their goal, they'd still have to find a way from the mainland to Catalina Island. That was going to be interesting, depending on what Jon's Earth was like. He wasn't sure if Jon had thought it through.

CHAPTER TWENTY-NINE

Drake built a small fire when they camped that night.

Jon had been eager to push on to the Earth where his ship waited, but he understood why Drake wanted to stop. Drake was afraid Jon would push himself too far or guide them astray. It was a valid concern; Jon was exhausted.

Drake was an enigma to Jon. He'd become a steadfast friend in the last week, which was something of a record for Jon. He didn't have many friends. Drake had saved him when he'd shown up back on that Earth. It was funny that Drake had been there to kill him. Maybe Jon didn't let it bother him too much because if Drake wanted to kill him, he was pretty sure Drake could have done it. Jon was faster, and he could apport, but so could Drake.

Actually, all of his companions had become friends. Geoffrey was young and eager for adventure, but he was steady underneath. Jason was older and wiser with a core of stony resolve. Jason also carried a sadness Jon didn't understand yet, but he wasn't going to push him. Jason didn't seem like the kind of man who responded well to being pushed.

Jon was certain Jason would open up to him eventually. If

not, well, Jon was okay with that, too. It wasn't as if he didn't have his own secrets.

Jon found it strange that they had all become friends. He was glad for it, though. Drake was a powerful ally, but Jon was also just glad for the company. He had to admit that he'd have been lost, trying to travel the worlds without someone like Drake around to guide him.

"What is your Earth like?" Geoffrey asked.

"First, it's not *my* Earth," said Jon. "I'm not from there. I get what you mean, though. It's... I don't know. Not a great place."

"Are you from Mars or something?"

"A bit farther away than that. Rhyddid is three jumps from Sol. My homeworld was settled mostly by the Welsh, originally, but that has been changing for a while. We've been taking in refugees from oppressed systems." Jon paused. "Well, we *had* been taking in refugees. I don't know what the planet is like now. I haven't been home in over a decade."

Geoffrey nodded. "I'm just wondering what we'll find when we get to Earth."

"Earth is a backwater shithole. It's the mother planet, but people didn't take very good care of it before they moved out to the stars. Now it's economically depressed, ravaged by climate change, and controlled by gangs and oppressive private corporations. Not a great place to spend any time, to be honest."

"You haven't encountered any other intelligent species?" asked Drake.

Jon shook his head. "No, just humans, so far. We know there's someone out there – the jump gate technology was found at Alpha Centauri. We reverse-engineered that technology and then made jumpships, too. If anyone has ever encountered any of the Precursors, I haven't heard about it, and I think I would have. It would be a pretty big deal."

"How far have humans expanded from Sol?"

Jon thought for a moment. "Maybe twenty, twenty-five light years."

Drake nodded. "I'm surprised you haven't encountered any other intelligent species." He shrugged. "There should have been at least one or two. Your Realm may lie outside the core populated clusters, though."

"What are those, exactly?"

"The populated clusters?" Drake sighed. "My people settled as colonists in many of the Realms. The core Realms usually have humanoid species descended from the first peoples."

"So humans leaving Sol might discover other people who look human, out there in space?"

Drake smiled. "The early colonists adapted to fit the worlds they found themselves on. I doubt many of them would look very human to you any longer."

"What kinds of people?" asked Geoffrey. "I mean, what would they look like?"

Drake shrugged. "Just about anything you could imagine. Erin is of a people descended from the first. She looks human enough in her trueform. Excepting the wings, of course. Not all of her people do. I've met other people who had the trueforms of dragons, elves, cat people, lizard people, and many other, more exotic forms."

"And they're all human?"

"No, they're all distantly related to *my* people. Humans are an indigenous species that usually evolves on Earthlike worlds."

"Then why do we look the way we do," Geoffrey asked, "like your people?"

"The universes were designed to have conditions my ancestors would find habitable. The first universe evolved a people who looked like us, so other universes built on that template evolve people who also look like us."

"But they aren't," said Jason. He'd been quiet since he'd

spoken to Drake that morning.

"Maybe not," Drake said, smiling. "Remember, my ancestors settled many places. Who is to say whether a given population is related to mine or not?"

"You always seem to know."

"I do, but I'm old, and I've met many different people in my travels. I know that people are people; form matters little. I make little distinction between those descended from colonists and the indigenous peoples who evolve in those universes."

"You have a better attitude than the people I met from the North," said Jon. "They acted as if those not from the Golden Kingdom weren't even people."

"The colonists who founded the Golden Kingdom split off from mine many tens of thousands of years ago," said Drake. "They left during or just after the ancient war. They were isolationist, scared, and running from unimaginable horrors. I don't blame them for their attitude. They spent most of their long reign forgetting about us in the South. I think it came as a shock to them to learn of their heritage."

"Many of them were rather arrogant," Jon said. "They acted like spoiled brats."

"The young ones often act thus. They are drunk with power and a heritage that says they're gods among the mere mortals of the Realms. Eventually, they'll learn that they, too, are mortal. It's not an attitude exclusive to the North."

Jon sighed. "People are people," he said.

"Exactly."

☉

Geoffrey was only half paying attention to the conversation.

His thoughts were mostly about the lovely Erin. He hadn't known her for very long, but he missed her, now that she was gone. That first night they'd camped, he'd had fantasies about her coming to him as he lay there.

It was absurd.

She was beautiful, and also alien and ancient. He was embarrassed by his feelings. He couldn't help being a young man, though. He was barely twenty years old, and he hadn't had a girlfriend in a while. Nor had he had any time to himself in a while.

He sighed.

"Doing okay, Geoffrey?" asked Jon.

"Doing fine. Just tired of walking all the time. My feet hurt."

Jon nodded. "I hear you. I'm not used to it, either. Once we get to my ship, we won't have to walk as much."

"You'll have room for us all?"

"Easily. That does bring up another problem, though."

"What?"

"We'll need new clothes. And we need to do something about the way you look, Drake."

"What's wrong with how I look?" Drake growled.

"Nothing, except you don't look human."

"I suppose I could always wear a bandanna," Drake said with a smirk.

Geoffrey laughed. "I don't think Jason will give his up. He never takes it off."

Drake shook his head. "Then I suppose I'll change how I look."

His ears rounded off as Geoffrey watched, and his skin darkened from the odd porcelain complexion he normally had to a normal human shade. Drake smiled, and his teeth looked normal, too. Other than being a dark redhead, Drake looked vaguely Chinese now, with his strong cheekbones.

"That is more appropriate," said Jon. "Can you maintain that look?"

"Once changed, my flesh will stay in the form I choose."

Jon nodded. "Your armor is going to be noticed, though. No one wears armor like that where I'm from. At least, I've never seen any."

"What would blend in?" Drake asked. "Tell me about your Earth Realm. I'm loath to be completely with protection."

"Earth is poverty-stricken and overrun with crime. The other stellar systems are better off, for the most part. Humans first journeyed to the stars centuries ago, and left an impoverished, resource-drained world behind."

"Were the clothes you wore before typical of the local fashions?"

"Pretty normal, yeah." Jon shrugged. "I don't think I'd call my clothes *fashionable*."

"Does no one wear armor?"

Jon shrugged. "The military does. Sometimes bodyguards and security forces. Just on the torso, though."

Drake stood, and his armor and clothes writhed and changed. It was bizarre, and Geoffrey felt a little envious. Being able to change clothes with the wave of a hand would be... *cool*.

Drake was still wearing armor, but now it looked like ordinary ballistic body armor, covered by the black leather trench coat he seemed to favor. Underneath, he wore black jeans and leather boots. Geoffrey thought the whole outfit made Drake somehow appear even more dangerous than he normally did.

"Your armor should blend in now," Jon said. "No one has swords that disintegrate people – just so you know."

Drake gestured, and the air around him was abruptly filled with blades. He placed his sheathed sword in the air with the others and spun them like a turntable until a small, Japanese-looking sword appeared; Geoffrey thought it looked too short to be a katana. The other blades disappeared as Drake sheathed it smoothly on his back. He pushed back his coat, and Geoffrey could see Drake was wearing a bulky pistol in a leather holster.

"That's just a normal sword? What kind of pistol?" asked Jon. "Energy weapons aren't common."

"The sword is just a sword, although it has an iridium blade. It won't eat people. I doubt many people would be able to identify the metal on sight. The pistol is a needler," Drake answered. "It's a rapid-fire, compact kinetic-energy weapon."

Jon frowned. "Steel needles?"

"Jagged hypercarbon over a samarium-cobalt core." Drake smiled. "Monomolecular point, and sub-sonic. Shreds flesh and penetrates most conventional body armor materials, but it won't puncture any decent starship hull."

"Has anyone mentioned *recently* that you're a little scary, Drake?" Jon shook his head. "You know way too much about killing people. Who would even develop a weapon like that?"

"My ancestors developed many deadly weapons. A pistol has little point if it isn't efficient at killing. As for me being scary," Drake said, "it has been mentioned from time to time. I believe Jason and Geoffrey will blend in well enough in their clothes from home, yes?"

Jon glanced at them. "Yeah, they'll be fine."

Geoffrey was disappointed; he'd been hoping for cool new clothes.

CHAPTER THIRTY

They set out the next morning for Jon's Earth.

Geoffrey had eaten that last of his rations for breakfast and hoped they wouldn't have to travel long. He was tired of walking. The luster had worn off the adventure. He wanted a burger, fries, and a milkshake.

Maybe that pizza he'd ordered some indeterminable time ago.

Jon led them for a few hours and then stopped, looking uncertain. He frowned and gestured back the way they'd come. Geoffrey just followed him. He couldn't tell much difference between the worlds they were crossing through at this point. Each place was just another stop on an endless freeway.

Finally, Jon stopped on a desolate highway under a stormy sky, ruins to either side half-buried under sand. Mountains loomed to the south, scraping the low clouds. There was very little vegetation. The world appeared to be dead.

"This feels right," said Jon.

Drake nodded. "This Realm has the same vibration as you."

"You can tell what universe I'm from?"

"Can't you?"

Jon shook his head.

"Here?" Jason asked.

"Told you Earth is a shithole," Jon said. He gestured south. "I think we need to go that way. Be careful. These ruins may look abandoned, but they aren't."

Geoffrey shivered as they walked. It wasn't too cold, probably around sixty degrees Fahrenheit, but the ruins were oppressive. Sand covered many of the buildings, with gnarled trees and shrubs peeking out here and there. It was only when Geoffrey saw the Walt Disney Studios sign that it really drove home to him just how different this world was from his own, and how similar.

They walked on, and Geoffrey felt as if they were slowly moving up in elevation. A ruined church was mostly intact to their right, and then Geoffrey saw the worn gravestones and monuments with unreadable dates and inscriptions. Weary trees bent under the constant wind down the mountains. They passed another church, this one broken-down red brick, and then began climbing into the hills.

They crested a mountain shrouded in fog, and the storm clouds began to rain on them. Geoffrey was thoroughly miserable by the time they crested the second mountain. They stopped by some skeletal ruins, which Geoffrey realized had once been the Hollywood sign.

That shook him a bit.

To him, Hollywood was a symbol of unattainable prosperity. It was that place where the movie stars lived and worked. The place where dreams come true.

This desolate world looked as if it had forgotten how to dream.

In the valley below them, Geoffrey could see a mostly intact-looking city stretching out into the fog and rain. At least the lights indicated that *somewhere*, people were alive on this ruined planet. He'd begun to wonder. Most of the lights were far away, near what he thought was the coast.

"Los Angeles," said Jon. "We're about thirty-five kilometers from the ocean. Then we have about fifty kilometers to Catalina Island. We'll have to find some way to board a ferry, or buy tickets for a shuttle. Either way, we'll need money."

"You don't have any money?" asked Drake.

"I doubt I have any left in my account at this point. I had enough to cover the docking fees for my ship for a few days, but I was relying on picking up a gig here to cover expenses. I don't know how long I've been gone. Can't you just wave your hand for money or something?"

"Doesn't work like that."

"You had cash back in Albuquerque," Jason said. "Where did that come from?"

"I earned that," said Drake. "We'll have to do the same here, if we need local coin."

"The common currency here is electronic credits," Jon said. "I have an imbedded chip in my hand. If we find a reader, I can check my account balance. I doubt I have much left, if any. Sometimes people use credit sticks, which store the banking data."

"So where do we find one of those?" Jason asked.

Geoffrey was a little weirded out at the thought of having a chip implanted in his hand.

Jon waved vaguely at the city below them. "We'll find work down there."

$\odot$

The Los Angeles of Jon's Earth was not what Jason had been expecting.

Jason had been to Los Angeles on his own Earth, years before. It had been sunny, warm, and full of beautiful people and things: everything that this Los Angeles was not. The day was cold, and it was still raining. Jason couldn't even see the sun thorough the clouds. It was funny, how much one could miss something like just seeing the sun.

The few people they saw as they made their way into the city were furtive and ran away from them. No one seemed to have cars. The wrecked hulks of unrecognizable vehicles rusted away along the streets, mixed with the trash and omnipresent rainwater.

The outskirts of the city seemed overgrown. Ferns and evergreens were the dominant plant life, along with green-grey moss on everything. Somewhere in the distance, a dog howled, and Jason shivered. He would not have wanted to live on this world. It looked far more cruel and barbaric than the world he'd spent much of his life on.

"We'll need money first," Jon said quietly. "I've got papers for the checkpoints, but we'll have to find someone who can forge those for the rest of you."

"You need to have papers?" asked Jason. "Identity papers?" He didn't like that idea at all.

"To get through the checkpoints, yeah. The whole planet is under martial law, which is to say, not much law at all. We're lucky we haven't had any trouble yet."

"So where do we start?" Drake asked.

"I may know a guy," Jon said. "Don't know if they're still in business. We can get what we need, though."

"For a price," said Drake.

"Nothing is free."

Deeper into the city, most of the people they saw looked hungry. Jason was hungry himself, but the locals appeared gaunt and starved. Many of them wore were ragged clothes, and some were barely dressed at all. He realized that to these people, he and his companions must appear rich.

Young men and women called sexual offers to them as they passed. Jason knew they were just desperate, but it chilled him.

Some were very young. Their hard eyes followed him with a hunger that had nothing to do with food.

"I hope your entire Realm isn't like this," Drake said quietly.

"Not my Realm – not even the planet I'm from," Jon answered. "But no, not all planets are like this. Most of the Earth is, though. At least the parts I've visited. Parts are far worse. Only the criminals live well on this planet. If you can call that living. Everyone who could leave Earth left a long time ago. Rich tourists sometimes come here. My understanding is that it's sex tourism, mostly. I've heard rumors of people coming here to hunt. People. For sport."

"It's sad," Drake replied. "Not that I haven't seen worse."

"Not much different, back where Geoffrey and I are from," said Jason. "Maybe not in the United States, but in other, less affluent countries, where people are poorer and more desperate? Yeah, you see this."

"I've read about it," Geoffrey said. "Never thought I'd see the USA look like this."

"Different Realm, Geoffrey," said Drake. "This isn't your Earth."

"What difference does that make?" Geoffrey demanded. "These people need help. Can't you do something for them?"

"Do something?" Drake asked with raised eyebrows. "You mean, wave my hand and make it all better? It doesn't work like that. Even if I could give them all money, someone else would just take it away. Remember, we don't have any money for ourselves, either."

"We can't do anything, Geoffrey," Jason said, "except not be part of the problem. Don't treat people like garbage. You know, don't be a dick."

"I try not to be."

"You don't, and I doubt you ever would. You grew up in a decent family as a rural, middle-class American. You have an idealized way of thinking about the world. Don't ever lose that."

"You're not from America, are you?" asked Geoffrey. "Originally, I mean."

Jason hesitated. He didn't want to have this conversation here, but he didn't want to keep lying to his friend, either. "No," he answered cautiously.

"Didn't think so," Geoffrey replied. "Was where you were from like this? Mexico or someplace?"

"It wasn't much like this," said Jason. "I grew up under better circumstances, in a place where this sort of thing could never happen."

"Must have been a nice place," Geoffrey said. "Maybe you'll tell me about it one day?"

"Someday." Jason was surprised to discover he wasn't lying. He trusted Geoffrey. When they were in a better place, maybe he would tell Geoffrey a little bit about where he was from.

He could see Drake smiling as they walked.

Jason was relieved that Drake hadn't said anything. That didn't mean he was comfortable that Drake knew about him. Jason had spent a long time hiding himself. It wasn't easy, knowing that someone knew.

CHAPTER THIRTY-ONE

Drake stayed alert as they walked through the city.

He could sense hungry eyes on them: people assessing his strength against the value of his weapons, and even the clothes they all wore. This Realm was the type of place the Ancient Enemy would have settled down in to feed.

He could almost feel it.

Drake wasn't here to liberate the planet, but he couldn't help but feel as if he should try. Although not responsible for the misery these people endured, the enemy would encourage it. That was what the Ancient Enemy did; they fed on the pain and suffering of others. If there was an opportunity to stop the Ancient Enemy, he would take it, he decided.

Patterns of movement around them coalesced. "We are being followed," he said quietly.

"I noticed," Jon replied. "I've been hoping they'll back off."

"Turn into this alley."

"That's a bad idea. They're almost certain attack us in there."

"Better a place of our choosing than an ambush on their terms."

"Damnit," Jon muttered, but he turned at the next alley, a long, narrow space between tall buildings. Drake hoped no one was waiting up higher, on the rooftop. He couldn't sense anyone hiding there, at least. Three tough-looking men with hard expressions moved into sight at the far end of the alley. Drake didn't need to be told that they were with the men following his group.

"Jason, Geoffrey, stay out of this if you can. Make yourselves small targets, in case someone starts shooting."

"Drake, I'm not into the idea of killing these guys," said Jon. "There has to be another way to deal with them."

"Nothing but force works on desperate men. If you don't want to get involved, then apport to the top of the building and keep watch. I can deal with this."

Two men entered the alley behind them, staying back and watching.

"Hey! Gringos, you on our turf," one of the men ahead of them called.

"Just passing through," said Drake.

"You gotta pay to pass through, *chinito*."

"Yo le pago a tu puta madre."

"For fuck's sake, Drake, can't we ever just talk our way out of these things?" Jon asked. He pulled Jason and Geoffrey into a deep doorway.

"Okay, *mamahuevo*, you gonna hurt now," the man said.

Drake smiled as he heard the men all draw knives. *No need to draw a gun for these,* he thought.

He drew his sword. It wasn't a katana, as the world he'd picked it up in hadn't had a Japan. It was, however, arm-length and slightly curved, with a two-handed grip and only a small guard. The blade was forged from an iridium alloy, which made it far denser than it looked.

The men at either end of the alley yelled derisively at him. Drake did a quick calculation and decided the two men behind them were a little closer and therefore more of a threat to his friends. "Last chance," he called. That was mostly for Jon, who would feel bad if Drake simply killed the men.

The men laughed – at least, until Drake apported.

A wet *swish,* and a man's head went flying. Blood sprayed six meters up the wall of the alley, but Drake was already moving, driving the point of his blade through the chest of the other man, and then apporting back to where Jon and the others waited, before the dead men even hit the ground.

The other men yelled and charged.

Drake moved a few steps forward and stood his ground.

A thrown knife came at him. He parried it into a wall and then stepped forward to drive the point of his sword through the man's eye. Another stepped under the thrust to stab at Drake, and Drake tore down through the first man to sever the arm of the second. That man fell back against the wall, screaming as the blood spurted, and Drake flicked his blade into the man's chest to put him out of his misery.

The last man fired a pistol of some kind directly at Drake. He managed to turn at the last moment, and something struck his shoulder. Drake brought his sword in low and pinned the man to the brick wall. The man screamed, but only for a moment. Drake jerked up with all his strength and split the man in half, bottom to top. Part of the wall collapsed over the bloody remains.

Drake wiped the blood from his sword. Only as he sheathed it did he notice the pain in his shoulder. Blood dripped steadily from his left hand. His leather jacket had a large ragged hole at the shoulder.

"You're hurt, Drake," said Jon.

"I noticed. Are we close to the person you mentioned before?"

"Just a couple of blocks." Jon picked up the fallen man's gun from the pavement. "He shoot you with this?"

Drake nodded.

"Damn. These things are highly illegal. Like *capital punishment, hunt down your family and everyone you ever knew* illegal, military-grade hotwire projector."

"Place it on the ground," said Drake. After Jon did, Drake crushed it under his boot heel. "No sense in getting caught with it."

"Are you all right?" Jon asked. "We should take a look at that wound."

"Not here," Drake replied. "Why don't you lead the way?"

Drake followed Jon and noticed that the pain in his shoulder kept getting worse. Normally his natural healing ability would be at work, along with the nanotechnology in his blood. He pressed his hand over the wound, but that only made it worse. It started bleeding more, and something cut his hand.

"Maybe you should look at it," he said to Jon after a block.

Jon directed them into an ally, where Drake sank down against the wall. He wasn't used to something hurting as badly as this did. For one thing, he was rarely injured; for another, he had a high pain tolerance. This burning pain in his shoulder was different, though.

Jon hissed when he looked closer at Drake's shoulder. "Do you have anything shorter than that shish kabob skewer that I can use?"

Jason handed Jon his dagger.

Drake watched with a certain detachment as Jon pulled a length of dull wire out of the wound on his shoulder. The wire shimmered and glowed dully red at times. There was a considerable amount of wire in there.

"Monofilament?" he asked.

"Yeah, nasty stuff. Tungsten ceramic, I think," said Jon.

"Well, that explains what cut my hand."

His right hand felt numb, except for the parts that burned. It was also dripping blood. His vision greyed out for a bit, and he came back to full consciousness to the feel of Jon working on his shoulder while Jason wrapped a bandage around his hand.

"You've lost a lot of blood, Drake," said Jon. "Anything we can do about that?"

"Not really," Drake replied. "My blood is a bit exotic for this place. I could take O negative, but why bother? I'll be fine, if we can get some food and drink."

"I still have some water," Geoffrey said, offering it.

Drake took the bottle gratefully with his bandaged hand. "Thanks." He drank all of the water in one long, slow swig. "And thank you, Jon and Jason, for the bandaging. Sorry I allowed myself to be injured."

"Well, as long as you don't make a habit of it...," Jon teased.

"Can't you just heal it," asked Jason, "like you did my arm?"

Drake shook his head. "Not without calling attention to us that we are ill-prepared for. There are worse than robbers on this planet. I naturally heal quickly; I will be fine."

He closed his eyes and focused on the injury. The wound on his hand was already starting to close up. His shoulder was another matter. The monofilament wire had gotten into the joint and cut the ligaments and cartilage. No wonder it had hurt so badly. He should have kept his powered armor on.

With that thought, he called upon the Instrumentality and restored his armor. The enemy had sent those men; he was sure of it. Their thoughts had not been entirely their own. If the enemy knew he was here, then there was little reason to disguise himself.

"Drake?" Jon sounded worried.

"I'm fine. Just trying to speed up the healing a bit."

"It's starting to get dark, and I don't think we should be outside at night in this part of town."

Drake opened his eyes and stood up. He couldn't do anything with Instrumentality for the blood loss, but he'd managed to knit the cut muscle and ligaments back together with his natural shapeshifting ability. He'd be able to use his arm if he had to. "We should go." His armor carried a reserve of compatible artificial blood; it would start to restore the missing volume.

Jon led them over two streets and then banged on a metal door.

A slot opened in the door. "Fuck off," came a voice from inside.

"The Margrave will want to see me," said Jon. "I'm Livingston."

"Whatever." The slot slammed shut.

It was only a few minutes before the door opened. The doorman was a huge man, as tall as Jon but built like a tank. He carried a bulky rifle casually in one hand. "Your lucky day," the man said. "The Margrave usually just has me maim intruders."

"We're just special that way."

Drake waited for the others to follow Jon in, then moved through the doorway. The doorman gave him an odd look as he noticed Drake's armor. He smiled at the man and wished he hadn't shifted away his fangs.

They made a better impression.

CHAPTER THIRTY-TWO

Jon smoothed the hang of his coat as he paced, waiting for the Margrave to see them.

He hadn't expected Drake to get hurt. He hadn't even truly believed that Drake *could* get hurt. The man seemed liked a force of nature most of the time; Drake certainly liked to project that image.

The other thing that bothered him was that he hadn't seen it coming.

He'd known the gang members were going to jump them. He'd even seen a few versions of it that got violent. None of the probable futures had ended with Drake getting wounded. Jon knew Drake was a problem for his prescience; Drake altered probabilities just by sheer force of will. There was something else at work, though. Something had pushed those men to attack Drake. Something more than just greed or desperation.

All of that came together to unsettle Jon as he and his companions made their way into the lair of the Margrave.

The Margrave wasn't the kind of person Jon would normally do business with. However, he'd delivered a package to the Margrave as part of the job that had brought him to Earth in the first place. Jon would never make the mistake of trusting the Margrave, but he thought they could probably do business.

He hoped so, anyway.

Quiet jazz was playing as a flunky led them into depths of the lair. Sycophants and other, less desirable types hovered around the edges of the ballroom-sized space. The Margrave was seated on a throne made of gold, surrounded by gilded skulls. Jon hadn't asked, but he suspected those were real human skulls. Rumor had it that the skulls were from people who'd tried to cross the Margrave.

Jon believed it.

Nothing happened on Earth that the Margrave didn't have their fingers in.

The Margrave was *aggressively* non-binary. They were dressed in a tasteful, dark burgundy velvet suit. They hardly wore any jewelry and just enough makeup to emphasize their noble features. Their skin was a rich coffee-with-cream, and their hair and eyes were as golden as the skulls around their throne.

No one stepped within three meters of the Margrave without being invited. Jon stopped at the requisite range and waited to be recognized. It didn't take long: Jon did stand out in a crowd.

"Mr. Jon Livingston, in the flesh!" The Margrave's richly textured voice managed to fill the room despite seeming to be unamplified. "Come closer."

Jon nodded to the others, stepped to a place a meter in front of the Margrave, and bowed. "Margrave."

"I have to say, Jon, I never expected to see you here again, and in such delicious company." The Margrave eyed Jon and his companions as one might a meal on a menu. "What can I do for you?"

"Actually, Margrave, I was hoping I might be able to do something for you."

"Hmm. I could think of a few things, but I suspect you mean something less... *intimate.*"

"I find myself without means, and in a position to provide a service."

"Let me consider it," the Margrave purred. "Tell me about your friends, and don't lie to me and say the big, pretty one is a bodyguard. We both know you couldn't afford *his* services. I'm not sure that I could."

☉

Drake stepped next to Jon and bowed. "Margrave, a pleasure. My name is unimportant. My services are not for hire, for as you say, you couldn't afford me. However, my companions and I are in need of local currency, and I suspect you have more need of me than you may know."

"If not for hire, then what?" the Margrave asked. They poured a glass of wine and deliberately sipped it before going on. "Do not mistake my flirting for an invitation. I have no need of one such as you. Not that way."

"A favor, then, for a friend. However, you may not wish to speak of it here, before so many others," said Drake. "You know of what I speak. The whispers in the darkness."

The Margrave stood suddenly. "Stop the music!"

The jazz screeched to a halt. Everyone in the room looked at the Margrave. Drake noted one who slipped from the room at that point. It couldn't be helped, though; the enemy would have spies everywhere.

"Everyone out!" the Margrave shouted. *"Out!"*

Within minutes, the ballroom was empty except for the Margrave, and Drake and his companions.

"You now have my undivided attention," said the Margrave. "We will speak of this now."

Drake stepped forward and poured himself a a glass of the

Margrave's wine. It wasn't bad. "My name is Drake. There is a darkness growing on this planet. I don't know how long it has been here, but it grows and festers, and corrupts everything it touches. I know you've felt it."

"I've felt it, and seen its influence," the Margrave said. "I don't know what it is. I do know that it sits here, in my city, and steals away the hearts of those who belong to me."

"We've identified your problem. Now to ours. My friend's ship is at the Catalina spaceport. He cannot afford his fees. Once I've dealt with your problem, deposit a sum in his account representative of the service I am performing for you."

"What are you doing," Jon asked quietly.

"Dealing with two birds at the same time," said Drake. "Now be silent."

"You look formidable," the Margrave said, "but I have sent mercenaries to deal with this problem before. All I received for my investment were their empty skins, somewhat ill-used. What makes you think you can succeed where they have failed?"

"Trust me when I say that none of them were like me."

"You are offering to hunt down and kill my rival in return for mere credits? It is certainly an intriguing proposition. I'm not sure I believe you can do it. I know that I'll not pay until it is finished. I must say, none of the other mercenaries were as arrogant, that is for sure."

Drake poured more wine.

The Margrave played with their lip while they considered Drake's offer. "Your offer is interesting but boring. Let us make it more interesting."

"What do you have in mind?"

"Motivation," replied the Margrave. "What is a game without a ticking clock? I will give you twenty-four hours to take down my rival. Your friends will be my guests during that time. They will be well-treated as such. However, if you fail, either to achieve your goal or to do so within the time limit, then they become mine. To do with as I please."

Drake swirled the wine in his cup as he considered. "You ask for much, without giving anything in return."

"If you succeed, you will all leave unharmed and much richer. I will even provide the services of one who forges excellent identification, for I suspect you need such. If you fail, I will have some playthings to amuse me for a while. You came to me. Those are my terms. What say you?"

"Drake! Don't you–" Jon began. Drake cut him off with a gesture.

"I would be a poor companion if I did not consult those whose fates hang in the balance."

The Margrave laughed. "You can all walk out now, for all I care. You have come before me as beggars. I offer riches. Discuss it, by all means, but don't take too long, or I may become bored."

Drake gestured for the others to follow him away from the gaudy throne. "You all heard. I am open to suggestions."

"I think you're crazy," Jon replied. "We can find something else."

"You brought us to the Margrave," said Drake. "This suits my own agenda, as well as yours."

"I don't like the idea of being bargained for," Jason said. "If you do this and fail, I will fight."

"I wouldn't make the deal if I thought I could fail," said Drake. "I am unhappy with the terms, as well, but I see little choice. The Margrave no doubt holds much sway in this city. We will not get Jon's ship back without money. I doubt anyone else will hire us, if the Margrave is displeased with us."

"Damn it to hell, Drake," Jon said, pacing. "I don't like this."

"Can I say something?" asked Geoffrey.

"Of course," Drake said. "Your life is also affected by this."

"I trust you, Drake. Just don't fail, okay?"

"Is this the will of all of you?"

They nodded hesitantly.

"Jon, if I fall, it will be up to you to get the others to safety," said Drake.

"I'm aware of that."

Drake walked back to the Margrave. "We have a deal," he said. "I suggest that you don't try to cheat me. You are a far less formidable enemy than the one I seek. Know that I am not a forgiving man."

"Splendid!" The Margrave clapped their hands. Drake could tell that the Margrave took his warnings to heart, even if they didn't show it. The would-be prince was afraid of him; Drake could hear their heart racing. "If you succeed, then we will all be richer. If you fail, I will have lost nothing and gained some amusements."

Drake nodded. "Now, tell me what you know of our enemy, so that I may effectively hunt them within the allotted time. The clock will start when I leave here, not before."

CHAPTER THIRTY-THREE

Drake left the warehouse an hour later.

He commanded his helmet to fold over his head, and felt himself relax back into his trueform. It was important to him to hunt his enemy completely as himself; he didn't want to hunt them as a monster, or even as a human.

The chronometer in his helmet display counted down the hours and minutes remaining until the Margrave's deal was forfeit. Drake didn't worry too much about the time. If he couldn't hunt down and kill an Ancient Enemy within the allotted time, it would be because he'd been killed by it. His friends would have to find their own way to escape whatever horrors the Margrave had planned.

Drake apported to the top of a nearby building and looked across the city. The Margrave had precious little actual information about the enemy Drake sought. The Margrave knew that someone had moved into the city in the past year, and twisted the loyalty of one of the criminal organizations. The gangs, normally under tight control, had become violent and vicious. Exotic drugs had flooded the city, drugs that drove people mad in fits of ecstasy and agony.

Drake lowered his mental shields. He was immediately assaulted by mental and emotional pressure from the millions of desperate people in the city. There was a darkness present here. He'd felt it before. It felt like a stain in his mind. He knew where the enemy was. He raised his mental defenses and took a few minutes to calm his mind.

It was difficult to open oneself up to that kind of onslaught. It had needed to be done, though. The Ancient Enemy he sought was on a decaying oceanic freighter in the bay. It directed the minions under its control from there. Drake didn't know what kind of criminal organization it had created, or more likely taken over. That didn't matter.

Drake was going to hunt it down and kill it, no matter what.

He apported from rooftop to rooftop, closing in on his quarry. On a high building overlooking the bay, he pulled his sword Maegril from the folded space where he stored it. The sword was the only weapon he needed against his Ancient Enemy. It would work well enough against the normal humans, as well. Not to mention his pistol. No, he wasn't worried.

The freighter was docked along a pier not far from him.

Drake could see guards on the decks and amongst the cargo containers on the pier. A sniper was positioned in a crane to the east of the ship. Drake had to assume there were others. It was unlikely anyone had weapons that could penetrate his armor. However, he didn't want the man there to sound the alarm too soon, either.

He wished he had all of the resources he usually had available. He hadn't wanted to bring everything with him, though, as he wasn't certain that this Realm wasn't being watched by those from the North. Drake had machines and resources dating back to before the war, and he didn't want anyone to know that, if he could help it.

A quick apport positioned him at the base of the crane. He climbed swiftly and tirelessly. Drake sensed the thoughts of the guard: He was bored with his duty. He'd been there for hours, and nothing had happened. The guards were expecting Drake to appear.

That made a certain amount of sense. Drake had known the enemy sent the robber in the alley earlier. It made sense that the enemy would be expecting retribution, knowing its minions had failed in their task.

Drake shuddered a little at just how close the assassination attempt had come to succeeding. He'd been sloppy and arrogant. A little higher, and the monofilament would have struck his neck or head. He'd have died then, the victim of some nameless gang member.

It was almost humiliating.

Well, Drake would be more careful now. He was wearing his armor and would continue to do so. If the locals had never seen anything like it, so be it. They would get over it, or he would make them. It wasn't hard to cloud the minds of ordinary humans.

The guard moved away from the door, and Drake attacked. He swung into the small cabin, catching the man by the back of the head and snapping his neck. The guard died instantly, without a sound.

Drake examined the guard's sniper rifle. It was large-bore, with an explosive tip on the bullet. He crushed the receiver in one fist while looking over the rest of the guarded area. The rifle hadn't been too much of a threat, although theoretically it could have penetrated the lighter powered armor he now wore. He was surprised to see a weapon so advanced in this Earth Realm. It may have indicated an asymmetric development of weapons.

The crane was positioned over the ship. It was almost too convenient. It was almost certainly a trap. The Ancient Enemy were often canny foes, but usually cowardly. The enemy would avoid a fight if it could. Drake didn't intend to allow it to do so.

Trap or not, the crane was the faster way onto the ship.

A frontal assault might allow the enemy time to escape. On the other hand, it might be somewhat unexpected, too. Drake smiled as he thought about that. There was really no place the enemy could run that Drake couldn't follow. For that matter, if it apported away, Drake could always grab the monster with an extension of the Instrumentality and jerk it back to this Realm. Yes, that would be best.

Drake set his display to track the positions of the guards, and apported down to the dock. He quietly drew Maegril and moved through the maze of containers. Drake timed things to wait for a guard to pass his position and then drove his sword into the back of the guard's head.

The guard died instantly, limbs feebly twitching. Drake kept Maegril from dissolving the dead woman, as he needed bodies for the Margrave. A clean battlefield told no tales.

Three more guards died before any of them realized something was happening. Drake strode forward then, heedless of the bullets that ricocheted from his armor. Anyone who got in his way got the sword; the ones farther away were quickly silenced with a few of the needles from his pistol.

The subsonic hypercarbon needles were heavy, barbed, and brittle. They tended to shatter as they ripped through flesh. It wasn't an easy death, but it was quick. The guards hit by those needles bled out in moments.

Drake didn't enjoy killing people. He did enjoy the thrill of battle. It was only slightly tempered by the inability of the fools to hurt him. They could have surrendered or run; they did not. Drake had no doubt that the Ancient Enemy would not be as easy to kill.

Those ancient ones were of his people, but fallen and corrupted by darkness. They were evil. Some were mindless beasts, but many knew exactly what horrors they inflicted. They fed on the pain and suffering of others. They were abominations that had be hunted down and destroyed.

The guards on the ship hardly slowed Drake. Barrels of oil exploded under stray shots and ricochets off the guards' weapons. The guards didn't seem to care, and Drake suspected they were under direct control of the enemy he was seeking. He could sense the presence of the Ancient Enemy nearby. It wasn't trying to run. That meant it wasn't afraid of him. Either it didn't know who he was, or it was a very powerful one.

The deck ahead of him suddenly bulged upward and exploded. Out of the hole rose a creature that was the stuff of nightmare. The Ancient Enemy was gargantuan – bigger than Drake had expected, and almost the largest he'd ever faced. Not that size was a measure of power. The thing wore a twisted form that seemed be a mass of tentacles the length of semi-trucks. Teeth gnashed in innumerable mouths along the tentacles. Eyes like fiery coals burned near the core. A dozen razor-edged beaks circled the stalk.

Drake had to give it credit for originality. If that wasn't the being's trueform, it was certainly imaginative. Rarely did a shapeshifter choose a body so huge. It required extra mass, gained either from living tissue or from the immense energy of the Instrumentality. Drake didn't think it had access to the Instrumentality. He hoped not, at least.

Maegril yearned to taste it, but Drake had other plans. He needed the thing alive for a while. The Margrave wouldn't simply take Drake's word that he'd destroyed the enemy. Drake would need to provide proof that the thing was dead. A difficult proposition, since the Ancient Enemy tended to dissolve rapidly within their own entropic fields.

Drake emptied his pistol into its eyes as he darted under the lashing tentacles.

It screamed with a thousand voices, but if it had wanted to run, it should have done so before Drake got to it. A tentacle grasped him and dragged him under the bulk of the thing. Teeth ground against his armor gratingly. His coat was shredded and dissolved in the powerful acids the mouths excreted, but his armor was unharmed.

Drake thrust Maegril into the closest mouth and tore a long gash through the tentacle that held him. The Ancient Enemy screamed again. The scream was psionic as well as audible. The few surviving guards on the ship fell to the deck, bleeding from eyes and ears. Drake was flung into the air as the tentacle spasmed from his attacks.

He curled in midair and came down hard near the center of the thing. Black entropic fire enveloped him, and white flames burst from his own body, as they did sometimes when he was fighting the Ancient Enemy. The white fire shielded him from the black; otherwise, he would have been consumed by it, despite his armor. His powered fist punched through an eye, and Drake used that to gain enough purchase to fling himself upward along the monster's bulky central stalk. At this point, the Ancient Enemy probably regretted staying to fight. Having been wounded with the white flames, it was bound to its energized form.

Drake clung to it as it tried to buck him off. He was close to where it stored its brain, and it was beginning to understand just whom it had chosen to fight. After untold millennia, the Ancient Enemy knew it was facing imminent death. Drake called on the Instrumentality and visualized the center of the Margrave's ballroom.

A rain of rainbows later, they exploded into the midst of the screaming crowd. Drake drove Maegril down into the thing's brain and unleashed the sword's full fury of annihilation into that dread mass. Drake slid down the side, Maegril still deep within it, opening a huge slash in the side of the dying creature. Nameless organs and rank fluids spilled out onto the ballroom floor, along with a dozen or so partially digested corpses.

Drake could still feel the power of the Instrumentality surging through him, and used it clean the ichor and other unspeakable fluids from his armor and sword. He then formed himself another coat, heedless of who might be looking on. Maegril, he kept in his hand.

His friends were near the throne of the Margrave, who appeared stunned. They all looked a little ill, and Drake couldn't blame them. The first glimpse of the Ancient Enemy was rarely settling.

CHAPTER THIRTY-FOUR

Jon had trouble fighting down his nausea.

The miasma rising from the rapidly decaying *thing* was simply the worst odor he'd ever smelled. When Drake proposed his deal with the Margrave, Jon thought he was going to fight some crime boss. Drake had mentioned the Ancient Enemy a few times, but Jon didn't really understand what was meant until he saw what Drake had ridden into the Margrave's ballroom.

Drake was glowing, covered in white flames. Jon didn't know how Drake was producing the energy. The light cast twisted and disturbing shadows across the steaming carcass of the thing he'd brought here.

The apport – Jon had no idea how Drake managed that – had blasted everyone out of the way of the thing. Still, a few of the guards who'd rushed forward had been crushed under the falling tentacles. One guard had been caught in a blast of highly acidic bile and was still screaming as he dissolved.

Drake walked into range of the Margrave without waiting for permission. Jon very much doubted anyone would have tried to stop him. Drake was wearing a helmet, which suddenly folded back until it was gone from his head, and he had reverted to his trueform. Jon didn't think anyone would notice or care; everyone was too much in shock. The flames seemed to fade as Drake caught his breath.

"Your enemy, Margrave, as promised," Drake said with a mocking bow. "Well within the agreed-upon time, I might add."

"What…?" The Margrave gestured feebly at the decaying thing taking up the center of the ballroom. "How?"

"When we spoke before, you indicated that you knew you couldn't afford me, and I agreed. This is what was guiding your rival organization from the freighter in the bay. Most of that organization is dead, too – you're welcome."

"What is it?" the Margrave managed to say. "What are *you*?"

"It's an alien, of course. I'm afraid this kind tend to rot rapidly in your atmosphere, so there won't be much left soon except the mess. As for me, I am tired and out of patience. Will you honor your bargain?"

The Margrave swallowed fearfully. "Of course." They gestured at Jon. "Come."

Jon stepped up to the Margrave, who produced a credit wand. The Margrave held their hand over it, and Jon was pleased to see a shocking amount appear on the wand. It was certainly enough to keep him in operation for quite a few years. The Margrave handed the wand over without any hesitation.

"Jon, are you satisfied with the amount?" asked Drake.

Drake still had his sword out.

"Very satisfied, Drake. The Margrave has more than fulfilled their bargain."

"Very well." Drake sheathed his sword without looking. "We'll need the promised identification papers and transport to Catalina Island."

The Margrave gestured, and a terrified little man ran up, holding a thick sheaf of papers and cards. He almost spilled the

IDs but managed at the last moment to get them under control before handing the whole stack to Jon.

Jon flicked through the papers. They seemed authentic and well done. He nodded to Drake.

"I thank you, Margrave, for your hospitality," Drake said with only a trace of irony. "Alas, we must now take our leave of you."

"I have several yachts in the harbor," said the Margrave. "Berth seventy, Venice Beach. One of them might be more discreet than a shuttle."

Drake bowed and gestured to his companions to follow him.

They all gave wide berth to the rotting thing in the center of the ballroom. Jon was glad when they got outside, and he was able to breathe in the cleaner sea air. Geoffrey gasped as if he'd been holding his breath.

"Drake, what was that thing?" Jason asked.

"One of the Ancient Enemy I have spoken of before," Drake replied. He was leading them through the maze of streets to the harbor.

"That… thing was one of your people?"

Jon hadn't considered that.

Drake paused and sighed. "I'm not sure, to be honest. It may once have been, long ago. I don't know. I've fought so many of them, in so many forms, I couldn't say."

"You're looking like yourself again," said Jason. "Thought you should know."

Drake smiled. "I refuse to hunt the enemy in disguise. I doubt anyone noticed back there. Even if they did, I am not that strange. Some humans have pointed ears."

"Not like yours," Geoffrey blurted. "Sorry."

Drake laughed. "Not at all, Geoffrey. I am not human, nor do I wish to be mistaken for one. If we are around others, I'll wear my helmet if need be."

"I think that would be fine, Drake," said Jon. "Now, I

suppose we just have to figure out how to get to the island. I think our paperwork would hold up on a shuttle."

"I thought the yacht sounded good," Drake said.

"Do you know how to sail?" asked Jon. "Because I don't. Not on an ocean, anyway."

"I do. With minimal, unskilled assistance, I can get us to the island."

"I've sailed," Jason said. "I can help."

Drake nodded. "Then we should get going. It will take a while to sail to Catalina."

☉

Jason was still somewhat in shock from what he'd seen.

He suspected Geoffrey and Jon were, as well. They didn't talk as they followed Drake down to the harbor. In the distance, Jason could see a freighter burning. He assumed that was where Drake had fought the creature and its minions.

Venice Beach wasn't in great shape. Garbage had been piled high by the tide, and dead fish and seaweed covered the lower area down to the waterline. Just south of the beach were smaller piers where yachts were moored. The three sailboats were smaller than Jason expected. He'd figured the Margrave would have huge yachts.

Drake selected a medium-sized sailboat, about forty feet long. She was a sturdy wooden vessel with the name *Dragonfly* painted in blue across her stern. Jason thought she'd make good speed.

The sailboat wasn't secured with anything other her anchor and a stern line. Jason was a little surprised, although he supposed no one was likely to try to steal a boat from the Margrave. That strange person didn't seem like someone to cross. Fortunately, the Margrave had been happy to give them a boat. They had probably just wanted Drake to go as far away as possible.

Drake moved confidently around the boat, only asking Jason to cast off the stern line while he used the boat hook to push off the pier. Jason thought they might need a rowboat to tow the yacht out of the inlet, but Drake had a deft hand and took her out under full sail. Jason was impressed; he'd never have guessed that Drake would be a master sailor.

Jon had helped Geoffrey get settled with a life-vest and belted into a seat. Then Jon sat next to him, looking a little ill. It had been a long time since Jason had been at sea, and he was enjoying himself. The salt wind off the ocean was brisk but clean. It washed away the last of the remembered horrors from his nose.

Seagulls followed them, crying shrilly. The setting sun cast a fierce red glow over Drake's hair and features as he stood at the helm. Jason thought Drake had a longing expression on his face as he looked west. Drake kept them along the coastline while they still had light, and then shifted them gradually more west of south as night fell.

"Will you be able to navigate without the stars?" Jason asked him.

"Catalina is the only island off the coast in this direction. I can sense the mass of the island to the southwest. We're making good way; we should see the lights in about six or seven hours. Then I can correct, if we need to. We'll be fine."

Jason nodded. If Drake said he could do it, he wasn't going to argue. He'd already seen Drake do the impossible. What was sailing a boat in the dark, next to slaying an eldritch horror?

"Are you doing okay, Jason?" Drake asked quietly.

"I'm doing surprisingly well," Jason answered. "Maybe I'm still in shock."

"One's first sight of an Ancient Enemy can be disconcerting."

"There's an understatement." Jason sighed. "You fight

things like that often?"

"First time for one like that," said Drake. "They have many different forms."

"What are the worst?"

"The ones that look human. They are ancient and evil, and they know exactly what they're doing. They always want to talk, to try to seduce you over to the darkness. Those are the worst."

"Are there many of them?" Jason asked, and then laughed to relieve his tension. "Does that even have meaning when we're talking about multiple universes?"

Drake smiled sadly. "Yeah, there are a lot of them. Some places are infested with many of the Ancient Enemy. I have an army for a reason."

Jason shuddered. "I can't imagine. Don't really *want* to imagine it."

"You guys sound like you're having a fun conversation," said Jon as he joined them. "Geoffrey fell asleep, so I figured I'd come listen closer. How many of them are *here*, Drake? Do you know?"

"Sorry," Drake said, "I can't know that. It was the only one I felt close to us here on Earth. I can usually sense the Ancient Enemy if I'm within a few thousand kilometers of them."

"How?" asked Jason.

"I'm just sensitive, I suppose."

Jason didn't think Drake was telling the whole truth, but he was willing to cut him some slack. Drake had just been through what must have been an epic battle.

"How are your shoulder and hand, Drake?" Jon asked.

Jason had forgotten Drake had been injured only a few hours before.

"Well enough," Drake replied. "My hand feels fine. My shoulder still hurts, but I may have reopened the wound during the fight. I wasn't thinking about it."

"You heal remarkably quickly," said Jon.

"You assume I do so naturally. I do heal rapidly, but not *that* rapidly."

"Magic?" Jason asked, teasing.

"Technology," said Drake. "My blood is full of technology to help me heal. My powered armor manufactures blood to replace the lost circulatory volume. The medical suite also injected me with some painkillers. Those helped a lot."

"More mysteries," Jon said. "Your tech is extremely advanced. Somehow, I don't think most of your people have access to that."

"I certainly hope not," said Drake. "One day, I'll tell you all the tale of how I came to have it, but now is not the time. Jason, do you mind tightening the jib? I think it's a bit loose."

"If I can see it."

"Then come and take the helm, and I'll go forward and take care of it."

Jason felt Drake take his hands and place them where he wanted them. Drake's hands were still in armor. It felt odd to feel the cool metal and know he was safe.

"Just hold this course. I'll be back in a moment," said Drake.

Jason heard Jon sigh next to him. "I wish I could see the stars," Jon said.

"We'll be at Catalina soon. Then we can get your ship. I have to admit I'm excited. I've never been in space."

"Yeah, I would guess not," said Jon. "Want to take bets about whether Drake has?"

"I think we'd lose if we bet against it," Jason said. "He knows too much about everything. I know he's old, but damn. He's really lived."

"That's what I was thinking."

They heard the deck boards creak as Drake move quietly back to the helm. "Don't make any bets," Drake said. "I don't talk about space, but yes, I've been there."

"You know, it really surprised me when Erin said that she

had," said Jon.

"Her people are not from an Earth Realm," Drake said. "They are older, and settled other star systems. You two should get some rest while you can. We're making good time."

"The starport is on the southern end of the island," Jon said, "just north of Avalon."

"We should be there in four hours or so," said Drake. "Rest. I've got this."

Jason decided he'd stay awake anyway. There was just enough light to see the waves and the open ocean. It was rest enough to know they were safe, at least for a while.

CHAPTER THIRTY-FIVE

Geoffrey had never been on a sailboat before, and he wasn't entirely certain that he liked it.

The boats he'd been on before were lake fishing boats, and a river ferry once, which didn't really count. He hadn't thought that he was prone to motion sickness. Of course, it could have had more to do with anxiety over what he'd seen in the last few hours. Despite everything he'd seen since he left home, he hadn't actually believed that monsters were real.

At least he hadn't vomited; he didn't have anything in his stomach to vomit. Geoffrey thought that he'd eaten that morning, however long ago that had been, but he couldn't remember. He wasn't used to being hungry. Growing up in the country, there was always something to eat, even if it was just the soup that was always on the stove.

Geoffrey unbuckled his seatbelt and carefully stood. The swaying deck made him wish for solid land, but it wasn't too bad. He made his way over to the others by the wheel. There were lights ahead, through the mist and fog.

"How are you doing, Geoffrey?" asked Jason.

"Hanging in there," he replied. "Hoping those lights mean

we'll be on land soon."

"Catalina Island," Jon said. "That's Avalon. The–"

Jon was interrupted by a loud roar and a bright light that ascended into the dark, stormy sky.

"The spaceport is just north of there," Jon finished.

Geoffrey watched in awe as the spaceship blasted off. He'd always wanted to see a launch in person. It had just never worked out. He could feel the sound of the rocket deep in his chest.

"Jason, take the helm," said Drake. "Just bring us into the end of the docks. I'll slow us, and guide us in with the sheet."

Jason stepped up and took the wheel, and Drake leapt forward to grab one of the lines from the sail. With Jason steering the rudder, and Drake shifting the sails, they slide directly into a berth with only the very slightest bump as they stopped against the pier. Drake leapt to the dock with a line and held the boat steady while they all disembarked.

Geoffrey was just happy to be back on something that didn't sway under him, although his inner ear hadn't gotten the memo yet. There were other boats at the dock, but he didn't see other people.

Drake patted the bow of the ship affectionately.

"Goodbye, *Dragonfly*," he said, tossing the rope back onto the deck.

The ship backed away from the dock and sailed off into the darkness.

"What did you do?" asked Jon.

"I just summoned a wind-daemon to return the yacht to its berth. She's a good ship," Drake said. "I thought maybe the Margrave would want her back."

Geoffrey wasn't surprised. Drake could be strangely sentimental. He also had a complex code of honor, however odd that might seem to Geoffrey's twenty-first-century mind. He wasn't even surprised about the daemon. Drake seemed like the kind of guy who would know a lot of daemons.

They walked down the pier toward the main part of the harbor. A faded sign with peeling paint welcomed them to the island. Seagulls swooped around them. Geoffrey could hear music from someplace. The air was cold and damp, but Geoffrey didn't mind. The pier also had a very familiar feel to it, like the Covington, Kentucky riverfront after dark.

"The spaceport is just a few kilometers to the north," Jon said. He sounded eager to get back to his ship. Geoffrey figured it was kind of like home for him.

"I think we should stop for some food first," said Drake. "After what has happened today, I need a drink."

Geoffrey's stomach growled loudly at the thought of food.

Drake laughed. "Come on, before Geoffrey wastes away."

Geoffrey privately thought that Jon was the one they should be worried about. The man looked as if he was about to blow away. He'd be invisible if he turned sideways. Geoffrey had never seen Jon eat more than a few bites of food.

It had to be past the middle of the night. Geoffrey had no idea what the actual time was, but apparently no one cared on the island. Near the harbor were several bars from which light, music, and voices spilled out. Drake picked one that was playing something that sounded like rock music. Geoffrey recognized a few of the tunes, if not the singers, and was happy Drake hadn't picked the one playing country across the street. One up the street looked a little nicer, but it was playing jazz, and after their encounter with the Margrave, no one wanted to hear that.

They found a corner table, and a sturdy waitress walked over to take their drink orders. Geoffrey had tried to order a Coke, but she'd laughed so hard that he'd just ordered a beer. She dropped stained menus onto the table for them to look over and left. Geoffrey was suddenly self-conscious. He didn't have any money of his own, and everything on the menu was really expensive.

"Don't worry about money, Geoffrey," Jon said. "Drake earned a nice amount that would buy meals here for us all for the next few decades, at the least."

"I was just going to get a burger, but it's, like, two hundred credits," said Geoffrey. "I don't even know how much a credit's worth."

"Vat beef is more expensive than fish," Jon agreed, "but get whatever you want. Trust me; we have enough to cover it."

"Vat beef?" asked Jason.

"Bovine muscle tissue grown in a lab," Jon said. "Why?"

"We usually buy free-range," said Jason. "I guess Earth can't really support herds of cows anymore, though."

"Yeah, no one eats actual animals anymore," Jon said. He sounded a little disgusted. "It's inhumane, and terrible for the environment."

"Does it taste the same?" asked Geoffrey.

"How would I even know that?"

Geoffrey decided that *had* been a dumb question. He ordered the burger anyway. If he and his companions were going to be in this place for a while, he might as well get used to the food. Drake ordered steak and eggs; the others ordered fish.

He was a little hesitant when the food arrived, but the burger smelled good. He tried it and decided he couldn't really tell a difference. It was better than a fast-food burger. The beer was draft, strong and amber-colored. It went well with the food.

"Well, Jon, where to now?" asked Drake.

"You mean after we get my ship back?"

Drake nodded.

"I'm not sure. I have a vague idea, but I'm not sure how to follow it. You see, I think you asking about my parentage is barking up the wrong tree, so to speak."

"What do you mean?"

Jon rubbed his face. He looked tired. "I don't know yet. Let's get to my ship, and maybe I'll have more answers. I'd rather not talk here." Jon waved over the waitress and settled up the account. "We good to go?"

They all stood.

Geoffrey felt better with some food in him, although he could have used another beer. At this point, he what he wanted most was a shower and some sleep. The next time he went on an adventure, he needed to remember to pack deodorant and a toothbrush.

Outside, Jon waved down the driver of a vehicle looking like a long golf cart that hovered. They climbed into the seats, and the driver drove them north. The sun was just peeking over the horizon when they arrived at the port facilities.

Two bored-looking guards, or maybe soldiers, checked their papers and then waved them through. It wasn't particularly crowded inside. A small group of people who looked like tourists were waiting to go through a gate. It reminded Geoffrey of a small airport.

"Jon Livingston!" a heavyset man in a uniform called to them. "I thought you were dead."

"People have thought that before," said Jon.

"I was getting ready to auction off that weird ship of yours. Your port fees were getting outrageous."

"Well, port master, I can pay them now."

The man looked embarrassed. "They've been settled."

"Oh?"

"The Margrave called up a few hours ago and cleared your debts," said the port master. "Had a message for you, too."

"What was that?"

"The Margrave said to tell you to 'get the hell off the planet and not come back!'" The port master seemed to think that was really funny. He was still chuckling when he unlocked the gate for them. "Docking clamps are removed. Just clear your takeoff with the tower."

"I'll have an expedited takeoff, then?" Jon said.

"I don't know what you did, but no one is going to slow you down, yeah."

Jon tapped the credit stick to the back of the man's hand and then went through the gate. Geoffrey assumed Jon had given the man a tip. That seemed strange to him. Why tip the guy who was being an ass?

The boarding passage was fairly normal looking, a long tunnel that ended at a short staircase. The stairs were a little rickety. There, Geoffrey got his first glimpse of Jon's ship though the open hatch.

It didn't disappoint.

The starship was as long as a large passenger plane, but wider and delta-winged. The hull was a dull bronze. Massive engines faced rear. It reminded Geoffrey a little of a Concord supersonic jet he'd seen once on television. The wings were folded down on the ends; he could see seams – he suspected that they moved. Massive clamps were retracted but visible nearby.

Jon ran his hand lovingly over the hull. He whispered something Geoffrey didn't understand. It wasn't in English or any language he recognized.

"Graceful," said Drake. "What's her name?"

"The *Chwyldro*," Jon replied.

Drake nodded.

Geoffrey wondered what the name meant, but he didn't ask. He was suddenly exhausted. He just wanted to sleep for a month. Jason looked about how he felt.

"How are you holding up, Jason?" he asked.

Jason laughed. "I keep thinking things can't get any weirder, and now I'm about to board a spaceship."

"Yeah, what the fuck, right?"

"Exactly."

Jon disappeared, and then a ramp unfolded from the back

of the ship. Jon was standing inside. The inside was painted neutral grey, and Geoffrey thought it might be a cargo area. There were a few crates lashed down with ratcheting nylon straps, and two spacesuits were on a rack by the forward doorway. Jon waved them in and turned to walk deeper into the ship.

The ship was smaller inside than Geoffrey had imagined. The main cabin was off-white, with a half-dozen strange-looking recliners. There weren't any windows. Six doorways led off the sides of that cabin: two forward and two aft, one to what Geoffrey assumed was the bridge, and the one they'd entered by.

"Sorry, my ship isn't really meant for a horde of passengers," said Jon. He gestured to the right. "There are three cabins to starboard – pick any you want. They aren't for much more than sleeping and storage. Galley is forward from there. Each cabin has a small toilet, but the only showers are forward to port. Please stow loose items. The inertial compensators have been acting up. I'll try to keep internal forces under ten gees during takeoff, but no promises."

Geoffrey tried the sliding door to the right. It opened into a narrow hallway. He opened the first door. The cabin was not much bigger than a closet. The bunk folded down and had a seatbelt. A place marked *toilet* opened when he pressed the button. It held a bidet that folded down. There were storage cabinets in the walls.

Geoffrey stowed his backpack and knife in a locker and made sure the door was secure. He used the toilet and then wondered what he was supposed to do. He didn't think the bunk looked right for a takeoff, so he went back out to the main area.

Jon was waiting there. The others came in just after Geoffrey. "All stowed?" Jon asked.

"We're good," said Jason.

Geoffrey nodded.

Drake hadn't had a backpack to stow. Or maybe he did but it had been tucked away in that pocket space he used to hold his swords. Drake was too secretive to let them know.

"Just grab an acceleration couch and strap in. I need to get to the bridge and do a preflight, and then we can get off this rock."

"Is there a television or something?" asked Geoffrey. "Any way that we can watch? I've never been to space."

Jon grinned and touched a panel on each wall. Suddenly, the walls lit up with the view outside. "How's that?" The panels showed a dark hanger.

"Perfect," said Jason.

Geoffrey nodded.

"Okay. I'll leave the intercom on, so just call out if you need anything." Jon left through the forward door, which closed and locked behind him.

Geoffrey settled into an acceleration couch, which was strangely comfortable. He watched the screen eagerly. This was finally an adventure he'd dreamed about.

CHAPTER THIRTY-SIX

Jason gingerly snapped the buckles into place, unsure what metal they were made of. The chair – or couch or whatever it was – shaped itself to fit him. He could look at the wall display without having to turn his head.

He felt a vibration roll through the ship and figured Jon had started the engines. Drake looked neutral, and Geoffrey looked excited. Jason wasn't sure how he felt. He was excited but also scared. He was aware, too, here in this enclosed space, that he really needed a shower. They all did.

Jon's voice came from overhead. "I've got clearance from the tower. Last chance if anybody wants off."

"I think we're good, Jon," said Drake.

"Okay. Don't say I didn't warn you."

Jason could feel motion now. There was a growing sensation of pulling to the rear as the ship accelerated. He could see that Jon was taxiing down a runway, like a plane. He wondered whether the ship always had to do that, or whether it could take off directly.

The pressure continued to build as the ship tilted up and left the ground. There was none of the noise of air screaming by or the roar of engines, as there would be on a jet. Jason sank deeper into the acceleration couch. The pressure was getting painful, and his vision started to blur. Geoffrey's head was lolling; Jason thought he might have passed out. He couldn't see Drake without turning his head, and he didn't want to do that.

On the screen, the grey clouds suddenly parted, and they soared above them. Jason could see the curve of the Earth and the thin envelope of atmosphere. The sun lit the clouds, and Jason was almost overcome with the beauty of it all.

The acceleration pressure eased off, but Jason could see the Earth still falling away from them on the screen. They had to be moving *fast*, for it to be that obvious. If there were other ships in orbit, he couldn't see them. The ship banked, and then there was nothing on the screen but distant stars.

Jon came back into the room and checked on Geoffrey. He pressed a place on the arm of the chair, and a display popped out. Jason couldn't see what was on it.

"Is he okay?" Jason asked.

"Yeah, just passed out from the g-forces," said Jon. "He'll be all right. His vitals are good. He's sleeping now."

"Let him sleep," Drake said. "We should talk."

Jon sighed and pressed a place on one the couches that made it fold into an easy chair. He sat down and stretched. Jason found the button on his own chair and did the same.

"I believe you were going to talk to us about your parentage," said Drake.

"Yeah, not a great subject," said Jon, "but I suppose it has to be dealt with. Listen, I *know* my mother wasn't from the North. She had brothers and sisters there on Rhyddid. She looked like them."

"But you still insist there was no father?" said Drake.

"I know there wasn't," Jon said. "I just can't prove it. The clinic was on Rhyddid, and I can't go there. However, I think something else may be going on."

"Please elaborate."

"I couldn't always apport."

"Very few people can," Drake replied.

"That's just the thing: I know a couple of other pilots who can do it, too. Or I did, anyway. You see, this ship is the key, I think."

"What do you mean?"

"Most starships in this Realm use jumpgates," said Jon.

"I think you mentioned that before," Drake replied.

"A few of the larger military ships can jump without a gate, but they have huge quantum computers devoted to navigation. The only other ships that can jump without a gate are like this one."

Drake's eyes flicked over Jon. "You're the computer for the jump."

"I couldn't apport before I was a part of the program that made us – maybe you would say *remade* us. There were sixty-six pilot candidates, from three star systems that opposed the expansion of the Federated Alliance, the government in this system. The Alliance is based out of Centauri. They've been aggressively expanding since before I was born."

"You said there were sixty-six pilot candidates," said Drake. "Could all of them apport after whatever was done?"

"No. Most died. Only a dozen pilots survived. All of us could pilot the jumpships, but three of us developed the ability to jump *without* the ship. We thought it was a side effect of how we were altered."

"And how were you altered?"

"Gene therapies and surgery," Jon said. He pushed up his sleeves so they could see the ports in his arms. He then showed them the jack at the base of his skull. "My nervous system was partially reworked to be hyperconductive. I interface directly with my ship to fly it. It becomes a part of me, and me of it."

"And the gene therapy?" asked Drake.

"We were told it was to make us heal faster, give us more endurance, etc. Mostly it was supposed to allow us to live through the surgeries. More than half of the candidates died from the gene therapy. It didn't work right. The rest who died, died while being reworked. Their bodies couldn't accept the modified nervous system."

"It seems that maybe we should focus on that, then. You said two others developed the ability to apport?"

Jon nodded. "When I jacked into my ship, I downloaded messages. One was from Terek, one of the other pilots who could apport. He said he was headed to Earth. He'd received a message from some people who said they knew where I was. I can only assume they did to him what they did to me. I had two other messages from other pilots who were worried that the three of us had disappeared. They thought our disappearance might have been because of Alliance security forces."

"Whoever took you certainly would have tried with the other two, as well," Drake said. "That is a lot to process. I've never heard of anything like it, and yet I can see how it could work."

"I'm not following," said Jason. "How *what* would work?"

"It would appear as if Jon isn't related to me, after all," Drake said. "His DNA was altered to make it seem as if he is. To be able to join with the Cynosure…" Drake shook his head. "I don't know why anyone would do it, but they have to be stopped."

"So you think I was altered to appear to be the son of someone up North?" Jon asked.

"Don't you?"

"I don't understand why."

"That is what we need to discover," Drake replied. "Why would anyone want a person who wasn't a part of the family to—?"

"What?"

"You don't *seem* to be related to them. You *are* a part of that family," Drake said. "You are related to them, *now.*"

"But why try to kill me as soon as they confirmed it?"

"I don't know. First, we need to know why they did it. It may even be more important than how they did it."

Jon shook his head. "Without going and asking them, I can't think of any way of getting that answer."

"Perhaps the scientists who altered you know something."

"Maybe. We'd have to try to track them down. The project was a joint effort of three star systems. My own system has since fallen to the Alliance, but when I left, the other two were still holding on. To be honest, I was hoping for allies to turn the tide of war."

"I didn't realize you were at war," said Drake.

"Well, maybe *war* is a strong term for it. These jumpships were modified scoutships, with jump engines from old probes repurposed into them. They're the smallest jump-capable vessels. We thought the Alliance would bring a fleet into our system; instead, they used infiltrators to overthrow the government. Last I heard, the planet was still seething with revolution. Governments hold for a few months and then fall again."

"Sounds like the French Revolution," said Jason. "Revolutionaries like to take out the people in power, and then they *are* the people in power and get taken out by other revolutionaries."

Jon nodded. "Sounds about right. The other two systems are under economic pressure to join the Alliance. Their jumpgates are inactive. The other jump pilots and I have been trying to take them medical supplies. Not a lot of money in that."

"I assume the Alliance doesn't know you have jumpships," said Drake.

"Oh, they do. They just don't care. We aren't making that much of a difference."

"So why do they want your system?" Drake asked.

"Strategic value. They murdered my entire family just to have unfettered access to the jumpgate, which gives them access to the other two systems. Only way in or out, without a jumpship."

Drake shook his head. "Wasteful. Why the jumpgates?"

"Why?" Jon shook his head. "Some ancient alien race left them scattered around. Might as well use them."

"It makes Alliance systems too vulnerable. Have you considered destroying the gates?"

"No, we haven't," said Jon. "Too many people rely on those gates. Many worlds can't support themselves without food shipments. We'd be condemning billions to a slow death."

Drake shrugged. "It might get the Alliance to back off."

"No, we won't do it. _I_ won't do it."

"It was just a thought." Drake smiled. "So, back to the topic at hand. How do we find the scientists from the original project?"

"I might know someone who can help. They're on Masir, one of the worlds involved in all this. We'll have to make a few jumps. It will take a while to get there."

"The scientists are our best lead," said Drake.

"All right, then I'll start making the calculations," Jon said.

"Can I take a shower?" Jason asked. "A change of clothes would be good, as well, if it isn't too much bother."

CHAPTER THIRTY-SEVEN

Geoffrey was annoyed and disappointed that he'd passed out during the launch; he'd wanted to see Earth from orbit. At least was able to take a shower when he woke up. Jason had found the laundry facility and tossed their old, smelly clothes into a washer. The clean jumpsuit he wore now was too long for him, but he didn't care. The jumpsuit didn't smell as if something had died in it, namely him.

Drake had conjured deodorant from someplace. Geoffrey didn't recognize the brand, or the language of the writing, for that matter. He didn't care, though. It worked, and it didn't smell weird, so he was happy. He sure everyone else was happier, too.

Space travel wasn't what he'd thought it would be. He'd imagined being weightless, but the ship had artificial gravity that felt normal to him. The stars outside the viewports didn't stream past, the way they did on *Star Trek*. In fact, there was almost no sense of motion at all. He could feel the hum of the engines, but it didn't mean anything to him.

It was about as exciting as the time he'd flown to Chicago. He'd traveled at night because it was cheaper. He just wanted to see the museum there. The museum had been amazing, but the flight had been really boring. There was nothing to see out the windows at night. The whole trip had felt a little unreal. It had also sucked up all his saved cash, the summer after high school.

Jason came back into the main cabin carrying two plates piled high with what looked like scrambled eggs. Geoffrey took one of the plates from him. It didn't smell like eggs. It didn't really smell like much of anything at all.

"Don't ask," said Jason, "because I don't know. There's a galley just up the way from our cabins. I selected bacon, eggs, and toast from the food processor. This is what I got. For yours, I tried steak and eggs from the menu. Got the same thing. I can't tell the difference."

"Do you think it is safe to eat?" Geoffrey asked. It didn't smell bad; it just didn't smell good. It may have had a taste, but he was struggling to bring himself to try it.

Jon came into the room with a plate of the same stuff.

"Is this safe?" asked Jason.

Jon paused and looked at his plate as if seeing it for the first time. "Yeah. You got it from the processor unit, right?"

"Yes, where else?" Jason said. "This isn't what I ordered."

"Oh, yeah, the processor has been broken for a while. Everything comes out looking like scrambled eggs."

Geoffrey tentatively tried a quivering forkful of it. Texturally, it felt like scrambled eggs in his mouth, or how he'd imagined brains to be. It was like chewing wet, firm foam. The only thing that saved it from being nausea-inducing was the lack of flavor. It didn't taste like anything at all.

Jon was digging into his with a gusto.

Geoffrey shrugged. The stuff was – probably – sustenance. He would never call it *food*. It made him long for a pizza. Pepperoni and extra cheese from LaRosa's: that was the best. He gagged on the next bite but chewed it and swallowed anyway. He needed calories.

"No wonder you're so damned skinny," said Jason. He'd tried what was on his plate.

"The food processor may be broken, but what comes out of it still has everything you need, nutritionally," Jon said. "To be honest, I sort of like it. This way, I don't have to think about food."

"Obviously," said Drake. He'd entered, carrying his own plate. "If you thought about this stuff, you'd never eat it. Which may indeed explain a few things, Jason."

Geoffrey choked back a laugh. Even Drake thought Jon was too thin.

Drake was wearing a black velvet robe, and his hair was unbraided and damp. Geoffrey had wondered if Drake ever bathed, or needed to. Of course he had to bathe. Geoffrey knew that he tended to idolize Drake, probably more than he should.

"All right." Jon had finished his meal. He stood up and took his plate to the galley, then returned. "I'll be in the cockpit. We'll make the first jump in about ten minutes."

"Do we need to buckle up?" asked Jason.

"No. If I do it right, you'll hardly feel anything."

"What if you don't do it right?" asked Geoffrey.

"If I don't do it right, you won't feel anything, either," Jon said. "Ever again."

O

Jon settled into his acceleration couch with a sigh. The cockpit was a small, grey space. There were no screens or controls, just the chair with its jacks. This was his home. Here, piloting this ship, was where he belonged. Jon carefully attached the cables to his arms and then pressed his head back into the rest before activating the last connection.

The acceleration couch slid out padded restraints over his

wrists, ankles, and forehead, holding him in place as the final connection was made at the base of his skull. There was a moment that was either intense pain or pleasure – he could never tell which, and maybe it was both – and a blinding white light in his mind.

Jon took a deep breath and opened his eyes. The artificial intelligence of the computer core was linked into his mind, and they were one. The cockpit was filled with displays of light, projected directly into his mind through the connection. His consciousness expanded until he could feel wispy interstellar gasses caressing the quasi-metallic skin of his ship, the faint vibration of his engines, the hum of the life support, and the faint buzz of his companions' voices. Time slowed for him as his racing mind flew beyond the confines of flesh.

He was the *Chwyldro,* and he was free.

Normally, Jon followed the jump sequence that the gate builders had used. To get to Masir, which was in the Eta Cassiopeia system, from Sol, he would normally have to jump through Epsilon Eridani, his home system. He didn't want to get that close to Rhyddid – not right now. Thinking of home clouded his mind. He didn't need that.

Instead, he called up his ideogram of the Cynosure. This was the first time he'd been home since joining with that strange Power, and he wanted to see how it would affect his ability to jump the *Chwyldro.* Maybe it would kill them all, but at this moment, fused with the cold artificial intelligence of his ship, he didn't care. He focused on the Eta Cassiopeia system, and the careful calculations for the series of jumps blurred away. A new equation formed in an instant, and he knew he'd somehow tapped into the machine intelligence of the Cynosure.

The equation was complex and elegant and so beautiful that he wanted to weep. It contained himself, his ship, and everyone aboard. The variable of the equation was in a math he could understand in his current state. That variable described his location within the spiral arm of the Milky Way galaxy, and indeed, it described the universe itself.

He knew then that he could fly between the worlds much as he had walked them.

Jon felt the energies of his engines charging up, coiling spacetime like a spring to launch them across the gulf of stars. He changed the variable to include their destination, and then fed the equation through the Cynosure and back to the onboard computer.

The pent energies unleashed.

Rainbows flowed through his mind. Jon could actually see the boundaries of the universe, the skin of creation itself, peel back. There was the void, hyperspace, a place of titanic energies, and then a rainbow parting of bent light, and they were here.

Masir lay nested in a web of vectors.

Jon sensed the positions of moons, asteroids, space debris, and other ships in the local planetary system. Looking outward, he could see the other planets with their moons and asteroids. A navigation buoy pinged his ship. Jon felt the computer respond, and the slow pulse of photons creeping away from his ship, carrying the name and registry information back to Masir.

Jon had done the impossible. He'd jumped from Sol to Masir in one instantaneous jump. Those Northerners may have been misguiding him, tricking him. They may have had other goals, but they had been right about one thing: he'd needed the Cynosure. Jon couldn't have done what he'd just done without it. No one could have.

CHAPTER THIRTY-EIGHT

Drake knew Jon had used the Cynosure to launch them across the stars.

He was always a bit uncomfortable when someone used Cynosure in his presence. Drake didn't know if that was an instinctive revulsion because of the Instrumentality, or something else. No one else seemed to notice it. A few people he knew, such as Emrys, had become attuned to both Powers. Drake shuddered at the thought. That wasn't something he'd have been able bring himself to do, even if he were genetically compatible with the Cynosure, which he was not.

Drake suspected that it had something to do with the two Powers being too similar, or maybe he was just sensitive. The Cynosure felt much like the Instrumentality but missing something. Maybe it was cultural: Drake had been raised to despise those who used the Cynosure, those people who had fled from the ancient war and taken a stolen part of the Instrumentality with them. He wondered what the Instrumentality must have been like before, when it was complete.

He watched the screens as Jon approached the planet. To

Drake, Masir didn't look like a habitable world. It was too large and brown and drab. Most Earth-like worlds were blue-and-white jewels, sparkling with water in liquid and vapor forms. Masir had few glints of water and only very small ice caps at the poles. Drake could make out what looked like dark forests clustered up near the ice, though. The planet couldn't be entirely desert. He didn't see any mountain chains. Masir might be an old world, cooling and losing water. Drying up, the way Mars had in so many universes.

The planet had more orbital traffic than Earth did. Drake could see other moving lights in orbit: ships, shuttles, and cargo haulers, mostly. The image quality of the display wasn't high enough for him to read the names on the ships, but the word *Masir* was Arabic. He thought that maybe the inhabitants of the planet were descended from those peoples of Earth. The Middle Eastern cultures of Earth had fascinated him for a while; they'd had such an advanced culture, before religion and politics had joined together.

Drake had noticed, in his travels, that humans often left their homeworld in ethnic clumps. He supposed it was one way to keep their cultural identities intact, but it still seemed odd to him. Where Drake was from, there was just the one identity: that of the Ruined Courts. The trillions of people there all spoke Thari, a debased form of the old language. Drake spoke hundreds of languages, but most of them had been picked up during his travels.

Granted, the ancient families of the Ruined Courts all had distinctly different cultures. The House of Drake, and all of their septs and allies, had a common culture. The House of Drake had been old when he was young. The warrior traditions of his people had been well ingrained, and as a youth, he had absorbed them like a man in the desert sucks up water from an oasis.

Drake smiled. Yes, the Arabic people who'd settled the

planet below him must have thought it a cruel twist of fate that they would settle a world so much like the biome of where they lived on the planet they had just left. Masir would be a dry world, and hot, this close to its binary orange and yellow dwarf star primaries. Life-giving water would be in great demand. That probably accounted for a high percentage of the orbital traffic: ice miners from the outer system.

"Looks like a barren world," said Geoffrey.

"It doesn't look hospitable," Drake agreed. "However, there are forests near the ice caps. I don't think the world is actually barren."

"It still doesn't look like a nice place to live."

Drake shrugged. "Life finds a way."

"Have you been to a lot of desert planets?"

Drake wondered why Geoffrey was so concerned. "I've been to many worlds with large deserts. Few of them were as arid as this one seems. Why?"

"I was wondering if they had giant worms," Geoffrey said. "Sand worms."

"I've never heard of such things. I doubt it. What would they eat?"

"Oh. Yeah. I hadn't ever thought of that."

Drake couldn't tell whether Geoffrey was relieved or saddened by the news.

The equatorial zone of the planet was probably uninhabitable. From orbit, Drake could see titanic dust storms raging, bands of dust and sand that raced around the planet. Masir probably had a low axial tilt and a slow rotational period. That would account for the strong winds.

Jon dipped the starship's wings and slowed. The ship shook as the atmosphere furled around the hull in a glowing wave. Jon was bringing them in for a landing in the high middle latitudes. *That's one benefit of a smaller ship*, Drake mused. It could actually land on the surface of a planet.

Drake's own starship was far too large for that.

○

Jon brought the *Chwyldro* in for a landing at a small spaceport outside Dümat al-Jandal, the capital city of Masir. His landing thrusters kicked up a considerable amount of sand and dust from the plascrete pad. He could see the man waiting by a rounded ground car cover his face with his shemagh. The man was dressed in desert robes over a business suit. This was probably the person Jon had come to Masir to meet.

It was with the greatest feeling of reluctance that he deactivated the integration systems. As he disconnected, Jon felt diminished. He always felt a certain post-flight malaise, but this was worse. Flying his magnificent ship had always been good; with Cynosure, it now bordered on intoxicating. He could easily become addicted to that kind of freedom. He could fly anywhere.

Jon finished disconnecting and stood.

He was weak and a bit shaky. Jon was glad Drake had reminded him to eat before making the jump. Jon tended not to think often about food. Something about the process that had reworked his nervous system had damaged his vagus nerve. The damage wasn't severe, so it didn't interfere with his digestion or breathing, but he never felt hungry.

Obviously, from what the others had said, he'd allowed himself to get too thin. Again.

When he reached the main cabin, his companions were waiting, having changed back into their traveling clothes. Drake was wearing his armor again, with the black coat over it. The coat couldn't provide any extra protection, and Jon wondered why Drake bothered. He had to admit that the coat did look good on Drake, though. Maybe that was the entire point.

Jon ushered everyone into the cargo bay and closed the

hatchway before lowering the ramp. He didn't want too much sand to get into the ship, although he knew it was probably a lost cause. In any case, the monomolecular repair robots would find all of the sand before it could get into vital systems. They always had.

Jon *was* aware that his ship was beginning to wear out, though – a little bit like Jon himself. The ramp closed behind him and his friends as they stepped onto the landing pad.

"*As-salaam 'alykum*," said the man waiting by the car as they approached: *Peace be upon you.* "We weren't expecting you for a few days, after your message. You must have traveled very quickly."

"*Wa 'alaykum as-salaam*," Jon responded: *And also with you.* "Perhaps we should get into the car and out of the wind before introductions are made."

"Of course." The man held the car door open. Inside, the vehicle was one large compartment, with seating all around. "It is good to see you, old friend," the man said as he settled inside with them, shutting the curved door. The car was spacious, and automated. It took off on a ground foil effect for the nearby capitol city.

"Dr. Yousef Shadid, may I present to you my companions, Jason Grey, Geoffrey Meeks, and Prince Daeren Drake. Yousef is one of the geneticists who worked on the pilot program."

"Just call me Drake. I've heard interesting things about your work, doctor," Drake said.

"You've had some interesting work done, yourself," Yousef said to Drake, who was in his trueform. "Or are you from a world I don't know about?"

Drake smiled, showing fangs. "I have not been altered genetically, and no, you wouldn't have heard of my world."

"I'd be curious to see your genetic scan," said Yousef. "You have some interesting mutations."

"I'm sure that you would, but I'm afraid I cannot allow

that."

"Al-ma'dirah." *Excuse me.* "I hope I have not offended you. I was simply curious. We see so few new faces these days. Not to mention how rare it is for a new colonized world to turn up."

"*La qalaq,*" Drake replied: *No worries.*

Jon should have guessed that Drake would know Arabic. He knew everything else.

CHAPTER THIRTY-NINE

Geoffrey watched the rolling dunes outside the curved ground car window. The planet was beautiful, in a dry, dusty sort of way. There was something wrong with the gravity; he didn't quite feel the right weight. The air was also a little thinner than he'd become used to. It reminded him of the mountain ridge outside Albuquerque, soon after all of this had begun.

How long has it been? Geoffrey wondered. He'd lost track of the days. So much had happened since he'd answered the door, and Jon had fallen into the house. How much time had passed back home? He had no way of knowing.

The doctor who'd picked them up at the landing pad was darker-skinned than Jason, with brown eyes, hair, and beard. Geoffrey thought his name sounded Middle Eastern. His professors back at the university would have killed to study this place.

"I wouldn't worry too much about where I'm from," Drake was saying. "I'm here to try to help Jon track down exactly what was done to him, and what has happened to the other pilots."

Yousef nodded. "I'd heard that a few of our pilots were

going missing. To be honest, Jon, we'd thought you were one of them. Terek sent me message when he got to Earth. He said he was following a lead that you'd been there. He thought you might have been abducted – the Alliance would love to have their own jump pilots. He went silent after that, and we haven't heard from him since."

"I wasn't abducted, exactly," said Jon. "I was almost killed, though. I don't think the Alliance had anything to do with it."

"Maybe not, but they tried to take me," Yousef said. "They got Dr. Hakubi."

"Dr. Hakubi?" Drake asked.

"She was the lead geneticist. It was her theorems that made it all work."

"They killed her?"

"No, worse than that. They captured her. Boarded the freighter she was on as it transited through the gate system at Von Maanen's Star."

"So they're trying to replicate her work," said Drake.

"It would appear so," Yousef replied.

"We cannot allow that to happen."

"I agree. The Alliance would make jump-capable fighter-bombers."

"I was thinking of the pilots. Jon said many died during the gene treatments."

"Many did, yes. I was more worried about them dropping atomics on us, though. I've struggled for years with the morality of what we did. Allah forgive me, I thought the work we were doing was for the benefit of many people."

"We were all volunteers," said Jon. "We don't blame you. I don't, anyway."

"We have other, more pressing problems, unfortunately. As urgent as your concern for the other pilots may be, I would need to settle things here before I could help you. I fear the Alliance is moving on us."

"You think they'll invade?"

"No, I think they are trying to destabilize the government, like they did on Rhyddid."

"Well, I suppose they think if it worked once…"

Yousef snorted. "They've had nothing but trouble from your people since then – no offense. They gained the jumpgates but lost a productive world."

"No offense taken. I could have told them it would be a bad idea to radicalize Celts. Not that they would have listened."

"Well, we have the same fear here," Yousef said. "Our people also have a troubled history."

Geoffrey thought that was an understatement. Middle Eastern people were the current bogymen back on his Earth. Of course, even back home, most people of Arab descent were good people. He shouldn't let the actions of a few radicals determine his impressions of a whole ethnic group.

He wondered if the history of this place was the same as his history. How close were the different universes? Drake said they were formed by parallel development, not splitting off each other like in stories. How could they have languages that were the same, though?

Yousef spoke excellent English, as did Jon. How could that be parallel development? Geoffrey wished he could talk to Drake about it, but he didn't want to interrupt what was obviously an important conversation.

Θ

As the ground car passed through the city, Jon thought about the Federated Alliance. If they had agents on Masir trying to stir up trouble, how much luck would they have? The people he saw out the window looked happy and prosperous. Of course, people had seemed that way on his world, too.

Jon had been an unwitting pawn in what befell his world.

There had been a widening gulf between those who had enough and those who had too much. In that way, it was much like any capitalist society. The workers at the bottom of the economic pyramid rose up against conditions that had gotten steadily worse during his brother's reign. Of course, the Alliance had made certain that the economy and social unrest had gotten bad on the Rhyddid.

Masir was like his world in many ways. There was a royal family, mostly figurehead, and a representational government. To Jon's eye, the difference between the economic classes here didn't seem as severe. Masir wasn't an industrial nation, as Rhyddid was. Masir's chief exports, before the Alliance embargoes, had been art, music, and handcrafted goods.

Jon didn't think the Alliance would be able to turn people's heads using the same tactics of class versus class. Not here. It would have to be something else. Religion seemed the obvious choice, but that didn't feel right, either. It was *too* obvious.

"What kinds of problems have you been having, Yousef?" Jon asked. "I'm not saying you're wrong, but why do you think the Alliance is moving against your planet?"

"We've been having civil unrest, for the first time in our history," said Yousef. "The problems have all been here in the capitol. It started out as a series of brutal murders. The victims were all women. When the police couldn't find the killer or killers, there were riots. There have been demonstrations against the police. It is somewhat outdated, but my people still feel protective toward women. There have been rumors that the murderer is someone in the royal family."

"Could it be?" asked Drake. "The simplest solution is often correct."

"No!" Yousef said. "That would be unthinkable."

"Obviously not, if there are rumors. Would it be possible for me to see the police files?" Drake asked. "I'm quite good at discovering truths that others don't want revealed. I could be of service."

"It would take a royal decree."

"Then it's a good thing that I'm a prince."

"Maybe I could arrange an introduction for you." Yousef shook his head. "I don't know. It would take time. Time we might not have. Also, if you are correct about the murderer being a member of the royal family, you might face obstruction."

"Well, it's either that, or I break in and steal the files," Drake said. "I'm good at that, too."

"Who are you, exactly?"

"Drake, don't do anything rash," said Jon. "It's known that I can apport. If files mysteriously disappear, someone will link the crime to me."

"Not if you're in a very public place when it happens," Drake replied. "Do you trust Yousef?"

Jon glanced at Yousef and nodded. "Yes, I do. I wouldn't have brought us here otherwise."

Drake smiled, and then his features flowed and shifted. In a matter of seconds, Drake's form matched that of Yousef. Even his hair had shifted. The only things that hadn't changed were his size and his armor.

"That's extraordinary," said Yousef. "Is it an illusion projection? I've never seen one so real looking."

"No, it isn't an illusion, doctor," Drake said in Yousef's voice. "I am a shapeshifter. Touch my face; you'll feel your own."

Yousef reached out, and then quickly pulled back his hand after touching Drake. "What are you?"

"I'm sure you could make a few guesses," Drake said as he changed back to himself. "Do you really want to know?"

"I am a scientist, sir. I *need* to know."

"I'm sure, as a geneticist, you've noticed that life across the galaxy shares many similarities."

Yousef nodded.

Jon thought he knew where Drake was going with this. While he might not have chosen to tell Yousef about everything, he trusted Drake's instincts at this point. Drake would say what he felt he needed to.

"I'm what you would call a Precursor," Drake said. "I'll allow you to see my DNA, if you promise to destroy it immediately afterward."

Yousef caught Jon's eye. Jon nodded. Drake hadn't told the truth, but he hadn't lied, either. Jon was starting to get a feel for how Drake operated.

"That is an extraordinary claim," said Yousef, "and yet I cannot deny what I have seen. That was no illusion. I hope you don't intend to commit a crime while looking like me."

Drake laughed. "I can shift into just about any living thing I can think of, although I need to keep my size approximately the same. I cannot easily change my mass, but I can change my density."

"I don't know what to say. I never thought to meet one of your kind. Can you tell me why the gate network is set up as it is?"

"That network is old, outdated technology."

"There is a better way to move through the stars?"

"You've discovered it yourself," Drake said, gesturing to Jon.

Yousef laughed and shook his head. "This is certainly an unexpected development. I am surprised you'd involve yourself in our problems. Are there many of your people in our part of the galaxy?"

"I certainly hope there aren't," Drake said with a smile. "I cannot guarantee it, however."

The car pulled to a stop outside a building, and the door sighed open.

"My lab," said Yousef. "You did say I could have a peek at your DNA?"

"You may," Drake said.

Jon and his companions piled out of the car and went inside. Jon saw a few people he vaguely remembered, and smiled to them when they greeted him. Yousef entered his key code on a reinforced door, and then they were in his lab.

It hadn't changed much from what Jon remembered. Masir wasn't a rich world, and genetic research wasn't a lucrative field. The equipment was old but serviceable.

"Are you the only... one of your kind in this party?" Yousef asked.

"My other companions are from Earth," said Drake.

Yousef retrieved a sample collector and took a swab from Drake's cheek. Jon was a little surprised that Drake allowed it. He supposed Drake wasn't too worried about what the genetic scan would show. To be honest, Jon was curious, too.

"It will take a few minutes for the sample to run," Yousef said. "Can I offer you all refreshments?"

"That's very kind of you," said Drake.

Yousef busied himself on the other side of the room, making tea.

"Drake, are you certain about this?" asked Jon.

"I wouldn't be doing it if I wasn't. You said you trust this man. We need allies here to guide us in our search. What he finds in the next few minutes will be informative."

Jon nodded. That was what he was worried about.

CHAPTER FORTY

Yousef served them all mint tea and then sat down at the computer to review the genetic material from Drake. Occasionally, he gasped and highlighted a section, or shook his head and then pulled up another part of the DNA sequence on the screen. Eventually he muttered imprecations that would have scandalized his ancestors and pulled up a second screen of data.

Drake could see that Yousef was running the two sets of code against each other. He suspected it was Jon's DNA sequence, or that of another pilot. Yousef marked several code segments, which flashed and were highlighted.

Drake wasn't surprised at the similarities between his code and that from the jumpship pilot program. Drake had already known someone had altered Jon's DNA to make him appear to be descended from someone in the Golden Kingdom. Drake also knew that the genetics of those in the North weren't so different from Drake's people in the South; their two species hadn't diverged that much.

Probably because they kept interbreeding.

Those in the North had been separate from his people for

only a hundred thousand years or so, time enough for some change, but nothing major. Even his own people had changed over that time. The ancient statues were somewhat… different in form.

Drake sipped his tea and waited while he watched the doctor look through his genetic code.

After about half an hour, Yousef finally turned to Jon. "Your DNA has similarities."

"So would your own," said Drake. "My DNA is compatible with that of humans. I am cross-fertile with your species. We are not that dissimilar."

"I would love to know why we are so similar. We know humans evolved on Earth."

"Your species did, yes," said Drake. "However, that doesn't mean that it didn't evolve according to a plan."

"Well, it looks as if someone had a sample of DNA very similar to yours to use in our jump pilot program," Yousef said to Drake. "Dr. Hakubi would never say where she got the core sequences. I never believed she'd created them in the lab, as she'd said. Now I wonder. She must have gotten them from one of your people."

"Yes, Dr. Hakubi could have gotten ahold of some Precursor DNA," Drake said. Or she was from the Golden Kingdom herself. He would put little past those in the North. It still remained to be seen why she had altered Jon and possibly the others. The list of people who could have accomplished the feat was short, and not something Drake wanted to think about. He didn't want any of them as an enemy.

"Now, you have seen that I am who I have said," said Drake. "Please destroy the data."

Yousef looked hesitant. "With your more complete code, we could fill in the gaps in the pilots' genetic sequence. Many of our pilots suffer from debilitating genetic illnesses. We could fix those."

"I did say *please*," Drake said. "You knew my conditions before we started. I will not ask again."

Yousef sighed and wiped the data from the computer. Then he stood and took the sample from the gene reader. He tossed the sample into an incinerator. Drake scanned the man's mind briefly: Yousef was being honest.

"Thank you, doctor," Drake said.

"I wish I could spend more time studying that," said Yousef. "It could take a lifetime to study the differences and similarities. I understand, though, why you want the data destroyed. I respect your bodily autonomy."

"Now, I think we should get on with the matter at hand. I will need clothes, to blend in. Preferably something dark." Drake could have made himself clothes, but he didn't want the doctor to know everything he could do. Not yet. "Then we will discuss how to make sure you are all in the public eye while I retrieve the data we need to solve your problem."

Θ

Geoffrey didn't know a lot about genetics, only what he'd learned in his high school science classes. According to the doctor, Drake's DNA wasn't that much different from a human's. Geoffrey found that very interesting.

Drake was an alien shapeshifter. He could change his form at will. If Drake really was genetically close to being human, did that mean humans might be able to shapeshift? Maybe those old myths and legends could be true. If so, that was really cool.

If he'd understood what Drake and Jon were talking about, then Jon had been altered to make him more like Drake's people. Or the people from the North, whatever that meant. Geoffrey wondered, if humans were so close genetically to Drake's people, why did so many of the test subjects die from the gene splicing?

Again, he wondered how humans could be the same across universes.

He'd just have to be content to hope he'd learn someday.

Yousef brought a change of clothes in for Drake: dark robes and a plaid scarf. Geoffrey wondered why Drake didn't just *make* clothes, the way he always did.

Drake took off his coat and folded it over the chair. Then he stepped out of his armor.

This was the first time Geoffrey had seen Drake take off his armor. Oh, Geoffrey had seen Drake out of his armor, in robes and in regular clothes, but he hadn't seen him actually take it off. The armor opened along seams Geoffrey hadn't even known were there and then closed back up as Drake stepped away.

Drake was naked.

He didn't seem to be embarrassed, but then, he didn't have anything to be embarrassed about. If Geoffrey had a body that looked like Drake's, he wouldn't have been embarrassed, either.

By the time Drake was finished dressing, he looked completely different. His skin was darker, and he was no taller than Geoffrey. He was little thicker in the middle, and his features were less sharp. His eyes were still green but not as intense. His hair was short and brown. A beard spouted from his face as Geoffrey watched. If Geoffrey hadn't seen him change, he never would have guessed the man was Drake.

"Well, that's disturbing," said Yousef. "If your people are all able to do that, they could infiltrate any organization or government."

"That is a part of why I wanted my genetic material destroyed," Drake said. His voice was the same, which seemed even stranger to Geoffrey. "We don't need *that* part of my genetic code being inserted into anyone. Now, tell me about the police station."

"It is two blocks up and one over to the east," said Yousef.

"The files will be on the main police server but can be accessed from any detective's terminal. The files are almost certainly password protected and fingerprint biometrically sealed. I'm not sure how you'll get past that."

"I have my ways." Drake's voice had altered and now had a trace of the local accent.

Yousef just nodded. "I'll take our friends here to a local restaurant that has very good food. It is two blocks north of the police station, just a short walk. You can join us there after you conclude your business. Although I prefer you to look different from how you do now, if it is not too much bother. No need to lead the police back to us there."

"You don't seem to have much problem with my lawbreaking," said Drake. "This surprises me, although I am too unfamiliar with your current culture to have a judgement."

"What could our human laws mean to you?" Yousef said. "Besides, you're doing it for a good cause. Allah knows sometimes one must do the right thing, even if others would disapprove."

"You understand that I will need to follow the investigation wherever it leads?" Drake asked. "I may even have to do things you wouldn't agree with."

Yousef sighed. "I understand. I don't want to think it could be our young prince, as the rumors would have it, but if it is, then *kama sha' allah*," Yousef said: *as god wills.* "I trust you will do what is right."

Drake nodded. "For your sake, and the sake of your people, I hope it is not as the rumors would have it. I will try to be discreet, no matter what I must do. If this Alliance is involved, I will uncover that as well."

"I think the Alliance must be. I just don't know in what way."

"They could be committing the murders and leaving evidence that implicates the prince," Drake suggested.

"I hope it is as you say."

"We will know soon enough. I will meet you at the restaurant when I have seen the files. And do not worry, I will have chosen a new shape by then."

Yousef shook his head. "I don't begin to understand the how, but I am very grateful you are here to do this. It has been a frustrating few months for my people. We never know when the slasher will strike down another young woman, and the civil unrest has everyone worried."

Drake bowed to them, touching his heart, lips, and forehead, and then left.

"You friend is quite extraordinary," Yousef said to Jon. "Where did you meet him, if I may ask?"

Geoffrey was curious about what Jon would say to *that*.

"We met on Earth," Jon said. "I'm sorry I can't say more at this time."

"Earth?" Yousef asked. "I wonder if he was there trying to find out what had happened to the pilots. Perhaps how you came to have genetic material from his people?"

"He certainly isn't happy about it," Jon replied. "Should we go find some food? It's been some time since I was here last. Do I remember correctly that the restaurant you indicated was Malouf's?"

Yousef nodded. "Well remembered."

Geoffrey had never had Middle Eastern food. He didn't really know anything about it at all. It had to be better than the egg-like stuff that had come out of the food processor on Jon's ship, though.

Anything would be.

CHAPTER FORTY-ONE

Drake felt naked without his armor, but it was too distinctively alien to be seen during the day on this world. He didn't expect to get into a fight anyway. He needed a way to sneak into the police station and steal what he needed. He *didn't* need to kill everyone and smash his way in. Sometimes subtly was in order.

He also didn't want anyone to be able to link him or his friends to what he was about to do.

The Dümat al-Jandal police station was an impressively large building constructed of glass and metal. The two suns glinted against the windows as Drake made his way inside. He didn't know the details about the murders yet, but he knew people, and police. He'd improvise and find what he needed.

There was a bored-looking sergeant at the front desk. "Can I help you?" the man asked in Arabic. He was filling in a crossword puzzle on an electronic pad.

Drake smiled. "I would like to confess."

"To what?" the sergeant asked. He still seemed bored.

"To the murders of the women," said Drake. "I killed them."

"You did, huh?" the sergeant sighed and pressed a button the desk in front of him. "Detective Bashar? We've got another kook up here claiming to have killed those women. What do you want me to do with him?"

"What's he look like?" came a faint voice from the intercom. Drake was surprised; the detective was a woman. He reevaluated his plan and his assessment of the local culture.

"Big guy, smiling weird. Dressed okay. Doesn't really look like the typical crazy."

"Hold him for me. Can't hurt to talk to him. Maybe he knows something. Probably not, but it is as god wills."

"You got it, detective."

Drake had to wait only a few minutes before a tall woman in a dark, striped suit and a dark red headscarf came out to meet him. She looked irritated. Drake could understand; the murders were unsolved, and the police probably had a lot of people claiming to be the killer, just for the publicity.

"I'm Detective Bashar," she said. "You have some information for me?" She carried a small notebook and didn't offer to shake hands.

"I do. I want to confess."

"Uh-huh. Do you even know where the bodies were found? Or how many there were?"

"More than you know," Drake replied.

She sighed. "What's your name, sir?"

"Younan Haddid." It was the equivalent of *John Smith* in America, so it should be safe enough.

"Look, we both know you didn't do it, so why don't you leave before I have to arrest you for wasting my time?"

"Maybe I want to get arrested."

"Sorry, you'll have to get your free meal somewhere else." She turned away.

Drake reached out and grabbed her shoulder. If the culture here was anything like other Middle Eastern cultures, he'd just committed a crime, but why stop there? He jerked her back against him, pulled free the pistol he'd seen hidden in her shoulder holster, and held it to her head. He hoped the police in this place weren't the type to shoot first.

Bashar cried out and struggled for a moment before she felt the gun.

Drake hated to do this to her. He knew she was afraid, but for his plan to work, he needed to be arrested. He had what he needed, though. He'd felt her hand against his. He scanned her mind and found what he needed there.

Within a minute, he was surrounded by police with drawn guns.

Drake released Detective Bashar and then stepped back with his hands up. She spun and snatched the gun from his hand, and for a moment he thought she might shoot him. After a quick pat-down, an officer pushed him to his knees and pulled his hands behind his back to bind them.

"Well, Mr. Haddid, or whoever you are, *now* you are under arrest," Bashar said. She read him his rights. "Place him in holding for processing."

The policeman who'd cuffed Drake pulled him to his feet and pushed him back through a set of automatic doors into the back of the police station. Dozens of police officers sat at desks, working on reports and taking statements. They looked at him with a mix of curiosity and hostility. The holding cells were in the back, through a set of doors sealed by handprint scanners, just as Drake had hoped.

He was pushed into a cell.

"Turn around and back up to the bars so I can undo the cuffs," said the officer.

Drake complied.

"You made a big mistake, you know," the officer said as he undid the cuffs. "We don't take kindly to someone doing what you did. You're lucky we didn't just shoot you."

"I've always been lucky."

"Whatever." The officer left the area, and Drake turned around, rubbing his wrists.

Drake punched the reinforced concrete wall next to him. His fist shattered the wall in concentric circles out to fifty centimeters in diameter. A heavy piece of concrete fell out into his open palm. *Perfect*, he thought.

He walked over to the bars and flung the piece of concrete at the camera, which shattered under the impact. Drake then called upon the Instrumentality and used it to change his clothes as he shifted into the form of Detective Bashar.

Drake placed his thumb over the scanner on the cell door, and it slid open for him. He'd seen a terminal in a cubical just outside the holding area. It would be perfect for his uses. He left the holding area and stepped into the cubical before anyone saw him. He didn't want to have to actually pretend to be the detective, if he could help it.

It was only a matter of a few keystrokes to bring up the files on the murders. They had been quite brutal, Drake realized. There was an element of madness in what he was seeing. There had been eleven murders; the police had managed to cover up three from the public. The police had no leads. The files included notes about possible suspects, including Prince Aziz, who'd been acting strangely and irrationally for a few weeks and before that had been known to be violent with women.

The prince was good lead, but Drake wanted to be fair, for Yousef. He'd have to investigate the crime scenes himself. He knew most of the physical evidence would be gone, but the killer might have left psychic traces behind.

Drake had what he needed. He cleared the terminal and wiped his prints – her prints – from the keys before leaving the cubical. He'd given Detective Bashar enough trouble today.

"Bashar!" a detective called as Drake moved to leave. "Heard you got yourself a fun one."

"Just some crazy," Drake said in her voice.

He pushed past the man and out of the building. He wasn't followed, and Drake let out a sigh of relief. It had been a while since he'd had to do things the hard way.

Drake found an alley and changed his form and clothes again. He stayed a woman but changed into one he'd known a few thousand years ago, on an Earth he'd visited. He'd liked her. Actually, he'd been in love with her, but it hadn't worked out.

He caught a reflection in a building window. Yes, he looked as he remembered her. She'd been small and compact, with dark hair and eyes. She had a stern look, and he smiled to test the face out. No, it looked better when he stayed stern, as she had been. She'd had great cheekbones.

The restaurant Yousef had mentioned was just up the street.

Θ

Jason was rather happy with the food at Malouf's.

That food was mostly meant to be eaten with the hands. Yousef had started them all off with plates of hummus and fresh pita bread. It was delicious. He was personally relieved to see that Yousef used both hands to eat. In similar cultures back on Earth, it was taboo to eat with the left.

Jason ordered kofta: minced beef mixed with onions and grilled on a stick. The waiter brought a plate full of the delicacies, along with a spicy yogurt sauce. The kofta was quite tasty. It was certainly the best food he'd had in a while.

A small, humorless-looking woman in a black suit and black hijab stopped by the table. She stared at each of them with a frown, and then nodded. "Yes, you're the ones," she said in accented English. "What can you tell me about a man named Drake?"

"I'm sorry, who are you?" asked Yousef. He sounded scared.

The woman laughed, and a chill ran up Jason's spine. He knew that laugh. She slid in next to him and picked up a kofta from his plate. "I always loved these."

The others still looked confused.

"It's Drake," Jason managed.

"What?" asked Jon.

"She's Drake." Jason felt a little lightheaded. Despite everything he'd seen, this shook him. He hadn't realized Drake could change genders – no, change *biological sex*. The realization made Drake even more terrifying.

"What do you mean?" Jon said.

"Too much?" the woman asked. "Jon, you didn't see this coming?"

"Do I know you?"

"Come now. Jason has figured it out." She gestured to the waiter. "Could I get a plate of these?"

"Certainly, madam. Lamb or beef?"

"Beef, if you please."

"Drake?" Geoffrey whispered.

"In the flesh, so to speak. Do you like it? Her name was Aaliyah; I knew her many thousands of years ago. I thought the form would blend in well enough here."

Jason thought that almost made it worse, knowing that the woman Drake appeared as now had been real, once upon a time. Could Drake change into anyone, or just people he'd known? Could he just invent a person and live their life?

"I didn't know you could do that," Jason said.

"I did tell you that I could change into any biological form," Drake replied in the dead woman's voice.

"I feel as if I have missed something," said Yousef. "Who is this woman?"

"It's Drake," Jason said, "thinking he's being funny."

"Drake?"

"You read my DNA yourself, doctor. What can I say? I

thought it would be amusing to tease you all a bit. Perhaps I have missed the mark slightly."

"But your genes were male!"

"What's a phenotype, amongst friends?"

"It's him, Yousef. Did you find what you needed?" Jon asked Drake.

"I did," Drake replied. "The detective on the case was very thorough. I'll need to visit each of the murder sites tonight. There may be psychic traces left by the killer. Almost certain to be. The killer is insane."

"Insane?" asked Yousef.

Drake nodded. "Those women were butchered with a manic zeal."

Yousef looked a little ill.

"Perhaps we should wait until we're back at the lab to discuss this," Jon said.

The waiter brought Drake a glass of tea along with the plate of kofta.

Jason snagged one of the meatballs on a stick from Drake's plate.

Drake laughed again.

Jason was still chilled by something in that laugh.

CHAPTER FORTY-TWO

Jon stayed silent during the trip back to the lab.

Drake had fooled him completely, and that wasn't an easy thing to do. He'd not seen it coming, as Drake had put it, and he hadn't caught on even after being told. Drake had changed his entire body language.

Jon still had trouble believing this was Drake sitting across from him in the car.

"Don't be too hard on yourself, Jon," said Drake. "I'm very good at what I do."

Back inside the lab, Drake winked at him, and those beautiful features dissolved and flowed into Drake's own handsome face. His clothes swirled and changed, as well.

Seeing the clothes change is going to be difficult for Yousef, Jon thought.

"How did you change your clothes?" asked Yousef, right on cue.

"Nanotechnology," Drake answered.

"But where does the material come from?"

"These are the same clothes you gave me before I left."

Yousef shook his head. "Is the shape-change technological,

too?"

"Not in this instance."

"Not in this…" Yousef shook his head. "Your technology is far ahead of ours."

Drake just nodded.

"You found the information on the murders?" said Jon.

"Yes. There have been eleven, so far."

"Eleven?" Yousef said.

"They're covering up the ones they can, to prevent public outcry."

"And you think you can trace the killer?" Jon asked. "How?"

"People impact their environment," said Drake. "A mind leaves traces on its surroundings. You focus on a lamp; that lamp has been touched by your mind. Those traces can be read by someone skilled. In the case of a madman, the traces are sure to be strong and splashed everywhere."

"You're speaking of psychic phenomena as if they were real," said Yousef.

"You've seen Jon apport – how do you explain that?"

"I can't, but I don't need to revert to pseudo-science."

Drake laughed. "Humans can be so narrow-minded."

Jon thought Drake was playing up the alien angle a bit too strongly.

"Okay, think of something no one else knows," said Drake.

"Think of it? Not write it down or something?"

"No, just think of it." Drake nodded. "Josephine. That was her name, right? The woman you loved when you went out of system for university, thirty-five years ago."

Yousef nodded. "I don't understand how you can know that. What became of her?"

"I don't know, because you don't know. I'm primarily a telepath, doctor. If you're that interested, go looking for her."

"All right, say I believe you. It is no stranger than you being a woman a few minutes ago. How does that help you uncover who is behind the murders?"

"I will be able to find a psychic trace from the killer. Think of it as a signature. Every person is unique. I'll be able to track down the killer or killers."

"You'll never be able to convince the police without evidence."

"I rather thought I'd take care of things myself."

"You mean to kill them." Yousef sighed. "I suppose if they are as mad as you say, then they cannot be redeemed. Allah, let it not be the prince."

"*In sha' allah*," Drake replied. *As god wills.*

☉

Geoffrey was quite relieved that Drake had turned back into himself.

When the woman first walked up in the restaurant, Geoffrey thought that she was just a pretty waitress. She'd looked stern but beautiful. That it had been Drake almost made him feel ill.

Geoffrey was straight. The thought that he could fall for a man, even one who looked like a woman, bothered him. Drake hadn't been a man, though. He had been a woman, completely.

What was he?

How could he…?

"Doesn't mean anything, Geoffrey," Jason said quietly to him. "I thought she was pretty, too."

"It just freaks me out."

"Me, too, buddy." Jason found a couch to collapse on. "Me, too."

Geoffrey laughed and sat in the nearby chair. The others were talking on the other side of the lab. Jason and Geoffrey had mostly been forgotten, and that was fine with him.

"What do you think of all this?" Geoffrey asked.

"What am I supposed to think?" said Jason. "Do you mean

about Drake? About him changing into the form of a woman? Jon? About this planet? This universe?" He laughed. "Hell, man, I don't know what to think about anything."

"Yeah, I guess a smaller question would make sense. I can't think about most of what you said. I was wondering about Jon's problem. How he's genetically similar to Drake."

"Yousef made it sound as if Jon was changed in an experiment."

"What about this *Precursor* stuff?"

"If Drake has been telling the truth about his people, then he wasn't lying."

"Just not telling the compete truth."

"That sounds like Drake, doesn't it?"

"Yeah." Geoffrey rubbed his face. "If he was telling the truth about his people."

"I think he does, when he can."

"You've changed your tune since all of this started," said Geoffrey. "You used to be angry all the time."

"What can I say? He's very convincing."

Geoffrey laughed. "I'm glad we don't have to walk everywhere here. My feet are a mess."

"Mine, too," Jason said. "I wonder how far we actually walked. How would you even measure that?"

Geoffrey realized he hadn't really talked much with Jason in a while. "I miss being home."

"I do, too. I miss my woodworking shop. I wish I could be there now."

"At the same time, I'm glad this happened to us. I'd never had a real adventure before," said Geoffrey. "Look at us now! Exploring the multiverse."

"Don't call it that," Jason said with a grimace. "Makes it sound like a comic book."

"Well, it kind of is," Geoffrey said. "Drake is a sorcerer and an alien. He's also a little like Stark, with his armor."

"Drake's armor doesn't look anything like that," said Jason. "Drake's armor looks like some kind of Gothic medieval stuff, but technological. It also seems much more advanced."

"True, although I can't imagine him flying in it."

They both started laughing.

"I'm glad you guys are having a good time," Jon said as he walked over to them.

"You getting things sorted out?" Geoffrey asked him.

"I think so," he said, collapsing on the couch next to Jason. "Drake is going to head out in a little while and try to track down the killer. Meanwhile, we're going back to my ship and stay out of the way."

"Your idea or his?" asked Jason.

"It was mutual. If the Alliance is behind the murders, it's going to get messy here, and we'll want to leave here fast. If the royal prince is guilty, we'll want to leave even faster."

"Do you think that's likely?" Geoffrey asked. "About the prince, I mean."

"I don't know. I heard nasty things about him, the last time I was here. I wouldn't put it past him, especially if he's slipped further into madness."

"Further?" asked Jason.

"Yeah, he was always unstable."

"That's scary," Geoffrey said. "Didn't the government do anything?"

"He isn't in the line of succession," said Jon, "and he doesn't hold any position in the government."

"Oh, I guess I thought it was a kind of monarchy or something."

"The government here is a representative monarchy," Jon replied. "The monarch is mostly a figurehead; the real power is in the legislature and the prime minister."

"Kind of like England," said Geoffrey, "or maybe Canada."

"That doesn't mean anything to me," Jon said. "I was never

great with old Earth history."

"Yes," said Jason. "The answer is yes."

They all laughed.

"Jon, can I ask you something?" Geoffrey said hesitantly.

"You want to know if I thought Drake was pretty as a woman."

Geoffrey blushed. "Doesn't it seem strange to you? Doesn't it bother you?"

"He's a handsome man. The woman he was imitating was someone he was in a relationship with a long time ago. I would assume he'd date beautiful women. As for it bothering me? No, it doesn't. I'm not interested in him either way."

"Neither am I!" Geoffrey blurted. "I just meant it freaked me out."

"If I understand your turn of phrase, then yes, it did me, too."

"Geoffrey is young," said Jason, "and he worries about his sexuality."

Jon shook his head. "If I were you, I'd stop worrying. Thinking the woman who walked up to the table was attractive, before you knew it was Drake, is normal. She was. Now, if you're having fantasies about Drake as a woman, that could be a problem."

"What? No!"

Jon and Jason both laughed.

"We're teasing you, Geoffrey," said Jon.

Geoffrey grinned. "Yeah, I guess I had that coming."

"Come on, let's head back to my ship."

They met up with Yousef in front of the lab. Night was falling, and with it, the temperature. Geoffrey thought about what Drake would find, and if it would affect the people of this planet much. Masir was a strange world, but the people had all seemed friendly and welcoming.

CHAPTER FORTY-THREE

Drake slipped out into the night.

He was wearing his armor and coat again, because he didn't know what he'd find in the darkening streets. The city was beautiful, he reflected, all glass, metal, and plascrete. He would have thought it even more beautiful if there'd been some green spaces, but he understood the limitations of the environment.

The first murder had been near the royal palace, which was partly why people had latched onto the prince as the perpetrator. The palace was in the center of the city. Drake passed very few people on his way there, and no women walking alone. That was one result of the murders: women felt less safe in the city. It was unfortunate, after the long cultural struggle to get equality in the first place.

Drake had never understood why humans always seem to have such an inequality of the sexes. Where he was from, women had always had equality, but then, where he was from, many women were warriors and sorcerers. That kind of power could right many injustices. He supposed it was possible that in the dim antiquity of his race, inequality must have existed. After all, humans had evolved from a template laid down by Drake's own people.

The police file said the first victim was a graduate student. She'd been walking home alone, later than usual, after a long evening in a research lab. Her file hadn't said what she'd been researching, and Drake didn't have enough data to determine if her studies were relevant to the case.

Drake easily found the spot where she'd been killed by the piles of wilted flowers and many candle stubs on the sidewalk. Many people had visited the site in the time since she'd been murdered, and there wasn't much psychic trace of anything anymore.

He hadn't had much hope that there would be traces left here. He knew the most recent murder sites would hold the answers he was seeking, but he'd wanted to visit them in sequence. He walked on to the next site.

The second woman killed had been a prostitute. Her profession didn't bother Drake, as the oldest profession was a noble one, in his opinion. He liked sex; most people did. It always confused him that people attached moral judgements to it. Sex was sex. If someone wanted to rent their body, that was their business. Soldiers did much the same.

In any case, she'd been lured into an alcove off the street and knifed – or more accurately, she'd been eviscerated. Such was the brutality of this murder, compared to the first, that the police hadn't even linked them until the third murder. Drake could sense echoes of the woman's terror as she died. There was also a trace of something else, a sour note of madness that itched in his mind. The killer was insane, certainly, but he hadn't been as unhinged as the savagery of the murder would suggest.

Drake wasn't sure what that meant about the killer.

He widened his perceptions and caught something unexpected: the murder had been witnessed. At least one person had been watching from a nearby rooftop. Drake didn't know what that meant, either. If someone had seen what happened, why hadn't the witness come forward? Unless…

Drake visited the other murder sites and noticed the same pattern emerging. The murderer was vicious but not unaware of what he was doing. The murderer took a disturbing satisfaction in the women's deaths; more than just a blood-lust, it was as if the killer was getting a kind of sick revenge upon them. The women were from a mix of backgrounds, and the only commonality among them, other than how they died, had been a certain similarity of age and appearance. They all looked a little like the murderer's first victim.

Drake revisited the murder sites, focusing on the observer. The same person had been witness to all of the murders. While it was important to uncover the identity of the killer, Drake also wanted to know who had watched and done nothing. Why they were there, and more importantly, how did they know where to be?

Another moon had risen above the horizon when Drake felt the radiating pressure of madness from the murderer. It came from only a few streets away. Drake apported to a nearby rooftop and carefully made his way toward him. The murderer was stalking someone but wasn't ready to kill the woman. Drake sensed the murderer's insane lust. It bored into his mind, touching the part of him that he unleashed in battle.

Drake had killed an untold number of people in the tens of thousands of years he'd been alive. None of them had been helpless victims. While he often killed brutally and without mercy, it was always to some purpose, usually war. He'd never hunted and killed someone simply for sport. He'd limited his revenge to those who deserved it, not innocents who happened to look like the target of his ire.

He sensed the mind of the mysterious watcher moments after apporting to the rooftop. The watcher was looking down at the street and hadn't heard Drake. The man was wearing a dark thawb over what looked like a military uniform, and he was armed with a rifle: large, with a scope and bipod. He didn't seem inclined to use it.

If the man was watching the murderer, why didn't he stop him?

Unless the man *wanted* the murderer to kill.

Drake carefully touched the watcher's mind. He was an operative for the Alliance. He and his team had been working on Prince Aziz for months. They were using an exotic cocktail of drugs to drive the prince insane. Not that it had taken much to push him over the edge.

Team? Drake thought. He'd only sensed the one man.

The high-caliber rifle round struck Drake between the shoulders with the force of a swung sledgehammer. Drake's armor protected him from the shot, but it still staggered him. He activated his helmet without thinking, and another round struck the side of his head an instant later. The Alliance had set up a crossfire of snipers, to stop anyone from interfering. The snipers were using some electronic sound suppression; the rifle rounds were hypersonic but almost silent.

The observer in front of Drake was diving for his rifle. Drake lunged forward and slammed the man's head into the roof's low wall, which crumbled under the impact. The man's head didn't fare much better.

A plan coalesced in a moment, and Drake raised the man's rifle. The prince was on the street below, trailing a pretty, young woman. Drake focused on the prince's chest; the weapon used a laser for targeting, and Drake could easily see the red dot as he pulled the trigger. The nearly silent round blew a hole bigger than Drake's fist through the prince. He had an almost comic look of surprise as he fell to his knees and then onto his face.

Drake dropped the rifle to the rooftop.

He knew where the other two shots had come from. Drake reached out with the Instrumentality and apported the men to him. They appeared, disoriented, in front of him on the rooftop. One of the men managed to get off a lucky shot as he appeared. The round stuck Drake's faceplate and splashed away with a scream of torn tungsten and depleted uranium.

Drake grabbed end of the rifle barrel just as the man fired again. The rifle exploded; the pressure of the round had nowhere to go. Both of the other men screamed as shrapnel from the explosion lacerated them. Drake snapped one's man neck and grabbed the other in a choke hold that lifted him from his feet.

A quick scan of the man's mind showed that these three were the only Alliance operatives on Masir, or at least, this one didn't know of any others. Once Drake was in his mind, the operative couldn't lie to Drake. The man screamed and writhed under the pain of the mental invasion, but he didn't know anything else.

Drake carried him to the edge of the building.

Screams from the street below indicated that the prince's body had been found. Drake could hear sirens in the distance. He forced the man to draw his own pistol and shoot the two bodies on the roof. Then the man shot himself in the temple. The side of the operative's head blew out across the building roof, and he and the pistol dropped over the edge of the building into the street. It would look as if the man had committed suicide to prevent capture.

More screams from below said the operative's body had been discovered, as well.

The police would find the body and naturally examine the rooftop, too. They'd find the other bodies and wonder what had happened. Drake guessed that with a prince dead and implicated to some degree in the murders, there wouldn't be a lengthy inquiry. The official story would no doubt be that the prince had been lured out in an attempt to stop the killer, and assassinated by Alliance operatives. The Alliance would be blamed for all of the murders.

Drake apported back the main cabin of Jon's ship, startling an oath from Yousef.

"What has happened?" Yousef asked then, looking at the blood on Drake's coat.

Drake folded his helmet away. "Your problem has been solved, Yousef. There won't be any more murders."

"The prince?"

"It's complicated," Drake replied. "He is dead. So is a team of Alliance operatives." Drake explained what he'd discovered and what he'd done about it.

"This is a classic example of why one should be careful of what one wishes for. The prince is dead. There will be weeks of mourning. You are certain that the deaths will be blamed on the Alliance?"

"I don't doubt that some will suspect the truth," said Drake, "but I left an overwhelming amount of evidence that it was the Alliance. Three bodies' worth of evidence. I think the royal family will grateful to be able to save face, as will the police."

"I wish it could have been done another way, but this was probably for the best," Yousef said. "I suppose you'd like to know what you came here for."

"It would be for the best," Drake said. "I feel that I have earned answers."

"I don't know where Dr. Hakubi is being held," said Yousef. "I do now someone who does."

Drake sighed. Nothing was ever easy.

CHAPTER FORTY-FOUR

After one look at Drake's face, Jon retrieved his best liquor from the cabinet in the galley. The changes to his metabolism meant that normal alcohol had little effect on Jon, but he sometimes had guests who relished a glass or two.

Drake tossed down the bottle in one long swallow. It was good to know that Drake had emotions, even if he was a little frightening when distraught. Drake was frightening at the best of times, though. Even after weeks together, Jon was still finding depths to the man he hadn't known were there. Jon wondered if Drake would ever open up, and how he would feel if Drake did.

"Yousef, you were going to tell us how to find Dr. Hakubi," Drake prompted.

"Indeed I was, and I shall. It is difficult, though," Yousef began. "You're probably not going to like what I have to say, Jon."

"I think it's been a night for that sort of thing," Jon replied. He hadn't liked Drake's solution to the murders, either, but it had been decisive. Jon didn't believe in killing if it could be avoided. Drake had probably had the right of it, though. The prince had been a beast that needed to be put down. The Alliance operatives... Well, Jon had little remorse for them, either.

"My information about Dr. Hakubi comes from one of the other pilots," said Yousef.

Jon had a bad feeling about what Yousef was about to say. It wasn't quite at the level of precognition, but it had weight nonetheless. "Are you going to tell us which pilot?"

"Lolani Ikaika," Yousef said quietly.

"Son of a bitch." Jon stood and began pacing. He and Lolani had once been close, but that had been several years ago. They'd had an argument, and Jon hadn't seen her since.

"Not a friend of yours?" asked Drake.

Jon stopped. "No, I wouldn't say that. She was good friend once. We've had... philosophical disagreements. There's more to it, but I'd rather not get into that. I don't think she'll want to see me."

"She's one of our jump pilots," said Yousef. "She's also a privateer. She felt that the better way to deal with the Alliance was to attack their shipping."

"Harming an enemy nation economically is a viable wartime strategy," Drake said.

"She's somewhat indiscriminate," Yousef added.

"*Somewhat?* She's become a murderer," Jon spat. "She uses her jumpship to hunt civilian ships and cripple them. She doesn't spare any of the crew or passengers."

"Sometimes war doesn't leave any elegant moral solutions. Look at me, Jon." Drake gestured to himself. "I'm standing here covered in the blood of three men I killed not less than an hour ago. Were they evil men? Did they deserve to die?" Drake shrugged.

"They were pushing the prince to commit horrific murders – you said so yourself."

"True. In this case, those men were guilty of that. It wasn't my job to determine their guilt, however. I judged and executed them because I had the agency and the means to do so. This other pilot is doing the best she can to cripple an enemy far too large and powerful for her to take on directly."

"She could damage the ships, take the cargo. She doesn't have to kill all those people."

"No, she doesn't have to kill them, but then her tactics would not be as efficient," said Drake. "If she spared the crews, the attacks would not serve to psychologically demoralize the enemy. You must think of the maximum gain in asymmetric warfare."

"Drake, can't you ever just think of the human cost?" Jon asked. Lolani had killed thousands of people. She'd wanted Jon to join her. He'd refused. She hadn't taken it well; there might have been a knife involved. He didn't want to dwell on the memory.

"Need I remind you that I'm *not* human, Jon? I cannot allow myself to think of the human cost. I've been fighting in a war for longer than your species has had civilization. If I did think of the cost, I would lose my mind. Anyone would. You see the power I have, and you think I'm powerful. I am, but my enemy is powerful, too. I fight the only way I know how. The cost is high. I could name all the soldiers I lost to the war, but it would take weeks. I fight anyway. I doubt your friend fights the way she does out of bloodlust."

"Damn you, Drake." Jon didn't like Drake's logic. He made the worst things sound proper.

"No doubt I am." Drake turned away from Jon. "Yousef, where can we find this other pilot?"

"I'm not sure where she might be at any given time. She returns to her home planet between strikes. She's from Kai. Your best bet would be to try to intercept her there."

"And you're sure she knows where Dr. Hakubi is being held?"

"Lolani came to me here on Masir, to try to enlist aid for a rescue attempt. I had to turn her down. We don't have the resources, nor do we wish to attract any more attention from the Alliance. She didn't take it well. She has a bad temper."

"Avoiding the Alliance's attention seems to have done you little good."

"We still couldn't fight them openly. A direct war would leave us subjugated."

"The Alliance prefers subterfuge," said Jon. "They like plausible deniability with their citizens. They prefer to let nations tear themselves apart, and then step in to restore order."

"In a representative government, the politicians are technically answerable to the people. Such nations rarely indulge in open war," said Drake. "These Alliance people know what they're doing."

"Yeah, they killed my entire family when they did that to my world," Jon said. "Forgive me for not thinking about how great they are."

"I didn't say they *should* be doing it. I said they seem good at it. If they did that to your world, then you should want to strike back at them," Drake replied. "Your friend Lolani is doing that."

"I do want to strike back against the ones who did it!" Jon said, slamming his fist into the table. "I just think that killing people not directly responsible for the crime is uncalled-for."

"No one is saying you have to kill anyone," said Drake, "but don't you think others should be allowed to make the decision for themselves? This Lolani sounds like a freedom fighter. You don't have to agree with her methods to respect what she's doing."

"Did you?" Jon asked. "Did you respect the men you killed tonight?" He knew it was probably a low blow. Drake had obviously been bothered by what he'd done.

"I did, actually. They did what they were ordered to do, but none of them enjoyed it. Even the prince was a pawn who had to be drugged out of his mind to commit those acts of violence. I didn't scan the prince's mind before I killed him, but I imagine he was confused and distraught. I can respect an enemy, and still do what I must. Lolani, however, isn't your enemy. Respect your friend. In any case, it seems as if we need her."

"Why is it so damn hard to win an argument with you, Drake?" asked Jon.

"This is hardly the first time such thoughts have passed through my mind. Do you think I've never had this conversation with other friends? I'm orders of magnitude older than you."

Jon shook his head. "I suppose you're right."

"Of course I am."

Jason snorted back a laugh. Jon had thought he was asleep. Geoffrey had gone off to his cabin before Drake had come back.

"You have something to add, Jason?" Drake asked.

"I think you like to think you're right," Jason said, "whether you are or not."

"Doesn't everyone?"

Θ

Jason had mixed feelings about them moving on to another world. He'd come to like Masir. It was a lovely planet, despite the arid climate, with a generally likable people. Jason also liked that it was culturally appropriate here to cover one's head. He normally wore a bandanna to cover his ears, but it wasn't always socially acceptable back in Cincinnati.

"You should wait until morning to return to your lab, Yousef," said Drake. "The city will be in an uproar tonight, with the prince having been found dead."

"I hadn't thought of that. The police will be rabid."

"Well, at least they have bodies to hold accountable. Luckily for the Alliance operatives, they are already dead."

"You don't think the police will find it suspicious that the Alliance Operatives are all dead?" Yousef asked.

"No, I don't, actually," said Drake. "I made it look as if one of the operatives killed the others, then shot himself before falling into the street. I made his suicide happen in front of witnesses. The authorities will be happy to close the case, and everyone will be relieved that the nightmare is over."

"Do I want to know how you made him do that?"

"Probably not."

Jason wished he had some whiskey or other strong alcohol. He didn't feel like going to the galley to search for some, though. Jason had known that Drake killed the Alliance operatives, but it was beyond disturbing to know that Drake had taken control of a man's mind and made him kill himself. He wondered macabrely if Drake had been in the man's mind when that happened. If Drake had felt the man...

"Have you thought about it, Jon?" asked Drake.

"You're right. We need Lolani. I just hope she doesn't try to kill me when we meet."

"I can be very persuasive."

"Lolani is a good person," said Yousef. "She has helped our world."

"Yousef, do you mind if I ask you a question?" Drake said.

"Not at all."

"Masir is a beautiful world," Drake began, "but it could be better. There appears to be too little water, and the magnetic field of the planet is weak. Too much stellar radiation reaches the surface. I was curious as to why this world hasn't been terraformed."

"Our world is not a rich one. We mine ice from the rings of the gas giants farther out. That helps. As for the magnetic field, what could we do about that?"

"I'd jumpstart the core, for starters," Drake said. "Increase the spin of the planet. With a proper magma cycle, the volcanoes would release more of the water that is trapped in the rocks. That might fix the problem with the magnetic field. If not, you could construct a plasma torus in orbit and generate a field."

"Our science is not advanced enough to do half of that."

"I would think you'd be motivated to develop the science."

"As I said, we are not a rich world."

Jason wondered if the Cynosure or Instrumentality could do what Drake was talking about. He suspected not. There was a big difference between making a change of clothes and remaking a planet. It was a strange thing for Drake to bring up.

Drake never said anything without a reason, though.

Jason wondered what he was planning.

CHAPTER FORTY-FIVE

Geoffrey was relieved that Jon lifted off the surface of Masir more gently than he'd left Earth. He'd already seen Masir from orbit on the way in, but at least he didn't pass out this time. Geoffrey was surprised to realize that he was going to miss that drab world.

Masir receded behind them, and Geoffrey wished he could see the other ships. At least he could sometimes see their engine glow. Traveling this way gave him a greater appreciation of just how empty space actually was.

"I'm going to take us out of the normal shipping lanes before I jump to 96 Gamma Piscium," Jon said over the intercom. "I'll let you guys know before I jump."

"Drake, what are we doing?" asked Jason. "I mean, why all this running around?"

"We need to understand what was done to Jon."

"I thought it was a gene therapy or something."

"Yes, but there's no way that I've heard of to alter someone so that they appear to be a direct descendant of a specific individual. The Cynosure thought Jon was a royal family member, descended from the founder of that family, who tied the Cynosure to his genes. Jon's DNA read correctly; he would have died otherwise."

"I wish I understood better what the Cynosure actually is. I mean, I know that it's an ancient machine with immense power, but that doesn't tell me much."

"I understand it can be confusing," Drake replied. "I'm not exactly an authority on Cynosure."

"So when you say we need to understand what was done, what you mean is *why*," said Geoffrey.

"No, I mean *what*," said Drake. "*Why* is another, more complex question. For now, we need to understand how a scientist from this Realm could make a person be able to attune to the Cynosure. The implications are frightening. Why they did it is also something we need to know, but I need to understand how first."

"You mean someone had to have DNA from a person who could attune to the Cynosure in the first place," Jason said. "They couldn't have accidentally stumbled on the correct combination of genes, right?"

"Correct. Humans don't even have all of the genes the scientists would have needed to use. At least, most of them don't. No, to fool the Cynosure, you'd have to use genetic material from a member of the royal family of the Golden Kingdom."

"Why do you think they did it?" asked Geoffrey.

"I can't even begin to speculate," said Drake. "I would think that if they wanted more of their kind, they'd make them the old-fashioned way."

"What?"

"Sex, Geoffrey. They would just have sex."

Geoffrey blushed. "When you said *make*, I thought you meant *genetically engineer* or something."

"Okay, I'm about to make the jump to Kai," Jon interrupted over the intercom.

Geoffrey gripped the hand rests on his acceleration couch. There was a feeling of tension, and then a wave of disorientating nausea swept over him. The displays blurred with rainbows, and then there was a beautiful, blue world on the screens.

"We made it," said Jon. "That took longer than I expected."

Geoffrey wondered what Jon meant. The jump had taken less time than a breath. His stomach was settling down, but the nausea lingered.

Kai was everything that Masir hadn't been, a swirl of white clouds and blue water. Geoffrey didn't see much land through the clouds; he supposed the continents could be on the other side of the planet. Earth wouldn't look much different if one came in over the Pacific Ocean.

As Jon moved the ship into orbit, Geoffrey saw a huge moon, much like Earth's own but larger and closer. Kai must have tremendous tides. Geoffrey still didn't see much land down there.

"What's the plan, Jon?" asked Drake. "Are we going to stay in orbit, or land and look for Lolani on the surface?"

"I'm speaking with orbital control now. They say she landed on the main island two days ago and hasn't left. I'm getting clearance to land."

"Please make sure your seat belts are fastened and your seatback trays are secure," Geoffrey said.

"What was that?" asked Jon.

"Sorry, just something they say on my Earth when coming in for a landing."

"Gotcha."

The ship bucked a little as ionized gas flowed up over the wings and sides. Geoffrey thought the glowing atmosphere was pretty. It didn't seem to last as long as it had over Masir, and then they were into the atmosphere. Jon flew through majestic, towering clouds laced with lightnings.

Geoffrey didn't have any of the fear he normally felt when

flying. This ship wasn't some aluminum airplane. It was made for space. Flying through clouds wasn't scary.

Under the cloud deck, the ocean was dappled and heaving. Tremendous waves raced them toward a string of volcanic islands. Geoffrey had never been to Hawaii, but he'd seen pictures. This place reminded him of that. The islands were green and lush with life. Massive reefs slowed the waves violently, the water exploding high into the sky.

Jon circled a large island and brought the ship down in a small spaceport. The field held a few other ships and shuttles, and hangers were just visible to the east. Jon taxied to a stop and then joined them in the cabin. It was raining heavily outside; Geoffrey could hear the steady roar of water droplets against the hull.

"Figures there'd be a storm," Jon said. "It's normally beautiful here."

Geoffrey stood and swayed a little. The gravity felt weird.

"Yeah, Kai is a little smaller than Earth. Gravity is only point-eight-six standard."

"Where do we start looking for Lolani?" asked Drake.

"Well, her ship is over there," Jon said gesturing across the field on the screen.

Through the rain, Geoffrey could barely make out a ship that looked similar to Jon's.

"She'll be either in her ship or one of the local bars."

"Should we go knock?" asked Drake.

"I'll let you knock. She might try to shoot me."

"Do you think that likely?"

"No, not really. Lolani is hard to read. She's a good person but has a bad temper. She might try to fight you just because you look tough. Please don't kill or maim her."

"Is there a history we should be aware of?" Drake asked delicately.

Jon smiled. "We're just friends. Not saying I wouldn't if she wanted, but Lolani always thought I was too tall. We're good. No history to worry about."

"I'm not worried about whether you slept with her," said Drake. "I just want to know the nature of the animosity she holds toward you. If she's a jilted lover, she could be a problem. If not, then what? You're worried, whether you say it or not."

"She's just hot-headed," said Jon. "We've had problems in the past, nothing major."

"How will we know her? What does she look like?"

"She's Polynesian, brown hair, brown eyes, brown skin, about a hundred fifty-two centimeters. She has a lot of tattoos." Jon shrugged. "I'm not sure what to say. She looks like most of the woman on this planet. I'll point her out."

"All right, then I suppose we should be about it."

"You okay, Drake?"

"I'm just a bit tired. Yesterday was a long day, and I am feeling as if we need to hurry. I'm not sure why, but I trust my feelings."

Jon nodded. "Okay. I don't sense anything, but you've been doing this longer than I have. By the way, you shouldn't wear your armor or sword. It's not that kind of place."

Drake left the cabin and came back a few minutes later in boots, black jeans, and a green tee shirt under a black leather jacket. He had his pistol on his hip. Jon didn't bother to ask him to remove it. Maybe no one would notice.

When Jon lowered the ramp, the air hit them like a wet pillow: hot and humid and smelling of rain and ocean salt. The humidity was a shock after the last planet.

Drake led the way across the field to the other ship. The rain didn't seem to bother him, but it bothered Geoffrey. He was soaked within the first hundred feet and miserable by the time they reached Lolani's ship. The ramp was up.

"Do we knock or what?" asked Jason.

He looked as miserable as Geoffrey felt, despite having a hat to wear.

"I paged the ship's systems," said Jon. "She's not aboard."

"So now what?"

Jon gestured toward the lights in the distance. "We head to the bars around the port. She'll be there."

Geoffrey thought the lights looked to be a couple miles away. "How will we find her?"

"We look for the most disreputable place," Jon said. "She'll be there looking for a fight."

Θ

Jon led them across the landing field.

It was a long, wet trip. Jon hated looking like a soggy mess, but he didn't have any of the electrostatic shells most people on Kai wore during storm season. He hadn't realized it was that time of year, and Yousef hadn't reminded him.

He knew which bars Lolani frequented. There were only a couple that would let her back in after she got into fights. Lolani wasn't truly aggressive and violent, but she sure didn't like pushy people. Guys who mouthed off to her usually got a powerful knee to the genitals.

Whatever else could be said about the jumpship pilot program, it had made all of the pilots who survived tougher and stronger. Lolani had the muscles of a heavy-worlder. The local toughs didn't stand a chance.

"I think this one is our best bet," said Jon.

He'd stopped outside a club that spilled light and a steady, heavy industrial beat into the night. The patrons sounded raucous, and a sign outside advertised cage fights. Lolani wouldn't have been able to resist.

Jon felt Drake do something as they entered, and a ripple, like an electric charge, flowed across Jon's skin. The rainwater was repelled and fell to the floor of the club.

"How do you do that?" Jon asked Drake quietly. "Could I do it with Cynosure?"

"I imagine the principles would be the same," said Drake. "Desire and focus, with the Power held in your mind. That's all sorcery is. All the spells and such are just dressing."

Jon nodded and stepped up to the bouncer, a man with fierce Maori tattoos on his face. "What's the cover?" he asked.

"Twenty," the bouncer replied. He had a surprisingly gentle voice. "Each."

Jon credited him eighty-five. "They're with me."

"Hey!" The man shot a thick arm across the doorway. "No weapons."

Drake unhooked the holster with his pistol from his belt and let go of it. It hung in the air. He blew on it, and it faded away.

"Cute trick," said the bouncer. He checked under Drake's coat. "Where'd it go?"

"It was just an illusion."

"Cool. Okay, you guys are good to go. You should go into business with that act. It looked real."

"I'll consider that," said Drake.

CHAPTER FORTY-SIX

Music pounded at Jon until he could feel it in his bones; his heartrate increased to match the beat, rhythmic and heavy.

The club was on two levels, with the entrance on the upper floor. That part was mostly tables around the balcony overlooking the large dance floor. Below, a sea of people seethed and rocked in a manner much like the ocean outside in the storm. Near the bar was a small empty area, where people stayed clear by unspoken agreement. It was dark and lit by neon lights and glowing patches on clothes.

A cage, currently empty, hung over the dancefloor. Jon's internal chronometer said the time was barely seven in the evening. The fights should be starting soon. Lolani was sure to turn up for those.

Jon gestured to the stairs and then made his way down into the mass of people. He didn't see Lolani, but that didn't mean much. She was average height, and there were a lot of people dancing on that floor. Most of the men were only around one hundred seventy centimeters tall, compared to Jon's two hundred three. He stood out. Lolani would find him. He just had to be available.

He pushed past the people to the bar, with Drake and the others following him. It was much quieter here; the club was using a silence zone around the bar. No wonder the dancers stayed back.

"I'm covering for these three," Jon said to the bartender.

She nodded. "What can I get you?"

"Beers all around." He tapped the credit pad and transferred a hundred credits over.

The bartender popped the tops on four bottles and placed them on the bar, then put four more with them. The beers were only ten each, but Jon didn't care. He took a long pull on his. The alcohol wouldn't do much, but the beer was refreshing.

The song wound down, and the crowd surged toward the bar, calling for drinks. The cage lowered to the dance floor, and the dancers slowly moved out of the way. When it had settled, an announcer said the first fight was in twenty – bets to be taken at the bar. Jon gestured for his companions to grab their drinks and move back up the stairs.

The lower level was packed solid with people, now that the cage was taking up part of the dance floor. There was a better view from the upstairs balcony. If Jon knew Lolani, she'd be one of the cage fighters. She never could resist a fight.

Suddenly she was there, pushing through the crowd to stand before him. Lolani wasn't a big woman, but she had a lot of presence. She was muscular and had full sleeves of tattoos on both arms, mostly tribal patterns. Her hair was shaved into a blue mohawk. She plucked the beer bottle out of his hand and drained it, dropping it to the floor when she was done.

"Never thought I'd see you on my turf again, Jon," she said.

"Heard you needed some help retrieving a mutual friend of ours."

"Not from you." She picked up his second bottle of beer and tossed it back. "I don't need no coward with me."

Jon winced. "I'm not, and you know it."

"Whatever, bruh. Who're your friends?" she asked. "They cowards, too?"

"Most assuredly not, *wahine li'ili'I*," said Drake.

Lolani laughed. "You come face me down there, *hapa*, maybe I think about listening to the *haole* here. I'd ask him to fight me, but I know I can kick his skinny ass."

"*Mahalo*," Drake said. "I'll see you in a moment."

Lolani laughed again and moved away from them.

"Drake, we need her," said Jon. "What are you doing?"

"She wants to fight. I'm happy to oblige. Don't worry, I won't damage her. Nothing permanent, anyway."

Jon sighed and waved the way to the stairs.

Θ

The club hadn't seemed too bad to Jason until he saw the large, steel cage being lowered from the ceiling.

He sometimes had nightmares about cages like that. They reminded him of those medieval European crow's cages in which prisoners were forced to stand in a cage until they died of dehydration or exposure to the elements. It had been a barbaric and sickening practice. Of course, the cage below was big enough for dozens of people.

Jason downed his two beers quickly and felt a bit of a head rush, since he hadn't eaten recently. Intellectually, he knew the cage was just a fighting ring, no different from a ring for boxing. The emotional part of his brain didn't give a damn about his intellect.

The spectators were jeering and screaming. They wanted to see blood, and they didn't care whose. Jason hoped Drake was as competent in unarmed fighting as he was with a blade, because the competitors all looked huge and cruel. Two of the men looked particularly fierce, covered in Maori tattoos.

Jason didn't have any tattoos; the idea of allowing someone

to stick a steel needle into him was the stuff of nightmare. He wasn't squeamish, but he just *couldn't* want that. He couldn't even think about it.

"You okay?" Geoffrey asked him.

Jason laughed nervously. "Not really. I'm just having a bit of a panic attack."

"Yeah, all these people and the noise are pretty overwhelming."

Jason nodded. That was a safe excuse.

He'd always hated crowds. Even going shopping was a bad experience. If Geoffrey thought his problem was just the noise and the people, and Geoffrey knew him… Jason relaxed a little bit. The alcohol helped to ease his tense muscles. Drake was going to be fine, and no one was going to throw Jason into that cage.

He felt inside his jacket. He'd wisely figured he couldn't openly carry and had left the large dagger, the one Drake had given him, aboard the *Chwyldro*. However, his broken ceramic knife was still in his inside jacket pocket. If anyone tried anything, even if they just thought they were being funny, Jason would let them feel the sharp edge of *that* knife.

That made him feel even better.

He was among friends, and he wasn't defenseless.

Everything would be all right.

⊙

Drake used Jon's credit stick to pay the entry fee.

He was the twelfth fighter to sign up. He didn't pay attention to who signed up after him. The tournament was a single elimination round-robin, fairly straightforward. The first two fighters were large, muscular men covered with tattoos. Their fight was brutal and short. There didn't seem to be many rules, other than no killing and no weapons. The bout lasted until one of the men was unconscious.

The winner of the first fight drew an immediate second and was defeated by a tall woman whom Drake thought looked vaguely Marathi. The next fight was Lolani against a bear of a man as tall as Jon but at least twice as heavy. Lolani fought with a style that reminded Drake of Muay Thai, although it may have simply been a descendant of that ancient martial art. Jon had indicated that humans had been settled on other worlds for several centuries, although Drake had no idea what the year it was in this Realm. Certainly enough time had passed for martial arts to have evolved.

Lolani won easily. She drew the next fight against the previous woman. Lolani obviously had the advantage. She was much stronger than her taller opponent. She was also much faster. He suspected Lolani was holding back a bit against the other woman.

Drake thought that Lolani must have had the same nerve enhancement treatments that Jon had. That would make for an interesting fight, if he and Lolani were matched up. Not that Drake was concerned about the outcome.

Drake drew the next fight, and stripped off his shirt and boots as he'd seen the other men do.

"Marcos the Lion vs the Drake!" the announcer called.

"My, aren't you pretty!" his opponent jeered. "I'm gonna mark up your pretty skin, boy."

Drake smiled as he let the man set the pace. Drake's own preferred style was closer to Tai Chi, although developed for brutal warfare rather than meditation. Most of the people in this tournament seemed to be trained in kickboxing or Muay Tai. Drake simply flowed around Marcos' strikes to get a feel for his opponent.

Drake's first strike skipped through Marcos' defenses and hit him in the upper chest. The man was flung around and into the side of the cage. Drake thought his opponent looked a bit scared then, as Marcos circled to catch his breath.

Marcos moved in with a flurry of kicks. Drake blocked the attacks and put him down with a series of strikes to the chest and then head. Marcos fell hard and didn't get up. Drake waited for the announcer to declare the winner and then left the cage and waited for his next bout.

Two more rounds, and then Drake fought two fights in a row. Both of these fighters were more cautious than his first opponent had been – not that it helped them. Drake took them down quickly. Lolani was just as fast to take down her next opponent. Drake was now certain she'd been holding back earlier.

Finally, it was down to Lolani and Drake as the last undefeated fighters. He suspected that the organizers had fixed the draw a few times to get them together. The crowd wanted a spectacle, and Drake and Lolani were clearly the best two fighters here. Drake thought the crowd was probably going to get their money's worth.

"So you can fight, bruh," Lolani said as she entered the ring. "You're not too bad."

"So can you," said Drake.

They began circling each other.

Lolani was fast, far faster than Drake had expected. She caught him with a light kick to the shoulder and then an elbow to the ribs that actually hurt. She was strong, too.

She was just as quick on the defense, and it took Drake almost a minute into the fight to hit her: an uppercut to the ribs that lifted her from the ground. She caught him with a kick to his face as she went down. He hadn't considered she'd stay that focused on the fight.

Drake circled her and wiped the blood from his cut lip. She was good. Drake smiled at her and then changed his fighting style. He'd been using the more passive Tai Chi style. He switched to the style he'd learned as a boy. His native martial art wasn't from the Earth and had never been seen there. He saw Lolani's confused expression as she noticed his stance change. She could tell he'd changed styles, but she didn't understand to what or why.

She started to circle him, and Drake moved in quickly. His native style was very aggressive. To match Lolani's speed, he had to push himself harder than he'd needed to in a long time. She was damn fast. He caught her with a kick; she blocked it but was lifted from her feet by the power of the strike. He delivered three rapid punches to her head while she was still airborne.

She hit the mat, unconscious.

The roar from the crowd was intoxicating. Drake could understand why Lolani fought in these matches. She was probably used to winning.

He almost felt bad for defeating her, but then, he was used to winning, too.

CHAPTER FORTY-SEVEN

Jon followed Drake as he carried Lolani back to the *Chwyldro*.

The rain had stopped while they were in the club. Jon wasn't sure how he felt about Lolani, or about Drake, for that matter. He was angry about them fighting, even if it had been in a contest. Lolani had obviously given as well as she'd gotten in the fights, even against Drake. She'd always been a good fighter, even before the enhancements she'd received in the pilot program.

Jon liked her. He'd been attracted to her when they first met, years ago, but she hadn't felt the same way. She liked men and women who were more muscular than he was. Jon had always been thin, and the damage from the gene therapy only made that worse.

It was hard to feel something for someone and know they didn't feel it back. Of course, it was better than not knowing. He'd spent the first couple of years hoping she felt the way he did. It had been painful to learn otherwise, but at least they'd been able to stay friends.

Then the Alliance had moved on his homeworld.

Jon lost everything. He wasn't even able to say goodbye. His family were all dead before he even learned of the revolution. He didn't know what had happened to their bodies, if they'd been buried. He couldn't return to Rhyddid without facing execution; as it was, he'd barely escaped.

Lolani had wanted to fight the Alliance. Jon didn't have the strength. That last conversation played itself out in his mind again now, as it often had over the years. Lolani had gotten it into her head to start attacking civilian ships, but Jon couldn't be a part of that.

"The Alliance is blockading our systems," Lolani had said. "They're cutting us off from essential supplies."

"Then I guess it's a good thing we have jumpships," he replied. "We can sneak around the blockade ships and buy what our planets need."

"Fuck that. We should *take* what we need."

"What are you talking about?"

"Their merchant ships are virtually unprotected," said Lolani. "We jump in, shear off the front of the ship to void it to space. Then we take the cargo. They won't know what hit them."

"You're talking about targeting civilians!"

"What the hell do you think *they're* doing? How many civilians have died on Rhyddid? It isn't just your family, Jon. People are dying in the streets!"

"You think I don't know that?"

"I think you're real good at hiding from the truth."

Jon had had a flash of insight he probably should have kept to himself. That's what was great about hindsight: it was so much more powerful than foresight. "What are you doing, if not hiding?"

"Fuck you, Jon. I'm doing this."

"I won't be a part of what you're doing."

"Then to hell with you."

Jon apported between her and the exit port. "Lolani, don't do this."

"Get out of my way."

"You know I have to try to stop you."

She pushed past him, and he grabbed her arm. The next thing he knew, he was on his back, laying on the deck. She had a knife in her hand, and that wild look she got sometimes.

"Lolani!" he pleaded with her. Not for his life, but for her to stop, to think.

She flicked the knife casually, leaving a line of fire across his cheek. "Don't ever get in my way again," she said. Then she left.

Jon had lay there for a while, bleeding, before he got up and cleaned the wound. He still had feelings for Lolani, even after that. Her leaving hurt far more than the cut. He even cherished the scar, until it faded. Jon had loved other women, but none of them had been like Lolani.

She hadn't spoken to him since, until she walked up to him in the club.

It wasn't as if he was pining away for her. He knew that whatever might have happened between them never would. His feelings were... complex. If nothing else, he still loved her as a friend, one of the few he had. To see her broken and bloody at Drake's hands had almost driven him to fight. It was absurd. Drake was bloody and bruised himself, from what Lolani did to him. He'd only taken her up on her invitation to fight; it would have been rude not to, plus it was probably the best chance they had of recruiting her.

Maybe it just rankled Jon that it had been Drake who'd gotten into the cage instead of him. Without using his apportation ability, Jon knew he didn't stand a chance in a fight against either of them. Even then, he didn't know if he'd have a chance against Drake. He'd never seen anyone move as quickly as Drake did. The man had been a blur.

Lolani's quip about Jon being a coward hurt, maybe even more than she'd intended. Jon had run from his responsibilities at home, and then run again when home had been taken from him. He wasn't a coward, but it bothered him that someone he loved and respected might think so.

He'd have to get up the courage to ask her later.

Jon smiled at the irony.

Θ

Geoffrey helped Drake settle Lolani on one of the acceleration couches.

She looked terrible. Not that Drake looked that much better. She'd really given Drake a beating, which Drake had returned in triplicate. Geoffrey wondered what Jon thought of what had happened. He knew that despite some differences, Lolani was Jon's friend, maybe even more than that. Geoffrey had seen the look of longing on Jon's face. He knew that look well from his own.

Unrequited love was tough to deal with.

"Geoffrey, if you don't mind, would you dampen a washcloth for me?" said Drake.

"You got it." Geoffrey ran to the washroom and back.

Jon had gotten a first aid kit from somewhere, and he and Drake were looking at Lolani's face. It looked pretty bad to Geoffrey. She wasn't bleeding anymore, but her whole face was swollen and bruised. She had several cuts over her eyes and on one cheekbone, like Geoffrey had seen on fighters in televised boxing matches. They looked horrible.

"I don't think the bone is broken," Drake was saying. "I pulled my punches. Ah, the washcloth. Thanks."

Drake carefully washed Lolani's face. Geoffrey had never imagined Drake could be tender, but he seemed to have a delicate touch when he wanted to. Her face didn't look much better after he was done. Drake handed the washcloth back to Geoffrey, and he went and rinsed it out.

Drake washed his own face then; it had been a bit bloody. His lip was swollen, but nothing compared to how Lolani looked. Drake stripped off his shirt, and Geoffrey could see a massive dark purple bruise on his side. It looked worse on Drake because he was so pale.

"That looks nasty," said Jon. "She do that?"

Drake nodded as he explored the bruise with his fingertips.

"No offense, but good."

"She may have cracked a couple of my ribs," said Drake. "She's a remarkable woman."

"She was remarkable even before the gene therapy."

"I never said otherwise."

Jon sighed. "She'll be okay?"

"She's bruised and battered. So am I," said Drake. "Does your medical science in this place include nanogel packs?"

"They exist," said Jon. "I can't afford them, even with the money you got from the Margrave."

Drake gestured, and a plastic crate appeared on the chair next to him. "Easier to pull them from the local universe than reach outside this Realm."

"Some hospital isn't going to find itself in need, is it?"

"No, I pulled them from a supply warehouse. There were six crates there."

Jason opened the crate and held up a squashy bag filled with grey fluid. "What are these things?"

"Medical nanotechnology," said Drake. "This kind is mostly used to repair soft tissue damage. The bags are filled with microscopic machines that bore down into the patient and repair the damage on a molecular level."

Jason dropped the bag back into the crate and rubbed his hand on his pants leg.

"You know I'm dying to ask you how you know about

those," said Jon.

"I hope not. I doubt these could help you, in that case."

"He jests."

"Is it so shocking that I have a sense of humor?"

Drake picked up two nanogel packs and placed them on Lolani's face. He did something with the edges of the bags, and they reshaped to fit the contours of her face, looking as if they'd stuck to her.

"How long will it take?" asked Geoffrey.

"A couple of hours for the bruising and cuts," Drake said. "The brain damage may take a little longer."

"Drake…" Jon sounded angry.

Drake sighed. "Any blow to the head resulting in unconsciousness results in trauma to the brain. She'll have swelling in the frontal lobe and her brain stem from the torsion. These are common martial arts injuries. She'll be fine and suffer no permanent impairment."

"Will they heal broken bones?" asked Geoffrey.

"These? No. Oh, they might help with swelling and such."

Geoffrey picked one up. "Do you need one for your ribs?"

Drake shook his head. "Better to save them for the four of you. I'll be healed in a few hours anyway. No need to waste one on me."

"I don't want you to ever use one of those on me," Jason said suddenly.

"They aren't made of anything you'd have a problem with," said Drake.

Jason shook his head. "Still, I don't want that."

Geoffrey wondered what Jason's problem was with the technology. Geoffrey thought it was pretty cool. He thought of all the times he could have used one of those medical packs, growing up. Maybe Jason was just creeped out at the idea of tiny robots crawling around inside him. Come to think of it, Geoffrey wasn't real keen on that, either.

"Well, hopefully you won't ever need one," said Jon. He picked up the first aid kit and crate of nanopacks. "I'll just take these to the galley."

Jason left for his cabin without saying anything else. He was always a bit weird after one of his panic attacks, and he'd had a hard time in the club, with all the noise and the people.

"Do you need anything else, Drake?" Geoffrey asked. He was wearing down quickly.

Drake gingerly pulled his shirt back on and settled into an acceleration couch. "I'm good. Thank you. I just need to rest a while to heal."

Jon came back in. "You staying up?"

Geoffrey yawned and shook his head. "I think I'll turn in."

"Okay." Jon did something that dimmed the cabin lights. "I'll be up front, if you need me."

"Thanks." Geoffrey went back to his cabin and fell into his bunk. It had been a long few days, and he needed to catch up on his sleep.

CHAPTER FORTY-EIGHT

Drake rose before the sun and got something from the galley. He wouldn't dignify it by calling it food, but at least it contained essential nutrients. He considered going out for food, but if the others had to eat this crap, he would, too. At least for now. To be honest, he just didn't feel like bothering with anything else. Maybe that was why Jon ate it.

His ribs felt better, and his lip appeared to be healed, although it was still a little tender as he ate. Jon had dimmed the cabin lights, and Drake didn't know how to brighten them. Not that it really mattered: his eyes saw well enough with any amount of light. He also didn't want to awaken Lolani.

The medical nanopacks were still attached to her face. Drake assumed they would fall when they had finished knitting her back together. That was how it usually worked. She was asleep, her heartrate and breathing slow and steady. Drake could see the jacks in her arms, like Jon's. He assumed she had one in her head, as well. He felt a bit bad about how hard he'd hit her at the end of the fight. He hadn't actually meant to damage her.

It had been some time since Drake had fought with just his hands and feet, and it had felt good to push himself. He was glad he was still just as fast as he should be. Of course, he hadn't been quite fast enough. His sore ribs and lip were a sign of that. He would need to get faster. If a human, no matter how enhanced, could hurt him, then so could the Ancient Enemy.

That was taking nothing away from Lolani. She was skilled, strong, and supernaturally fast. Whatever gene therapy had been done to Jon and the pilots in the same program, she'd gotten a good mix. She'd had good genes to begin with, Drake decided. She was small in stature but fit and muscular. She'd also been quite pretty, before Drake had smashed her face. He could understand why Jon had fallen for her.

Perhaps if it had worked out between her and Jon, their children would have averaged out to a normal height. Drake chuckled at the thought.

"I'm glad you're in a good mood," Lolani said groggily. "I feel like shit."

"Well, you look more like raw, tenderized steak."

She laughed a little and then cut it off. "Oh, don't make me laugh. That hurts."

"Can I get you anything?"

"Maybe a drink? Water, not alcohol," came her muffled reply.

"Just a moment." Drake got her a glass of water and returned to the cabin.

Lolani had adjusted her acceleration couch and was sitting up. The medical nanopacks were still adhered to her face. They looked a bit like grotesque ticks. Not that Drake had seen ticks that large in some time, fortunately.

Drake helped her drink a little of the water.

"Thanks," she said. She sounded stronger. "I don't think I got your name, or maybe you beat it out of me."

"Daeren Drake," he replied. "Most people just call me Drake."

"Dayeren… dayren… Yeah, I'll stick with Drake," she said.

"I'm Lolani, in case no one told you."

"I was aware. Jon spoke of you, of course."

"Of course." She settled back into the couch and dozed.

Drake watched over her.

After about half an hour, the nanogel packs fell off, and Lolani sat up and carefully rubbed her face. She still had some faint bruising there; it would take a while for her body to clear out the dead blood cells. Her cuts had closed and were now just pink scars, which Drake was confident would fade over time.

"So, I don't know you," said Lolani. "You're enhanced. Alliance Special Forces? You a jumpship pilot, too? Did that crazy doctor make more of us?"

"I'm not enhanced," said Drake. "Not the way you mean it, anyway. I'm just me."

"No way. You were faster and stronger than me. No human can be that fast without enhancement."

"As you say."

"Okay, you didn't hit me in the head *that* hard, or the nanopacks would still be on there. What do you mean, because I'm not following."

"You said *no human* could be that fast. Didn't you wonder where the genetic material came from?"

Lolani rubbed her face again. "You know, if you hadn't just kicked my ass, I'd say you were full of shit. There aren't any aliens, and you look human."

"No, *you* look Precursor," Drake replied. He hated using the lie, since he had no idea who that Precursor race had been. At least no one else did, either.

"Bullshit."

Drake was in his trueform, but she probably wasn't looking closely. He studied her for a moment and then shifted to look like her, bruises and all. He even used the Instrumentality to change his clothes. Lolani didn't say anything to him as he changed; he supposed she might be in shock.

"That's some kind of illusion, right?" she asked. "Damn, if I look like that, then you really messed me up."

"Not an illusion," Drake said in her voice. He stood up and walked to her. "You should have seen what you looked like before the nanopacks. Touch me."

"No, thank you. Then I might have to believe."

Drake reverted to his normal form and grinned, showing his fangs. He sat back down on his acceleration couch. "No one is trying to fool you."

"Didn't think you were. I just think I have some brain damage."

"Fortunately, no, you don't," Jon said as he came into the cabin, "although Drake can certainly make you think you do."

"So let me get this straight," Lolani said. "You found some Precursor drifting around and decided to bring him here to beat me up? You got a twisted sense of vengeance, Jon."

"Well, at least you haven't tied to cut me again yet."

"Nah, you liked it, bruh." Lolani started to shake her head and then thought better of it. "Seriously, what the hell?"

"Actually, I found Jon," said Drake. "I think Precursor DNA was used in the jump pilot program. I want to know how and why."

"Everything points to Dr. Hakubi," Jon said.

"Yeah, she was pretty whack." Lolani frowned. "You don't think she was a Precursor, do you?"

"We don't know," said Drake. "I'd like to meet her and find out. At the very least, she can tell me where she acquired the DNA she used for the gene therapy."

"You're taking this pretty well," Jon said.

Lolani shrugged and gestured at Drake. "Dude is definitely superhuman. He says he's a Precursor, who am I to argue? What do you really look like, anyway?"

"Like I do now."

"Cool ears. I like the fangs. How do you get the clothes to

change? Are they a part of you? That would be weird."

Drake chuckled. "Nanotechnology," he replied. In a way, it wasn't even a lie.

"Okay, I can buy that. You got any cool tech I can see? That would help me believe."

Drake apported his armor into the cabin.

"Armored space suit? Powered? I've heard the Alliance was working on stuff like this, but in the images of theirs I've seen, it was really bulky." Lolani stood up and walked around it. "How you put it on?"

Drake commanded it to open. "Don't touch the sword, though. It might eat you."

"Why do I think you're not joking?"

"Because I'm not."

"Right." Lolani pressed around on the inside. "You can't wear clothes in there."

"No, but I think now is not the best time for a demonstration."

"Can't blame me for trying."

Jon rolled his eyes.

"That armor isn't very thick," said Lolani. "What's it good against?"

"Just about anything. It will protect against everything up to fifty-megaton nuclear weapons. After that, the failsafe stasis field engages. You could fall through the heart of a star with it. I also have heavier armor available."

"Can you engage the stasis field?"

Drake closed the armor and triggered the stasis field remotely.

Lolani ran her hand over the silvery surface of the field effect. "This is the stasis field?"

"Yes. It's bubble of spacetime, a perfect mirror. Nothing can affect the interior while that's in effect. Time nearly stops inside."

"Nearly?"

"I set the field to last one nanosecond inside, about a minute outside the field."

The field blinked off, and the armor stood looking as it always did.

"Okay, I'm a believer," said Lolani. "That isn't anything we could build."

Drake apported his armor back to his cabin. "As you can see, I am what I say."

"So why are you hanging out with this loser?" Lolani asked, gesturing at Jon.

"That is unkind, lady," said Drake.

"Lady? I'm many things, but not that."

"To answer your question, Jon and I have become friends. People have tried to kill him. We are trying to discover why."

"People have tried to kill you?" Lolani asked. "You mean, other than me?"

"*Actually* trying to kill me, yes," Jon said. "We don't know why, but it seems to have something to do with the gene therapy."

"I could see why they might want to get their hands on Precursor technology, and even the genetic material, considering what it did to us, but why try to kill you?"

"We don't know that," said Drake. "We are hoping Dr. Hakubi can tell us."

CHAPTER FORTY-NINE

Geoffrey thought Lolani was looking much better this morning.

He got a plate of the stuff from the galley. At least when eating it for breakfast, he could pretend it was scrambled eggs, although it really could have used some pepper and salt, or just about any flavor, actually.

Jason came in with his own plate and settled into the chair next to Geoffrey. He looked about as enthusiastic to eat the stuff as Geoffrey did. Jason had also found a glass of something that looked like orange juice.

"Is that really juice?" asked Geoffrey.

Jason shook his head. "No, but at least it tastes sort of orange."

Geoffrey got up and found a glass for himself.

Drake, Jon, and Lolani were deep in conversation about that doctor they were looking for, and how they were going to break her out of prison. Geoffrey thought it sounded cool, like one of those jailbreaks in movies. They were talking about guards and when they could infiltrate the place.

"You're not planning on all of us going in there, are you?"

asked Jason.

Drake looked up from the portable screen he'd been studying. "No, we'd want the two of you to stay with the ship, unless you prefer to go to Masir. Honestly, I'd prefer Lolani to stay out of the prison, as well."

"No chance," she said.

"Jon and I can both apport," said Drake. "We can escape if things go poorly."

"Then either take me, too, or come back and get me," Lolani said. "I'm not staying behind on this one. This my operation, remember? I'm the one that got the intel."

"I merely stated what I would prefer," said Drake. "You may do as you wish, of course."

"Thank you." She glared at Jon.

Jon held up his hands in mock defense. "I didn't say anything."

"You didn't have to, bruh. You're always too overprotective."

Geoffrey grinned at Jon's discomfort. It was amusing to see someone else being embarrassed by things like that. To Geoffrey, it usually seemed to be *him* caught in embarrassing situations.

"Sounds good to me," Jason said quietly. "I don't want to go anywhere near some alien prison."

"Yeah, me, either," said Geoffrey. "You're not regretting coming along, are you?"

"Bit too late for that, don't you think?"

"Okay, guys, come over here, if you don't mind," Jon said.

Geoffrey and Jason stood and walked over to the others. "What's up?" asked Geoffrey.

"We need to know what you want to do. We can drop you off here or on Masir, or you can come along. We can't guarantee your safety, whatever choice you make."

"I got some good people you can stay with here," said

Lolani. "They'd take care of you two *haoles*."

"I don't know what that word means," Jason said.

"Not an insult, bruh. Just mean you ain't a native here."

"When you say *come along*, you mean in the ship, or into the prison?" asked Geoffrey.

"If you came along," said Jon, "we'd want you to stay with the ship."

"I think we'd rather stay with the ship," Geoffrey said.

Jason nodded.

"Okay, that makes things easier," Drake said. "We'll leave here later today and then make the jumps to the prison facility at Wolf 359."

"We're looking at a total of nine jumps," said Jon. "It will take a couple of hours, total. Lolani and I will need to rest before we assault the orbital facility."

"If there is heavy resistance in orbit, I'll apport into the prison complex and try to find Dr. Hakubi myself," said Drake. "Otherwise, we'll dock both ships at the facility and go from there. I'll leave you both firearms to defend the ships if you have to," he said to Jason and Geoffrey.

"Ships?" asked Jason.

"Lolani will be piloting her ship. It has better armaments than Jon's. I'd like one of you to travel with her."

"Sure, I can do that. Why, though?"

"So you can defend her ship after it docks."

"I doubt either of us can hold a ship by ourselves."

"You won't have to. We'll leave the coms open; you can talk to each other and to us. If you get in trouble, let us know, and we'll apport back. I should be able to neutralize just about any threat."

Jason blew out a long breath. "Okay, yeah. We can do that."

Geoffrey nodded. He didn't feel as confident as Jason sounded, but he was pleased that Drake was trusting them with guarding the ships. He wondered what kind of guns they'd get, and hoped he wouldn't have to use them.

☉

Jon wasn't sure it was a good idea for Jason to go over to Lolani's ship, but he didn't have any good reason to argue against it. It wasn't that he had a premonition of doom or anything – quite the contrary. Splitting up increased the odds of success by at least thirty percent.

Jon just wasn't sure how he felt about Jason being alone with Lolani.

Of course, she was going to be busy piloting. Of the two, he supposed Jason was the better choice. He was far less likely to be seduced. Jon wasn't even sure whether Jason liked women or not. He hadn't seen much indication one way or the other. Not that it mattered.

"Jon, quit sulking and come eat, bruh," Lolani called.

"I'm not sulking."

"Uh-huh."

Lolani had decided to take them all out to dinner before the mission. Jon would just as soon have avoided going, but Lolani was insistent. He knew that she thought she was going to die breaking Dr. Hakubi out of prison. With Lolani, everything was like that. She wasn't melodramatic, exactly, just a bit fatalistic.

Jon sighed and left his ship.

His companions were waiting for him outside. Lolani gestured impatiently. Jon just shook his head and followed along.

Despite what Lolani might think, Jon was looking forward to finding Dr. Hakubi. He was finally going to have some answers about what had been done to him. Whether or not he liked those answers hardly mattered. He wasn't the sort to pray, but he wished he could have faith that they'd find Dr. Hakubi.

He needed to know the truth.

"C'mon, Jon, you're slowing us down. You walk like you fly, bruh," Lolani taunted.

Jon smiled. Lolani had always been competitive. Even just walking to the bar, she had to be first. Jon had never felt that compulsion. He didn't need to be first, or win everything. He was happy enough just to breathe in the salty air.

The sun was high in the sky, and the surf boomed in the distance. The air smelled of the local flowers and the sea. The island was just as beautiful as Jon remembered it, when it wasn't raining. Granted it did rain a lot on Kai, but it wasn't raining now. The day was glorious.

The bar Lolani led them to was much quieter than the club from the night before, with an actual musician strumming a guitar softly in a corner. Several of the patrons, recognizing Lolani and Drake as they came in, congratulated them on a great fight.

"Hey! *Kolohe!* No! No! No! You trouble!" a large man shouted at them from the bar.

"Hey, now, you got the best *grindz makai!* We just here to eat, not fight. Didn't you see my bruh here kick my ass last night? He keep me straight!"

"Ainokea!" the man said. He'd come around the bar. "You trouble!"

Drake moved to intercept him. "Come now, friend. Lolani says this place has the most *ono* food on the island. You'd not deny me a good meal, would you?"

"You? No. I don't know you. She short me last time she here and broke two tables."

"Then how about we settle up?" said Drake. He held up Jon's credit stick.

Jon hadn't even noticed that Drake had taken it.

"Two hundred," the man said sullenly.

"You lie!" Lolani shouted and stepped forward.

Jon moved in front of her. "Lolani, just let Drake deal with it."

"Here's three hundred," said Drake. "We good?"

"Yeah, *hapa*, that do, but if she start up, we gonna get into it."

"She'll behave."

Jon thought Drake didn't know Lolani very well.

A pretty, young waitress in a split skirt and bikini top brought them water and menus. Jon had to grin at Geoffrey's obvious, instant infatuation. The young man had a lot growing up to do.

"I don't know what most of this stuff is," said Jason.

"*Manapua* is a bread roll with pulled pork, at least in most places," Drake said. "I assume the pork is vat-grown here. *Poke* is a raw fish salad. I don't recognize the fish names; they must be local. Not sure about some of these others."

"How you know our language?" Lolani asked suddenly.

"I know many languages," said Drake. "I visited Hawaii back on Earth, long ago."

"I would kill to have done that," Lolani said. "Place been gone a long time now. How old are you?"

Drake just smiled and ordered a round of beers. "Try the *poke*, Geoffrey. It's better than it may sound."

Geoffrey looked a little ill. "Raw fish?"

"Just order a burger, *haole*," said Lolani.

When the waitress came back, Geoffrey asked her about the food. He settled on the pineapple burger. Lolani rolled her eyes, and Jon kicked her shin under the table before she could say anything. Geoffrey couldn't help being young; he'd be more willing to try new things as he matured.

Drake ordered enough food to feed four people, just for himself. Jon couldn't figure out where Drake put all of it. They sat and ate and talked for several hours. There was an unspoken agreement not to discuss what they might be facing soon.

CHAPTER FIFTY

When they got back to Jon's ship, Drake went inside for a moment and then came back out with a bulky, black rifle. Jason was amused that Drake didn't want Lolani to know about all of the things he could do. He didn't think it was a matter of trust; Drake just didn't ever let anyone in on everything.

"The rifle is made of hypercarbon, almost indestructible," said Drake. "Fires a meson particle beam that shouldn't damage the hull of Lolani's ship but will shred flesh."

"I hope I don't have to use it," said Jason.

"Me, too."

Jason shook hands with Geoffrey and Jon. "If we don't make it…"

"We'll be fine," Geoffrey said quickly.

Jason nodded.

"Come on, Jason. I'll show you some real flying."

"Ready when you are, Lolani."

She led Jason across the field to her starship. It looked much the same as Jon's, except it had been coated in a matt-black ceramic paint. It also had more weapons: Jason could see what looked like missile pods mounted under the wings.

"Welcome to the *Ahi'iwa*," said Lolani.

The inside looked the same as Jon's ship.

"You want the screens on?"

"Yes, please."

She turned on the wall screens. "You too nice, bruh. You sweet as *poi*."

"Fuck off."

"There you go!" Lolani moved forward to the cockpit. A moment later, her voice came over the intercom. "Find a seat. We lift in five."

Jason settled into an acceleration couch and wedged the rifle by his side, under the straps. He wasn't happy to be on a ship piloted by someone he didn't really know. Lolani was nice enough, for someone completely insane, but he didn't trust her. It wasn't her fault; Jason didn't fully trust anyone.

Jason was on Lolani's ship, the *Ahi'iwa*, because Jon had asked him to. He understood why it had to be him and Geoffrey who stayed behind on the ships once they reached the prison. It was actually something of an honor: Drake was showing them trust.

Lolani took off without warning. She was much rougher at the controls than Jon had been. Jason felt his breath crushed out of his lungs and the rifle digging painfully into his side. Just when thought he couldn't take any more, the pressure eased off. His ribs hurt. That takeoff had been much higher-gee than Jon's had ever been.

He could see the blue curve of the planet receding on the left screen. The *Chwyldro* was visible on the right, flying very close by. Jason thought the bronze of Jon's ship was prettier than the matt black of the *Ahi'iwa*.

He wondered what the name of Lolani's ship meant.

Either one of the ships' names, for that matter.

Geoffrey voice came over the intercom. "Jason, can you hear me?"

"I hear you."

"Jon said Lolani took off at fifteen gees. I was worried about you."

"I'm doing fine."

"We're headed out to the closest LaGrange point," Jon said over the com. "We'll jump from there to Gamma Eridani. That will be a big jump."

"Why not tell everyone in the system, Jon?" said Lolani.

"You know our coms are entangled. They can't be intercepted."

"Your point?"

Jason could imagine Jon rolling his eyes. "We'll have eight more jumps after that. Lolani, I have a better nav computer interface. I'll feed the jump coordinates to you before each jump. I'm going to take them fast."

"You in a hurry, hotshot?" said Lolani. "Okay, you do got balls; I stand corrected. Feed me the nav points. If we implode, I'll see you in hell."

"Implode?" Jason heard Drake ask calmly.

"If I'm wrong in any of my variables by even a small amount, the engines won't be able to pull us out of the jump vortex," Jon said. "We'll punch a microscopic hole into hyperspace and get pushed in, one atom at a time, very quickly."

"Sounds like fun," said Drake. "Please attempt to be precise."

Lolani laughed.

Jason wished they would shut the hell up and get it over with.

"Okay, on three," said Jon. "Three, two, one, mark."

Jason closed his eyes. The disorienting nausea of the jump punched him in the gut. He didn't know whether that was because the jump was covering more distance or due to a difference in the engines on the *Ahi'iwa*. Maybe the pain was just because he'd eaten recently.

He didn't know, but the jump had caused him pain just below his solar plexus. He clenched his teeth. He wasn't going to allow himself to vomit. Lunch had been very good, but mostly he didn't want to vomit because he didn't think Lolani would stop jumping just for that. He'd have to spend who knew how long covered in the mess.

"Mark."

The jump hit him again, hard.

Jason felt a little bit disconnected from himself. He knew he was biting down on his lip to keep from being sick or crying out, but he was also floating, weightless. His thoughts moved into the past. He remembered people he'd known over the years. Friends long gone. Enemies he hoped were dead. He wasn't even sure who he was. Everything blurred and streaked, and he cried out; he didn't want to leave his memories.

"Jason!" Someone was shaking him. "Jason, come on, bruh. You scaring me."

A woman's voice. He thought maybe he should recognize it. His face hurt. He touched it, and his hand came away wet and sticky. That made him open his eyes.

His hand was red.

"Jason?"

He turned his eyes toward the speaker. "I know you," he said. "You're Jon's pretty friend."

She laughed and smiled. "Do you remember my name?"

"Lolani?" he asked. "That sounds like a *you* name."

"Hey, guys, he's okay!" said Lolani.

"Jason? Are you all right?" Drake asked from the intercom.

"I'm okay, I think. What happened?"

"We jumped in too close to an uncharted asteroid," said Lolani. "We can't jump that near a mass. I still don't know how Jon pulled us both out of that. I thought it was the Big Slurp for us."

"Big Slurp?"

Lolani didn't answer but instead began washing his face. Jason was pleased to note that he hadn't vomited. He'd bitten his lip, and his nose was bloody and swollen, but he hadn't gotten sick.

"What we call it when a ship implodes," Jon said over the com. "That's what it sounds like over the com if you're talking with a pilot when they make an error."

"Sorry about the blood," Jason mumbled.

Lolani laughed. "Jon pulled us out of the vortex at twenty gees. I was out cold while he did it. Still waiting to hear how."

"I recalculated the field radius on my engines to include the *Ahi'iwa,*" said Jon. "Then double jumped us out of the vortex."

"Which shouldn't be possible, but I'm not complaining," Lolani said. "You win, by the way. You're the better pilot. You don't have to show off anymore. The rainbows were a nice touch, though."

"Though you said you were unconscious," said Jon.

"Maybe that was just wishful thinking on my part."

Jason thought he knew what Jon must have done: somehow, he'd used the Cynosure to save them. Jason was just glad to be alive, although the near-death experience did make him wonder about the nature of the Cynosure and the Instrumentality. Drake made the use of the Instrumentality seem like magic but called it science. Jon called the Cynosure science but made it seem like magic.

"Is Geoffrey okay?" Jason asked suddenly.

"He's fine," came Drake's calm voice. "A little the worse for wear, and unconscious at the moment. He'll be fine."

"Well, let's not do that again, okay?"

"We're at Wolf 359," said Jon, "in the ring system of the gas giant. If all goes well, we'll leave a little more slowly."

"If all goes well," Drake said.

"I'm going to head back up to the cockpit," said Lolani. "You going to be okay?"

"You tell me," Jason replied.

"Yeah, you're good, bruh." Lolani punched him lightly on the arm and left.

Jason pushed himself up in his couch. His chest hurt badly, and it was difficult to breathe. He suspected he'd cracked a couple of ribs against the seat harness. He shifted the rifle to a more comfortable place. He stretched and then saw his bandana lying on the deck.

He sighed, and then snatched the bandana up and put back on his head. Maybe Drake was right, and it would be easier not to hide anymore. What did he have to fear out here? Who knew if he'd ever even make it back home again?

☉

Jon adjusted the straps on his seat again. No matter how he shifted, the straps hurt. The maneuver that saved them had been closer to twenty-five gees. He'd never been as scared in his life as he had then. Not even when he'd first seen the Cynosure, or when the asshole with the crossbow had tried to kill him.

The Big Slurp wasn't something you flew out of.

When they'd come out of the jump and the proximity alarms rang out, Jon had known they were all dead. The double vortex formed as the engines of the *Chwyldro* and the *Ahi'iwa* twisted spacetime into a knot near the implacable mass of the asteroid.

A ship couldn't be pulled out of a vortex, much less a double one. Without thinking, he'd reached out to the Cynosure and calculated a way through the jump. He'd somehow taken the *Ahi'iwa* with them through the shift. Running the situation back through his mind, he knew that they had jumped to the next universe over, where there wasn't an asteroid in that position, and then jumped back into his own, all in less than a heartbeat.

No other pilot could have made that jump. Jon was just glad he'd been able to save Lolani and Jason. He suspected he'd be shaking for a while. One didn't stare into the jaws of death and laugh.

"How is the local shipping looking, Jon?" Drake asked.

Jon wondered if Drake knew how close they'd all come to dying. *Probably*, he thought. Drake didn't miss much. If Drake seemed to overlook something, he'd probably just chosen to ignore it.

"Some ice miners, a few light minutes away," Jon was surprised at how steady his voice sounded. "I don't detect any military vessels near us."

"Then we should head into the inner system without delay."

Give me a minute, Jon thought. "Yeah, I set up a route for us."

"Jon?"

"Yes?"

"Good job back there."

"Thank you."

CHAPTER FIFTY-ONE

Drake checked on Geoffrey and then went to change into his armor.

He wasn't oblivious to the fact that they'd almost died. However, he'd had faith that Jon would pull them out of the near miss. It was hardly the first time Drake had faced death, after all. He'd almost died on numerous occasions. He'd lost count of the times he'd awakened, thinking he had died, only to find his body had healed while he was unconscious. Of course, being torn apart in a spatial maelstrom was a bit different from being run through with a sword.

Drake pulled his coat on over his armor and checked his weapons. He had his pistol and his sword. He considered and then discarded the idea of a more formidable weapon. If he needed something more than Maegril and a pistol, he'd use Instrumentality.

Thinking of that, he summoned a suitable rifle for Jon. The man would need to be able to fight with when they stormed the prison. Drake doubted the guards were going to simply hand the doctor over to them.

Geoffrey was awake and rubbing his face when Drake

reentered the cabin. "How are you feeling?"

"Rough," Geoffrey replied. "Did I pass out again?"

"We had a difficult reentry after the last jump." Drake saw no reason to tell Geoffrey how close they'd come to death. "Jason also passed out aboard the *Ahi'iwa*, but he is doing well now."

"Well, at least he won't give me shit for passing out again."

"He didn't before, did he?"

"No, he didn't, and he wouldn't." Geoffrey carefully stood and stretched. "Are we there? At the prison, I mean."

"We're dropping down into the system," Jon said over the intercom. "We'll be at the prison in a half an hour."

Drake retrieved Geoffrey's rifle from the floor and placed it on his couch.

"Thanks," Geoffrey said. "I'll try to take better care if it."

"No worries. I told you it was almost indestructible."

Drake could see that the ship was moving toward a stark-looking planet. In another Realm, that planet held domed cities. Drake had loved someone there. They were gone now, though, a victim of some nameless enemy. The planet in this Realm didn't look as if it had any cities. There was little orbital traffic around the icy world. Drake could see a single orbital habitat, which must be the prison.

He didn't see any ships patrolling near it. Drake focused on the screens, wishing the resolution was better. He didn't detect any drones or spatial mines. He saw turrets on the habitat, but those were most likely for asteroid defense.

"The prison is undefended?" asked Drake.

"It certainly looks like it," Jon replied. "My sensors don't detect any military vessels in range of us. The Alliance doesn't have any powerful enemies, and not even the criminal syndicates would attack a prison. They'd have little to gain from it. The prisoners are mostly political."

"They don't lock up criminals?" asked Geoffrey.

Drake could tell Geoffrey was thinking that the mafia back on his Earth would love undefended prisons.

"No, mostly they just space everyone else," said Lolani. "Commit a crime, and you die if they catch you. The Alliance will have entangled communications on that heap. I don't think they have any military ships in system, though. I figure it would take a little over three hours for a ship to get here from their base at Lalande 21185. Assuming they have a ship prepped and ready."

"I think we can assume they have at least one ship on patrol. Still, it would take two hours to get to the prison from the jump point," Jon said. "That's our window for rescuing Dr. Hakubi."

"What about defenses on the prison?" Drake asked.

"There will be automated gun turrets. We'll have to take them out on the way to the landing bay."

"Can you fire the guns and fly?"

"I can fire the forward guns. The turret has to be manned separately."

"Geoffrey, why don't you take the gun turret?" Drake suggested.

"What?"

"It'll be just like a video game. You can do this."

"Okay." Geoffrey took a deep breath. "What do I have to do?"

The door forward slid open. "The compartment on the right as you come forward contains the gunnery chair," said Jon. "Come on up, and I'll talk you through getting logged in."

Drake smiled encouragement to Geoffrey.

Geoffrey nodded and went forward.

Now they just needed to reach the landing bay. Drake studied the prison's defenses. Getting to the bay shouldn't be a problem. As for what was waiting for them, Drake would apport out first and soften the resistance.

Θ

The hatchway opened into a small, grey room with a chair sitting in a ball in the middle of it. Geoffrey sat down carefully in the strange chair. The gunnery chair had many odd straps and connectors. The whole contraption made him nervous. It was like a cross between a hamster ball and a dentist's chair, and he didn't like it.

"Now what?" he asked.

"Strap in," Jon replied over the com. "Don't worry about the ports. The seat was designed to work manually or with neural interface. Once you're strapped in, I'll activate the controls."

"Okay." It took Geoffrey a few minutes to figure everything out. He had to strap down his legs and body, then his head, and then his arms, which was tough. "I think I have it."

"All right. You look secure. Let me bring up the controls."

Suddenly, the room went dark. As Geoffrey's eyes adjusted, he saw stars, and the other ship next to them. Ahead was a formidable-looking structure orbiting an icy planet. As he looked around, a crosshair followed his eye movements. It was difficult to get used to. Then he looked down.

The chair swung around to keep his vision centered. There was no feeling of gravity, but the vertigo was terrible. Geoffrey got lost for a second, and then his inner ear settled down.

"Sorry about that," said Jon. "The artificial gravity turns off in there when the chair is activated. Feel in front of you. There should be stick controls close to your hands."

"I feel them."

"Good. The left controls the vertical axis of the chair; you must have bumped it before. Grasp it and use subtle movements to right yourself."

Geoffrey was able to get the chair oriented the way he thought he'd first been.

"Okay, the other stick has a trigger. That controls the gun turret and the left-right motion of the chair."

Geoffrey spun the chair around and accidentally pulled the trigger. "Shit!"

"The guns aren't enabled yet. You're doing fine. Try using both sticks at the same time."

Geoffrey did, and the room spun around him. He centered back up on the station.

"Good job. How do you feel?"

"I wish I had some Dramamine."

"I'm not sure what that is. Don't worry," said Jon. "You'll get used to it. Just stay focused on your target."

"And what is my target?"

"The orbital station ahead has automated gun turrets. The targeting computer will highlight them in red when we get close. Just target them and pull the trigger."

"I'm worried about hitting the other ship."

"Don't be. The friend-foe systems will disable the guns if they're pointed at the *Ahi'iwa*. In fact, you can't shoot anything the targeting computer doesn't flag as a threat."

"That makes me feel a little better."

"I'll take out anything directly in our path. Most of our threats are going to be on your right as we come in. You might have turrets on both sides once we get to the landing bay."

Geoffrey shifted the chair to the right. "I'm ready."

"The effective range on the lasers is line of sight, so you can start firing as soon as we start our run. Keep in mind that their weapons are the same."

"What happens if we get hit?"

"Well, those weapons are designed to deflect or destroy asteroids…"

"Right, so get them first." Geoffrey let his breath out slowly and tried to relax his shoulders. "No pressure."

"You've got this, Geoffrey. Okay, Lolani is ready. She'll be shooting, too. I'm starting the run now."

Suddenly Geoffrey's display lit up with red target icons. The habitat was covered with them. The closest ones strobed. Geoffrey focused on those and pulled the trigger. At first, he thought nothing had happened, and then the turret he'd been aiming at exploded.

"What happened?" Geoffrey asked.

"You shot the turret. Good job."

"But I didn't see anything!"

"You can't see lasers unless they act upon something like dust or atmosphere. Hold on a second. I can probably add a false overlay to your screen, if it would help."

"Thank you."

Geoffrey focused on another turret and pulled the trigger again. This time, he saw two beams of red light lash out and carve across the turret. It was just computer-generated, but that actually made it easier for him. It *did* feel like a video game.

Of course, if he died here, he'd be dead for real.

The *Ahi'iwa* crossed his field of vision, and Geoffrey saw dozens of missiles fly away from the ship. The entire side of the habitat exploded, and his sensors were overwhelmed for a moment. Lolani's attack had taken out many of the enemy turrets. Geoffrey just kept focusing on new targets and firing. A strobing on his left made him spin his chair, and he fired at the turrets there without even thinking.

He could see the docking bay ahead.

The *Chwyldro* jerked to the side, and a beam of light flashed past the *Chwyldro* from inside the bay. Geoffrey had no idea how Jon had managed to dodge the attack. He pulled down on the trigger and swept the bay, hitting three turrets in succession. A ship about the size of the *Chwyldro* exploded to the right of him.

Geoffrey let go of the sticks. He didn't know whether he'd done that or not. What if there'd been people on board that ship? He suddenly felt sick.

"Lolani fired the shot that took out the patrol ship," Jon said quietly. "It wasn't you, Geoffrey."

"How can you be sure?"

"Because that ship was never targeted by my computer. You couldn't have fired on it, even if you wanted to."

"I just don't want to hurt anyone. It was like a game."

"You didn't, and don't feel bad about that, either. Not wanting to take a life requires courage and conviction. Don't let the callousness of others color your judgement."

"Thanks. Can I get out of here? Do you still need me?"

"We're good. You did very well. Thank you."

The chair spun around, and the display turned off. Geoffrey could feel gravity again, and it was a relief. He unbuckled the chair straps and took a few deep breaths to calm himself. Once they landed, he was going to have to defend the *Chwyldro*. He might actually have to shoot someone, and he wasn't sure he could do that.

CHAPTER FIFTY-TWO

Drake apported out of the *Chwyldro* as Jon brought the ship in for a landing. A small team of guards in light armor were trying to set up heavy gun of some kind on a tripod. Drake drew Maegril and cut them down before they could finish. There were no other guards visible.

Drake searched the remains quickly. One of the bodies had a keycard that looked as if it could be useful, so he pocketed it. He was prepared to cut his way through bulkheads, if necessary, but he'd rather not, if he could help it. He knew the Alliance would have cameras recording everything that happened and didn't want them to know all that he was capable of.

The melted turrets were still radiating intense heat, and the patrol vessel Lolani had destroyed was still burning. Drake could see a field of blueish energy holding the air inside the landing bay. Lights flashed, and a klaxon blared. He shot the speaker to silence it, and then he turned and watched as Jon and Lolani landed their ships. The *Ahi'iwa* had a melted streak down one flank; Lolani wasn't quite as fast as Jon at dodging.

Drake met Jon and Lolani between the two ships. He nodded to Geoffrey and Jason as he passed the ships. They both looked nervous. If all went well, they wouldn't have to do anything. He hoped for their sakes that nothing happened. Neither of them really had the killer instinct, which was probably for the best.

Lolani wore a pair of bulky energy pistols on her hips.

Drake unslung the rifle he'd gotten for Jon and handed it to him as he walked up.

"Drake, I'm not going to kill the guards. You should try not killing, too, if you can help it."

"It's non-lethal," said Drake. "Fires a sonic pulse that stuns."

Jon checked the rifle again and nodded. "Okay, thanks. I don't know that I'll have a chance to use it, but thanks for respecting my wishes on the matter."

"I only ever kill when I think I must," Drake said. "Granted, that is most of the time I face an enemy, but you've seen what I normally fight."

Jon nodded again. "I can see how that might lead to a bit of overkill."

Drake gestured to the direction the ships had come in. "What happens if the enemy disables the force field holding the air in this bay?"

"The outer hatches on the ships will close automatically. Our friends will be safe."

"Very good."

"Call me crazy," said Lolani, "but can I ask why you have a *sword?*"

Drake smiled and pointed across the bay to the dismembered bodies and the still-glowing parts of the heavy anti-ship gun. He hadn't allowed the blade to destroy the bodies; he didn't want the Alliance to discover his advanced nanotechnology.

"You cut the cannon apart with that?"

"And the guards, yes."

"So... You have a magic sword that cuts through anything?"

"It projects a quantum field effect along the edge that annihilates matter, energy, even space itself."

"And that means what?"

"I have a magic sword that cuts through anything."

"Gotcha. Still weird, bruh. Swords on a space station?"

Drake ignored her. "Where do we find Dr. Hakubi?"

Jon looked at Lolani, who shrugged. "Don't look at me; I've never been in prison before," she said. "My source just said Hakubi was here. I didn't get any information more specific."

"We'll need to find a computer terminal," said Jon.

Drake nodded. "I think I saw one at the end of the bay, near the doors."

Lolani drew her pistols. With her speed, she'd be able to neutralize most threats before they became a problem. Jon had slung his rifle over his shoulder; he'd probably realized that it would be practically impossible to stop Drake and Lolani from killing.

Jon studied the terminal. "We'd need a keycard."

Drake held up the card he'd pocketed.

"Do I want to know?"

"One of the guards had it on him," Drake replied. "I didn't conjure it out of the air."

Jon took the card and accessed the security system. "Here we go: *Hakubi, B., cell two-one-eight-seven.*"

"That should be level twenty-one, if they follow any logic here," said Drake.

Jon nodded. "We're on level eleven. There should be an elevator through those doors ahead of us."

"Can you do anything about the alarms?" said Lolani.

Jon shook his head. "Don't have clearance from this terminal."

"Can you find a route to the doctor?" Drake asked.

"I believe I can, yes. Should be fairly simple."

"Then take point. Lolani, keep an eye forward. I'll watch

our flanks."

"You keep your eyes on your own flank," said Lolani.

Jon gripped her shoulder and then moved through the door. Lolani grinned and followed him. She seemed in good spirits.

Drake followed them, feeling something that wasn't quite dread: not concern about what they might face, but about Dr. Hakubi herself. He didn't know why, but he suspected that she would turn out to be more than she seemed.

Θ

The alarm was annoying, and the flashing lights distracting.

Jon used the keycard to activate the elevator and then punched in level twenty-one.

The assault on the prison was turning out to have a higher cost than Jon had anticipated: the unknown number of crew aboard the patrol ship Lolani had destroyed, and the guards Drake had slain in the landing bay. *Even one person was too many,* he thought. The Alliance was going to respond to this attack with force. They probably wouldn't limit that response to a bounty on Jon and Lolani, either.

Drake never seemed to consider the consequences of his actions, but then, what need did he have to do so? He could always just walk away to another universe, if he didn't like the one he was in. It wasn't as if anyone could really threaten the man. He was ancient, practically immortal, and armed with technology that made him a god.

Jon wasn't sure whether he envied or pitied him. Drake enjoyed a freedom few other people ever could. Jon wondered if *he* would be like that eventually. The power the Cynosure granted him could certainly be tempting.

The elevator opened on level twenty-one, and Jon had a bad feeling as the doors opened. He stepped to the side, pushing Lolani out of the way just as a powerful blast of energy shot through the doors and blew a hole through the back of the elevator. Drake had stepped aside the precise distance to avoid being struck. Jon glanced out of the elevator and saw that a team of guards had set up a particle cannon at the end of the corridor.

Drake apported to the cannon and kicked it hard enough to send it flying away. The guards in the path of the cannon were crushed as it tumbled by. It exploded against the far bulkhead. The two remaining guards dove for cover as Lolani opened fire on them from the elevator.

Those two guards had almost seemed to be in shock. Jon could certainly understand the feeling. Drake had exploded out of the elevator in a whirlwind of death. One of the guards recovered and fired his pistol into Drake's chest. Drake punched *through* the man's head and then threw the body into the other guard, who was still trying to draw her pistol.

Jon silenced her scream of horror with blast from his stun rifle. She didn't need to die. Enough of the guards died had already. Leaving a witness wouldn't matter; there were cameras everywhere. The Alliance knew who was attacking. They just couldn't do anything about it. Jon felt sick from all the carnage.

Drake glanced at him from up the corridor and nodded.

They didn't face any more resistance as they raced down the corridor. Either there weren't any other guards the prison could send out to fight, or more likely, the guards were refusing to face Drake. Jon didn't blame them.

"We should free all of these people," said Lolani.

"What would we do with them?" Drake asked. "We can't take thousands of people on two ships. They would fight and die trying to board. Better to leave their lives to fate."

"Do you really believe in fate?" she asked.

"No. I make my own way through life."

Jon found the right door, but it wouldn't open to the keycard. The prison must have finally caught on and disable it. Jon opened the lock panel, but it was solid-state circuitry; there was nothing to hotwire.

Drake stepped past him and punched through the door, then wrenched it open.

A petite red-haired woman whom Jon remembered well lay on the cell bunk, wearing a grey prison jumpsuit. She didn't look much different from what he remembered. Her dark hair was cropped short but still spiky. She hadn't aged in the years since he'd last seen her, but with her skills in genetic manipulation, she wouldn't have. She still looked absurdly young.

She stood when the door opened, and her bright green eyes flashed as she looked at Jon, Lolani, and Drake. Jon couldn't interpret her expression: surprise, but also something else. *Anger? Bemusement? Fear?*

"*You?*" she said, focusing on Drake. "Just how much trouble am I in, Dad?"

CHAPTER FIFTY-THREE

Drake frowned and glanced at Jon and Lolani.

"Don't look at me," Lolani said. "This is between you males. I've been called many things, but never *Dad*."

"I'd invite you in and offer you some tea, but I think that would defeat the purpose," Dr. Hakubi said. "You are here to rescue me, aren't you? I hope so, because I don't have any tea, and that would be awkward."

"Who *are* you?" asked Drake.

"Obviously, I'm Dr. Brygida Hakubi. At least, that's my name in this place," she said. "Surely you knew that, or did you just open the wrong cell?"

"That doesn't answer my question, or why you said what you did."

"Oh, you mean calling you *Dad*? Because you are, you oaf. Although I suppose we've never actually met."

"Could we have this conversation someplace else?" Lolani said nervously. "We're coming up on two hours since we attacked, and I have a bad feeling. We need to get out of here."

Drake gestured and used the Instrumentality to envelope them all and apport them to the base of the *Chwyldro*'s ramp.

Geoffrey cried out and fired as they appeared. Drake caught the blast in his outstretched hand before even Jon could react.

"Show-off," said Hakubi.

"Be more careful, Geoffrey," Drake said. He nodded to Lolani, who ran to her ship.

"I should ride with her, just to spite you," Hakubi said.

"Get aboard," Drake snapped. He didn't know who this young woman was. She looked as if she might be related to him, but looks could be altered. He sensed the Cynosure about her, so he knew she was from the North. She didn't look like anyone he knew there. *Maybe somewhat like Monika, in the eyes,* he thought. *No, she couldn't be.*

"What now, Drake?" asked Jon.

"We'll rendezvous back at Kai for now," Drake said. "Maybe we can try to sort out some of this there. I suggest you take a little more time on the jump calculations."

"I'll let Lolani know." Jon moved forward to begin prepping the *Chwyldro*.

Geoffrey looked confused. "Who's this?"

"I'm Dr. Hakubi. Who are you?"

"Nobody," Drake replied. "Sit down and shut up. We'll talk when we get to Kai."

"Wow, you're a real charmer," she said. She settled into a couch and buckled in.

Drake shook his head at Geoffrey; he wasn't in the mood to answer questions.

If Brygida really was his daughter, then he had a few things he needed to say to Monika, the next time he was in the Eternal City. He and Monika had once been lovers before certain *ideological* differences when it came to dealing with the Ancient Enemy caused them to go their separate ways. Of course, there had also been that ridiculous war between their two peoples. Drake had always regretted parting from Monika. He had loved her.

Drake looked over at Brygida; she certainly bore a family resemblance. In particular, something about her eyes and cheekbones was familiar. Her ears had distinct points. Her teeth, he hadn't seen, but he suspected they would look more human. Her eyes were slightly slanted, and her skin was darker than Drake's, but that could have been an expression of his and Monika's genes mixing.

Brygida turned her head and smirked at him, aware of his regard.

Monika was a beautiful woman. Drake's people were fertile with just about every species, but they rarely had children. *If* Monika was Brygida's mother. The more he thought about it, the more likely it seemed. Something about this young woman called out to his heart. It had been decades since he'd been with Monika. If she'd had a child, that child could easily be the person he saw in the acceleration couch next to him.

There was an uncomfortable silence aboard the *Chwyldro* as Jon made the jumps to take them back to safety. Drake wanted to have his conversation with Brygida in private, but that wasn't possible aboard the ship. Once they got to Kai, they would go for a walk, and he'd discover the truth.

⊙

Jason strapped down in a hurry when Lolani rushed by.

He'd placed his rifle in another acceleration couch first. His ribs still hurt badly, and he didn't want more bruises.

Whatever had happened seemed to have shaken Lolani. She spun her ship around violently on its axis and blasted out of the landing bay. Jason could see the *Chwyldro* keeping pace with them. He hoped Geoffrey was doing okay. In the last few weeks, they'd spent almost every waking moment together. Now he hadn't talked to his friend in almost half a day. He missed the damn kid.

"Did you find the doctor?" he asked.

"Yes, we found her," Lolani answered. "We're on local, by the way. Jon cut off communication over there."

"Why?"

"I'd say he doesn't trust Hakubi. Can't say I blame him. There's something strange going on with her."

"Can you tell me what?"

"Sorry, bruh, not my story to tell. Ask Drake when we get back."

Jason nodded. He was getting used to not knowing what was going on.

"We're coming up on the jump point," said Lolani. "Shit!"

The *Ahi'iwa* suddenly jerked to the side.

"Fuckers!"

Jason could see three ships decelerating past them, drives plumes bright in the displays. Those ships had materialized out of nothing a moment before. He realized they must be Alliance jumpships.

Lolani fired a salvo of missiles at the ships; he could see the dozens of bright drives from the missiles' engines. Some of missiles exploded as the Alliance ships defended themselves.

"We're jumping. Hold on."

Jason felt a kick in the gut, and then the stars looked different. Then there was another sudden burst as the *Ahi'iwa* jumped again. Jason thought he was going to be sick. He just couldn't get used to the feeling of the jumps.

"Okay, we're safe for a few minutes. Alliance ships rely on computers. They can't jump as quickly as we can. I hope some of those missiles I fired take out at least one of the bastards," Lolani said. "Are you okay?"

"It hurts when you jump," Jason managed to say.

"Did it feel the same on the way out?"

"Yes."

"Hold on." She came out of the cockpit a minute later.

"Sounds like you're sensitive to the spacetime field. It affects some people worse than others. I've got something I can give you for it."

Lolani pulled out a large syringe from a box on the wall.

"No!" The pain was almost unbearable. He hadn't hurt like this after the other jumps; the pain then had been momentary. He was embarrassed to feel tears on his face.

"It's just a drug that eases the symptoms."

"Can't," Jason gasped. "Allergic."

"How would you know if you're allergic to it?"

"Allergic to the needle." He hated admitting that, but he couldn't let her inject him, and he wasn't strong enough to stop her. The pain was too much. He was almost willing to take the needle, to get something to stop the pain.

"Hold on," she said. "Jon, we got a problem."

"What kind of problem?"

"Jason is having a bad reaction to the jump, but he doesn't want me to inject him with the meds."

"Yeah, that would probably be a bad idea. Let me talk to Drake."

Jason heard a *whoosh* and then a startled oath from Lolani.

Drake had apported to the *Ahi'iwa* from the *Chwyldro*.

"How the hell did you do that?" asked Lolani.

"Should I take the time to explain or to check on Jason?"

Jason thought Drake sounded angry. He hoped Drake wasn't angry at *him*. Drake laid a cool hand on his head – he'd taken off his gauntlet, Jason realized.

"I'm not upset with you, friend. Tell me about the pain."

Jason realized some of the pain had faded. It was still there, but it was blocked from affecting him. Drake had done something with that light touch. "Started with the jumps," he said. "Got worse each time."

Drake felt around his abdomen, where the pain was centered. "Is it worse this time?"

"Yes. I don't know why."

"Jon thought you knew what this might be," Drake said to Lolani.

"Jump sickness," she replied. "Some people have a vagus nerve response to the spacetime stress. No one knows why. We have a medication for it, but he didn't want me to inject him. He said he had an allergy to the needle."

"He has a severe allergy to iron," said Drake. "The needle could kill him."

"That's a weird allergy to have," Lolani said. "Is he...You know, one of you?"

"One of me?"

"One of your people. A Precursor."

"Why would you think that?"

"After the near miss, when I was helping him, his bandana had fallen off."

"Ah, I see. No, he isn't a Precursor. It is rare, but some Precursor genes exist in the general population. Ask Yousef about it sometime. Sometimes someone is born with a superficial resemblance to us."

"Are you allergic to iron, too?"

Drake reached out and gripped the needle in his fingers. "No. That's just a quirk of his particular genetics."

"Whew. I was worried it might be something those of us in the jump pilot program might develop."

"It is highly unlikely." Drake frowned down at Jason. "You don't have a hypospray?"

Lolani shook her head. "Sorry, no. I don't have much medical stuff aboard. Just stuff to stitch up cuts. I get into fights sometimes."

"You don't say." Drake smiled and shook his head. "How bad is jump sickness?"

"It can kill," Lolani said quietly. "When it's as bad as he has it, it might only take another jump or two."

Drake pulled a disk out of his pocket; Jason would have bet anything that it hadn't been there a minute before. "Jason, I think the best thing I can do for you is to put you into stasis for the rest of the trip."

"What's that?"

"You'll be in a bubble of spacetime. No time will pass for you. Nothing from outside can affect you. You won't even realize the trip back to Kai happens. You'll just blink, and we'll be there."

Jason swallowed hard. He trusted Drake. "Okay."

Drake placed the disk on his chest. Then Drake picked the disk up and placed it back in his pocket.

"What went wrong?" Jason asked.

"Nothing. We're on Kai." Drake undid the buckles on his harness. "I told you no time would pass for you. Let me help you up."

Jason leaned on Drake as he walked down the ramp. It was night on Kai, the moon high in the sky. The air smelled of salt and rain. His pain was already fading.

"Drake, thank you. For everything." He knew Drake would know what he meant.

"You're welcome. Now, why don't you go join the others? I need to speak with Dr. Hakubi."

From the way Drake said it, Jason would not have wanted to be the doctor.

CHAPTER FIFTY-FOUR

Drake left Jason with Geoffrey and walked over to Brygida.

She was above average in height; her one hundred sixty-seven centimeters matched that of her mother, more or less. He'd have expected her to be taller if she was his daughter, but genetics was strange.

"Shall we take a walk, so that we may speak privately?"

"I don't know," Brygida said with a faint smile. "Are you going to knife me in the dark? My mother said never to talk with strangers."

"I am not a stranger by choice. I wish to talk with you privately, nothing more. If, after you listen to what I have to say, you no longer wish to speak with me, I'll arrange passage for you back to the Eternal City."

Brygida sighed and gestured toward the beach.

Drake walked with her until they were out of earshot of the others. The surf was loud enough to drown out most voices, and they were speaking quietly. "Is *Brygida* your real name?"

"Yes," she said.

"It suits you. Your mother is Monika?"

"Of course, or have you slept with others of the Royal

Family?"

"Just with Monika," said Drake. "That was some time ago. She never suggested she was pregnant."

"I'm older than I look."

"Yes, I say that often myself."

"You really didn't know?" she asked. "I mean, about me? That I existed?"

Drake breathed deeply of the pure, clean salt air before answering. He felt a mix of emotions, difficult to quantify. He'd loved Monika. She was a lovely woman with an incredible intelligence. "No. I take it that your mother didn't tell you that she'd kept you a secret from me."

"We didn't talk about you much. She told me you were from a Southern Realm, and she told me your name and what you look like. Sorry, you weren't her prime concern, or her favorite topic. After a while, I learned not to ask."

"I was *never* her favorite topic," said Drake. "I think perhaps she was embarrassed by how she felt about me."

"Well, we're a hell of a family, aren't we?"

Brygida, he thought. *I have a daughter whose name is Brygida.* "You should see the other half of your family," he said.

"Then you don't deny me?"

"Why would I? Not to mention our similarity of bone structure, hair, and eyes. Monika's hair is not as red as yours. You have the classic Drake family look."

"I thought you might deny me. Mother didn't think very highly of you. Although you are obviously a powerful sorcerer like her."

"Monika thought highly enough of me to almost marry me," Drake replied, shaking his head. "Then that whole succession thing got in the way, and then the war with the Ruined Courts."

"They're real?" Brygida asked. "The Courts, I mean."

Drake nodded. "Quite. I am a prince of those courts."

"I'd like to see them."

"I'm sure I could arrange that," Drake said with a smile. "However, there are a few more pressing issues right at the moment."

They walked along the beach in silence for a while. Drake didn't attempt to read her thoughts, and her mind was too well disciplined to broadcast. Whistles and clicks sounded across the waves, and Drake wondered idly if dolphins had been brought to Kai.

"When you came to rescue me, you didn't know I'm your daughter," said Brygida. "That means it must have been for another reason. Is Jon doing all right? He was always the sickly one of my kids."

"Your kids?" Drake asked sharply.

"Just a figure of speech, Dad. Do I call you *Dad*? May I?"

"Of course you may," Drake replied, "although not everyone should know. There are those in my party whom I would wish to remain ignorant."

"You don't trust them?"

"I don't think they could keep the secret if put to the question. There are those who would harm you to get to me. I wish to avoid that."

"Mother told me a little of ancient horrors from beyond the Realms. I thought she was talking about the Ruined Courts, most of the time."

"Entirely possible," said Drake. "Those in the North often think of us in the South as demons. How did Jon put it? *Madmen and sorcerers*, I believe he said when we met."

"So not too far off the mark?" Brygida said with a faint smile.

"Indeed."

"Anyway, back on topic. I called all the volunteers who survived the gene treatment *my kids*. I'd used my own genetic material to alter them, after all."

"You didn't stop to think about how dangerous that could be?"

"I'll grant you that I didn't expect so many of the volunteers to die. I didn't get chance to study that before Rhyddid fell and the program collapsed. However, I don't see what's so dangerous about enhanced speed and injury recovery."

"Jon has attuned to the Cynosure," said Drake.

"That's impossible." Brygida stopped and sought his eyes in the dark. Drake realized his daughter must have inherited many of his natural abilities, including excellent vision.

"It's true. I've traveled with him as he walked the worlds using the Cynosure."

"I'm telling you, it's impossible. There is no way that what I did could have allowed him to attune to the Cynosure. I was extremely selective with the genetic material I used."

"And yet he has."

"I will need to look at his genetic code," said Brygida. "I need to see what's going on."

"There is more."

"What?"

"Someone is trying to kill him, and I think your mother might be behind it."

"Is this some kind of plan to get back at her? Turning me against her?" Brygida shook her head. "No, because you didn't know who I am. Who's trying to kill him?"

"Most recently? Sergei tried to kill Jon after Sergei walked into a closed Realm I protect. He could only have entered that Realm with coded information that few people possess. You mother is one of those people."

"Closed Realms with codes? I've never heard of such things."

"It's advanced work with one of the Powers."

"Hmm." Brygida shook her head. "I suppose I should have stayed in the Eternal City for more advanced lessons on the

Cynosure."

"Why did you leave?"

"I wanted to go to university. I wanted to study science at one those universities in the central Realms. I wanted to understand what the Cynosure is, and how we can do what we do. I got my Ph.D. in physics first, then another in genetics. I studied genetics because I wanted to understand myself."

"I assume you have figured out that the Cynosure is a machine," said Drake.

Brygida looked startled. "I did, but I didn't think anyone else knew that."

"One day, when we have more time, I'll tell you the convoluted history of our people and the great Powers that we built and have now forgotten. In the South, we have the Omphalos; I know it as the Instrumentality. It's a machine intelligence of unimaginable age and power."

"I've seen references to the Omphalos in the palace library, but I never heard it called the Instrumentality. That would have aided in my studies. I wish I had met you sooner."

Drake reached out and touched her shoulder. "I wish I had known you sooner, as well."

Suddenly she turned and hugged him.

He realized she was crying, and he patted her back awkwardly. He wasn't sure what he should say or do. He'd never been good at being a father.

"Sorry," she said, wiping her face. "Just a bit overwhelmed."

"No need to apologize," Drake replied. "Shall we get back to the others? They're probably beginning to wonder about us."

They began walking back up the beach. Drake saw someone waiting by the stairs to the landing pad. He thought it might be Lolani. The moon came out from behind the clouds, and he was sure it was her. She looked anxious.

"I need to speak to Jon, too," said Brygida. "Anything else I need to know about him?"

"You knew he could apport?" Drake asked.

Brygida nodded. "Three of the kids developed the ability. It was quite unexpected. You seem to have exhibited something similar."

"I used Instrumentality for the apport back at the prison. I can apport without it, but that takes more effort."

"So the Instrumentality is like the Cynosure?"

"Older and more powerful, but yes, they are similar in nature and function."

"Is it possible to have both Powers? It would be interesting to compare them."

Drake smiled. "The Emperor of the Ruined Courts is of mixed ancestry. His father is Prince Joseph."

"Really? Do many people know about the Courts, then?"

"The Royals in the Eternal City certainly do. You don't remember the war?"

"I think I was away at university. No one would tell me what it was about, other than the succession. I know Uncle Andrzej ended up on the throne. I didn't realize it involved the Ruined Courts."

"Some of your uncles – Joaquim and Giovanni, in particular – didn't like the idea of a son of Joseph on the throne in the South. They thought one of them deserved the throne instead, not realizing that Emrys' claim to the throne was through his mother, not his father."

"Did you fight in the war?"

"I did not. If I had, Emperor Emrys would have both thrones."

Brygida laughed. "You're certainly as arrogant as Mother said."

Drake smiled. "Arrogance can be earned."

Lolani waved to them when they got close. "You guys figure out all the secrets of the universe?"

"Not quite all of them," Drake answered.

Brygida startled Lolani with a hug. "Good to see you. You doing okay? You look healthy. How did you cut your face?"

Lolani laughed and pushed her away. "I'm fine. Stop mothering me." Lolani didn't seem displeased. She turned her gaze to Drake. "Is she really your daughter?"

Drake nodded. "Yes, she is."

"So you're a Precursor? I guess that explains the genetic material."

"Precursor?" Brygida asked with a raised eyebrow.

"Well, how would you explain us?" said Drake.

"Good point." Brygida grinned. "It might even be true," she added in Thari.

"Come on," Lolani said. "We ordered lot of food at the bar. Come help us eat it."

"We'll be there presently."

Lolani left.

Brygida gave Drake another hug and then followed Lolani.

Drake gazed out across the ocean. It had been a long and trying few weeks, but this new revelation was a welcome one. He didn't have many children – not who were still alive, anyway. Whatever it was that had allowed him to live as long as he did, didn't seem to be passed on to his children. They usually lived no more than a few thousand years.

He thought then of a woman he'd known in his youth. They'd had a child together. That had been before he left to follow the call of battle. He'd gone to right a great wrong, and he never returned to that Realm. He wondered if it even still existed, and how much time would have passed there. One day, he would return, when it was safe to do so.

CHAPTER FIFTY-FIVE

Jon watched with something between amusement and anger as Drake, Lolani, and Dr. Hakubi came back from the beach. Dr. Hakubi and Lolani obviously liked each other far better than Jon liked Dr. Hakubi. He'd never been able to forgive her for all the candidates who had died. Some of them had been friends of his.

Dr. Hakubi was very petite, with an ethnic mix Jon couldn't quite identify. Her eyes were bright green, and her hair was dark auburn like Drake's. Seeing them together, he could see the family resemblance. Jon wondered how Drake couldn't have known about her. He wondered, too, who her mother was.

Hakubi – Brygida, or whatever her real name was – looked as if she couldn't be older than fifteen, but she was a medical doctor and had worked on the genetics project that made Jon and Lolani into jumpship pilots almost twenty years ago. Now that Jon knew more about her parentage, he could understand why she hadn't aged.

Drake introduced Dr. Hakubi to the others.

"Call me Brygida, please."

"I thought you always insisted on being called *Dr. Hakubi*," said Lolani.

"Well, it seemed best to cultivate a professional atmosphere at the time."

She acted very friendly. She kept giving everyone hugs. Geoffrey looked smitten, as Jon could have guessed he would be. Even Jason appeared interested in her, although he was difficult to read.

Jon couldn't blame them.

They didn't know her the way he did.

He still remembered the endless screaming, the nightmarish pain as the gene therapy took effect. The transformation had been worse than the monomolecular surgeries that carved apart his nervous system and made it into something new. The gene therapy had even taken his identity away from him, altering his face in subtle ways that made people who had known him doubt his identity.

On the other hand, with everything that had happened on his world, maybe it was for the best that he no longer looked like the youngest prince of Rhyddid. Everything else from his previous life had been taken from him, so why not his identity? He had vowed that one day he'd return home, even if he had to wait a hundred years. Looking at how Hakubi hadn't aged, that might even be likely.

Lolani had ordered an indecent amount of food, but Jon wasn't hungry. His anger roiled his stomach, and the day had been long and terrifying. He had almost died, too many times to count. He didn't want to sit around and eat now as if nothing had happened.

As if Hakubi wasn't someone who'd tortured dozens of people to death with her experiments.

"Eat, Jon," Brygida encouraged.

"Will you please stop?" Jon snapped, slapping the table. "I'm not a child."

"Stop acting like one, then. Still have problems with your

vagus nerve?" Brygida asked. "You always were the worst patient."

"I wasn't a *patient*," Jon said. "I was a lab rat. An experimental animal for you to play with."

"Jon, it wasn't like that," said Lolani. "Come on, bruh, chill."

Jon pushed himself away from the table. "Don't follow me."

"I don't think anyone had planned to," said Drake. "They just brought the food. You should at least stay for that."

He wasn't going to win an argument with Drake. Jon turned and walked away. He was angry: Angry that he'd let Hakubi get under his skin. Angry that he'd lost control. Most of all, he was angry because, for the first time in years, he actually felt hungry.

The irony of *that* was too much to think about.

Θ

Jason wasn't sure what was wrong with Jon.

Maybe he was just tired, but Jason thought it was rather more than that. Jon had actually been angry. Jason had never seen that side of his friend. Geoffrey had left just after Jon, but he seemed genuinely exhausted. Jason had learned that Geoffrey had operated the *Chwyldro*'s guns during the battle to get into the prison. That was pretty amazing. It was no wonder Geoffrey was tired.

Jason glanced at Brygida, who was laughing and chatting with Drake and Lolani.

He thought Jon's problem might have something to do with Brygida, but he didn't know what it could be. Jason only had the vaguest idea of who this woman was. He knew she was a geneticist who'd somehow given Jon his abilities. He didn't have much more of an idea than that, other than that she seemed nice.

Watching her with Drake, Jason could see there was

something going on with the two of them, but he didn't know what. They had a similar look to them. Could that be it? Could Brygida be one of those people like Drake? *If she is, she's much less scary than Drake,* he thought.

Jason excused himself and walked back to Jon's ship.

The moon had gone down, and it was dark outside. Jason was at the ramp into the *Chwyldro* before he noticed the figure standing down by the beach. As tall and thin as the man was, it could only be Jon. Jason considered just going to bed, and then he sighed and walked down the stairs to the beach.

The tide was low, as the massive moon was on the other side of the planet. The beach was strewn with seaweed and broken shells. Whatever lived on this world, the sea life wasn't so different from that on Earth. Many of the shells even looked familiar to him.

Jon had his back turned to him as he walked up. "Hello, Jason."

"Hey, Jon," Jason replied. He didn't ask him about his anger. Jon would either tell him or not. Asking might discourage him.

"They still at it back at the bar?" Jon asked.

"Geoffrey went to bed."

"Yeah, I sensed him walk past."

Jason was feeling as if he should have walked past, too. "The ocean is beautiful," he said.

"It is, isn't it?" Jon said. "I've always loved the ocean."

"I haven't seen any boats on it."

"No, they don't sail much around here. The harbor on the other side of the island holds a fishing fleet, but they don't venture outside the barrier reef."

"The waves too high?"

"That, and the huge sea creatures," Jon said. "*Here there be monsters.*" He shook his head. "They killed off all the native animals inside the reef and imported Earth animals and fish."

"Are there people on other parts of the planet?"

Jon nodded. "There are lots of islands like this one. This is just the first place humans settled when they landed on Kai. It's the only island with a spaceport."

"Is that important?"

"Not really. I could land on any field. The *Chwyldro* is a tough ship. I don't even have to refuel that often."

"What kind of fuel does a ship like that take?"

"Oxygen for the life support system, and deuterium for the engines. Food for the pilot and passengers."

Jason had a vague idea that deuterium was heavy water. He sat down in the sand; it was very fine. After a few minutes, Jon sat next to him.

"I suppose you'd like to know what I was angry about," said Jon.

"Only if you want to tell me."

Jon sighed. "I'm just angry at Brygida, or whatever her name is. I shouldn't be. I got myself into that mess."

"You volunteered for the jump pilot program," Jason said. "You didn't know what you were getting into?"

Jon laughed bitterly. "Not really. Oh, they explained it all before they did anything, and they let people leave if they didn't want to be a part of it. I suppose I can't complain too much: I got the *Chwyldro* from the program, and the ability to fly her. It's just that so many of us died."

"You think that's her fault?"

"Who the fuck knows? She was the lead designer of the gene therapy, though."

"Any idea if she was behind you… being changed to… you know?"

"Attune with the Cynosure? Almost certainly. She's Drake's daughter, after all."

"What?"

"You didn't know?" Jon asked. "Oops. Oh, well, fuck

Drake, too."

"So you're saying she *is* his daughter?"

"Apparently. Drake seemed just as surprised. I don't have that story, but I bet it's interesting."

"Wow, just when I thought things couldn't get any stranger..."

"Been a hell of a few weeks, hasn't it? You know, I don't even know what I'm angry about. She didn't do anything I didn't ask her to do. Except maybe whatever she did that has people trying to kill me. I'm not even sure it was her who did that to me. There was talk of a third doctor. After discovering that Brygida is Drake's daughter, who the hell knows who or what that other guy is? I don't remember there being another doctor, but that doesn't really mean anything."

Jason nodded. "I know you're pissed about what was done to you, but it did make you a jumpship pilot, right?"

"Yeah, but a lot other people died."

"You don't think she did that deliberately, do you?"

"No, dammit. She is exactly what she seems to be."

"Except for the *related to Drake* part," Jason added.

"Yeah, except for that. I wish I knew what it all means."

"She's right back there in the bar. You could go ask."

"Then I might get answers, and I wouldn't have anything to bitch about," Jon said. "What about you?"

"I'm not a pilot," said Jason. "I don't have a problem with her."

Jon laughed. "I meant, are you going back to the bar?"

"No, I'm going to your ship, to sleep. I was on my way there when I saw you moping down here, and I thought what the hell, at least it's the beach."

"Fair enough. Hell. I may as well go back."

"Good luck."

"Thanks. I think I might need it."

Jason went on back to the *Chwyldro*. A part of him wanted

to join Jon in the bar. Another part of him just wanted to sleep for a week. He suspected he wasn't going to be able to do that, so he'd settle for what he could get.

CHAPTER FIFTY-SIX

The morning sun crested the central peak of the mountain and set fire to the clouds in the east. Geoffrey thought it was one of the most beautiful things he'd ever seen. He had never been to Hawaii, but he could understand why Pacific Islanders would want to settle Kai. Everything about this planet was perfect.

"Good morning, Geoffrey. Sleep well?" asked Drake. He'd been down at the beach swimming, and had a towel wrapped around his waist.

Geoffrey suspected Drake didn't own a swimsuit.

"I did," Geoffrey replied. "You?"

Drake shrugged. "I never sleep much. Have you eaten?"

"Brygida brought breakfast wraps."

Drake nodded. "We'll be leaving for Masir soon."

"Why are we going back there?"

"Brygida needs a genetics lab. The only one we know we can get access to is Yousef's, on Masir."

Geoffrey sighed. He wished he could just stay on Kai forever. The weather was perfect and apparently always was. It rained often but never snowed. Jon had said the planet had a low axial tilt, so it didn't really have seasons.

It didn't hurt that almost all the women wore bikinis all the time, and looked good in them.

"We have a few hours before we need to leave," said Drake. "So if there was something or maybe someone…"

"I'm good," Geoffrey said quickly. He'd been thinking about the waitress who kept smiling at him, at the bar where they'd been eating. He suspected Drake was reading his mind.

"You were thinking about her quite… hard," Drake replied.

Geoffrey blushed. He didn't want to have this conversation with Drake, of all people. "I'm ready to leave when you are."

"All right. You might want to say goodbye to Lolani."

"She isn't going with us?" Geoffrey was disappointed. He liked Lolani. It was scary to think that the genetically enhanced warrior with the chip on her shoulder was the most normal woman he'd met on this entire adventure.

"Lolani has her own life and her own adventures," said Drake. "We asked her to help rescue Dr. Hakubi, and she did. I'm headed over to her ship after I shower, to repair it."

"They almost got hit, didn't they?"

"They *did* get hit, but she managed to dodge most of the blast. Fixing her ship is the least I can do, under the circumstances. I owe her for her part in this. I will not forget that."

"I hope we can come back here someday," Geoffrey said. "I think I would like to live in a place like this."

"It is beautiful," Drake acknowledged.

"You know, it's funny," said Geoffrey. "I always craved adventure. I wanted something more than what I had back in Kentucky or even Cincinnati. I never thought about how you travel and meet people, and then you move on and maybe never see them again."

"It can be difficult. I probably understand that better than most. Sometimes I remember someone I liked. Then I return to them, only to find a thousand years have passed, and they are now dust."

"I guess one day that will be me, too," Geoffrey said. "I'll just be dust, and a memory."

"It happens to everyone eventually. Even me, I suspect. I don't know how I've lived as long as I have. In the lifetime of the universes, even I'm just a speck of fleeting dust."

"Wow, how can you guys get so moody on a morning like this?" Brygida said as she walked up. "Cheer up!"

Geoffrey liked Brygida. She was much friendlier than the other women he'd met since leaving home, except maybe Erin. Of course, she was from the North, the Eternal City. Geoffrey hoped that one day he'd get to see that. No offense to Drake, but he thought it sounded nicer than the Ruined Courts.

"I think I'll take my leave," Drake said.

"How are you, Brygida?" Geoffrey asked. "And thanks again for breakfast, by the way."

"I'm good," she replied. "And you're welcome." She leaned against the wall he was sitting on.

Geoffrey was struck again by just how small she was. He'd thought Erin was small, but Brygida was tiny, barely shoulder high on him. She was exotic, and pretty, in a way. She was a little odd looking. He wondered how old she was.

"A gentleman never asks a lady her age," Brygida said.

"I didn't!"

"No, but you thought it real loud."

Geoffrey blushed again. He wondered how much of his thoughts she'd overheard. He hadn't meant anything by them. She was pretty, just different looking compared to other women.

Brygida laughed. "You need to work on your mind shields. I took no offense."

"I would if I knew how," Geoffrey said. "I am sorry."

"Don't be, Geoffrey. I know you didn't mean anything

negative with your thoughts about me. To be honest, I wish I didn't hear what everyone was thinking all the time. I don't do that deliberately. I just hear most thoughts as easily as I hear people talking."

"That must get annoying for you."

"I can shield, if I need to. Besides, I'm used to being different. I look different because I'm mixed-race – hell, I'm mixed-*species*," she said with a laugh. "I had a parent from both the North and the South. Not too many like me."

"I think the emperor is like that."

"So I've heard. Maybe one day I'll meet him."

"You've never been to the Ruined Courts?"

Brygida shook her head. "I didn't even know they were real."

"Wow. I feel you, though; I didn't know any of this was real until a couple of weeks ago."

"You're from an Earth Realm?"

Geoffrey nodded. "Yes, Cincinnati."

"There's a Realm called Cincinnati?" she asked.

"What? No, that is the city I was living in."

"I'm teasing you, Geoffrey. I went to school in an Earth Realm. University of Tokyo."

"Oh, yeah, you'd probably fit in there."

"You mean because of how I look?"

"Well, I did think you looked Japanese."

"I thought so, too," Brygida said. "Apparently not a lot of people there with red hair and green eyes, though." She shrugged. "You'd think that in a place where people dye their hair green and blue, red wouldn't really stand out."

"When were you there?"

"Let's see. I received my Ph.D. in physics in nineteen ninety-one. Got my Ph.D. in genetics a few years later."

"I was born in nineteen ninety-one, back on my Earth."

"You *are* a young one, aren't you? I was thirty-five when I moved to Earth to go to school."

"Well, you don't look it."

Brygida laughed. "I know. I kind of stopped developing when I was a teen. It was around the time I attuned with the Cynosure. I've always thought something about my genetics went wonky."

"That the technical term?"

"You bet!"

Geoffrey grinned. "Drake said we're going to Masir next."

"Yep. Dusty, sandy place."

"Yeah, I like Kai much better."

"No genetics lab here, though," Brygida said. "We need to figure out what happened to Jon."

"You didn't intend for him to be able to attune with the Cynosure?"

"No, it shouldn't have been possible. I screened all of the applicants to the program. Jon wasn't from the North. I only enhanced the subjects' speed, strength, and recovery. He should have turned out like Lolani. Instead, something went wrong. I think it has something to do with all the people who died during the therapy. That shouldn't have happened, either."

"You think you can figure it out?" Geoffrey asked. "Drake thinks that's why someone is trying to kill Jon."

"I'm certainly going to try," Brygida said. "Which reminds me: I need to get a genetic sample from Lolani before we leave. I want to compare her genetic code to Jon's."

Geoffrey smiled as she ran off. Brygida was strange, but he liked her. He wondered if everyone from the North was like her. He doubted it. She was weird and definitely unique.

O

Drake took a shower and changed back into his armor.

It had been a long time since he'd let his guard down and

taken a swim. It had been pleasant. He agreed with Geoffrey: this world would be a good one to live on. It was poor, and technologically backward, but the people seemed kind and happy. There was little economic disparity. Everyone had enough to live and be comfortable.

Lolani was inspecting the damage to her ship.

"You took some scoring back there," Drake said as he walked up.

Lolani nodded. "Gonna cost me a fortune to fix her, too, bruh. If I can find a place to do it."

"That is what I wanted to talk with you about. I think I can fix your ship."

"Now you a starship mechanic, too, eh?"

"I'm a lot of things," Drake said. "This technology isn't overly advanced by my standards."

"Yeah, I can see that."

"I'd like to try, if you'll let me. I owe you for your assistance. This won't repay that, but it gets us closer."

"I helped Jon," Lolani said. "That Brygida happens to be your daughter was just a bonus for you."

"Be that as it may, if you need anything from me, I'll give it. I do feel as if I owe you."

"You really didn't know she's your daughter?"

"I did not."

"I guess you Precursors aren't so different from us, huh?"

"No, we aren't," Drake replied. "We just have access to older, more advanced technology. Our patterns of behavior are much the same. We have the same desires and motivations."

"Her momma must have been beautiful, to turn your head."

"She was, but many women have beauty. You're beautiful yourself."

Lolani laughed. "Gods, if I had a week free, I'd climb you like a tree. You're leaving, though, and I don't need my heart broken. I think once I had you, I'd never be satisfied with another man."

Drake smiled. "Well, I'd happily be climbed by you, if you'd like to know. Now, shall we look at your ship?"

"Yeah, we better, or I'm gonna do something stupid."

Drake tested the wing and then leapt up onto it. "This is the only damage?" he asked.

He was thinking that Lolani was lovely, and wishing he had that week free. It had been some time since he'd been with anyone. He hadn't had a sexual partner in years, in fact. He'd been too busy.

"Yeah, I didn't quite move out of the way fast enough."

"You dodged a blast from a laser cannon," Drake said. "That takes considerable skill."

"Hurt like hell," Lolani said.

"You feel it when the ship is damaged?"

"Yeah, supposed to make us react better."

Drake called upon the Instrumentality and inspected the damage. The beam had melted a perfectly straight line down the side of the ship. The metal of the hull had bubbled and flowed a little. The hull had been weakened. They were lucky the pressure of the interior hadn't blown it wide open. As it was, air had leaked out. He'd noticed that when he'd apported to the ship to help Jason.

He removed his armored glove and placed his hand at the beginning of the damage. The metal felt rough under his hand. Drake focused the Instrumentality upon it, willing the power of that ancient machine to flow into the hull and fix it. He felt the metal soften and smooth under his hand, and he walked along the wing. As his hand passed over the hull, it repaired itself.

Inspecting it afterward, he could see it had been fundamentally altered by what he'd done. He could sense the monomolecular machines in the hull; they crawled over the entire ship, strengthening it. Lolani would have a better ship than she'd started with.

Drake jumped back down next to Lolani, replacing his glove.

"What did you do?" She sounded awed.

"I used some of that advanced technology to repair your hull. I suspect it may continue to repair itself."

"What do you mean?"

Drake drew his sword and slashed the wing.

"Hey!"

After a minute, the torn metal began to flow back together. Within two minutes, it was if the damage had never been done. Drake hadn't intended to make her ship capable of self-repair, but he didn't regret it.

Lolani ran her hand over the smooth wing, where the cut had been. "It will fix itself, now?"

Drake nodded.

"Bruh, I ain't got nothing to repay you for this."

"I still owe you," Drake said. "I just want to make sure you're still around when we do have a few weeks free."

Lolani blushed. "Yeah, that'd be good."

Drake gently embraced her and kissed her cheek. "You take care of yourself."

CHAPTER FIFTY-SEVEN

Jon received clearance to lift off from Kai and accelerated down the runway. He was going to miss this watery world. He was going to miss Lolani, too. He'd enjoyed being able to spend some time with her again. Jon always hoped that somehow Lolani would feel differently about him someday, although he knew it was just a fantasy.

Lolani had talked to him privately before he left. She wanted him to know she was sorry things hadn't worked out between them. Lolani was and always would be a good friend. Jon would do almost anything for her. She'd also asked him to smooth things over with Brygida.

Jon wasn't quite ready for that.

He wasn't ready for either of those things, actually. He still loved Lolani; he always would, even if they never had anything other than friendship. Brygida was another matter.

He had mixed feelings about helping Brygida determine what had been done to him. He didn't trust her, even if she was Drake's daughter. He hadn't spoken to Brygida since the night before, when he went back in to ease the memory of how he'd left the bar.

He wasn't sure he wanted to talk to her again. He wasn't as angry as he'd been, but that didn't mean he forgave her for what she'd done. Deliberately or not, Brygida had been responsible for a project in which many people had died. Many of those people had been Jon's friends.

"Jason is safe in the stasis field," Drake said over the intercom.

"Good. We'll be at jump range in five minutes. Sending the updated calculations to Lolani now."

Jon wasn't sure about the stasis field technology. If it worked the way Drake said, it would have interfered with the jump. Obviously it didn't, but Jon couldn't explain why not. He didn't have a good enough grasp on the technology Drake was using to understand the field interactions. Well, Lolani hadn't imploded on the trip back to Kai. He'd just have to trust Drake.

Jon brought up the Cynosure for the jump. He didn't need to use it for this, but he'd discovered he was relying on it more and more. Was that an aspect of the Power they hadn't warned him about, that it was addicting? He certainly understood how it could be.

As they came up on the jump point, Jon engaged the engines and spun the *Chwyldro* out of existence. With the Cynosure held in his mind, what had been a moment of nearly-instantaneous nausea became a slow eternity of strange sensations. He knew that the flow of time hadn't changed; he could feel his heart working to push the blood out during its slow beat.

Jon sensed something in the void around his ship, something alive in the nothingness he was jumping the *Chwyldro* through. It didn't seem hungry or malevolent. He mostly just sensed curiosity. Then the prismatic effect started again, and Jon felt his perception of time speeding up as the ship entered the spacetime occupied by Masir.

"We're through the jump," he said.

"Jason is fine," Drake replied.

"Disoriented," said Jason. "That stasis field is weird. I just blink, and we're someplace else. Not that I'm complaining, considering the alternative."

Brygida started telling Jason about jump sickness, and Jon shut down the intercom and brought up the long-range com. "Masir Orbital Control, this the *Chwyldro*, requesting permission to land at Dümat al-Jandal."

"Roger, *Chwyldro*. You're cleared to land at the Dümat al-Jandal field. Be advised that there's a haboob over the city now. You might want to wait to land."

"Acknowledged, Masir Orbital Control. That shouldn't be a problem. I'm heading in now."

Jon could see a massive wall of dust and sand as he skipped down through the atmosphere. The haboob was a big one. High winds rocked the *Chwyldro* as he fought his way down into the edge of the storm. He lived for times like this. He loved to fly, and when it was difficult was when it was the most fun.

Jon's awareness expanded. He could actually *see* the vectors of the grains of sand as they flowed past his ship. There was a pattern to the haboob he'd never noticed before. He altered his course slightly, and the *Chwyldro* slipped into a gravity current.

Just like that, it was easier to fly through the storm.

He circled the landing field once, noting the additional ground cars. Usually when Jon traveled to Masir, it was just Yousef at the landing pad to greet him. The hundred-kilometer-an-hour winds buffeted the *Chwyldro* on the final approach, but he brought her down smoothly and taxied into the shelter of the electrostatic shield near the ground cars.

He didn't like the look of the people waiting.

"We may have company," he said over the intercom.

"Trouble?" asked Drake.

"Maybe. Looks like police."

"They shouldn't be any trouble."

"Drake, play nice."

"You know me."

"Yeah, *play nice*. Don't cause any trouble for Yousef."

"How about we see if they're even here for us before we worry about what I might do to them?"

"I don't think you should take your armor and weapons off the ship, Drake."

"Why is that?"

"Because police tend to open fire on people with swords and guns."

"I will consider it."

"Fine. I'll be back there in a moment."

Jon shut down his ship and locked the controls. He didn't think anyone else would have been able to operate her, but he didn't want to take any chances. The police waiting at the landing pad made him worry. He hadn't spoken to Yousef before they set off, and he hoped his old friend was okay.

Θ

Drake led the way from the *Chwyldro*.

If there was to be a confrontation with the police, he wanted to be in front of everyone else, to shield them. As he approached, he was somewhat surprised to see Detective Bashar step from the lead vehicle. She was wearing her red headscarf across her face to block the dust, but Drake recognized her anyway.

"Hello, detective," he said in Arabic as she walked toward him.

She stopped. "Have we met?"

"Not in the flesh."

She gave him a sharp look. "I'm Detective Bashar. I was wondering if you and your companions would be willing to come in for a statement."

"About what, if I may ask?"

"The murder of Prince Aziz, for one thing. The timing of your departure from this planet was suspicious. Also, several witnesses put someone very much like you at the scene of the crime."

"We left because we had pressing business on Kai."

"And why have you returned?"

"Because we have pressing business on Masir."

"You speak very good Arabic, for someone not from here."

"This is not the only world where the language is spoken."

"Good sir, will you come with me or not? I do not wish to stand in this dust for longer than need be." As she said that, other police officers exited their vehicles.

He could see Yousef and his vehicle behind them. Yousef looked worried.

Drake sighed. There was no easy solution to this situation that wouldn't result in bloodshed. He wanted to avoid that, if he could. The police here were not bad people. "Perhaps we could compromise."

"What do you have in mind?"

"I will come with you peacefully, and you allow my companions to leave with Dr. Yousef Shadid, over there, so that they may conclude their business. It is rather urgent, and medical in nature."

Bashar glanced at the doctor and then at Drake's companions. "Okay, as long as they agree to remain on Masir until we've resolved all of this. The *Chwyldro* won't be granted clearance to leave and will be fired upon if an attempt is made to run."

"I doubt my friends would leave me behind. May I speak with them before I join you?"

Bashar frowned and then gestured assent.

Drake walked back over to the others.

"What's going on, Drake?" asked Jon.

"The police have a few questions for me. I may have been too clever when I was here last. As of now, they only wish to speak to me. However, your ship is grounded until the situation is resolved."

"I hope you aren't planning to fight."

Drake turned his back to the police and then opened his coat so Jon could see he was unarmed. He hadn't even worn his armor, although he felt naked without it. "I have agreed to go with the officers if they allow you all to go with Yousef."

"You're sure about this?" asked Brygida.

"I'll meet you all at the lab later. You can show me the result of your investigation into the changes made to Jon's DNA. The detective is looking impatient, so I had better go. Yousef is waiting behind the police cars."

"I'll make sure everyone is safe," said Jon.

"Thank you." Drake walked back to Bashar. "I'm ready when you are, detective."

"Do I need to cuff you?" she asked.

"I wouldn't try it. However, I have given you my word to cooperate. Do not make me regret it. It would be unfortunate for us all, I think."

"Come on." Bashar opened the door for him.

Drake waited for his companions to climb into Yousef's car before he seated himself. Two burly officers were in the car already. Neither the police nor the flimsy shell of the ground car would stop him if he wanted to leave. The detective was true to her word, however. He watched Yousef drive away and then turned to meet Bashar's brown eyes. Her scarf covered the rest of her face.

"Do we speak here, or at the police station?" he asked.

"We should probably wait until we reach the station," said Bashar.

"Very well."

It was short trip by car to the same police station he'd been to before. The haboob was dying down as they exited the vehicle. Drake thought the number of police officers was somewhat excessive. Surely, the two men with Bashar could have been sufficient to handle any problems a normal man would give them.

Unless, of course, they knew he wasn't a normal man.

CHAPTER FIFTY-EIGHT

Detective Bashar led Drake into the police station, escorted by the two officers who'd been in the car with them. They went through the doors into the back area where all the desks and cubicles were. Bashar stopped at the desk of the intake sergeant.

"We'll need fingerprints and a DNA sample," she said.

"I'm afraid I cannot comply with that request," said Drake. "I agreed to come and answer some questions. I do not agree to allow you access to my genetic material."

"Sir, this is standard procedure."

"I'm sure it is. I cannot and will not comply."

"Want us to make him?" asked the burly officer to Drake's left.

Drake glanced at the man and smiled. The officer lost his own smile and took a step back. "I don't think it would be wise for you to touch me," said Drake.

"Do you have any weapons on you?" Bashar asked.

Drake pulled back his coat so she could see that he was unarmed.

"Let's step into the room over there and talk," she said. "You men can wait out here."

The Sorcerer
409

"We'll keep an eye on the monitor, detective."

She nodded and led Drake into the room. The interrogation room was normal-looking enough, with a table, two chairs, a flat screen television, a single camera in a corner, and a mirror on the wall. The mirror was undoubtedly one-way, the kind of mirror common in such rooms. Drake could hear the officers talking from behind the glass. They didn't like him being alone in the room with the detective.

Drake thought that if being in the middle of a police station, surrounded by officers, wasn't enough to deter someone, then having more people in the room wouldn't help. He did wonder why they were bothering. He'd left a lot of evidence that the prince had been killed by the Alliance.

Drake sat in a chair facing the window. The chair creaked a bit under his weight but held. In armor, he weighed much more than an average human. Even out of armor, he weighed more than he appeared to.

The detective sat opposite him. She laid a folder with some hardcopy on the table but didn't open the folder. She'd noticed the chair creak as he sat down. She seemed far more nervous than Drake could account for. Her heartrate was elevated, and she was sweating even though the air in the room was only twenty degrees Celsius.

Bashar's voice was steady, though. "Let's start with your name."

"I am known as Daeren Drake."

"*Known as?*"

"It's the name I have used since I was young. The name I was born with would do you little good. The world on which I was born is far away from here."

"And where exactly was that?"

"What form of coordinates would you prefer? I don't think anything I said to answer the question would make you happy. Why am I here?"

"I told you, we have questions about the timing of you leaving after the prince was murdered."

"Then ask your questions."

Detective Bashar glanced at the mirrored wall behind her. "Where were you on the night of August the twenty-seventh?"

"I have no idea."

"You said you'd cooperate."

"I don't even know the date *today*. I have no idea when August the twenty-seventh was."

"It was the night you first arrived on Masir."

"Ah. I believe I spent the night at Yousef's lab."

"Where were you before that?"

"I think we had dinner at Malouf's"

"You were not there with your companions."

"Then I must have stayed in the lab."

"Hmm. Do you know these people?" She pulled two pictures from the folder. Drake recognized them both as himself. Of course, he didn't look like himself in either picture. The first was the form of the man he'd used to infiltrate the police station. The second was the female shape he'd worn to dinner.

"I can't say I've met either of them."

"What about him?" Bashar slid a picture of the Margrave across the table.

"I believe the Margrave prefers to be referred to with a gender-neutral pronoun." If she knew he'd met the Margrave, then Drake could guess why she was upset. He decided to let her tell him, though; he could be mistaken.

"Apparently you've been a busy man," said Bashar. "You were seen on Earth, then here, and then Kai. The Alliance put out a kill order on a man matching your description. Apparently, there was an assault on a prison facility by someone who looked much like you."

"I was under the impression that Masir is independent of

the Alliance."

"We are, but your movements start to form an interesting pattern. There is also a matter of a video that was smuggled off Earth."

"A video?"

Bashar pointed at the television, and one of the men in the other room activated it. The view was from a camera overlooking the Margrave's ballroom. The scene was momentarily overwhelmed by a flash of rainbows, and suddenly Drake was visible, riding the monstrous horror. The video showed him slicing the Ancient Enemy apart with his sword. The video cut off as he stepped away from the dissolving corpse, then looped back to the beginning.

"What do you call that?" asked Bashar.

"Good television." Drake smiled. "How long did it take the effects team to create it?"

"I think we both know it isn't faked. That *is* you, isn't it? With the sword? You're dressed just as you are now."

"Excepting the gore, of course," said Drake. Actually, he'd been wearing his armor under his coat then, but the coat was the same. "Yes, I think the look becomes me."

"Apparently. You were also seen at several crime scenes on the night in question." She gestured, and surveillance camera video showed him investigating the crime scenes. He hadn't thought about the possibility of being recorded.

The images on the screen changed again. A street-view camera showed a section of rooftop wall exploding. For a moment, Drake was clearly framed in the broken wall. A brilliant flash illuminated the rooftop, and a man on the street below collapsed in a spray of blood. Drake knew he was seeing the death of the prince, from a different perspective. People rushed to the body. A man stood on the top of the wall, shot himself in the head, and then fell to the street.

"Do you see now why we're interested in you?" asked

Bashar.

"It seems to me as if the man who shot himself in the head must have shot the prince."

"So you recognize the man on the street as Prince Aziz?"

"Wouldn't anyone?"

"Anyone from Masir might, but we wouldn't expect an outsider to know him by sight."

"Is that a crime?"

Bashar sighed. "I think you were on that rooftop."

"That's an interesting opinion."

"We're certain the three other dead men were Alliance operatives. They were armed with Alliance weapons. The same type of weapon that killed the prince."

"Then they must have done it."

"The problem is this: We have also *you* on that rooftop. Plus, two of the operatives were dead before they were shot. The third man, who killed himself, had torn muscles in his right arm. It almost seemed as if he was trying to keep from killing himself."

"I've heard the Alliance can create some powerful post-hypnotic suggestions in people."

"Here is what I think happened, Mr. Drake. I think you investigated the crime scenes, possibly after stealing information from this very station. I think you tracked down a team of Alliance operatives and killed them. I believe you also killed Prince Aziz."

"That is a very interesting conjecture, detective."

"I think all of these people are you." She spread out the pictures.

"You're sounding a bit crazy, detective. How could I be different people?"

"I don't know. Why don't you tell me?"

Drake smiled. "I'd have to possess some powerful illusion technology, I would assume."

"Not illusions," said Bashar. "The man in this picture grabbed me and took my gun away in this very station. We stuck him in a holding cell. A few minutes later, *I* apparently walked out of the cell, accessed case information, and then walked out of the building."

"Maybe you should be a suspect, then."

"I was in a meeting with the police chief at the time."

"What answer are you hoping to hear from me, detective?"

"I want to know what all of this means!"

"Perhaps you should just take the win."

"What do you mean?"

"The murders stopped with the death of the prince, didn't they?"

"How would you know that?"

Drake liked this woman's tenacity. She wanted the truth. Perhaps he should give it to her.

"Do you really want the truth?" he asked.

"I do."

"You should be careful what you wish for."

"You're no djinn, even if you do look like one."

Drake called forth the Instrumentality. He directed its energies with a glance, and the camera shorted out explosively. Bashar pushed away from the table and drew her gun. Drake clouded the mirror and welded the door shut. That should give them a few minutes to talk.

"The truth, detective, is that your prince was a psychotic murderer. He was being goaded by the Alliance. I believe the intention was to discredit the government and incite civil unrest. I think it worked, in that regard."

The detective kept her gun on him as she tried the door. "You killed him, didn't you?"

"And the Alliance operatives," Drake replied, staying seated. "It seemed the easiest way to defuse the situation."

Someone began pounding on the door. Drake could hear

the officers shouting to one another. It would take the other officers a while to get through the door. Shots rang out, and someone screamed from a ricochet. The officers had discovered that the clouded mirror was now bulletproof.

"What are you?"

"Call me an interested third party."

"What is that supposed to mean?"

"You've determined that I'm not human. You tell me."

She stopped moving, and for a moment, Drake thought she was going to shoot him. "Are you a Precursor?"

The favorite bogyman of this Realm. "In a manner of speaking, yes."

"And you've taken an interest in Masir?"

"I've taken an interest in this star cluster. The Alliance might be a threat."

"And you're going to do something about that? Alone?"

"I'll do whatever I have to."

"What did the prince have to do with any of this?"

"He was a monster."

She glanced at the screen, which was now blank. "You mean like that thing you were fighting on Earth?"

That surprised him; he hadn't expected her to make the connection. "No, the prince was just the human kind of monster. You knew that, though."

"We couldn't touch him."

"Now you don't have to."

Bashar took a deep breath. "You're still guilty of taking the law into your own hands."

"Yes, I am," said Drake. He stood up. "But your laws don't apply to me, do they? I'm not human, so I certainly can't commit homicide."

She lowered her gun. "What are you doing here now?"

"Just visiting with a geneticist about another matter. Nothing to concern you. I don't intend to kill anyone. I won't, unless they try to kill me."

"I wish… Oh, hell. Maybe I *should* just say thanks."

"You're welcome," said Drake. "Your officers will be through the door in a moment. I think I'll take my leave before then."

"Go with god," said Bashar.

Drake nodded and apported away.

CHAPTER FIFTY-NINE

The automated ground car bucked, and the sand and dust howled by as it drove to Yousef's lab. The streets of the city were deserted. Most people had the sense to stay indoors during a haboob.

Jon worried about Drake, or more accurately, he worried about what Drake was doing to the local police. The man wasn't easy on a person's sanity. Yousef didn't need trouble from the police on top of all his other concerns. The doctor was wanted by the Alliance, after all.

Brygida was quiet. She'd greeted Yousef and then settled into the car and kept to herself. Jon didn't know whether her silence had to do with their talk last night or something else. He didn't think she was worried about Drake.

"Drake will be okay, right?" asked Geoffrey.

"Worry about the police," Jason said.

The storm died down as they reached the lab. Jon had a bad feeling about what Brygida might uncover in his genetic material. He didn't want to go into that building. He didn't want confirmation of what his precognitive sense said was coming. His genetics were somehow tied into the visions of war he'd had since meeting Drake.

"You coming, Jon?" said Jason.

Jon climbed reluctantly out of the car and followed the others inside.

The lab was mostly empty, it being late in the day; only a few of the lab techs were still working. Yousef and Brygida started Jon's genetic sample scanning and sat catching up. The two doctors were old friends, although Jon could sense some tension between them. The sheer mundanity of those two chatting while the fate of universes hung in the balance struck him as odd. His premonitions were tearing his mind apart, while these two had no idea what was coming.

Of course, considering how vague his premonitions were, neither did he.

"Would you like to do the honors, Brygida?" said Yousef.

"Thank you, Yousef." Brygida sat down and typed rapidly on the keypad. Jon could see lines of code displayed: she was obviously writing an algorithm to find the differences between Jon's current DNA and the genetic samples from the other people who had been augmented in the jumpship program. Jon understood the math there, if nothing else.

After a while, Brygida sat back from the computer and shook her head at Jon.

"What?"

"I didn't do this," she said. "Look at Lolani's code, next to yours." She pointed to certain areas on the screen.

"You know I don't understand any of that stuff."

"Then take *my* word for it," said Yousef. "Your genetic material was altered from the original pattern. I suspect we'd see the same changes in the other pilots who were able to apport."

"The coded changes are supposed to be regular and predictable," Brygida said. "The changes to *your* DNA are neither. Your genetic material shows alteration in physical appearance, as well as other areas. I never coded that. It shouldn't be possible, unless..."

"What?"

"Dr. Preta. She was in charge of the actual administration of the doses."

"I sort of remember a woman administering the injections," said Jon. "I don't remember that her name was Dr. Preta."

Just then, Drake apported into the lab, startling Yousef. "Who did you say?"

"Dr. Timira Preta," said Brygida. "She was the other doctor on the project. She administered the doses of retrovirus used to augment the jumpship pilot candidates. Why? Is the name familiar to you? I believe she was Indian, originally from Earth."

Drake laughed softly. Jon didn't think it was a laugh of humor, though. The look on Drake's face sent chills up his spine, not quite a premonition, but Jon still dreaded whatever Drake was going to say.

"What is it?" Yousef asked.

"We need to track down this supposed doctor," said Drake.

"I'm not sure why. She was very knowledgeable about genetics, but hardly more so than the two of us," Brygida said.

"I suspect you may be mistaken there."

"I'm sorry, I don't think I understand," said Yousef.

"I remember Dr. Preta kept asking to see the original samples," said Brygida. "You don't think she would have tampered with the dosing, do you?"

"Why would she?"

"What original samples?" asked Drake. His voice was flat and cold. Jon wasn't sure he'd ever heard Drake sound so angry.

Apparently, Brygida heard it in his voice, too. She looked uneasy. Her voice was small and low as she answered; she sounded scared. "I had samples of genetic material from all of the Royal Family."

"What's this?" asked Yousef.

"Could you all excuse us for a few minutes?" said Drake.

Jon nodded and gathered up Jason and Geoffrey with a glance. They moved into the outer part of the lab. Jon was sure they were as happy to leave as he was. An angry Drake wasn't something any of them wanted to be around.

Jon could hear Drake's raised voice in the other room. Drake was shouting; something Brygida had done frightened him. Jon wasn't sure he wanted to know what could do that. If Drake was afraid, then they should all be cowering. If there was any place safe to be.

The few techs in the outer lab were talking about a report that the Alliance fleet was massing. Rumor had it that the Alliance was going to pacify the current rebellion at Rhyddid. From their conversation, the techs were also worried that the Alliance fleet was coming to Masir.

Jon's mind filled again with visions of worlds burning and endless fields of rotting corpses, war on a scale he couldn't even comprehend. Drake was somehow pivotal to that. Jon just didn't know whether Drake was going to stop it or cause it to happen.

He hoped Drake managed to uncover something in the genetic material that would help Jon prevent that war. Ever since he'd met the people from the North in that bar on Avalon, his reality had spiraled into chaos. Every move he made seemed to make things worse.

Something was coming. Something horrible.

Jon sensed that a major event was close, temporally. There was sorrow and pain associated with it, but also a sense of hope. Jon clung to that hope like a drowning man. He needed something to shield his mind from the madness.

☉

Drake waited until the others had left and then turned on

Brygida.

"Tell me exactly what you meant by that," he demanded.

"I had genetic samples from everyone in the Royal family," she said. "I wanted to know why my relatives had different traits. Why some were better at healing, and some had much faster reflexes. Some even have other, more exotic talents."

"I'm sorry – what royal family?" asked Yousef.

"Brygida is my daughter," Drake said.

"What?" Yousef looked confused.

"Drake is my father," Brygida said.

"You're actually a Precursor?"

"And she has been playing with things that she doesn't understand. Things that are dangerous. For everyone."

"I wasn't playing," Brygida snapped. "I am a scientist. I have been trying to understand what makes our people different from humans. Why is our birth rate so low? As promiscuous as our people are, we are nearly sterile. They are hardly any children born. Why is that? We're more fertile with humans than we are with each other! It wasn't as if I actually had parents around whom I could ask!"

"So you have mommy and daddy issues, and decided to experiment on humans by injecting them with genetic material from your family?" Drake asked coldly.

"I didn't do anything of the kind! I told you, I only enhanced their strength, speed, and healing abilities. Look at Lolani! She was one of the first to receive my treatment. She turned out perfectly."

"And Jon?"

"I don't know what went wrong. He was from one of the later candidate groups. Dr. Preta would have administered the dose."

Drake sighed. Brygida hadn't known any better, and she was right that he and Monika had essentially abandoned her. He hadn't even known about his daughter, but he hadn't questioned Monika about the possibility, either. As Brygida said, his people weren't overly fertile.

"I'm still somewhat confused," said Yousef. "Even if Dr. Preta did alter the dosing, what does this have to do with Jon? And why is it so terrible, that you are so angry?"

"Jon has genetic changes that I didn't code for," said Brygida. "Because of that, his genetic material reads as if he's a member of my mother's Royal Family. That has given him access to a… technology that he shouldn't be able to access. I assume that's why my father is so angry."

"Actually, no," Drake said. His anger at Brygida had run its course. "I couldn't care less about that. What I *am* concerned about is what other technology Jon might be able to access."

"I don't understand."

"I know. I'm sorry I yelled at you. What is done, is done. We need to know the specific person whose genetic material was used to alter Jon. I promise I will tell you all that I suspect, but I wish to determine this first. Can you do that?"

Brygida frowned. "Maybe. I don't have that material any longer. It was in the lab on Rhyddid."

Drake laughed sourly. Of course the genetic material was unaccounted for. If he ever got to the Golden Kingdom again, he was going to have some harsh things to say to Monika about the way she had raised Brygida. His daughter was too impulsive. She hadn't thought about what might be done with the DNA samples. The knowledge it represented. The power, and the danger.

There were Powers in the Realms that could only be accessed by specific bloodlines. His sword, for example: Maegril was tied to his bloodline. Only he, or one of his children, could use the blade without being destroyed. Maegril was an ancient relic of his House, and there was a terrible secret tied to the sword.

With that blade, or one of its sister Plaza blades, a person with the correct knowledge could unleash an ancient horror, a tide of darkness that would sweep across all of creation, condemning untold hundreds of trillions to torment and death.

Drake knew that there was at least one of the Plaza blades in the North. He's encountered the wielder once, at a distance. He knew of only one living descendant of that man: the emperor on the throne of the Ruined Courts. Emrys was fairly safe from being used by anyone.

Drake hoped he was wrong about what had been done to Jon. He hoped Jon wasn't now effectively Joseph's son, because if that was what had happened, it meant that someone wanted to use Jon for some unspeakable act. That Jon would be destroyed in the process was secondary to the horror he'd unleash.

"We'll have to travel to Rhyddid, then," said Drake.

"I don't think you know what you're saying," Yousef said. "Rhyddid has been directly blockaded by the Alliance. There are rumors that they are going to do the same to us. They already stop traffic at the jumpgate. They may actually invade. If they do, we'll be unable to resist "

"Not only that. Rhyddid is an anarchy," said Brygida. "I don't even know if the lab would still be there."

"We need to find out," said Drake. "I need to know whose genetic material was used. If it was just some random royal, then I can stop worrying."

"And if it was the person you seem to be worried it is?"

"Then we have a long and terrible road ahead of us."

CHAPTER SIXTY

"We need to go to Rhyddid," said Drake.

"You want to go *where*?"

Geoffrey thought Jon sounded pissed off. Not that Jon didn't have a right to be. He'd made it very clear that he couldn't go back to his home planet.

"We need to go the lab where all this began, to examine the DNA samples there."

"What makes you think the lab is even still there?"

"It was a government facility, Jon, built and run by the military," said Brygida. "I know there have been multiple revolutions on Rhyddid, but I think it's possible the facility is intact. Very few people knew about it."

Geoffrey wondered if that was what Drake had been yelling at Brygida about. Her voice had a bit of a waver in it now, as if she was upset. It would be almost impossible for Jon to go back to his home planet; he'd said before that they'd kill him on sight. He was a member of a royal family that had been overthrown. He'd be lucky if they just chopped his head off.

"No more games, Drake. No more lies. No more secrets. I want to know why you think it's important to go back to

Rhyddid."

"All right," Drake said quietly. He summoned his sword from the air, the way he did sometimes.

"Am I supposed to be intimidated?"

"Not in the least. This blade is tied to my bloodline. Anyone who isn't a direct genetic descendant of mine will be destroyed if they try to wield it." He held it out to Brygida. "If she isn't my daughter, it will kill her."

Brygida didn't even hesitate. She reached out and grasped the sword. She grinned and then handed it back to Drake.

"What's that supposed to prove?" asked Jon. "I know I'm not related to you."

"It isn't just a sword," said Drake. "There is a place, beyond the Eye, where untold millions of the Ancient Enemy are locked away. In my youth, the place was called the Stasis Tombs. Now, almost no one knows they exist. This sword could unlock those Tombs and release the horror within."

Jon looked shaken. Geoffrey didn't blame him. The only thing he knew about the Ancient Enemy was that they were like the thing Drake had killed on Earth. That millions of the horrific creatures could exist was terrifying. No matter what Drake said, those Tombs were not someplace he ever wanted to go.

"So don't go to the Tombs," said Jon. "Hell, if I were you, I'd destroy the damn sword."

Drake sheathed the sword. "This blade is one of the best tools I possess to destroy the Ancient Enemy. The weapon is essentially indestructible. It is also, sadly, not entirely unique."

"What do you mean?"

"There are other blades out there similar to this one. They all have different powers, but they can all be used a key to unlock the Tombs."

"Why would anyone make such a thing?" asked Brygida.

"Because those who built the Tombs knew the people they

were locking away – I should say they knew those that had once *been* people. Our ancestors were weary of war, and they locked the worst of the monsters away in the Tombs. They carried the keys so that they could lock others in there later if need be. But a key can unlock a cage as easily as it locks it. Over the years, the keys were lost, some probably destroyed. Some were even used to unleash horrors like the one I destroyed on Earth."

"There was an Ancient Enemy here?" asked Brygida.

"Yes. I presume your mother spoke of them."

Brygida nodded.

"Okay, I still don't understand what this has to do with me," said Jon.

"At least one of the swords is in the Golden Kingdom."

Geoffrey realized what Drake was saying at about the same time as Jon did.

"Are you saying that if I've been altered to match the genetic code of the Royal Family, enough to fool the Cynosure, then it may be enough to fool one of those swords? Why would anyone do that?"

"If someone wanted to use a sword to unlock the Tombs – and I hope I'm wrong – but if they did, they'd need someone who could use that sword. If you wouldn't use it in that fashion, and I don't think you would, then the Ancient Enemy would *make* you."

"I'd refuse."

Drake laughed sourly. "You'd try."

"Drake, I swear, I'd kill myself before I let myself be used that way."

"You would if you could," said Drake. "Imagine an enemy older and more powerful than me, with no compassion or kindness. Imagine what they would do to you if they had you alone to play with as they pleased. How long could you resist the torments they would bring? Remember, you wouldn't be allowed to die. They would keep healing you, to torture you more. How long would you hold out against that?"

Geoffrey felt ill.

He had read enough of history to know about the kinds of horrific torments that people used to devise. The Spanish Inquisition had driven people mad with inventive tortures designed to cause pain without allowing the victims to die. He could easily imagine what someone with Drake's power could do.

Jon wouldn't have a chance against that.

"So what do we do about it?" Jon asked. "Are you going to kill me?"

"No," Drake said. "I'm going to try to stop whomever or whatever is trying to use you like this."

"Why, Drake?" Jon asked. "Why not just kill me?"

"For one, because we are friends. Also, because the enemy would just find someone else."

"Promise me you'll kill me before you let them use me that way."

Drake nodded sharply.

"Did you know about this all along?" asked Jason.

"No. I didn't. I still don't know it for sure."

"It would explain my premonitions of madness and pain," Jon said.

"We have to make sure it doesn't come to that," said Drake. "That's why we need to go to the lab on Rhyddid. If there is any chance that we'll find the answers we need, we have to go. If there is any chance that the enemy could make more people like you, we have to stop it."

"The Alliance kidnapped me for a reason," said Brygida. "They wanted their own jump pilot program. At least, that's what I was told. Now I wonder."

Drake nodded. "There are answers we must discover. We should make haste. I cannot help but feel as if time is pressing."

"I can drive you all back to Jon's ship," Yousef offered.

"Thank you."

"Drake, is the situation with the police resolved?" Jon asked as they stepped outside.

The last rays of the setting sun cast the world in red. There was still some dust in the air, even though the storm was over. Fine dirt and sand coated everything outside.

"It is, and I didn't even kill anyone. I don't believe any of us will have any more problems from them. The detective is taking the situation as a win, although she is inquisitive. She may come around asking more questions, Yousef. I trust you to be discreet."

"I certainly will be, although I don't understand half of what you were talking about."

"You're staying here?" asked Brygida.

"I think so. I still have my research into the genetic diseases our pilots have developed. I want to help them, if I can."

Brygida gave him a hug.

"I'm driving you all back to the spaceport," said Yousef. "It isn't quite goodbye yet."

"Thank you. For everything."

Geoffrey thought Drake looked impatient and annoyed. He obviously wanted to get to Rhyddid as quickly as possible.

Geoffrey frowned. There was a spot of red on Drake's shoulder. It looked like what his mother always called a *shiny bug*: a laser cat toy. It had to be a reflection; the sun was behind Drake. Geoffrey looked around but couldn't see what it was reflecting off.

The dot moved until it was centered over Drake's chest.

Suddenly Geoffrey knew what it was. "Look out!"

He dove forward to push Drake out of the way.

There was a sudden pain between his shoulder blades, and his chest felt as if it was on fire. Drake looked startled. Geoffrey realized there was blood on Drake's face. He worried that he hadn't warned Drake in time.

He looked down and noticed his hands had blood on them, too. His vision greyed out, and he fell to his knees. There was a hole the size of his fist through his chest. Blood weakly pulsed from the hole, and he realized he'd been shot.

The last thing he heard as darkness closed in was Drake's voice.

"*No.*"

About the Author

Paul B. Spence is a practicing archaeologist who hopes to one day get it right. He currently lives in New Mexico, where all the cool kids hang out, with too many cats.

Like most authors, he had an eclectic career path. He's worked as a retail gofer, a food service monkey, brute laborer, a rennie, a writer for the RPG industry, and many other rewarding jobs that didn't pay enough to feed him or his cats.